MISSION PARK

Linda Twist

PublishAmerica
Baltimore

ISBN: 1-4241-3472-2
PUBLISHED BY PUBLISHAMERICA, LLLP
www.publishamerica.com
Baltimore

Printed in the United States of America

I dedicate this book to my very good friend Judy Beth Morgan.
She has given me the confidence and encouragement to keep writing.

Acknowledgments:

My daughter-in-law, Pamela Morgan, who told me a few years ago to follow my dreams. She gave me a beautiful granddaughter, Katey Beth.

To Publish America who is allowing my dreams to come true.

Chapter 1

"Well, Chris, what do you think? Should I tell him tonight or just wait for him to tell me first?"

"That's for you to decide, Pam. You've been seeing Joe for a couple of months but I can't tell you when to make that big step about your feelings for him. It sounds like you two are in a big standoff about who'll commit first."

"I called you because you're a guy and I wanted a male point of view. I'm in the dark about males in general. I didn't even have a brother when I was growing up."

"You don't know this but I never went to my senior prom. I was extremely afraid of girls growing up. Asking me about females is like asking the devil about asbestos." He heard Pam give out a small sigh. "Okay, seriously, men would like sex often without bringing up feelings or love. This is our mentality, if you really want to know."

"You sound like men never fall in love only females."

"All men fall in love with sex and I don't think women do. I think he cares about you but I'm not sure just how much, only he knows."

"Chris, he's the guy I've been waiting for since I first started dating and I would hate to break up with him. I am so ready to hear the 'L' word or make some changes."

"Do it and then call me, if you get a chance. On second thought, you'll either be laughing or crying and you won't have to tell me a thing." Pam liked Chris's sense of humor. It was always right to the point. No hemming and

7

hawing around for him.

"I'll call you tonight and you will immediately know," she told him. "Thanks for your input and I'm sorry for waking you up." Pamela hung up the phone and still stayed in her bed. She had Joe on her mind at the moment. She had called her friend and co-worker Chris to get his opinion on her plans for the evening. He was such a nice guy and the first male friend she had ever had. Chris had a rather small and wiry type of build with blue eyes, light brown hair and he was just a little taller than her 5' 5'' height. He came across loaded with energy and was very emotional for a guy. The very same traits that went along with him being somewhat outspoken. Some of the dispatchers thought he was gay but she wasn't so sure. He looked all male to her but she knew that could be misleading. He hadn't mentioned any girlfriends since they became acquainted. The officers at the police department tolerated his dispatching but didn't really like him.

She decided to do some shopping and look for a new outfit. She would wear something nice for Joe this evening. Pam was hoping he would declare his love. She had all day to rehearse her speech to him. She would be the one who would have to take the initiative if she was to ever find out his intentions. Pam kept busy during the day shopping for clothes and buying groceries. She made his favorite wine cake to share with him.

In the early evening she started getting dressed. She put on a royal blue blouse and white pants. The blouse was not too tight across her full breasts and she unbuttoned the top two buttons only. The pants were smooth and a perfect fit. No body parts were showing that shouldn't be exposed. Her dark blond hair was naturally curly and she kept it cut down to her shoulders. What stood out were her large blue eyes. From the time she was very young, her eyes were on the receiving end of a lot of compliments, not necessarily for their color but their size.

The doorbell rang and she was thinking that the outfit could make or break her this evening. She opened the door and he was smiling. He was tall and rugged looking with dark brown eyes and hair. The cleft in his chin stood out and he was handsome to her. She liked the way his hair kinked a little around his ears. As soon as he saw her outfit he gave her a low whistle. "That outfit is great but I thought we were staying in this evening?"

"We are, I just wanted to wear something new. My friends keep telling me I don't dress stylishly enough so I'm trying to change my ways."

"You don't need to change a thing but you look really pretty. The darker blue blouse makes your lighter blue eyes stand out more. Is it okay if I hug you, I don't want to wrinkle the clothes?"

"You know by now you don't have to ask." Pam was in his arms before he could say another word. She kissed him long and hard and then pulled back from him. "Can I get you a beer or a glass of wine?"

"A beer would be fine." She left him sitting on the couch and returned from the kitchen with two bottles of beer. She was sitting real close to him. They drank and talked for a little while about work.

"Have you lived with Webb since you came to this office?"

"I lived with another guy but he transferred out so Webb came here and moved in with me. Truthfully, I'd prefer to live alone because guys are really slobs. If they would have had my mother, they wouldn't be but I wouldn't wish that on my worst enemy. Webb and I work the same shift but have different days off so it isn't that bad." She was admiring his looks very much. She put her beer down on the coffee table and leaned toward him. Her breasts were up against his arm.

"Joe, there's something I want to talk to you about this evening." She got his attention. She looked into his eyes and then couldn't help kissing him on the neck. She kissed him around his ears and he groaned a little. She found his lips and he found her breasts. He moved his hands over her breasts as she kissed him some more. His thumbs moved to her nipples where he worked them around that area. He slowly started unbuttoning her blouse. His mouth traveled down her neck to the tops of her breasts. She let out a small moan. She reached for his waist band and unbuttoned his jeans. He was moving his body towards her for her to continue. She unzipped his pants slowly as he was reaching to unhook her bra. The doorbell rang and they both jumped. His jeans were bulging and he was trying to zip them up. She scurried to get her blouse back in order as the doorbell was rung again.

"Pam, you're home so open the door," her grandmother called out.

"Oh, God, not her, Pam whispered to him. They got themselves back intact. Joe grabbed his beer and held it in front of his jeans to hide the bulge. She hurried to open the door to let her grandmother in.

"I didn't think you were going to let me in, Pam. Why are your cheeks pink, are you coming down with something?" Lee stepped inside the door wearing her all too familiar blue jeans with a jean jacket. Her short curly blond hair and eyes to match Pam's, completed the picture. "Oh! you have company, dear. Hi, Joe, how have you been?" He mumbled hello to Pam's grandmother. "I don't have a lot of time but I haven't seen you in a couple of weeks. I had to check in on you this evening after closing the nursery. Is something wrong, did I interrupt something? You both look like you were up to no good. How long have you known him, Pamela?"

"Almost two months now, why do you ask?"

"That's not long enough to start making whoopee, young lady. Joe, you need to leave and come back when you can act like a gentleman to my Pamela."

"Nana, what do you think you're doing coming in here like this?"

"He's older and shouldn't be taking advantage of you like this."

"I invited him here and he's not doing anything."

"What does that big bulge between his legs mean? I would guess you weren't holding hands in church just now." Pam could have died at her grandmother's tirade. "Men only want one thing and they'll promise the moon to get into your pants. You haven't known him long enough to get intimate with him."

"Nana, you need to leave right now and stop interfering in my life."

"I'm going to leave but he needs to before I do." Joe got up and started for the door.

"Joe, please don't go," Pam called out after him. He kept going. "How could you do this to me, Nana?"

"You'll thank me in the morning. I'm disappointed in you after all the times I have told you about men and their evil ways." Pam sank down on the couch.

"Joe is not evil and you have no right to run him off. Nana, just because you had a shitty life doesn't mean I will. I can't believe you did this. This night was so important to me and you just ruined it."

"Well, if he was half a man, he would have stayed. Do I have a weapon or did I threaten to shoot him? I just told him to leave."

"He happens to be a gentleman, in case, you weren't aware of it. Acting this way, Nana, is not good if you really care about me. Maybe I'd see you more often, if you would treat me as an adult." Lee shook her head at Pam. The older woman stiffened her back and left the apartment. Pam couldn't believe what had just happened and he didn't stick around. It wasn't long before her phone started ringing. She was not about to pick it up and talk to him tonight. If he wanted to talk with her, he would have to come back. She disconnected the phone line from the wall and did the same in her bedroom. She didn't even want to hear the damn thing ringing. It was only 7:30 PM. Here she sat with an evening off, all alone, and upset at that. All she had in mind was to find out his feelings for her. She didn't even have a chance to ask

10

him. Pam wanted to talk to Julie, even though, she was working. She took her cell phone out of her purse and dialed the Communications Center's private phone number.

"Hi, Dave, this is Pam, could I speak with Julie, if she isn't busy?"

"Hold on a minute and I'll have her pick up this line."

"Hi, Pam, what's up?"

"We can't talk on this taped line but I need to talk to you, Jules. Can you come over after work?"

"Sure, I'll be there as soon as I can."

Pam watched "Cops" and "America's Most Wanted" on TV waiting for Julie. She thought she would get enough of this cop stuff at work and not want to watch it at home. She had been working for the Mission Park Police Department for two months so maybe she hadn't gotten her fill of it at work. Her friend arrived and she poured them both a glass of wine. She told Julie what had happened earlier in the evening. She couldn't believe her grandmother told Joe to leave and he took off in a hurry. "Pam, your Nana scared him off and good. He doesn't know her real well so it was best that he left. He'll be back because I think he must be seeing you because he wants to or he likes getting into your pants."

"I was all set to tell him my feelings when she came by."

"Pam, let me tell you a little about Joe's history. We started working here four years ago just a few weeks from each other's starting date. As you already know, I've been around a lot in the dating world so I decided to get friendly with him. I went after him big time. I couldn't get him to even ask me out. Deep down I felt it had something to do with my reputation. Some guys don't care how many guys you have been with and others do mind and will ask. He asked and I told him and that was that?"

"Jules, I didn't realize this."

"That's why I'm bringing it up now. I don't know who he has dated since being here. I don't believe he's ever gone out with a dispatcher or the whole office would know. He and I could talk easily to one another so we would meet at The Den in our little group and talk. He mentioned once about his very religious upbringing so deep down, it could have something to do with his actions. We all know when he met you, something happened to him. He seemed happier than he ever had been. I think he either cares about you or he's enjoying having a fling with you."

"Has he ever told you this or what his feelings are?"

"No but friends know about these things. I take it you didn't want me to come by to listen but you wanted some advice?"

"Yes, I need help because I don't want to screw up what he and I now have. Did you ever come right out and ask him why he wouldn't go out with you, Jules?"

"I hinted about it once and he used the excuse that he didn't want to get involved with someone at work. Well, we know he has gotten involved with you so that was just an excuse to me. All you can really do is wait and see what happens next. Did you expect him to be disrespectful to your Nana?"

"No, but I didn't expect him to run out either. I only wanted to ask him what his feelings were for me. I thought after a couple of months, it would be okay to bring it up. Jules, I care about him so much. I've never felt this way about another guy before. Why keep going the way we have been because I would like to know how he feels? Maybe I'm expecting too much."

"Pam, you have only been to bed with one other guy and you went with him for six months. Did you have these same feelings for him?"

"God, no, I thought I was very much in love or I never would have gone to bed with the jerk. It's different with Joe. I feel that he cares about me but I don't want to second guess his feelings. I want to hear those words from him."

"He could be a little on the cautious side since you work together and I really don't know what to tell you."

"Jules, that doesn't make any sense. If you meet someone and fall in love who cares, if you work with that person or not. I thought falling in love meant meeting someone and right away having good feelings about him. I guess I may be wrong. How can you be picky and choosey about who it turns out to be? I could never go to bed unless I cared about the guy."

"Pam, guys are different and they can usually have sex with any woman or so I have been told. Love doesn't even have to be in the picture. I have to admire you for not jumping into bed with every guy you meet. At times, I wish I had been more like you. In high school I wanted to be popular. If you didn't have sex with the guys that wouldn't be happening. I must admit, I wasn't reckless about it and carried condoms all the time. It just got me a loose reputation and a weight gain." Julie had a cute face framed by short mousy brown hair with blond streaks. She was small over most of her body but she was thick through her waist. She always wore long loose blouses to cover her fat. "Pam, how did you stay pure in high school?"

"I was never a member of a popular crowd. My classmates all seemed to like me but I didn't get invited to many parties. I had some real nice friends and that was all I needed to get me through the teen years."

"See, Pam, I wish I had been like you. Look at me, 25 years old and fat. You would never know I had a real good figure in high school. Now, I stay home on my nights off, sit in front of the TV, and snack when I'm not even hungry. I'm constantly comforting myself with food and that's pathetic. I could see me like this, if I was older and alone. Sitting on my ass as a dispatcher isn't helping me either. I need to stop eating and start exercising. I find myself looking for a nice guy who wouldn't mind screwing a fat hen." Pam felt bad for her friend. "Here I am going on and on about myself when you wanted advice."

"Hey, I'm here for you, too, Jules. Friends do help each other."

"I need to get home and I hope talking has helped you some tonight. I want to tell you that I'm releasing you from training status on Sunday. You'll be on your own, girl, and you caught on so fast."

"You really think I'm ready to be on my own?"

"I'm very sure of it. You have all the good traits of being a real good dispatcher."

"Thanks for coming by, Jules. I'll figure something out without scaring Joe away completely. I'll see my grandmother tomorrow and I'll make sure this evening will never happen again."

"Oh, I almost forgot to tell you that you'll be going out on patrol next week. It was penciled in on the schedule. You're going on Wednesday with none other than Officer Webb, better know, as the 'Loose Cannonball'."

"I have the best luck on my rides with officers. If nothing else, it'll be exciting since he can't stay out of trouble." She walked her friend to the door.

"Now, Pam, hang in there and don't let this night get you down. We have no control over our grandmothers and Joe didn't want to cause problems between you and Lee. He's quite the gentlemen and he respects his elders."

"That may be true but it was a big let down for me." They both said goodbye.

At least the night was no longer young and she might be able to sleep. She went into the bathroom to brush her teeth and she thought about Julie and Joe. Pam often thought that Julie was a borderline flirt with Joe and now she knew why. She was sure her friend still cared for Joe. She wondered, if it could ever turn into a problem for them. Pam climbed into bed knowing this was the only time of the day that she could really do some heavy thinking. She couldn't help but wonder how it'll be, if they ever declare their love for each other. They certainly had made out on most of their dates and had been intimate for

13

the past month only. Two months was long enough to know how much they cared about each other. They would have made love this evening, if her Nana hadn't shown up. Since they first made love he seemed to like being with her and she definitely enjoyed being with him. They were getting more comfortable with each other but still no words from him about his feelings. She didn't know what he was waiting for unless he wanted her to be first. They were at a big standoff and things between them definitely needed to change. Maybe men resisted change more than women but she wouldn't be happy, if things were to stay the same. Her Nana always said that talk was cheap and it was important to keep the lines of communication open for a good relationship. She adored her Nana but she wasn't going to let her run her own life into the ground. She cared a lot for Joe and wanted him in her life for a good long time. She felt that he wanted the same thing.

Chapter 2

Pam woke up the next morning to a small ray of sunshine from a faulty blind hitting her pillow. The digital clock said 8:15 and it was a perfect time to rise. She wasn't a late sleeper, even if, she went to bed after midnight. She had gone off to sleep with a lot going through her head and she was waking up in the same manner. After getting the coffee pot started in the kitchen, Pam went into the shower. The sprayer felt good cascading over her body. It didn't take her long to towel off, don her robe, and grab a cup of coffee. She took her cup out onto the patio to sit down and enjoy the morning sun and sounds. The sun was splashing over the lemon trees with its golden rays. She looked across at the grove that came right up to the back of the apartment complex. The trees were glistening along their perfect rows as the dew on their leaves was kissed by the sun. She loved this time of day. Pam had two rose bushes in pots and they were in full bloom. Listening to the birds singing their happy songs was enjoyable to her ears. Atticus her favorite mockingbird was diving relentlessly at a cat near the edge of the grove. How he loved to tease the cat and make loud squawking sounds? Sometimes he sat on the roof overhang and sang his little heart out. Working the swing shift made it possible for her to enjoy much of the morning. She made herself a mental note to call her Nana, in case, Pam hadn't gotten through to her last evening.

Her whole young life had been overshadowed by her mother and nanny telling her what to do and with whom. She left her rich life on the Northern Coast of California to be near her grandmother on the Southern Coast. Nana

Lee was the poor side of the family and the side that Pam truly belonged in. She made the decision to stand up to her parents and move on with her life in a down to earth middle class atmosphere. Her mother was appalled that she would leave their lifestyle of grandeur to make it on her own. She traded her Mercedes in for a Chevrolet Malibu and stopped buying her dressy clothes in the Nob Hill section of San Francisco. She, now, shopped at clothing store chains which she liked to do very much.

Lee Duncan, her Nana, had made it possible for her to end up in Mission Park. Pam fell in love with this Area on each of her summer visits for the past ten years. She enjoyed visiting her Nana for the whole month of July. Lee sent her an application a few months ago that dispatchers were needed for the police department. She traveled down the coast and stayed with Lee while going through the complete hiring process. Pam had a job interview with them and they gave her an extensive background check. She passed all the stages of the hiring process. Pam was happy to be on her own. She was glad to leave her family and the boyfriend she had just broken up with. She had finished three years of college at Redwood University where she had worked part time for the past year in the college admission's office. Her dad was instrumental in her finding that job by his hefty contributions to the college's athletic programs. Her mother wanted her to stay with them and finish her final year of college. She wasn't happy with Pam's choice of moving away from them. She had been very protective and yet over indulgent to their daughter and she didn't think her own mother was the best influence for her. Pam didn't care for the rain and misty weather that was prevalent for the North Coast. She did miss the giant redwood trees. They stood so tall in the forest and made other normal size trees around them look like bushes. Her mom kept busy with her charitable causes and country club membership. Pam had no siblings and never cared for her rather lonely existence.

When Pam moved to Mission Park she wanted to be accepted as just a regular person. She told no one of her wealthy family background. She thought she could pull it off and live a happy and normal life.

She went out into the kitchen and poured herself another cup of coffee. She sat down again and was thinking about Joe and herself. On May 1, 2004, two months earlier, she started working at the police department. She thought about the first time she had seen him in his uniform. He stepped into the Dispatch Center and she looked up into his friendly brown eyes. Joe gave her a wink and introduced himself. She was hooked from that day forward. They met socially for the first time at the Den, a local bar, her first week completed.

She had just turned 21 in April and it was her first time drinking legally. They talked and hardly knew anyone else was present. After the others went home, they stayed and talked until the place closed. He walked her to her car and they talked even longer. He asked her to lunch the next day and she accepted. They have been seeing each other ever since, always enjoying each other's company.

Pam thought he might call her this morning since she was sure he tried last evening. She didn't understand why he left when she asked him to stay. Her Nana had scared him off and she would have to deal with her. She was aware that she had a lot to learn about men. She plugged her kitchen phone back in and dialed her grandmother's number.

"Well, Pam, have you been thinking about what I told you last night?" Nana Lee asked her.

"You had no business telling him to leave and bossing me around either. I'm an adult and I'll live my life as I see fit. I'll be lucky, if he ever sees me again, thanks to you. I care about him and I want him in my life."

"He'll be back or he isn't the man for you. You should be upset with him not me. I asked him to leave but he didn't have to do it. He may need to grow some balls. I see that you have two choices either ignore him completely or talk to him like nothing is wrong. Knowing you the way I do, you'll choose to ignore him. You don't really need my advice after all."

"I'm not calling to ask for advice but to tell you to let me live my own life."

"You're not handling your own life very well, my dear, I need to help you along. You should be grateful that I care enough to want to do that."

"I'll admit I don't have the experience you have had but I need to learn on my own. How did you ever get through your younger years?"

"It was easy in the fifties and I think the easiest generation in many years. Life was simple and nice. I went to school dances and not always with a date. We had rules to go by, we obeyed, or suffered the consequences. Girls went out on dates and kept their clothes on and guys did the same. There was no real pressure just good clean fun. Pam, let me give you a little advice, don't be in such a big hurry to live your life. You have so many years ahead of you. I made hasty decisions back then that I have regretted and I don't want you to do the same thing."

"Nana, it's hard to imagine that you have regrets. You got a divorce but you raised my mother and started your own nursery business that you love so much."

"Which reminds me, Pam, I have a shipment of plants coming in any minute and I need to decide where they are to be unloaded. Hope you don't mind, if I hang up now."

"Not at all and I'll be over to visit on my next days off."

She was beginning to wonder what was going to happen at work. He was always in the office doing reports when she arrived for her shift. They would talk for a few minutes and it was always nice to see him before he went out on patrol. He stood out from the other officers in her opinion with every crease in place on his uniform and all his equipment shining. The swing shift started at 1:45 for the officers and 2:00 for the dispatchers. The officers stayed until 10:15 and dispatchers left at 10:00. Her current days off were Fridays and Saturdays and he had signed up for the same ones. Their first month together was hard because they didn't share any days off. They got to eat lunch together but there were no chances for regular dates. This past month they were together a lot more and she was glad.

It was hard for her to enter the building. She always got to work 15 minutes early and today she was earlier than that. She figured he would be in the locker room getting into his uniform so she would be able to miss seeing him. The business office was in the front of the building with a long hallway to the dispatch center. In between the main office and Communication's Center were the briefing room, locker room, evidence locker and the sergeant's office. She entered the building and put her sunglasses on top of her head. She was approaching the locker room door when it opened wide and Joe walked out almost touching her. She jumped back and her sunglasses fell to the floor.

"I'll get those," he said as she started to kneel down to retrieve them. With one swoop, he picked them up and handed them to her.

"Thank you," she told him. She avoided his eyes and kept walking towards the Center's door.

"You're not even going to say hello, Miss Pam?" He asked her.

She stopped. "You may not like what I have to say, Mr. Pellerini."

"Go ahead and say it because it can't be any worse than what your grandmother said to me last night."

"I didn't think she would run you off when I asked you not to leave."

"I try and respect my elders and I didn't want to cause any problems for you."

"You left because that's what you wanted to do so I got the answer I was looking for last night. I won't bother you anymore." He turned and went into the briefing room and she continued down the hallway to the Center.

"Oh, God," said Julie as Pam entered the radio room and closed the door.

There was sadness in Pam's eyes. "You must have run into Joe."

"Yes, I did," said Pam as she opened her locker to get her headset. The dispatchers had small boxlike lockers located at one end of the long but narrow kitchen.

There was, also, a full size stove, refrigerator, microwave and cupboards. A sink and small counter top area completed the room.

"What did he have to say?" Julie asked her friend.

"He left because he didn't want to cause problems for me with my grandmother. It doesn't make me feel any better. I was hoping I could avoid him today but I couldn't." They both took their headsets and went out into the radio room. Part of the Center's equipment consisted of two radio consoles, one for police business and the other for fire and ambulance calls. There were three desk positions used to answer the many telephone lines. The supervisor had a small office in a back corner of the room. The officers were frequently going in and out of the Center for one thing or another. She was wishing he would not come in today.

"Hey, Chelsea," Mike bellowed out to Pam, "come over her and let me watch you breathe." Mike Barton had a nickname for everyone especially his co-workers. He called Pam, Chelsea Chest and liked to admire her ample breasts. "You need to work day shift so I can look at you for eight hours instead of just at shift change." She was ignoring him. "You don't look so good today did you have a bad night? Don't tell me, Peckerini, kept you up all night savoring those lush melons?" He called Joe this particular name because his last name was Pellerini. She gave him a look that made him decide not to tease her anymore. He explained to her what was going on with the troops. Mike was a 15 year veteran of the dispatch center with a boisterous personality. He didn't care what he said or to whom he said it. He had a graying beard and thinning hair. He has walked with a cane since an accident left him crippled in one leg when he was young. He described to Pam about a non-injury accident that was pending. The sergeant would send an officer out from the office to handle it. There was not a lot happening on this Sunday afternoon but Pam knew things would pick up as the day progressed into the evening. Chris walked in and yelled hello to everyone.

"Chris, what are you doing here?"

"Dave called in sick so I was nominated to come in. What a nice way to spend my day off." He gave them a thumbs down gesture and they knew how he was feeling.

"I have a project for you today, you can try and cheer us all up," Pam told him. She was just getting comfortable at her position when Joe walked into the Center. He made a beeline for Julie who was seated at the fire console waiting to dispatch engines and paramedics. Chris was working one of the phone positions and the phone lines were ringing frequently.

"Jules, would you please run a driver's license number for me?"

"Sure," she told him, "and how are you today?"

"I'm not good and who in hell cares." He gave her the license number and the information appeared on her computer screen. She shut up.

"I wouldn't try talking to him, Jules, his underwear is too tight," Chris told Julie. Joe gave him a dirty look and he didn't say anymore.

"Do you want a copy to take with you, Officer Pellerini?" Julie asked.

"No, I just need the status of the license, please?"

"He's expired and not much else on his record."

"Go ahead and print it. I may need it later." She gave him the printout and he left the room. Chris had a worried look on his face.

"What's going on?" He asked Pam. "You didn't call me last night as you promised so I thought you were happily romping in bed. Did you break up with him?"

"He was visiting when my Nana showed up and it went downhill from there. I don't think she cares for him and she likes to boss everyone around."

"What did the asshole do?"

"It just isn't working out between us. He left because she asked him to leave."

"Did she catch you doing the dirty deed.? What are you not telling me? You two are like dogs in heat around each other so what in the fuck happened?" Pam could tell his curiosity had gotten the best of him. "I warned you about dating officers when you came to work here but you wouldn't listen to me. Tell me what happened?"

"Chris, I just told you what happened. He didn't want to be in my company and that was it. Why does everything have to be so dramatic for you?"

"Did he tell you what his feelings were before he left?"

"We didn't get that far so there's nothing else to tell." Pam was getting a little annoyed at all of Chris's questions.

"How can I give you advice, if I don't get any details?" His emotions were getting the best of him. "Tell me what the prick did and I'll take care of him. He'll be chasing loose dogs every time I'm on the radio with him. I have an idea, let's go to the Den after work and discuss things. You can drink a couple of beers and spill your guts to me." He was chuckling to himself.

"Sure, I'll go," Pam said. "I don't have another damn thing to do this evening."

"Same here," said Julie, "that sounds better than going home and going right to bed all alone. Maybe I might pick up someone who'll be glad to take me home and make me happy."

"So it's settled," Chris told them. "We can go out and howl the rest of the night away." He always enjoyed going out with his friends to the Den.

The Lion's Den was a family type restaurant with a bar at one end and a few booths to accommodate the drinkers. The rest of the room had tables for dining. They had a barbeque pit at the rear of the building and were well known in this area for serving outstanding steaks and ribs. Officers and dispatchers were known to end up there at the end of their shifts. They all called it going to choir practice, after Joseph Wambaugh's book of the same title. It was a good way to have a couple of beers and unwind after work. They would talk about all the events that had gone down during the shift. They had fun and enjoyed the time together. The three friends sat down at a large booth, the one they normally occupied, and ordered a round of beer on tap. The bar was fairly quiet, even though, there were quite a few people in the place.

"Okay," said Chris looking at Pam, "what's the scoop?"

"He and Nana had words and he left my place. I asked him to stay but he left anyway so that was the big fucking deal, Chris."

"There has to be more to it than that. What did the dick head do to you? You know there's a reason they call cops dicks? They only think with their dicks and it gets them into trouble all the time." The beer came and Pam was thirsty. She downed half her glass at one time. Chris and Julie looked at each other but didn't say anything. He told the women how he had sent Webb to a simple accident the other day and it turned into a major incident. "He's a loose cannon ball and they're going to send you out on a ride with him?" Chris asked Pam.

"I don't like it when he's on the radio and his voice gets higher when he is excited which is most of the time," Julie added. Chris and Pam grinned knowing exactly what she was talking about. Pam finished her beer and asked the waitress for a second one. Her two friends were not quite ready for a second round. They chatted some more about the officers. Soon, Julie and Chris were ready for a second and Pam ordered her third.

"Don't look now but the Cannonball and Peckerini just walked in," Chris said. The booths were all taken so the two officers walked over to the dispatchers.

"Do you guys mind, if we join you?" Webb asked. "We really don't want to sit with some strangers." The dispatchers scooted over and Joe ended up next to Pam. The waitress took the officer's orders as she delivered Pam her fourth beer. Webb was a clean cut looking guy, short brown hair, and had a medium build. He was an ex-Marine and he let everyone know it. He and Joe were friends on and off the job. Joe dating Pam had curtailed a lot of time they once spent together.

"How's it going?" Webb asked the dispatchers.

"We were wondering why you were so quiet this evening over the radio?" Pam asked. "Couldn't you find any trouble to get into?"

"No, I couldn't and it wasn't because I didn't try very hard." The others grinned, including Joe.

"You can turn a quiet shift into a nightmare," Pam added. The beer was talking now. Her words were starting to slur. Joe took a good look into her eyes. She signaled the waitress for a fifth round who promptly returned with a fresh one. She started drinking it immediately. "If you would please excuse me, I need to go to the restroom." Pam looked at the officers and they stood up to let her out. She had to steady herself at the end of the table before walking off. The guys sat back down. She came back to the booth in a few minutes and sat back down. "What did I miss?" She asked.

"How many beers has she had?" Joe asked Chris.

"This is her fifth one," Chris told them.

"Why are you letting her drink so much?" Joe questioned Chris. Pam didn't know what to think.

"Look, asshole, she's a big girl now and we're not spoiling her time here. We would like to know what in hell you did to make her drink so much beer?" Chris was speaking in a defiant tone. "Don't blame us for something you have obviously done to her." Joe lowered his eyes as he knew Chris was right.

"Well, Pam, I want to take you home," Joe said to her. "You never drink this much and you're way out of control."

"I'm fine, Mr. Pellerini, you're not my keeper and you don't give a damn whether I'm okay or not."

Joe turned to her and said, "please let me take you home, that's all I want to do."

"I don't want to go home," she shot right back at him. "There is nothing at home for me. My life stinks right now, thanks to you, so I might as well be out with my friends having a good time."

"You don't look like you are having a very good time," he shot right back at her. "You're having trouble walking and you're slurring your words."

"It's none of your damn business what it looks like, this is my life and I'll do as I please." Joe got real quiet and so did Pam after this exchange. Chris tried to joke and ease the situation but he wasn't successful. "If you two will let me out, I'll go home now," Pam said slurring every word. "I bet tonight I'll be able to sleep the night away."

"Pam, just let me drop you off, it's on my way home."

"I'm just fine." They got up and let her leave the table. Joe was determined so he followed her out the front entrance. He went out into the parking lot and saw her trying to get her keys out of her purse.

"Pam, as a friend, I can't let you drive home tonight. You must know you shouldn't be driving after five beers. Don't do something stupid and get hurt or take the chance of hurting someone else. Don't forget that you work for the police department."

"What do you mean, me get hurt?" She looked into his eyes. "After you walked out on me last night and made me feel like a fool." Joe ignored her words.

"You could hurt an innocent person by driving drunk and I know you would never want to do that. Just leave your car here and I'll drop you off."

"Okay, you're right, I shouldn't be driving." He opened his passenger side door and she sat down on the seat. He closed the door and got behind the wheel. She was fumbling with the seat belt and he leaned across her to belt her in. "Why do you have to be so damn good looking, Joe?" He finished with her belt and was close to her face.

"Is that what you think?"

"You're one handsome guy." She put her hand on the side of his face and kissed him on the lips. "You're one sexy guy, too." Joe started the car and drove off. Her head was back against the seat and she had turned to look at him. "I must be a sorry sight?"

"You're beautiful, Pam, even when you're drunk."

They arrived at her apartment and he helped her inside to her bedroom. "Do you think you can get yourself into bed?" She sat down on the edge of the bed.

"Yes, I can manage, if you don't want to help me."

"It'll be better, if you can do it yourself tonight."

"Joe, last night I invited you here to ask you what you thought of me. I dressed up nicer than usual because I thought you would like me better that way. We have never told each other our feelings and I wanted to tell you that

I was falling in love with you." Joe hung his head. "I guess you don't feel that way about me, do you? Is it because we work together and you don't want to get involved? If that's the case then you should have been honest with me before we first went to bed."

"I care about you, Pam, but this isn't the time or the place to talk about it. You need to be stone sober for us to talk on this subject. I'll come by in the morning to pick you up and take you to your car. We can talk then. I'm sorry about last night but your grandmother pissed me off. She came into your place ordering me around so I thought it was best that I leave. I didn't really want to go."

"I talked to her today about that and told her to never do it again. She still thinks of me as being very young and she always will. I wanted you to make love to me last night and I was so disappointed when you left. Joe, do you think I'm sexy enough? Is there something I could do to make myself more appealing?"

"You're the sexist woman on earth to me. Do you know what makes you sexy?" She shook her head. "It's those big, beautiful, innocent eyes."

"You don't want to make love to me now since we didn't last night? You could undress me and go from there. I really want you, Joe."

"Yes, I could undress you but I don't want to take advantage of you when you're drunk, Pam. I have to be going and I'll be back in the morning around 10." He leaned over, kissed her on top of the head, and left. How disappointed she was that he wouldn't stay longer. Something must be terribly wrong with me for him to leave she thought. Why won't he tell me?

Chapter 3

True to his word, Joe arrived the next day in the middle of the morning, to take Pam to her car. He had a worried look in his eyes just like last night when she told him she cared about him. She couldn't wait to find out what he had to say. She didn't think his facial expression looked good for the two of them. They got back to her apartment and they both sat down on the couch. He couldn't even look her in the eyes. He sat with his head bent over and his eyes cast down. "Pam, the night before last I did a real stupid thing. I left your apartment and went to the Den for a couple of beers. I called a few times but you didn't answer your phone. I was hoping you'd show up there but I guess you were upset with me for leaving your place. I drank more than a couple of beers and I took a female to her place and spent the night." The tears quickly filled Pam's eyes as his words hit her hard.

"Thanks for being honest with me, Joe. I want you leave now." Her heart was pounding fast and she felt the air space around her body falling into a million pieces.

"Pam, you have to let me explain," he pleaded.

"Why in hell do I need any details? I don't want to hear about your big night with someone else and I mean that. Who do you think I am that I would want to hear something like that? You did what you wanted to do and that's that." She wished she could stop her tears but she couldn't.

"Pam, I care about you a lot and what I did had nothing to do with you."

"How can you sit there and say that." If my grandmother had not interrupted us, we would have made love. You ran out on me and turned immediately to another woman for your sexual needs. How can you say it had nothing to do with me? You could have come back here after Nana left but you chose not to. I didn't even know that you had someone else you were seeing. I must be the biggest idiot in the universe to think that I was the only one in your life."

"I'll leave now." He headed for the door and then turned back around when he touched the door knob. "Look, I didn't know your feelings either but I can't take back what I did. I wish I could but I can't. Please think this through and give me a second chance. Pam, I want only you in my life and no other woman." He left and she cried her heart out.

A short while later her phone rang and she picked it up. "Pam, I'm calling to see, if you're okay," Julie said to her.

"I'm just fucking wonderful so what did you expect?"

"I was worried because Joe called and told me the whole story."

"Jules, I don't want any details from you or him."

"I won't say a thing to you but you should know the whole story. That woman doesn't mean anything to him and I know how much Joe means to you. He feels really bad about what happened. Do you think you'll be able to give him a second chance?"

"This may sound crass to you but it's none of your business what I'm going to do. I'm not able to talk about intimate details of my life the way he can. He should have told me there was someone else he was seeing. It would have made a big difference in our relationship. I have a question for you, Jules. When he wouldn't date you, did you take the rejection in a grand way or did you cry and carry on like I'm doing right now."

"Joe, didn't care about me as a girlfriend, we became friends only."

"Jules, I truly thought I was the only woman in his life and then he drops this bomb. He must know her quite well to spend the night with her. He must have a whole bunch of secrets he's keeping to himself."

"You won't let me give you any details and there's more to his story."

"Oh, I bet there is," Pam said sarcastically. "I'm sure he's full of excuses for what he did. He was here with me that evening and my Nana shows up so he leaves. He spends that very night with another woman. He could have returned when Nana left but he didn't. He made the wrong choice, if he expects to keep seeing me."

"He didn't have to tell you what he did."

"He most certainly did have to. I'm assuming the reason he told me is because he didn't practice safe sex. What other reason would I have to know?"

"You should ask him that because it's important."

"I have every right to know the answer and it was not forthcoming. I don't care about getting a sexually transmitted disease and he should care about me and himself. It makes me wonder if there have been other times with other women."

"You had better ask that question before you jump into bed with him again."

"Don't worry, Jules, if I was going to jump into bed again with him, I certainly would. I don't have any plans to do that. Life is hard enough without being disease ridden for the rest of it. What he did brought up a lot of questions for me. He could be seeing others and I'm surprised that he told me because you're right he didn't have to. It makes me wonder what he's saving me for in his scheme of things."

"Pam, he doesn't want to lose you. This is the first woman he has been with since you two met. He told me that when he called. He was completely taken by surprise when you admitted you were falling in love with him. He felt good about you but he didn't know your feelings."

"I should feel so good about him that I go to a bar, pick up a guy, and have sex. Do you think he would like that?"

"That wouldn't solve a God damn thing and you know it."

"I wouldn't stoop that low to hurt the person I care about. I thought we would be good for each other but this isn't the first time I've been wrong. At least, I'm not afraid to admit it. I'm upset and I need to pull myself together before I go to work so I'm hanging up, Jules."

Pam glanced at the clock. She had time to eat a quick lunch and then get ready for work. After eating, she checked her face in the mirror and saw redness around her eyes. Her skin, also, had red splotches from crying. The Austin skin tone was prevalent all over her body. She would keep her sunglasses on inside the building and hide from the cruel world.

In ten minutes she arrived at the office and parked her car. She noticed his car as she rushed into the building. Pam looked down the hallway and he was waiting for her outside the dispatch center door. She took a deep breath and walked towards him. She didn't feel like talking to him. "Pam, I need to talk to you," he said as she approached him. "Please give me a few minutes of your time."

"I believe we said it all this morning. You were extremely honest with me and you got your point across."

"We haven't even scratched the surface. Can't we start over with our relationship instead of throwing it away? You said you were falling in love with me so it should be worth fixing. Not talking about it and trying to avoid each other, is not going to work."

"I need to know, if you practiced safe sex or not, Joseph? This is my main concern at the moment." He didn't look too good. "It should be an easy question to answer."

"No, I did not use a condom."

"Joe, are there going to be anymore surprises and why would you act in such a reckless manner? This hasn't even had a chance to sink in."

"Did you see me jump into bed with you last night?"

"Thank you for sparing me and not going to bed with me."

"I would never do anything to cause you harm so that's why I left last night. Just meet me after work to talk."

"I don't know what to think, Joe. I'm so disappointed in you."

"If it will make you feel better, I'm more disappointed in myself. Talking never hurt anyone and just give me a little bit of your time." She finally agreed to meet him at the Den. She continued into the Center and grabbed her headset.

"Hey, Pam, what's with the sunglasses?" Chris asked her. Julie already knew the reason and she hadn't had a chance to fill Chris in."

"My eyes are real sensitive to the light today and I have a headache. I would like to work the phones, if that is all right with you two." They both said it was fine.

"Pam, we know you've been crying so why don't you level with us for once," Chris said. "We're just friends here today and you're free to talk."

"You might consider minding your own business for once." For Pam to volunteer to work the phones was punishment and the least favorite part of her job. She was glad the phones were busy and the time passed quickly. Chris sent her a message and told her to find some loose dogs for Joe to chase. She smiled at the thought of Joe chasing dogs all around the streets. Joe didn't come into the Center during the shift and this was unusual for him. She guessed he was giving her eight hours to think, like he said he would.

She was reluctant to meet him but she had given her word. She wasn't in any hurry to get there ahead of him but she didn't want to hang around the office either. She arrived at the Den and took their usual table. There were only a few people in the place. She noticed a lone female sitting at a small booth. The female had long dark brown hair and was rather plain looking. Pam wasn't close enough to get a real good look at her. She surely can't be the one. Pam knew that every time she came in to this bar, she'd be looking around to see her. I now have a new hobby, she told herself, looking for the tramp in the den of inequity. She glanced at the entrance in time to see Joe come through the door. He got to the booth where the dark haired lady was sitting and the woman said something to him. He turned his head and said something back but didn't stop. Pam knew it had to be the woman he spent the night with. He came up to the table with a big smile on his face and she was not in the mood to smile back.

"Is something wrong?" He asked her.

"Is the woman you just talked to the one you spent the night with?" Pam asked.

"You're not even going to say hello without asking me questions about who it was." The waitress came by and they both ordered a beer.

"Well, hello, Joe, it's so nice to see you. Is the woman you just talked to the woman you spent the night with?"

"Yes, she's the one but I need to tell you about Saturday night."

"Joe, I don't want details and I'm damn serious."

"Yes, you do and hopefully I can make you see everything in a different light and you can forgive me."

"I don't need to forgive you, Joseph, because we're not a couple nor are we even going together."

"I thought we were only dating each other for the past two months."

"I was only dating you, Joe. I don't know how many women you have been with. You have every right to sleep with whomever you wish. I want no explanations or apologies. This should be easy for you."

"This is not easy for me but very difficult. If we didn't care about each other, it would be easy."

Pam started to get up from her seat. "Joe, I swear I'll leave if you continue." He stopped talking and sat not knowing what to do. "I do not want any details. She's not big enough to carry you to her place so you went with her voluntarily."

"I didn't come by here to pick her up; I came by hoping you would show up."

"Well, the scenario is getting better all the time."

"I didn't show up so that gave you the right to pick up any female in here and take her home." He shook his head. "I'm not being sarcastic now but I'm trying to convince myself that you had every right to do what you did. Do you see a ring on my finger or anything else to show that we are committed to each other? No, I don't think so. I've been thinking this over a great deal and you're right and I'm wrong for being upset with you. If you're looking for me to forgive you then I forgive you. I don't want to discuss all the details."

"I won't feel good about it, if I don't tell you what happened."

"Go ahead, Joe, give me all the wonderful details."

"The female that I spoke to hangs around here and all the officers know her. They turn to her, if their marriage is unhappy or if they are between girlfriends. She is always available. I have never had anything to do with her before Saturday. I never wanted a thing to do with her but she came in and sat down at the booth I was in. She kept telling me how good she could make me feel, if I would go to her place." Joe stopped for a minute before continuing and she knew it was difficult for him. "The beer got in control of me and I took her home. I did not have intercourse with her but she gave me a blow job without a rubber being used." Joe stopped again.

"Did you spend the night?"

"Yes, I did."

"Why would you spend the night?"

"I told you I was drunk and she promised another one in the morning. When I woke up in the morning, I got the hell out of there as fast as I could. I was disgusted with myself but I couldn't change what had already happened."

Pam had heard enough and ordered another beer. "When I first came in here I looked around to see, if she might be here. I knew that every time I came in here I would be looking around. She's staring this way. Saturday night I was going to tell you that I loved you and I felt you would tell me the same thing. I wanted you to sweep me away to my bed and make love to me to cement a commitment between us. How pathetic is that? It's bad, if you think about for a few minutes."

"Why are you putting yourself down like this?"

"There are so many loose women around that I don't stand a chance. Why did you go home with her and not want to take me to bed?"

"I never said I didn't want to take you to bed, Pam."

"I know I'm very inexperienced but I felt when we started making love that you would be patient with me. I've never given a guy a blow job because I'm not a woman of the world. They didn't teach such things in school but I'm willing to learn. I know guys like that or so I've heard. I just need some lessons."

30

"I don't know what to say because you're right. I should have turned to you instead of a stranger who I know nothing about. I'll be going to the doctor to be checked because I never want to cause problems for you."

"This conversation is going nowhere so we need to talk about other things."

"What would you like to talk about?" he asked her

"Let's talk about your family? Every time I have brought up your family, you get quiet and you don't say a thing. I'm very interested in you and what your family might be like."

"I have a mother, two sisters and my father died a couple of years ago. I was brought up in Reno. I left home and joined the Navy as soon as I turned 18 and graduated from high school. I wanted to travel in the Navy but my recruiter talked me into the Shore Patrol so I could go into law enforcement when my hitch was up. I found out that Mission Park was hiring so I took the test, passed everything, and ended up here right out of the Navy. That was the luckiest break I have ever received. I met you and we're here so now you know it all."

"Do you see your family very often?"

"No, I do not. Mother is living with my sisters. Her health isn't very good. They had me a little late in life and I can only assume I was a big mistake."

"Why do you say that?"

"My dad was an alcoholic who somehow managed to make a living for us. Mother went to church everyday and she liked to beat me up. I was her little hobby. I thought I was a bad kid until I got older and found out I wasn't so bad. I think she took my dad's drinking out on me. The last time I saw her was at Dad's funeral and I'll never see her again. My sisters are taking turns taking care of her. Every six months she goes back and forth between the two families. They know I don't want anything to do with her and they understand."

"I knew there was something about your life that you didn't want to tell me."

"Do you have any secrets?" He asked.

"I'm sure there are things I haven't told you but I wouldn't refer to them as secrets. My life was nothing compared to yours. I wasn't brutalized physically but my mother did a number on me mentally. No matter what grade I brought home it was never good enough for her. She always said I wasn't trying hard enough. She wanted me to go to college for four years and have a remarkable career. I was suppose to meet a rich guy, live in a big house, have two children, and belong to the country club. Her dreams were suppose to be my dreams, too. At least once a week I heard the same old phrase from her, 'you can have all the brains in the world but if you have no ambition then you have nothing'. I've had a rough day, and I need to go home and try to sleep."

"I need to leave, also." They walked out together into the parking lot.

"Joe, I'm sorry for all that you had to go through when you were young. I had no idea things were so bad for you."

"I'm sure there were kids who were treated a lot worse than I was."

"Just the same, your mother had major problems and took it out on you." She looked back at the entrance and the tramp was standing by the door watching them. "I guess your girlfriend is wondering, if you'll be with her again this evening."

"She is not, nor will she ever be my girlfriend. Pam, I hope you'll reconsider seeing me and I'll give you all the time you need."

"I'm so disappointed in you, Joe. I had such hopes for the two of us but now I don't know. I told you I was falling in love with you and you tell me that you care about me. You can care about a damn dog, a friend, or even a stranger that you read about. I wanted to hear so much more than just caring. Do you think you could give me a hug, Joe?" He took her into his arms and held her close. She pulled back from him and looked into his eyes. "It does feel so good for me to be in your arms."

Chapter 4

She and Joe had lunch together at the beginning of the week but being with him did not seem the same. They talked about work and their friends but nothing was said about his little escapade. She figured he was giving her time to decide, if she still wanted to see him steadily once more. Pam didn't need a cooling off period. She definitely wanted to be with him and over time she would be able to forget about the big mistake he made with the tramp. This particular situation was taking its toll on him. She cared about him so much. He said he cared about her but he did not declare his love. Maybe caring and loving was the same to him. She was spending a lot of time rethinking their relationship.

She showed up for work on Tuesday and the dispatchers started talking about her ride along for the next day with Webb. "You're lucky to be going with Webb," Chris said.

"Of all the officers to get to go with, I'm stuck with him. He'll probably end up in a remote area of the county, miles from the city, backing up a deputy."

"Now that would be a little bit off his beat don't you think?" Chris asked. "I can see him doing it though. The guy knows no boundaries when he's out there fighting crime."

"You must know they would never send you out with Joe since you have been dating," Jules said to her. "God only knows what could happen, if he took you out in that big cruiser. It sticks out like a sore thumb and you couldn't hide it very well, even in, a remote area."

"You mean he and I could end up in a lemon grove necking for the whole shift," Pam added. "That would be a big no-no." They all laughed at this thought.

"You're the first one to ride on swing shift. It surprises me that Marge will allow you to do that," Julie offered. "She must trust you to behave yourself. She has never let one of us ride in the evening."

"She figures Pam being new wouldn't know much about getting into trouble," Chris told them. We haven't had time to teach her how to be an errant person."

"I'm surprised, too, because once the sun goes down you never know what wild things could happen," Pam told them.

"If the old heifer heard you talk like this she wouldn't even let you go," Chris said. The dispatchers were well aware of Marge Stewart the Communications Supervisor's strict rules of conduct. She runs the Center in a very tight manner. There had been rumors flying around about her husband having a fling with an 18 year old co-worker and he had gotten her pregnant. It appears they may have been more than just rumors because Marge's unhappiness was being felt in the Communications Center. She was not liked because she took her frustrations out on the dispatchers. Chris seemed to be in her office quite often and he couldn't stand her. He nicknamed her office the Blue Room. She was a 50 year old, short, heavy set woman with dark stringy hair and thick glasses. He vowed to them all, if she was dying on the Center's floor, he would not pick up the phone and dial 9-1-1. She made it known, she did not like to send dispatchers out in patrol cars with officers, even though, the rides were mandated by the Department.

"Hey, let's do a little howling tonight after work at the Den?" Chris asked his co-workers. "The three amigos here don't get out often enough."

"I don't know, Chris, I'm not in a very good mood," Pam told him.

"I'm not either and I have a headache that will not mix well with drinking," Julie said. "Come to think of it, a headache doesn't mix well with anything."

"Getting out with a friend might help you both. When are you and Joe going to get back together so you can be your old self, Pamela?"

"Chris you get way too personal at times. I don't even know what I'm feeling right now and it's still none of your business." Pam decided against revealing too much of her feelings because Joe and Julie still talked with each other.

"So go out with me to unwind and you'll have a good time," Chris said. He

34

liked to prod his friends into doing things he cared to do. "You both don't even have to drink alcohol. Have a coke and let me drink and I'll even let you drive me home."

"Okay, I'll go with you but don't expect an evening of happiness to radiate from me," Pam said.

"I knew you wouldn't let me down, my friend. It's terrible, if you have to drink alone and don't have a buddy to keep you company."

"Chris, you know I would go but this headache is too much," Julie said. "You, two can have a good time and I'll catch you next time." The rest of the shift went well and before she knew it, they were out the door. She wished she was seeing Joe and everything was fine between.

On her way over to the Den she wondered, if Joe was still seeing the tramp to take care of his needs, even though, he told Pam he only wanted her in his life. It was definitely a black cloud hanging over them. She parked at the side of the building so that no one driving in would know she was there. Chris had arrived at the bar just ahead of her and secured the booth. She passed the tramp sitting by herself in the small booth. Pam figured the woman had probably been coming here for some time but she never noticed her before. She guessed Joe would go for a real foxy lady and she was not. Pam noticed she had a small figure and wore too much make up. He must like his women on the plain side she thought since he settled for her and Pam knew she was not spectacular.

The woman's heavy make up only made her look worse.

"Don't look now but Peckerini is in the building," Chris said. Pam couldn't believe it when he walked over and sat with the tramp.

"Oh, my God," she said out loud.

"What do you see?" Chris turned and saw Joe sitting with another woman. "Is she the one he dumped you for?"

"Yes, it is but I didn't think he would ever sit with her like this." The tears welled up in her eyes as she looked at them together.

"She looks like Elvira without tits." Chris said. "He could have almost any woman and he trades you in for her. I have absolutely no respect for him at all."

"When you're drunk looks don't always matter or so I have heard," Pam said.

"If you drank a six pack of beer and Quasimoto asked to take you home, I think you would know the difference."

"Chris, he would look ugly to anyone, even in the dark."

"Look, Pam, don't let him see you cry. That's the last thing you want to do. Jesus, make him think you're out having a good time. Wipe those tears away and straighten up because there's no crying in bars."

"I can't play act, my friend, I wear my heart on my sleeve and I always have."

"So what do you plan on doing? Wait until he leaves and follow them, in order, to make a big scene so that the neighbors will call the cops? That would make for some nice gossip to go around the Center tomorrow."

"No, I would never do that but I'm getting up and going to the restroom and walking right by their table. I'll not say one word." She did just that and Joe's mouth fell open as she walked by. When she returned she did the same thing.

"That was great, Pam, I have never seen a guy as surprised as he was."

"It doesn't make me feel any better to do that. I just want my guy back."

"Well, you just walk over to that booth and tell him you want him back. He would be stupid to go home with the tramp there. She would be a good candidate for gonorrhea, syphilis, or some other dreaded disease. I've seen her in here before so she's probably very popular."

"Chris, I'm going home and going to bed to get ready for my big ride with Webb tomorrow. Pray for me while I'm out there and please try and work the police radio. I'd rather hear you on the radio than Jules." She walked out through the front entrance and Joe was not far behind.

"Hey, Pamela, wait up for me." She ignored him. As she approached her car he called out her name again. She stopped and he caught up to her.

"Joe, I'm really tired and I don't want to hear anymore of your bullshit. You have her all lined up for the evening so go for it."

"I don't want another woman." She turned to face him with a hurt look on her face. "I don't like hurting you either."

"I saw you enter the bar and go right for her table. Why did you do that when you told me you didn't want anything to do with her or any other woman?"

"I looked around and didn't see anyone and she waved at me to come over. I guess I feel sorry for her because she's used by men and doesn't have any friends."

"If she had made better choices in her life, she might have amounted to something. You can't change people by feeling sorry for them."

"You mean you've never felt sorry for anyone before?"

"I always feel sorry for abused children. They're young and at the mercy of adults. She looks like an adult to me who could change her life, if she wanted to. She would rather hang around bars and go to bed with anyone who'll have her. Why would you feel sorry for someone like that?" He didn't say anything. "I'm sorry that I let myself fall in love with you and I let you hurt me. You know what I think, Joe, your mother abused you so badly that you are trying to do the same to me. Maybe you don't even realize this is what's happening."

"Oh, so all of a sudden you've become Miss Freud?"

"The other night when you told me about your little escapade, you said you wanted me to think about seeing your again. You haven't even asked me since then how I feel. I never said you had to stay away from me, Joe, that all came from you. I love you with all my heart but I wonder about your feelings. You have every right to have any woman for sex. It hurt me but I'll get over it. You shouldn't have even told me unless it's part of your 'Abuse Pam Program.' "You're single and you can go out with anyone." She got into her car and sped off leaving him alone in the parking lot.

Her phone rang shortly after she got home. She picked it up hoping it would not be Joe and she got her wish.

"Hi, Pam, I just wanted to make sure you got home all right."

"Sure I did, Chris so now I'm strictly a loner. You can find me at work or at home waiting for my life to get better."

"I saw Joe follow you outside so I left and stood at the entrance to see, if you were going to be all right. It looks like you were doing most of the talking and then you left so fast like you were on fire or something."

"What can I tell you? I'm not having very good luck with men and I just have myself to blame."

"I didn't call to rub it in your face about cops or I told you so shit. I just wanted you to know that if you need to talk I'm here. I do know all about Joe's one night fling. The other night Jules had too much beer and called me. She spilled her guts out to me about you, Joe, and the tramp."

"Chris, I don't want the world to know my private business."

"Pam, I consider you a friend and I'll never talk about this to anyone, except you and Jules."

"I'm not so sure that Jules is a good friend, Chris. I have this feeling that she still likes Joe and she's waiting for something to happen so she can claim him. She talks to me like she wants Joe and me to be happy, but deep down she doesn't want that."

"Just tell me what happened tonight before Jules tells me."

"You want me to bring you up to date?" She revealed to him her conversation with Joe this evening.

"I think you may be right. He could be treating you bad and not even realizing it. I, also, agree with what you said when you told him it was none of your business who he went home with. You haven't had any commitment pledged between the two of you. You aren't living together so you're a couple who started dating and you haven't gotten off the ground yet. I know you haven't asked me but this is what I would do. Start treating him like he has done nothing wrong and what he did, doesn't bother you at all. I know you just screwed your nose up at me but it's the truth. He can go to her anytime he wants to but I think he'd rather be with you. I doubt if he's sitting around his apartment moping. He's waiting for you to give the signal so he can be back with you. Guys don't sit by the phone waiting for a woman to call but I bet you know plenty of women who do that very thing. He knows that there are guys at work just waiting for you two to break up. I think he would like to keep you but he doesn't know how to act until you make the next move. You should buy all kinds of sexy clothes and wear them everyday. To hell with him and how he thinks."

"Chris, I'm not comfortable wearing revealing clothes. I could never have been a hooker. I just want a good and happy life with a guy I'm in love with. Maybe I'm expecting too much and I know I have a lot of years ahead of me. I don't want to talk about my stupid life. How is your new roommate working out?"

"Sam is okay and I knew him before he moved in so we're not exactly strangers. He's having relationship problems so it must be in the air. I'm giving all my friends advice lately. I should start a 'lonely hearts' column for the newspaper."

"Where does Sam work?"

"If you think we have a rough job, he's a guy with a tough one. He works at the Head Shop down on Main Street giving the old ladies perms and blue tints to their hair. Everyday he comes home with some really funny stories. I have to tell you this one that happened not very long ago. First of all, Sam's a nice looking guy and one old gal called him on the phone to ask him, if he would dye her twat hair at her place. She really had an itch and she wanted him to take care of it."

"My God, Chris, we think our jobs are stressful and demanding. We don't have a clue what others have to put up with. I think most dispatchers all over get caught up in their own little world."

"I'll let you go, Pam, get some good sleep if you can."
"Thanks, for lending me your ear and you sleep well, too."

Chapter 5

The next morning Pam's thoughts were mostly about her ride along. She had already been out on a couple of rides to learn the area since she started as a dispatcher. One officer had been assigned to drive her over the city streets to acquaint her with problem spots that she might receive calls about. Mission Park was a community of 50,000 with not a lot of high crime to deal with. This particular ride was to demonstrate to the dispatcher what the officer has to go through during his shift. She would like to see someone arrested and taken to jail. She thought that would be interesting to observe and learn what the officer is faced with going through the booking process. Each new officer to the area was assigned an eight hour shift in dispatch so they could see what the dispatchers had to endure. She had to carefully dress for the occasion. No dresses, skirts, nor high heels could be worn by orders of the Dispatch Supervisor. You couldn't be ladylike sliding in and out of a patrol car with a dress and heels on. Pam picked out a green knit top, matching pants and tennis shoes. She would be looking good and still casual but comfortable. They could go into a foot pursuit and she especially wanted comfortable shoes on. She grinned at the prospect of running after a crook. She looked at the clock and needed to get moving, if she was going to attend briefing.

She walked into the briefing room and she was the first one there. She could hear some of the officers coming down the hall from the locker room. Pam sat near the back of the room, trying to be inconspicuous. Joe and Webb walked in together and made their way toward her. They both said hello and

Webb sat next to her. Joe sat on the other side of him. The Sergeant had yet to show up at the podium. "Pam, I asked Joe to meet us for dinner at the New Horizon's at six, if that is okay with you? That is, if we're not tied up on some big case or event."

"That'll be just fine," she told him. She glanced at Joe who gave her a wink. The Sergeant entered, picked up a clipboard, and read the briefing items. He introduced a new officer Ken Iverson to the rest of the troops. Ken would be training with Officer Lopez and this was his first day on the job. The Sergeant reminded Webb to check the back streets in and around the downtown area later in the shift for anyone driving under the influence. He told them all to stay safe. She followed Webb out the back door and Joe was right behind them. They got into their patrol cars and she looked over at Joe and gave him a little wave. She didn't think he looked too happy. Chris was on the radio and she was glad of that. He had a nice sounding voice to listen to for eight hours. Joe had complained how awful it was at times to have a dispatcher on the radio for the whole shift who sounded terrible. Rose always worked the graveyard shift and she was a good dispatcher. Her voice sounded like fingernails going down a chalk board. The shift started out quiet and Webb wrote one ticket their first hour on the streets. Pam pointed out an expired license plate to him so he stopped the vehicle and told her to write the ticket.

"No, I don't think so right now but maybe I'll try later on."

"She's a dispatcher on a ride along," Webb told the citizen. The man was not impressed.

A little later, Webb asked her a few personal questions and she was sure Joe was the reason. Joe was dispatched to a vehicle into a building and it was unknown, if there were any injuries. She and Webb responded to give him a hand. They arrived at the scene and both got out of the patrol car. An old lady was involved and not injured. She was frightened to death. Joe was having a hard job trying to calm her down. They figured she stepped on the accelerator instead of the brake when she stopped at the cleaners. The car hit the large plate glass window and was wedged right into the building. People were gathering from other shops in the area to look at the mess. She and Webb hung around until the tow truck removed the vehicle from the building. Joe drove the old lady home. A half hour after the accident they were on patrol again.

"You're doing great, Pam, most dispatchers are afraid to step outside the patrol car when they ride. Maybe you should think about becoming an officer. It would be a good pay raise for you and you could easily do the job."

41

"I think you have to want to do the job first and I have no desire to be out on the streets fighting crime. I like my radio and helping on that end." They still had a couple of hours to kill before they met Joe at the restaurant. They were sent to a minor accident between two cars and then Webb wrote a couple of speeding tickets. A sheriff's deputy needed back up on the outskirts of the city and the Sergeant told Webb not to respond. He was closer and would handle it.

"I guess, if I wasn't here, you could have gone to help," she told him.

"The Sarge worries when we have a passenger and he doesn't want you to get hurt. It doesn't bother me not to go and I know the dispatchers would not believe me but

It's true."

"Don't worry what we think, tomorrow I'll tell them what a great guy you are, and that'll be the end of all their speculations."

"Thanks, I could use some nice words. I like to keep busy and you can't do that by ignoring things." Joe received a call to respond to take a vandalism report and Lopez spoke up and said he would handle it. Pam could hear the car-to-car traffic and Joe told him thanks. Lopez told him he didn't mind handling it and maybe Joe could help him out some time. Joe said he would.

They drove to the New Horizon's Restaurant located on the outskirts of the city. It was near a busy intersection where many produce trucks frequented the area. The PD had a problem with the speeding trucks and trying to enforce the 50 MPH speed limit. The two patrol cars arrived at the restaurant at the same time. She was happy to see Joe and she gave him a full smile. They had a very nice but short dinner together. When they went outside to leave Webb had to get something out of the trunk and she and Joe stood next to each other. "Pam, I wish I could hug you right now," Joe told her in a whisper. She discreetly put her little finger into the palm of his hand and he gave it a little squeeze.

"There you just gave me a hug," she said with a giggle.

"What are you two giggling about?" Webb asked as he came around the car with a new ticket book in his hand.

"Just a silly joke between us," Joe said. "I think I'll stay here in the parking lot a little longer and write some on my accident report. You two take it easy and I'll you see back at the office, if not sooner." After getting into the cruiser she turned back and gave Joe a little wave and a big smile. Webb drove out of the parking lot and was proceeding towards the intersection with a green light in their direction. A large truck entered the intersection on their left side and T-boned the patrol car on the driver's side. Joe was sitting in the parking lot and saw the whole thing. The impact was loud and his heart jumped into his throat. He grabbed his mike after he started the patrol car and called for help. "Mission Park, we need fire and an ambulance at Main and Citrus streets."

"Send the Sergeant, too, Webb has been hit in the intersection." He could not drive over there fast enough. The patrol car was totaled and he couldn't get the passenger side door opened. The frame was bent too badly. "Pam, I'm going to get you help real soon. Please don't die on me." He glanced at Webb and knew he was dead. She had hit the side window with her head and was unconscious. She had a gash in the side of her forehead and was bleeding. "Mission Park, we need the Jaws in a hurry, I can't open the side door and Pam is bleeding a lot. Send the coroner to the scene." Chris's voice was shaking over the radio but he knew he had to get them help. He called the fire department again with the new orders that the "Jaws of Life" were needed and the coroner. Joe kept trying to open her door but it was jammed really bad. It seemed like an eternity before he heard the sirens and saw the yellow trucks coming down the road. "Pam, don't give up," he yelled at her through the window. Other officers arrived and he asked one to check on the driver of the truck. He had been too busy to check on his condition. Another PD unit arrived and Joe asked the officer to put his yellow plastic blanket over Webb behind the wheel. The Jaws were already being used on the passenger door but they had to be careful and not hurt her. A fireman opened the rear door on the driver's side and put a plastic cover over Pam to protect her from the tool. Sparks were flying right and left. They worked hard cutting the metal and soon had the door opened. The paramedics put a neck brace on her before they carefully removed her from the wreckage. They laid her on a back board next to the vehicle. The ambulance crew got her secured and she was still not moving.

The Sergeant was now at the scene. He told Lopez to handle the accident report. He didn't want Joe handling any part of it. "Joe, you go to the hospital and I'll be over later. Be careful driving over there, she's in good hands."

"Thanks, Sarge, I really appreciate this." As soon as Pam was in the ambulance, Joe took off behind them. He didn't remember the trip to the hospital and it was only a few miles away. He arrived, parked the patrol car, and ran into the building right behind the gurney. They raced down the hallway and put her into a cubicle. The emergency room doctor was waiting, as well as several nurses. Someone took out a pair of scissors and cut her clothes off from head to foot. They checked her all over for bruises and trauma to the body. She had bruises on her shoulder and right side along with the gash in the side of her head.

"Do you need to be in here, Officer?" A nurse asked him.

"Yes, I do, she's my girlfriend." A nurse kept trying to wake Pam up but she was non-responsive. They needed to know where she was hurting. Joe told them the position and condition he found her body in to help them out. They would do a complete body CT Scan and go from there. All of a sudden her eyes opened and she called out Joe's name.

"I'm here, Pam, you'll be okay." A nurse asked her, if she hurt anywhere and she told them her head did. She was looking all around the room trying to see him with a panic look in her eyes.

"Joe, where are you?" she asked.

"I'm over here, babe, just to the left of you." She turned her head a little and saw his worried face."

"Please cover me up," she pleaded to the emergency room crew. Someone got a sheet and put it over her body. "Joe, where's Webb? Did they bring him in, too?"

"Honey, if you're asking about someone else being brought in from your accident, you're the only one," a nurse with short curly red hair and a slim build volunteered.

"Joe, where is he, you must know where they took him?" Joe did not want to tell her right away. A doctor was barking orders and they wheeled her to the lab to do a CT Scan. Joe waited outside the room. Pam was upset because Joe was not with her. "Please let him come in with me," she pleaded to the hospital staff."

"Look, if you cooperate we can get this over with and you'll see him in no time." Pam tried to settle herself down and do as they instructed. It seem forever before they were finished with her. She waited on the gurney as the doctor and technician got together to look at the pictures. The doctor finally came out of the adjacent room not looking as worried.

"Young lady, your CT scan shows no trauma to the brain but we have to be cautious."

"We are putting you into ICU for tonight and another doctor will see how you are doing in the morning. Is it okay, if the officer stays with you, he says he's your boyfriend?"

"Yes, I want him with me, if I may."

"You can't have any other visitors until you get moved to a regular room tomorrow."

"Thanks, doctor for everything. Can I see him now?"

"I'll get him for you and you take it easy." They let Joe back into the room. "How are you doing? He asked her. "You gave me quite a scare." "Much better now that I'm awake and you're here with me." "I want to be with you forever, can't you feel it?" "Yes, I can and you're so good looking, my Joe. I'm proud to be your girl and I hope I always can be." "You're number one with me and I want to take care of you." "I need to talk to you about so many things, Joe. I feel if I don't do it right away something else could happen. My brain is on overload but I'm glad you're here with me." "First I have to say something myself. Pam, I have fallen in love with you and I know I just said that I cared. What I feel for you is more than just caring. I would like to stay with you tonight. I just called the dispatch center and told them what was going on. I thanked them all for getting help so fast. I couldn't get you out of the car no matter how hard I tried."

"Were going to take you to ICU now," the nurse told Pam. She told Joe that he could see Pam after they got her settled in about 30 minutes.

"Pam, I'm going to the office, take the patrol car back, and get my car. I'll see you as soon as I can." He bent over and kissed her cheek.

"I'm so glad you're going to be here with me tonight." He gave her a smile and she tried to give him one back. Pam thought they would never stop working around her in the ICU bed. Her head was killing her and they finally gave her some medication. She felt weak and tired but she wanted to talk with Joe. She had so much to tell him. A nurse was taking her blood pressure and her temperature.

"I haven't heard anything about the officer in the accident. Could you tell me where is he right now?"

"Yes, he should be at the morgue. It was a terrible thing to happen to such a young guy and a good cop to boot. I would think worrying about getting shot on the job would be bad enough but being hit in your patrol car and dying is terrible."

"You mean he died in the accident?" The nurse nodded and told her to call, if she needed anything. Her tears were coming so fast and she wondered how she would ever get through this. She could not believe that Cannonball was dead. How could this have happen she asked herself? She lay in bed and was crying so hard and she needed her Joe to be with her. "Joe, please help me," she called out. She yelled until the nurse came back in to see what was going on.

"You mustn't do this to yourself," the nurse told her. "Getting upset like this won't help your recovery."

"I need to see my boyfriend right now."

"I'll check and see where he is but you need to calm down." Pam didn't know, if she would ever calm down. It seemed like an eternity before Joe came back in with the nurse right behind him.

"Joe, she just told me Cannonball is dead, I can't believe it." He looked disgustedly at the nurse.

"You had no business telling her tonight that he died." He sat down next to her bed and took her hand."

"Joe, I'm so sorry that your best friend is gone." He leaned over and kissed the back of her hand that he was holding so tightly. She knew it would be awhile before she could stop her tears. He kept telling her to calm down but she didn't know how. "We need to talk about so much, my Joe." He nodded his head. "I know one thing that I'll never bring up that woman again to you. The night with her is in our past and I just want to think and talk about our future. I just want to be with you and love you, if you'll let me."

"What do you mean, if I'll let you? Pam, you know I'll let you love me from now on and I'll love you the same. We're a couple for good and it sounds nice."

"Life is so precious and I want to live it to the fullest with you. Webb dying has me so upset and it'll change my life forever."

"I want that, also, but you need to sleep because we have the rest of our lives to talk. I'll be here in the morning for you. Chris and Jules both came by but they wouldn't let them in to see you. When they move you to another room you can see them. They are very worried about you. They wanted me to tell you that they love you and they're praying for you. Chris wanted me to tell you not to eat the food because you'll never recover, if you do." She smiled at her friend's humor.

"Thanks so much for telling me and I'll be glad when I get to see them." Maybe you should go home tonight and get some rest yourself. I'm not going anywhere and the nurses will take good care of me."

"I'm not leaving you tonight and I'll be just fine. I couldn't sleep, if I was away from you. I'd be wondering, if you were hurting or not sleeping good. I want to keep a good eye on my girl all night long. I want to make sure you're going to fully recover before I leave you alone." She gave him the best smile she could muster up.

"How can I not get well with the best guy in the world taking care of me? I want to love you so much." The medication was starting to take over as her eyes closed and she drifted off to sleep. She still had his hand in her own.

Chapter 6

Early the next morning Pam moved a little and she opened her eyes. He was still clasping her hand and he looked awfully uncomfortable to her. The clock read 4:20. She was wishing he would never let go of her hand. She started to remember the awful accident and Webb dying. How could something so terrible happen to him? "Joe, I need you to wake up and talk to me."

He lifted his head up and looked at her. He gave her a sleepy looking smile. "You're the most beautiful sight in the whole world, my Pam. This is a new day and I'm lucky to be looking into those precious eyes. When I first got to the accident, I thought you were dead. I'm sorry, I shouldn't be talking about it with you."

"Now you can't be telling me the truth, officer and I've never known you to lie. You're not looking at anything beautiful, at least, not in this room. Don't worry about saying the wrong things. I'll get over that soon and we can talk."

"Well, the fact that you're here with me is beautiful and you'll clean up okay."

"What a nice compliment when I feel like shit but I'm glad you think so. The reason I woke you up is because you're lying bent over and I don't want you to get a stiff neck. Why don't you get over in the other bed and let me look at you?"

"Do you know what I'm looking forward to right now?" She shook her head. "Lying in bed next to you, holding you all night, and keeping you safe."

"You have some mighty big plans for us, officer, I can't wait for that to happen. I woke up thinking that you should spend the nights at my place until I find out when I'm getting out of here. It'll be too hard for you to go to Webb's and stay."

"You wouldn't mind me doing that?"

"Of course I wouldn't, and you can keep my bed warm."

"Whenever you decide, you want to hear about it, let me know ?"

"Not right now but I want to talk about it with you soon. I'm just not up to it." Joe stroked the left side of her face and showed a lot of love to her in his eyes. "I feel so bad right now for Webb but I feel so good about you. Have you thought about what, if you had been in the accident with me?" He nodded but didn't say anything. "I would be grieving for you right now and my heart would be broken. The tears came once more and filled her eyes.

"We shouldn't talk about that because the most important thing is you're getting better. We can't help Webb but we can make you better and that's my number one goal."

"Joe, please lay down on the other bed because I'm worrying about you not being comfortable." He walked over, took his shoes off, and climbed into the other bed. He turned to face her and he gave her a wink. "You're so handsome, my Joe and I hope I'll always make you happy."

"You need more sleep, too, so close those beautiful eyes and rest." They both dozed off again.

A little while later a nurse woke them both up to check Pam's vital signs.

"You're doing much better this morning," the nurse told her. "The doctor will be in shortly."

"I do need to brush my teeth and wash up some," Pam told her.

"We'll take care of that after the doctor comes in." The nurse gave her a smile and left the room. Joe had gotten up and put his shoes on. He walked over and gave her a kiss on her cheek.

"Joe, why don't you go to my place, clean up, rest, or do what you have to do. The doctor will check me and they'll put me into another room, I hope. I can clean up myself and I'll miss you terribly. You can't neglect yourself."

"Are you sure you don't mind, if I leave? I can wait until Chris or Julie shows and go at that time."

"It's really okay, if you go now. I don't think the accident has hit me completely and I may need you more later." She told him to get a spare key out of her purse.

"Pam, I want you to know that I care about you so much and I do love you.

48

It took this accident to show me just how much I do care." Joe gave her another kiss and left the room. She thought about her Nana and wondered, if she knew. There was a possibility she didn't know because Pam knew she would be at the hospital. Joe probably forgot to tell her amid all the excitement. The doctor came in and checked her over and told her she was well enough to go into a regular room. Pam told him she wanted a private room. A nurse's aide came in later and Pam was able to get washed up and get her teeth brushed. She was wishing something could be done about her hair. It was matted and needed a good washing. They got her moved into a private room and Pam was looking forward to seeing her friends. There was room for a cot to be brought in for Joe, if he wanted to spend the night. She waited for him to come back and for her friends to show up. She soon got her wish.

"Hey, I had trouble finding you since they moved you and you left no forwarding address," Joe said. "I went over to Webb's and got some of my things and took them to your place. It'll be much nicer there for me."

"I'm glad because you need to be comfortable right now."

"His folks should be coming over from Phoenix sometime today and they'll stay at his apartment. His funeral is Saturday afternoon and the office is making big plans for it."

Pam closed her eyes for a few seconds. "I have to go to the funeral, Joe. I hope the doctor will let me."

"Pam, Webb wouldn't expect you to attend because of the condition you're in."

"I have to go for me and I wouldn't feel right staying away."

"We can check with the doctor and see what he says. I talked with Jules and she'll be by soon. You'll probably have more visitors than you can handle."

"Did you call Nana because she'll be upset, if she's not told?"

"No, I didn't call her and I should have but I didn't have her number either. Let me go out to the phone and call her because she'll never forgive me for this one." Pam gave him Lee's number and he hurried out the door. He was back shortly with a scowl on his face. She knew it didn't go well with her Nana.

"I didn't make any points with her about this. She reamed me good and is on her way here." They talked about her injuries and about how long she may be in the hospital. They were still talking when Lee slowly opened the door to Pam's room and stuck her head in. The look on her thin but square shaped face could kill. She walked over to Joe with her jaw held tight and her eyes glaring. She was 62 and didn't look a day over 50.

"Just when did you think you were going to let me know that my granddaughter was in a terrible accident? I had to read about it this morning when I opened up the newspaper. I'm very upset so you had better start talking to me."

"I'm sorry about this but it has been a terrible thing for all of us." He explained to her all that Pam had been through.

"Nana, please give me a hug and listen to us." Lee walked over and hugged Pam.

"I'm sorry, Lee, but I don't carry your phone number with me and Pam was too upset last night."

"I really don't know who died in this family and left you in charge but you're making way too many decisions on her behalf."

"I'm sorry that you feel that way and it was not my intention to take over. I was only concerned about Pam last night."

"Do I have your permission to see my granddaughter now in private?"

"You don't need my permission; you can see her anytime or under any circumstances." He glanced at Pam and then went out the door.

"Oh, Nana, it's so nice to see you. Don't be upset with Joe because he saved me last night. He spent the night with me and it helped me. I'll see that he has your phone number with him from now on."

"He should start carrying it around, if he is going to be in your life. I can't stay too long, dear. I have a large delivery due this morning and I have to be there. I'll come back later in the day, if that's all right with you? I'll call your mom later and I know she will want to come down."

"No, I do not want her here and I mean that. Don't even tell her I've been in an accident. Nana, I just can't deal with her."

"My God, Pamela, it's your mother and she needs to know what's going on. What is your problem about her coming down?"

"Nana, you know that no one here knows about my rich family and my upbringing. I'll not have mother here flaunting her money and looking down her nose at everyone."

"You can't help being born into a rich family. Do you think your friends will dump you, if they find that out?"

"No I don't think they will but she'll let the world know how much money she does have. You of all people know how she is."

"I have to leave and I'll be back later." Lee gave Pam a kiss on her cheek and left.

Joe was back in the room in no time. "I'm sorry I screwed that all up for you. I have a feeling she'll never forgive me for not calling her."

"This is not the half of it, Joseph. She wanted to call my mother but I talked her out of it. If you think Nana is bad then wait until you meet Anne Austin."

"What's wrong with your mom being here?"

"I don't want her to come right now because she's my mother. You'll understand, Joe, when you meet her for the first time. She'll want to sue the police department and the city for putting me in harm's way."

"They're not going to upset you or they'll not be in this room. I'm looking out for you, Pam, and your health is coming first."

Julie showed up around 9 AM and let out a whoop when she saw Pam. She first gave Joe a hug and then Pam.

"You're not looking too bad this morning, Pam. How do you feel?" Julie asked.

"I'm hurting some but at least, I'm alive," she said and the tears came forth.

"I didn't come to see you and make you cry."

"It's hard knowing Webb died and I just have to get through it." Joe was still sitting next to her bed and holding her hand. Pam told Julie about her Nana's reaction and that she wanted to tell her mom to come down. Pam, also, told Julie all about her ride along up until the time they left Joe at the restaurant. "I told Webb that I would tell all the dispatchers that he's really a nice guy. We knew only one side of him and I got acquainted with his other side."

"I'll help you spread the word around. I can spend the day with you, if you would like that. I even brought a book to read when you take a nap. Joe, if you need to leave go ahead because I'll be here with Pam."

"I was going to leave for awhile but it doesn't have to be now," he told her.

"Joe, go ahead and go while you have the chance. I'll be here when you get back."

"Well, if you don't mind then I will. The office wants to see me sometime today. I would like to see Webb's parents and talk with them a little."

"Joe, tell them I'm sorry and take your time. I'll see you later." She gave him a grin but her eyes were full of tears.

He went over and gave her a kiss. "Don't forget that I love you, blue eyes." He rubbed her cheek with his thumb and gave her a wink. "Bye, Jules, I'll see you later."

"I see he told you that he loves you so things are okay with you both?" Julie asked.

"I'm so happy and I'll be so good to him. I can't wait to get well."

"Don't you think it's funny that he would tell you that he loves you after the accident and not before?"

"You mean you think he said it because he feels sorry for me?"

"I don't know, Pam, you wanted to hear those words and he wouldn't say them. You get in the accident and they come pouring out of him."

"I've been wanting to hear them and I feel he means them."

"It may be true, Pam, I just thought it was a little strange." She figured Julie was jealous but she had Pam wondering a little, too.

Chris popped in a little later. "Hey, girl, let's go out howling tonight at the Den. We could rent you a wheel chair and take real good care of you."

"I think I'll have to pass this time, Chris. I'd rather walk into that place than be wheeled in."

"I've seen some people wheeled out of the Den that walked in and I've seen friends of mine stagger out. You don't know who I'm talking about, Pam, do you?"

"I'm trying to ignore you and your drama."

"Joe seemed very concerned and upset when I came by last night. Losing his best friend must be hard on him."

"Yes, it is but he's trying to be strong for me."

"God, I hate hospitals. There's too much gloom between these walls," Chris told his two friends.

"Pam, what, if it had been Joe that you were riding with and he was killed?" Julie asked her.

"I actually mentioned that to him but he didn't say anything. I would be feeling much worse." Pam was getting a little weary but she didn't want to tell her friends to leave. They were excited to see each other and the three friends got caught up once more.

"Pam, didn't you tell us that your mom was rough on you growing up?" Chris asked her. "What's she going to say when she sees you like this?"

"I asked Nana not to call her because she would blame the world for me being in an accident that couldn't be avoided. She'd want to sue all the parties involved with me riding with an officer. That's how she was when I left home."

"She could meet Joe and get that over with," Julie said. Pam was telling Chris about her ride with Webb when Joe came back into the room. He gave her a kiss and Chris rolled his eyes.

"You weren't gone long enough to do much," Pam said to him.

"Did you sleep any?" He asked.

"No, but I will soon. When I'm sleepy enough, I'll fall right off into slumber land and take a real long nap."

"Chris and Julie, I hope you don't mind that I ask you to leave. She has not slept enough since the accident. She has got to try and sleep and these are the doctor's orders not mine." Chris said he would see her in the morning and Julie told her she would be back in the evening.

"I'll call first and see, if you need anything," said Julie.

"I only want you and Chris to see her for a couple of days. The doctor wants the visitors limited for now."

"Pam, I'm going to walk Chris and Jules to the elevator and I'll be right back." He returned to find the nurse giving Pam something to make her sleep.

"You see this, I agreed to a sedative so I can try and sleep but I'm not very happy about it."

"I'll stay right here and I guarantee you'll feel better when you wake up."

"Joe, I really don't expect you to baby sit me everyday. It must be boring for you, here with me, and sitting around."

"Being with you, babe, is never boring. I go back to work Saturday and then I can't be here. Are you tired of me hanging around already?"

"I'll never be tired of you being with me," she told him. "Will you promise to teach me to love you properly? I don't want you seeing other women because I'm not good in bed."

"I never said you weren't good. You're very good and we'll discuss it later. Go to sleep for me, please," he told her. Pam only saw love in his eyes for her and she was sure that Julie was wrong.

"I'll try," she told him and she was already starting to drift off. He walked out quietly to let her sleep.

Two hours later he was back in her room and she was still sleeping. Good he said to himself as he sat down in the chair next to her bed. She had slept for about three hours, altogether, when she woke up hearing Officer Lopez coming into her room.

"Pam, this is Raul and he's handling the accident report. He knows you don't remember much but he still has to see you."

"Raul, it's so nice to meet you," Pam told him. "I haven't even asked about the person who hit us. Could you tell me who it was and how are they doing?"

"It was a man and he suffered a few bruises and they'll throw the book at him. He ran a red light and hit the patrol car. There's no excuse for that," Lopez said.

"Was he drinking?" She asked.

"The drugs tests aren't back yet but it appears he was stone sober." Lopez left.

The same doctor that treated her when she was admitted came in to examine her cuts and bruises. "I would like to see you up and walking a little in the morning, if you're strong enough. I'm not going to push you for a few days but you can at least try."

"I'm looking forward to it," she told him.

"I'm so proud of you for sleeping a few hours," Joe said to her. He told her that Webb's parents had arrived and he met them when he went over to drop off some of his friend's things from the office. They seemed concerned about Pam and asked how she was doing. He brought them up to date on her recovery.

The rest of the day was rather quiet. Lee called Pam and told her she wouldn't be by this evening but would see her in the morning. Pam let Joe know and he told her he would be there with her to face Lee.

Chapter 7

The next morning she woke up to find Joe not sleeping on his cot. She immediately worried that something could be wrong. An aide brought a walker in for her to try and use. She was told that when she could get around real well, she could take a shower. She really wanted that shower. She sat on the edge of her bed with her legs dangling over the side. Joe came into the room and her face lit up. He went over to her and gave her a gentle hug and kissed her softly.

"I went out to make some phone calls because you were still sleeping."

"Do you think you could bring in my nightshirt later. I hate these hospital gowns."

"I'm sorry that I didn't think about it because I saw it hanging in your closet yesterday. How do you feel?"

"Much better today but my head still hurts some. They said I could take a shower, if I start walking around."

"We'll take care of that and I'll help you."

"I need to go to the bathroom right now."

"I'll help you, if you don't mind." Pam didn't know what to say. "If you don't want me to help, you can ring for the nurse. I'll just put you on the toilet and when you're finished I'll get you back to bed." She nodded at him and she stood up with the help of the walker.

"I feel a little light headed but I can make it," she told him. He put his arm around her waist to help steady her. They slowly walked to the bathroom and he helped her sit on the toilet. He went out and closed the door.

"I'm finished, Joe," she told him. He helped her over to the sink to wash her hands.

"You're doing real well and I feel in another day, you'll be doing this all by yourself. I talked with the nurses and told them to wash your hair this morning."

"Thank you so much, Joe."

"They have the equipment where you can lay back in bed and they can wash it. Someone made a good invention. I know what my girl needs and I want you home real soon." They brought in her breakfast but she didn't feel like eating. He told her that she had to eat a little to keep up her strength. She was enjoying him waiting on her and taking care of her. After she ate he told her that he was going to her place and clean up and go by the office. He would be back as soon as he could. He kissed her and left. An aide brought in the equipment to wash her hair after she washed up. It was so nice to feel her hair being cleaned. She had no idea they had such equipment and it was just what she needed. After she was shampooed she used a towel and was drying her hair the best that she could. In walked her grandmother with a smile on her face for Pam. Lee was holding a beautiful bouquet of cut flowers.

"Oh, my God, Pamela,you look dreadful, let me help you dry your hair." Her Nana took the towel after hugging Pam and helped her finish. "Where is that man who just took over your life?" Lee asked her.

"Joe, had to do some running around while I was getting cleaned up."

"Did he spend the night in here?" Lee was looking at the cot in the corner.

"Joe, and I love each other and he spent the night. I wanted him here."

"Is it wise to be sleeping in the same room with you?" Lee gave Pam a 'you should know better' look. Pam knew her Nana was still seething over not being called after the accident so she started telling her about the ride along.

"I don't care about the ride, I just want to know about Joe's intentions? When your mother finds out he's just a cop she'll go through the roof."

"That's too damn bad. He's a good guy that I love and she'll have to accept him." Joe came back into the room and sat next to Pam's bed.

"Lee, if you're still upset about me not calling you, I'm sorry. We were a little tied up and I was concerned for Pam."

"I would have been concerned, too, if you had called me right after the accident," her Nana said to him.

"Please don't do this to him, Nana."

"He's a good guy who's been great to me and he doesn't deserve an ass chewing this morning."

"Well, Joe, you must fill me in on the accident," Lee said.

"No, he can't because I'm not ready to hear about it yet."

"That's fine, Pam, I'll talk with Joe about it later. I hope I didn't come over here to find out you're up to no good. We need to have a big talk as soon as you're out of the hospital."

"Anything I do with Joe is good and you can save your words, Nana."

"She needs her rest, Lee, so I'll walk you out to the elevator."

"Pamela, I'll be back this evening," Lee told her. She said goodbye to Pam and followed him out the door. Joe came right back in and told her, he was taking Lee to the cafeteria to fill her in on the accident. He would be back as soon as he could. He wanted her to try and rest. She wanted to talk privately with him for a little while. They had hardly been alone since the accident. Her Nana had worn her out and she dozed off.

After awhile she heard the lunch trays being delivered to the rooms and it woke her up. Joe was still not back and she wondered, if her grandmother was giving him hell. She still didn't want to eat but felt that she should. She was given a plate with meatloaf on it that looked a little gray. She squirted ketchup all over it and it wasn't too bad. Joe came back in as she finished her tray.

"I'm glad you're eating and you look like you napped."

"I dozed off until they brought the tray. What did my Nana have to say?"

"She told me to keep my clothes on tonight, if you can believe that."

"Oh, you're making that up, aren't you, Joe?"

"You know her better than I do and I can't believe she would think I'd take advantage of you in a hospital bed. I know I rub her the wrong way but she isn't being very nice. I've never done a thing to her, except not call her after the accident."

"Joe, that's Nana's way and she and mom are a lot alike. You can't change either one of them. She used to embarrass me so much when I was younger. Never forget that you're stuck with your relatives." She gave him a big smile.

"You're nothing like her and I'm glad. I don't dislike her but she's too pushy where you're concerned. I'm surprised that your family allowed you to grow up."

"They didn't want me to that's for sure but I surprised them. You have no idea what I went through when I told them I was moving here to go to work. I was suppose to get my college degree and work up there. I already told you my mother wanted me to find a rich guy, stay home, and have babies. I would rather find someone that I really love than be unhappy."

"Do you think you've found him?" Joe asked.

"I know I have and I'm so very, very happy. I'm kind of disappointed right now. We haven't hardly had a minute to ourselves since the accident. Someone is always coming by or popping their head into this room."

"What do you have in mind?"

"I just want to be close to you and talk about different things."

"We can do that now, although, I can't guarantee a nurse won't come in. I'll go out and tell them not to come in for an hour unless we call them." He bounded out the door and was back in a few. He had a "do not disturb" sign that he put on the outside door handle. "No one is allowed in while this sign is on the door," he told her. He went over to her bed and told her to move over. She scooted over and he lay down and took her into his arms.

"Okay, now we're alone and we can talk." She gave him her nicest smile. They were face to face and she was enjoying the closeness.

"I have dreamed for some time what it will be like the next time we make love. I picture us kissing and undressing each other. I dream about you making love to me a lot. In the ER I didn't mind you seeing me naked but I didn't want the other men to see me. I only want your eyes on my naked body from now on. I hope you never get tired of looking at me."

"I know you were embarrassed when you realized I was there and you didn't have a thing on. You asked them to cover you up. It was such a nice thing to see your innocence like that. It was too cute. Your body is beautiful and I'm looking forward to undressing you and making love to you real soon." Joe got up on his elbow and kissed her all over her face. Just gentle sweet kisses and they made her feel so good. He kissed her on the lips and she responded with her tongue. She felt his penis getting hard against her leg and she reached over and caressed it slowly. "Do you have any idea what you're doing to me, my babe?"

"I can't help it, Joe, I want you so badly. I've been turned on to you since the night Nana interrupted us. I can't get rid of the feelings I had for you. I was so ready for you to make love to me and it didn't happen." He stopped kissing her and buried his face in her neck. She stopped caressing him as she knew it would not be happening now. "I'm sorry but if we were home I wouldn't let you stop," she told him.

"I wouldn't want to stop either."

"I'm going to tell the doctor tonight that I'm going home tomorrow. I'll go to the funeral and take it easy the rest of the day. You'll look out for me at the funeral, won't you, Joe? I can rent a wheelchair to help me get around in and it'll be okay."

"Of course, I'll look out for you but we need to see what he says. If he knows you have someone staying with you, he may agree to release you." She enjoyed their private time together.

The doctor told her she could go home but it was important to take care of herself. Chris had stopped by on his way to work but the "do not disturb" sign kept him from going into her room. Julie came by in the evening and so did her Nana. Lee was not happy with her plans to go to the funeral. She felt Pam should go home and rest and not be doing much. Joe brought in a long dress for her to wear home and to the funeral. They spent the rest of the evening talking and he slept on the cot in her room.

The next morning Joe took care of her and helped her get ready for her trip home. He packed her bag and stood vigil outside her shower. The doctor checked her and Pam was allowed to go home. She left the large bouquet of flowers and two small ones she had received with the hospital staff. On the way home he stopped at a rental place and got a wheelchair for her trip to the funeral. They pulled into the complex and she was so glad to be home. She went into the living room and there was a beautiful bouquet of red roses on the coffee table.

"Oh, Joe, these are perfect for my homecoming."

"How do you know they're from me?"

"I know they are because it's something you would do for me." He gave her a big smile. She leaned over and smelled the flowers. She noticed the answering machine light was flashing. "I wonder who would call and leave messages knowing, I'm in the hospital?" She said to him. She pushed the button.

"You need to leave my boyfriend alone. He doesn't want you because you're not woman enough for him." Pam looked at Joe and he turned his head.

"That's Suzy the one I spent the night with but I had no idea she would start calling you. Please don't be upset, Pam."

"How would she get my number? The PD wouldn't give it out."

"There's something I need to tell you." His eyes were sad.

"Go ahead and say what it is."

"I wanted this to wait until after the funeral but I have to tell you now. When I went to Webb's yesterday, she had left a message on my answering machine." Pam could tell it upset him to tell her about the calls.

"Joe, you have no control over it but how did she get your number?"

"I have a little address book I carry in the back pocket of my jeans so it's the only way she could get it."

"Your number is in it too?" Pam asked.

"When I moved here and didn't want to forget my new number, I jotted it down in the very front of the book. She must have gotten it from there."

"This means that all the numbers in your book could be used as she wishes."

"She could have taken them all down or a few."

"Not just numbers but addresses too."

"I'm afraid you're right and I didn't realize it would come to this so I'm to blame."

"Joe, I'm not going to get terribly upset over a stupid phone call. I know that being with her was a mistake you made and I'm over it now. Life is too precious to think about things that can't be changed. In the hospital I said I wouldn't mention her or you being with her. We come home to a message from her. It's going to be hard not to think about it." He took her into his arms and he felt so good. He made her lie down to rest and then eat a little lunch before they left for the church. He was in full dress uniform and they went to the office to get a patrol car. They had given him permission to drive Pam to the funeral and be with her during the eulogy. He would join the procession of police cars to the cemetery after the funeral.

"Joe, you look so handsome in your uniform today. I'm proud to be going with you but it's such a sad time."

"You always know how to say the nicest things at the right time," he told her. She was able to walk but rather slowly. The wheelchair would allow her not to get too tired out. She was looking forward to meeting Webb's parents and brother. The PD asked her, if she would like to say something at the service and she said she would. She was the last one to see him and talk with him. It seemed proper that she should speak. Joe would stand with her at the podium for physical and moral support. The funeral started at 1 PM and they left for the office at 12:30. It didn't take them long to get the patrol car and make their way to the church. The church was in the downtown section of the city with plenty of parking around the old brick building. It stood out from the rest of the city because of the bricks used in its construction. This was not a Southern California type of building. There were a lot of people gathering when they arrived. Joe helped Pam out of the car and into the wheelchair. He was pushing her towards the main entrance when a hush came over the crowd. They all knew she was the one who had been with him in that terrible accident. They found Chris and Julie after they entered the church. It was a most somber occasion. Julie gave her a hug and Chris did, also, along with a kiss on her forehead. They were seated down front because of the wheelchair. Pam was on the aisle and Joe sat next to her in the end pew. An older couple walked over to them and introduced themselves as Webb's parents. His mom gave Pam a big hug. She could tell they were very upset with his death. His brother walked over and introduced himself. He told Pam that he was glad she wasn't hurt very badly. They were all glad he didn't die alone. The service started at exactly one with several music pieces being played. The police chief talked and then a state assemblyman. It was not going to be a long funeral. Soon it was time for Pam to speak. Joe got up and wheeled her over to the dais where she had to get out of the chair and walk up three steps. She tried but it was difficult so Joe picked her up and carried her up the steps to the podium. She stood up with both arms laid across the podium for support and Joe had one arm around her waist. She adjusted the microphone and started speaking.

"I was asked today, if I wanted to say something, and I said I would. I don't have any speech prepared but I wanted to tell you about Cannonball's last few hours. Yes, that's the pet name that we dispatchers had for Curtis. He had such enthusiasm for his job that he loved and we all told him he was like a loose cannonball. He liked that name. He would drive to the ends of the earth to help a deputy, a CHP officer, or a fellow policeman in trouble. He would drive old ladies home who were lost. He loved going to the schools and talking to the kids about the police department. He loved life in general. Webb told me about playing catch with his dad when he was little and how his mom always hugged him when he got hurt." The crowd heard his mom let out a small cry. Pam voice was starting to falter a little. "He loved teasing his younger brother about collecting rocks. He missed his dog Dino who had slept with him every night when he was small. Last but not least he's missing his best friend Joe who's standing here next to me. He told me how much Joe helped him when he came here. They became roommates and best friends." Joe could not hold back the tears. "He would be so pleased to see everyone here today paying their last respects. He'll be here always in our hearts." She put her hand over her heart. A gentleman in a Scottish kilt was at the back of the church and he started playing *Amazing Grace* on the bagpipes. Pam's voice rang out as he walked toward the front of the church. She was singing the lyrics along with his pipes. Her voice was beautiful and the crowd was mesmerized. There wasn't a dry eye in the church when she finished. Joe couldn't believe what he had just heard.

"That was so beautiful," he whispered to her. He lifted her up, carried her down the steps, and put her in the wheelchair. She looked over at Chris and Julie and they were smiling and wiping their eyes, too. They all got in line to pay their respects to his family. Joe pushed Pam over to his mom and she said some nice things to her. She would always remember Pam's kind words and her beautiful voice. They got through the line and went outside. Everyone was telling her what a nice job she did for Webb. They got over to the patrol car and Joe was helping her stand up to move her into the passenger seat.

"Joe, do you think you could take me home and drop me off real quick. I don't think I can make it through the cemetery service. I hope you don't mind."

"Of course not, Pam, you did well to come to the funeral." They hurried to the complex and he got out and took her inside.

"Joe, thanks for taking me and I hope I'm not letting you down by staying home."

"I love you and I want you to rest. Cannonball won't mind, if you're not at the cemetery. Can I get you anything before I leave?"

"You need to hurry back there and get into the procession. I hope I haven't screwed it up for you. You won't be coming back here, will you, since you have to work?"

"I'll come back on a break or my lunch time and see you."

"Joe, please call me, if you get tied up and can't make it. We haven't even discussed tonight or plans for us."

"I'll be here for you so don't worry about it." He gave her a big kiss and left. She lay down on the couch and dozed off as the day's events caught up with her.

The doorbell rang and woke her up. She slowly got up from the couch and went to answer the door. It was her Nana.

"Pamela, I want you to pack a few things and come to my place so I can take care of you. You should not be alone right now."

"Nana, I'm staying here. Joe will be with me later."

"You should have someone looking out for you all the time not just a few hours a day. Don't argue with me, I want to take you to my place."

"You don't understand. This is my home and this is where I belong."

"Joe can take care of you before and after work but not in between." Joe walked in as they argued some more.

"What's going on here?" Joe asked Lee.

"I'm taking my granddaughter home with me and take care of her. You can't possibly think that you can give her proper care when you're working."

He looked at Pam and saw that she was upset.

"I was telling Nana that I was going to stay here and you would stay with me."

"Yes, I was told to come home and stay with Pam after the graveside service so I'm here now and I'll take care of her."

"You don't have to go back to work?" Pam asked him.

"No, the sergeant told me to take the rest of the day off. I came home to take care of a brave and courageous woman."

"Well, what about tomorrow and the next day?" Lee asked him. "She'll still need to be taken care of."

"I can come over here during my shift and check on her and she has other friends who can be with her." Joe was irritating Lee and he knew it but he didn't care. "I promise she'll be well taken care of."

"I want to say one more thing to you, Pam, you should be with your family during a time like this not with some guy who's trying to control you."

"He isn't doing that, Nana. You have him all wrong."

"If you have something to say to me, Lee, than say it and don't talk to Pam about me as if I'm not even here."

"She belongs with her family in a crisis like this but I don't want to upset Pam. I'll leave and you know where I am, if you need anything." Lee went out the door. Pam hurried over to Joe as quickly as she could and fell into his arms.

"I'm so glad to see you and we can be together this evening."

"Anything you want will be yours." He rubbed her back as she stayed in his arms for a little while longer.

"Please tell me about the graveside service, my Joe." He proceeded to tell her what took place as they both walked over to the couch and sat down. He told her Mrs. Webb had collapsed as each person with a rose filed by and laid it on top of his casket. "It must have been awful for her and the rest of his family. I feel that I let you down by not being there with you. I knew I wouldn't be able to make it until the end."

"Don't even talk that way, you haven't let me down and you never would. It was sad but they were still talking about, my girl, singing so beautifully in church."

"It was the least I could do for him." The phone rang and Joe walked over to answer it. Whoever it was hung up.

"It must have been a wrong number," Joe told her. "You were right when you said before I left that we haven't talked about the two of us."

"Joe, let me start. I don't want you to think that you have to stay here with me. I can be alone because I don't want you feeling uncomfortable being here."

"Do you think I could ever feel uneasy in your company after what we have just been through?"

"I hope you won't feel that way. What would you like to do about us?"

"I never want to leave your side if you want the honest to goodness truth." She smiled at his words. "I take that as a yes and you feel the same way?"

"You have just made me so happy."

"You're sure this is what you want knowing what you do about me?" She put her index finger over his lips and hushed him.

"I know that you love me and you want to be with me. It doesn't get any better than that." It was all settled that he would move his belongings in with her the very next day. They spent a quiet evening with Joe waiting on her and they were enjoying each other. When it was time to go to bed she got ready first and climbed in. He finished in the bathroom and came out and climbed in beside her. She was in her nightshirt and he in a pair of briefs.

"This is going to be so nice with you in my arms tonight," he told her.

"I'm so happy right now, my Joe. I couldn't be happier than I am right now." They kissed and she cuddled up next to him. They were still hugging each other when she fell asleep.

Chapter 8

Pam woke up first and she smiled immediately when she felt his arms around her. Oh, how good it felt being with him. She never dreamed they would be a couple so soon and what changes they had made from just a few days ago. He would move in this morning and she couldn't wait. She slowly tried to move away from him to get up and shower.

"Where do you think you're going?" He asked her.

"I was trying to sneak out of bed to take a shower, officer, but you spoiled it." He hugged her even closer and wouldn't let her leave the bed.

"Let me tell you my plans. I should shower first so that I can go to Webb's and get some stuff to bring over here. You can shower while I'm over there. How does that sound?"

"It sounds great and I'm glad I wasn't dreaming when you told me you would move in with me." He had his arm under her breasts and it was touching them. She was wondering what he was thinking.

"It's going to be hard being close to you and not getting intimate," he said. "We should not take that step too soon. I want you well and happy before we make love."

"You must be reading my mind because I was just wondering about that. I know you would never force yourself on me until I'm ready."

"There's something I have to do right away and that's go to the doctor to be checked for anything that she could have given me. It won't be right, if I expose you to something bad." Pam nodded but didn't say anything. He got up and showered. She lay in bed a little longer. She was thinking about her mother and dad and their rather disdainful relationship. Her dad, Lake Austin, spent most of his time in San Francisco where his computer business was headquartered. Her mom, Anne, refused to live in that city and he built her a home in the redwood empire. She wanted a house that matched the Carson Mansion in Eureka with its magnificent construction and grandeur. Lake would come home on weekends and during the week stayed at their penthouse in the Saint Francis Hotel. Her mom would visit him at times during the week when she went to the city to shop and visit friends. Pam never remembered them being affectionate in front of her when she was allowed to be in their company. She had Sarah her Nanny from the time she was born until she started college. She was more of a companion to Pam after she reached puberty. She would answer the many questions Pam always had about life as a normal person. Pam went to the local public high school and enjoyed every minute of it. The month of July with her Nana, was the highlight each year of her life.

She got up and put her robe on as she heard the shower stop. He came out of the bathroom and she went into his arms. "It's so hard being near you and I can't love you completely."

She backed away from him. "I guess I shouldn't be hugging you so much but it makes me feel so much closer to you. I can't get enough of you right now."

"Pam, it's going to be so nice waking up to you each morning."

"Do guys think much about what they want in a woman?" She asked him.

"I don't know about all men but I have thought a lot about what I don't want in a woman. I'm sure my mother had something to do with that."

"I wish I could change your childhood, Joe. I have fairly good memories of growing up and you had mostly bad ones."

"What's important to me now is having good memories with you."

"I promise that you will and I will too."

"I hate to get up and run but I want to bring some things over."

"I wish I could cook you some breakfast before you get started."

"You are not lifting a finger until the doctor says you're much better. I like taking care of you, in case, you haven't noticed."

"I did notice and I like it, too. The same goes for me and I'll try and be more patient." He gave her a kiss and left the apartment. She got into the shower. After she was dressed she started moving some of her things around in the closet and the dresser drawers. The phone rang and she went to answer it.

"Well, I'm so glad you're okay and you sound pretty good this morning," Chris said to her. "We were worried yesterday when you didn't show up at the gravesite."

"I didn't realize what the funeral would do to me and I didn't want to come home. My body gave out so I had to leave."

"Mrs. Webb was having a rough time of it so I'm glad you didn't get to see that. When I die, my parents will probably be dancing on my grave."

"Chris, what an awful thing to say. They'll miss you terribly, I'm sure. You must have brought some smiles to their faces growing up with your famous antics."

"When I was real young it was okay but turning into an adult did not endear me to them. I didn't turn out they way they would have liked me to."

"We all go through some rough times and my mom was harsh on me with her high expectations. Yours probably had the same high hopes for you."

"You just blew us all away when you sang, Pam. It sounded like an angel from heaven had come down to sing for us all. I know you couldn't see Joe as you sang but he was so emotional. Losing Webb was hard on him so let's talk about nice things today."

"What would you like to discuss, my friend?"

"Are you going to be okay, taking care of yourself or can Jules and I help you out? We can take turns waiting on our good friend. We're glad you're okay and we know you'll recover and get back to your old self."

"Joe is helping me right now. I know he goes to work later but I should be fine. He'll keep in touch with me."

"He stayed last night with you?"

"Yes, and he's moving in with me today."

"No shit, Sherlock. Aren't you two moving like a train out of control? Are you sure this is what you want? Playing house will make it all serious and things will change."

"We both want this, Christopher, and why do you sound so surprised?"

"Well, after his one night stand, you were plenty upset and now you have completely turned everything around."

"If you truly care about someone, you don't stop loving them because they made one mistake."

"I understand that, Pam, and he said he cared about you. You didn't hear the L word, if my memory is correct."

"He didn't realize what I meant to him until the accident happened. He does love me, Chris. He told me in the hospital and I can see it in his eyes."

"As a friend, I just want you to be happy and I'll always be here for you, either to talk or to do any favors that you need."

"I know you're a good friend but I have a request for you. Please don't discuss me with anyone else. That's the nicest friend you can be for me right now. I have issues about Julie and I don't want her to know everything."

"I won't discuss you with anyone, I promise. When do you go back to the doctor?"

"I have an appointment on Wednesday and I'm going to ask about going back to work."

"What in hell is your hurry? Don't count on going back too soon. You should take some R & R until you're completely well."

"I just sit around here and I can do the same thing at work."

"If you're real serious about coming back so soon, I have an idea that might work. Tell your doctor you want to work half a day and he might go for it, if you say full time, he may not."

"That's a good idea, Chris and I'll try that on him. I think you have something."

"If you get to come back, Pam, let's go to the Den to celebrate on Friday night. We can meet for a couple of hours and you don't have to drink any alcohol."

"I like that idea so it's all set. I'll go to The Den a little early and reserve our booth." They hung up and she went back into the bedroom to make more room for Joe clothes.

A little later Joe showed up but he was a little upset with her for moving her clothes. "You shouldn't be doing anything, Pam, I can do what needs to be done. I know it's hard for you to sit or stand by and do nothing but you have to do that for the time being."

"I feel useless but I know what you're saying. I want to go back to work real soon and in order to do that I have to take it easy."

"Oh, you plan on going tomorrow?" He asked with a chuckle.

"Not that soon but I see my doctor on Wednesday and I hope he'll release me soon."

"Don't get your hopes up too high. I'm here to take care of you for the duration and I'm happy to do it."

"Chris called while you were gone to see how I'm doing. I told him you were moving in here today and I hope you don't mind that I told him. I figured Jules would know soon and then everyone would."

"I don't mind you telling him. As soon as I give them my address at the office, they'll all know. What did he say about it.?"

"He thinks we may be moving too fast in our relationship. I told him no we weren't that we love each other very much."

"If he was a normal guy, he would see things differently. We do love each other and we'll just have to let our friends see this."

"He thinks I should ask the doctor about working just half a shift when I return. I'll ask the doctor because I don't think he would agree on full time work just yet. If I'm released to go back to work, he wants to go to the Den Friday to celebrate."

"Half a shift might be better and going to the Den is up to you and how you feel. It might not bother you for a couple of hours."

"Does Jules know that you're moving in?"

"Yes, I called her from Webb's and gave her the news. She said the same thing about moving too fast. What do they know? We're the important ones and we do know what's in our hearts." He put his things away and went to the New Horizon's to pick them up some lunch. All that mattered to her was that they were happy. Their friends would just have to see for themselves. Her family was a different matter but she would deal with them, also.

He came back a little later and dropped a box of condoms on the coffee table.

"I thought we could discuss personal stuff over lunch today, if it's okay with you? I have to use these until the doctor says I'm all right. I know you're on The Pill and this will keep you safe."

"It's what we have to do. This is an awful lot of condoms, Joe."

"They will probably last us a week or so." She smiled at him.

"I'm hoping I'll be woman enough for you. This is a worry for me right now since you spent the night with that woman."

"We can overcome the problem and we can teach each other what we would like when we make love."

"I want you to be happy with me, Joe, and I don't want to have to worry about you being with someone else?"

"You look at me with love and I see desire in your eyes, also. I'll never turn to someone else. I promise you I'll be faithful and true to you."

"Joe, you make everything seem nice and I like that in you."

"I got you a Chinese chicken salad for tonight because I don't want you not eating. I'll check on you often or stop by when I can."

"You seem happy that you moved in, Joe, and I want you to be happy everyday."

"Happy isn't the word I would use but thrilled is better and I can tell you are. We can lick the world, the two of us can and we'll show our friends how happy we can be all the time." The phone rang and Pam answered it.

"I know Joe moved in with you today but this won't last very long," a female voice told her. "Enjoy him while you can because I'll win in the end. He enjoyed his night with me very much and there will be more nights with me."

"Don't call here anymore," Pam told her and hung up. Joe knew she was upset.

"What was that all about?" Pam told him what Suzy said to her. "What's her fucking problem? I don't want to be with her and she'll never accept that. I don't want her to upset you all the time."

"I'm not going to let her upset me, Joe. She must have her eye on you but she'll have to get over it."

Joe got ready to leave and took her into his arms. "Please don't let her bother you. If this keeps up, we can change our phone number."

"If we do that then she might call me at work. I'd rather she called here than there. She must be following you around, Joe, to know that you moved in here today. That scares me more than anything. Do you think she's capable of doing bad things?"

"Well, I didn't think so but with the phone calls she has made, I don't know. I have to leave and we can discuss this more later. Keep the doors locked and I'll come by later to check on, my girl." She kissed him long and hard. She turned the TV on to see, if she could catch a movie or something to pass the time. It was going to be so hard being a shut-in.

A little while later her Nana called to see how she was doing and said she would come by in the evening. The nursery was quite busy on this Fourth of July. Pam didn't even realize it was a holiday until Lee mentioned it.

"Nana, you don't need to come because Joe's keeping close tabs on me."

"What do you mean by close?"

"He moved in this morning and you don't have to worry about me being alone ever again."

"You let him move in with you; what are you thinking, Pamela?"

"He wants to take care of me because he loves me and I do him."

"He's a man and he can't be trusted, young lady. I had to learn the hard way about men and I don't want you to go through what I did."

"Nana, I love him and I want him in my life. He's a kind and sweet guy who loves me. I'll never find another guy like him."

70

"Men will say anything when they're screwing you. You're too naïve, Pam. There's another thing that bothers me a little that you haven't told him the truth about your wealthy family. He may have a problem with that when he finds out."

"You need to let me live my own personal life and not interfere. That's one of the reasons I came here because my folks interfered so much. I thought you would be more understanding and compassionate about my life."

"I'm trying to help you, my granddaughter, not destroy your life."

"Why would it bother him, if my family has money. It should be a plus in our relationship."

"Your mother will croak when she finds out you're not just dating but living with a cop. He won't be making enough money for her tastes."

"I don't care about her tastes or what she likes. I love him and I want to be with him. You let me handle her and I don't want you saying anything to her. I'll do that when I'm damn good and ready."

"I only want what's best for you and I'll check on you from time to time. You can always come here, if you feel like it."

"I know I can, Nana, but I'll be fine with my Joe." Pam hung up thinking about her grandmother's rather peculiar life. Lee only hired women to work for her and she was sure this attributed to her success in the small city. She preferred not to have anything to do with men in business or in private. The many rough years she spent being a battered wife had taken its toll on her and her thinking. Pam thought most men were nice and she'd rather work with Chris and Dave than all the female dispatchers. Women were too catty and jealous most of the time.

Chapter 9

Pam and Joe were enjoying being together very much. Marge, her supervisor, called her to see how she was doing and if she needed anything. Pam told her that she had a doctor's appointment and she was going to try and come back to work as soon as she could. This pleased her boss very much. Joe was checking on her when he worked or calling on his cell phone when he couldn't come by. She felt so very special. Ken Iverson, the new officer they all met just before the accident dropped by to see Joe. The two officers got more acquainted with each other at the accident scene. He showed up at the event with his trainer who was asked to handle the accident report. Ken was a local guy who's family was in the produce business. He was tall, sandy haired, and good looking. He joined the police force because selling blueberries, strawberries, and raspberries was not what he envisioned for his life. Enforcing the laws and helping citizens was what he wanted to do.

"Well, Pam, you're looking a lot better today than the last time I saw you."

"I clean up quite well as Joe reminded me after the accident."

"You're not by chance related to Lake Austin the computer multi-millionaire who lives in the redwoods are you?"

"Gee, Ken what do you think?" She gave him a big grin. Pam was stunned that Ken would bring up her dad. I guess money knows money she thought.

"As you already know, your accident was my first day on the job. It'll be a day I will never forget and I hope I never have another day like it."

"It must have been terrible to see an officer killed like that. What an awful beginning to your new career. The tears filled her eyes as she thought about Webb dying in the crash.

"I apologize, Pam, maybe I shouldn't be talking about the accident with you." Joe took her hand.

"No that's okay, I'm still real sensitive about the whole thing."

"I was thinking it may help me in my career," Ken told them. "I won't take things for granted and I'll be more cautious when driving. I do have to say one thing, if I may, I have never heard *Amazing Grace* sung as well as you did. It got to everyone. Here you were in a terrible accident but you still stood tall and sang your heart out for Webb. There's one other thing, Joe here was trying so hard to get you out of the car and he couldn't open the door. He's a real calm guy but he was feeling bad for you. We were all real glad when the fire department showed up." She looked at Joe who had lowered his eyes at Ken's words.

"I'm so lucky to have such a nice guy care about me," she told both men. Joe gave her a wink and she gave him one back.

"I think you're both lucky," Ken said to them. "I have to go and do some running around, Pam, you take it easy now. I'll see you at work, Joe."

"Yes, I'll be there and you take care."

"It was nice chatting with you, Ken, and I'll see you when I get back to work." Ken left and Pam looked at Joe. "I wonder, if he would be interested in getting acquainted with Julie."

"He met her yesterday in the Center and she got all shook up. I guess that means that you're not interested in going after him."

"I'm disappointed that you would say something like that, Joe."

"I was only joking. I don't want you going after him or anyone else."

"Don't worry I only want you. I'm not a matchmaker so I'll let them figure it out for themselves." She gave Joe a long kiss with the help of her tongue. He responded by putting his hand on her breast and caressing her nipple gently. "Oh, Joe, this feels so good. We have to leave for the doctor's appointment but I wish we had more time."

"I know," he told her. "I don't want to keep my hands off you for another minute." He took her by the hand when they got outside the apartment. She was feeling so good being with him. "I'm sorry for doing that, Pam, it isn't right until you are feeling better."

They arrived at Dr. Cho's office and went inside. Dr. Cho was a second generation Korean born in this country. He got his medical training in the Navy and at UCLA. Julie suggested him to Pam and she liked him right away.

Joe stayed in the waiting room while she went in to be checked. He did a thorough job and told her he wanted to see her in two weeks. She pleaded with him to let her return to work on Sunday for half a shift. He didn't think that was a good idea. She talked a little longer with the doctor and finally convinced him to release her for part time work. She was overjoyed when she came out of his office into the waiting room.

"You don't even have to tell me what was said. He had to release you."

"He sure did for part time and I have to go by the office to see Marge. If I don't show her this paper, she may not believe me."

"I'll take you there right now so you can get your schedule all set up. When does the doctor want to see you again?"

"I have to be checked in a couple of weeks. I'm doing great and I know it's because you have taken such good care of me. We make a good team."

"It's nice of you to say that but us being together is probably what really did it. When you're very happy things just seem to work out right."

"Will you make love to me tonight? If we just take it easy, it should be okay."

"Is that what you really want, Pam?"

"Joe, it's all that I think about since you moved in. Being close in bed at night and not being able to make love is terrible for me."

"I thought I was the only one thinking that way. You know we'll make love and I'll be gentle with you."

"Now I have something wonderful to think about for the rest of the day, Joe." He took her by the office and waited in the car while she went inside. The dispatchers were pleased to see her. Marge was glad that she could come back to work. She allowed Pam to keep her same days off and wanted her to work from 6:00 PM to 10:00 PM. Pam was happy. She went back out to the car smiling.

"Do you feel up to a little lunch in town since we're already here?"

"Sure, I'd like that very much." Joe drove to the New Horizon's. They were seated and the waitress took their orders when a dark look came across Joe's face. Pam turned to look and see the tramp standing at the entrance waiting to be seated. Joe looked into Pam's eyes and he was sad.

"Don't worry about it, Joe. We just can't let her bother us too much. She must have followed us all around this morning." Suzy was seated a couple of tables away where she could constantly look at Joe. "I love you, Joe."

"I love you, too but it's hard to relax when a big mistake is looking right at you." They didn't talk too much during the meal and they were both glad when it was over. After they got into his car, Suzy came out of the restaurant and was staring at them until they couldn't see her any longer. They were soon back at the apartment. Joe started getting ready for work and Pam was trying to cheer him up.

"Don't forget our big date tonight, my Joe. I can't wait for you to come home and love me all over." He grinned at her comment.

"I already love you all over, I just haven't shown you physically lately just how much. I'll keep checking on you throughout the shift and I'll try and come by." He left and she called her Nana to see how she was doing.

"It's so nice to hear from you, Pamela. Usually I'm the one who has to contact you so this is a nice switch. Do you have good news for me?"

"Well, I'm unemployed so that's clue number one that I'm more available to call you at the present time."

"Are you still with that man and are you happy? I want to make sure you're getting well and Joe is taking good care of you."

"Yes, to both your questions because our relationship is not going away, Nana. I wish that you could get to know him more and you would like him a lot."

"I prefer to take it slow and easy unlike my granddaughter who does everything fast and furious."

"That's not true, Nana, and you know it. You have always told me that I'm a sensible young lady. Have you stopped feeling that way?"

"No, but this time you may have put your emotions ahead of your brain. Are you staying in touch with your mother?"

"Yes, I e-mail her all the time but I'll not telling her about living with Joe for awhile. She would cause us too many problems."

"I wouldn't wait too long she might just show up unexpectedly and you would be up the creek without a paddle. She can be impulsive as you well know. I have a personal question to ask you and don't get riled up. Are you practicing birth control because that would be the last straw with your mother, if you came up pregnant?"

"Nana, I have been taught quite well about practicing birth control, in case, you have forgotten about my mother. How did my parents ever have me, Nana?"

"What do you mean, have you?"

"I never saw them close or even hug and kiss in front of me so I wonder how I was ever born."

"As you know your mother was a stewardess and met your dad on a flight

75

from New York to San Francisco. She knew he was loaded with money so she used her female wiles to get him to notice her. After the wedding they became a man and woman living together under the same roof on the weekends. He had his business life and she her social life. They were married two years and your mom got pregnant with you. How they pulled that off, I will never know. They both love you dearly in their own way."

"Nana, I don't want that kind of a life. I want to be with my Joe everyday and sleep with him every night. I love him and I always will. Money is nothing, if you don't have happiness. We care about each other and this is going to last a long time, Nana."

"I believe you, Pam, and I'll try and respect him because you love him so much."

"You just made me so happy, Nana. If we can convince mom, I'll be overjoyed."

Pam felt like doing some things around the apartment in the afternoon. She cleaned the bathroom and did some laundry. Anything to keep her busy and not watch the clock. She wanted tonight to be perfect for the two of them. He called her twice but wasn't able to come by on his dinner break. She understood his job quite well but she was a little disappointed. She tried to get interested in TV during the evening. She watched an old movie and then her phone rang.

"Hi, Pamela, what's going on?" Chris said to her.

"Hi, yourself Chris, I'm just taking it easy and it's starting to wear on me. I don't make a good patient and I'd rather be at work."

"Peckerini just called in and asked me to call you to make sure you were okay. His cell phone is out of power so that's why he hasn't called you. I'm afraid we gave him a big crash so he won't be getting off on time. Whatever you had planned for the evening will not be happening."

"We had no plans but he knows I'll worry, if he doesn't get home at the usual time."

"It has been one fucked up shift, Pam, if you ask me. A night like this is suppose to happen on the holiday weekend not a few days after."

"I have some good news, Christopher."

"Let me see, you're coming back to work so we can celebrate at the Den."

"Did Joe tell you today? Men talk more than women."

"Friday night we can howl once more and it seems like a long time since we were there. I'm glad you're coming back because work isn't the same without you to tease all the time. I'm losing my teasing skills. Marge has been real nice to us since you've been out. She's been kissing our asses to cover the overtime."

"I wanted to know, if you and Jules could come by for lunch tomorrow. I know she's off and you both can meet here at 1230 and we can have a good old time together. Joe will be here but he won't mind, if we gossip. I can fix some sandwiches and we can get caught up."

"I'm all for it. Jules is busy right now but I'll tell her and we should both be there. We need to celebrate you coming back to work with us."

"I can't wait to see you guys again. I won't kill you for sending Joe to a late crash. Shit happens all the time." She was very disappointed about Joe not getting off on time. You couldn't make too many plans when going with a cop. She learn that right after she started at the police department. She was trying to be positive in their relationship. She was determined to never turn into a whining female. That could make their commitment to each other go South in no time. Sometime during the night he crawled into bed and took her into his arms. She could now relax more knowing that he was home safely.

The next morning she had no problem getting out of bed without waking him up. He was still sleeping soundly. She loved looking at him while he slept. She went to the kitchen and put the coffee pot on and jumped into the shower. She came out a little later to see Joe sitting at the kitchen table having a cup of coffee.

"What a nice surprise," she said as she walked over and gave him a big hug. "You haven't had enough sleep and I was trying to be quiet getting out of bed."

"It's just me. I always get up around this time and my body thinks I went to bed earlier. It would be nice, if our minds and bodies could be synchronized perfectly but it will never happen."

"I've done that before. Brains and bodies sometimes work against each other."

"I could smell the coffee so I got up. I'm sorry about last night. I bought you a peace offering during the shift." He pointed to a white bag on the table.

She opened it up and gave him a big grin. "Chocolate donuts for me, how nice."

"I got in at two and didn't have the heart to wake you up."

"The next time just start nuzzling my neck and playing with my nipples and it'll work for you."

"Is that what your first boyfriend used to do?"

"No, not at all but it's what I would liked done." Pam was not expecting that from Joe. He knew she was hurt.

"Pam, I'm sorry that was not right for me to say that. I'm just tired and disappointed that I couldn't come home on time."

"I invited Chris and Jules over for lunch at 12:30 and you can join us. Jules is off but I thought she might like to come over. Chris said he would but she was too busy on the radio for me to talk to her. He relayed the message to her from me but I never got an answer."

"I can leave a little early, Pam, and get a bite in town before I go to work. I think you need this time alone with them. Thanks for inviting me though."

"Now I feel bad, Joe. This is your home, too and I feel like I'm booting you out to entertain my friends. Is Chris the reason you're doing this? If I just invited Julie, you would stay and eat with us?"

"If you're going to make a big deal out of it, I'll join the group. I just thought you might like to gossip without me."

"Please have a donut so I don't look like a pig." Her door bell rang and it was her Nana with more flowers, some home baked cookies, and a big pan of lasagna. The older woman walked in and seemed more polite to Joe then she ever had been.

"Nana, would you have some coffee and a donut with us? I know you just made Joe happy with the lasagna." He grinned at Lee. "No, dear, I just wanted to drop these off and I can't stay long."

"If you ladies will excuse me, I have some stuff to do this morning. It was nice that you dropped by, Lee."

"Joe, you haven't had enough sleep and you need more rest," she pleaded.

"It was nice seeing you again, Joe, have a good day," Lee said. Pam explained to Lee about Joe's late night out working the crash. He went to the bathroom and got into the shower while the two women talked. "Pam, you look awfully cozy around each other and for me to visit you under these circumstances is uncomfortable."

"I can't control how you feel but you're in my house now. I wish you wouldn't keep bringing this up."

"Why don't you come by the nursery later and visit for a little bit. You need to get out and the fresh air will be good for you."

"I just might do that and I think you're right about needing fresh air." Lee gave Pam a big hug and left. She was having a fairly good day so far. Joe finished his shower and said he would be back for lunch. He kissed her and she went into his arms. She did not want bad feelings between them.

She fixed some lettuce leaves, cut up a couple of tomatoes, and sliced an onion to put on their tuna salad sandwiches. Just a few minutes before 12:30, Chris rang her doorbell. She gave him a big hug and thought he looked a little pale. He was carrying a small Winnie the Pooh and a bouquet of flowers. "I wanted to give them to you in the hospital but first you were in ICU and you couldn't have anything like this. Then I forgot to bring them in." He gave her a big smile.

"Chris, you're so nice." She smiled too. She put the bear on her coffee table and got a vase for the flowers and put them on her dining room table.

"This room looks like a funeral parlor with all the flowers. Sorry I shouldn't have said that I just wasn't thinking."

"I know what you mean, Chris, you don't have to apologize."

"I'm not sure, if Jules is coming. I tried to talk to her last night but she wasn't very receptive. She has a guy that she is going ape shit over. Did you meet, Ken, the new hunk in the office?"

"He came by to visit Joe and I got to meet him at briefing before the accident." Joe came through the front door into the living room and said hello to Chris.

"What's this talk about Ken?" Joe asked.

"Jules, met him and she's all excited about a new hunk to go after." Chris said. "She thinks he's the one for her and I hope it works out but I don't know." The doorbell rang and Joe went to answer it. Julie bounded into the room and gave Joe a hug. She said hello to everyone and gave out no more hugs.

"We were just talking about you and Ken doll, Jules." Chris said to her.

"What were you saying about him?"

"The way you went ape shit over him the other day."

"I did not. I think he's good looking but there are a lot of good looking men around and she made a point of looking at Joe."

"Pam, didn't you think he was good looking?"

"I guess so but I'm not interested in the looks of other men. I thought he was very nice to talk to but I really don't know what he's like. Why do you call him Ken doll?"

"Pam, he looks just like Barbie's boyfriend, Ken."

"Oh, I guess he does resemble him." Pam fixed their sandwiches and they sat down at the table.

"Okay, I'm ready to hear more about what's going on at work," Pam said.

"It has been too serious around there since the accident and I think we need to lighten up a little," Chris told them. "I don't think Cannonball would want

79

us moping around forever."

"Have you been in the Blue Room lately?"

"No, too much else going on for the bitch to bother with me. I've not missed going in there so that's good. Mike comes in hung over as usual. It's kind of quiet without you, Pam."

"How are you and Joe doing living together?" Julie asked. Pam and Joe looked at each other.

"Everything is fine with us. He's taking great care of me but it'll be nice when I can do everything on my own again. I'm a piss poor patient."

"We just got Pam's version so how do you feel about playing house, Joe?"

"We're not playing house, Jules," Pam said to her friend before Joe could answer. "We're serious about each other."

"Why don't you let him answer, Pam? You, two just don't look as happy as I thought you would be since you moved in together."

"We just went through a lot and it isn't a happy time when a good friend dies."

"Pamela, I'm not talking to you why won't you let him answer?" Julie was getting upset at Pam and Chris didn't know what was going on.

"Jules, when a guy is getting regular sex, he's on cloud nine so what do you want him to do, turn cartwheels?" Chris asked. "This lunch is good, Pam. I'm getting anxious to go to the Den so let's not forget choir practice Friday night. We do need to get out and howl and it'll be fun. Jules, you should ask Ken doll to join us."

"Are you sure you're up to going out, Pam?" Julie asked her.

"I'm sure it won't hurt me to be out for a few hours as long as I don't drink and stay up too late." Joe finished and took his dishes to the sink.

"It's been nice you guys but I have to get going," Joe told them. He gave Pam a nice kiss. "I'll check in with you later or come by. I love you."

"I love you, too, my Joe. Take it easy and watch your back." Julie jumped up and gave him a hug.

"I'll walk out with Joe because I have to be going," Julie told the others. She followed him out the door.

"What's with her today?" Chris asked Pam. "She was denying she even likes Ken doll and she gave Joe two hugs. I didn't get a hug and neither did you."

"Chris, I told you before that I think she's still carrying a torch for Joe. She knows that he doesn't want her but she still wants him. I can feel it. Maybe she plans on trying to get Joe jealous by going after Ken. Women can be like that."

"Well, anything is possible and you women have all that intuition that man don't even understand. It's now time for me to depart and I can't wait for tomorrow night." Chris gave her a hug and left for work. She thanked him for his gifts.

Pam called her Nana in the afternoon to tell her she would not be visiting. She didn't quite feel up to going out. She spent the afternoon watching a couple of movies on TV.

Joe called on his lunch break and she was hoping he would have dropped by.

"You sound a little down," he said. "What can I do to pick you up?"

"It does get a little lonely when I'm here by myself. I'm missing you a lot because I didn't see enough of you today."

"I've never been told I was missed before."

"I miss you all the time when we're apart."

"I really like hearing that so you can tell me anytime."

"Lunch wasn't as nice as I thought it would be. Joe, I don't understand Jules and why she's acting the way she is. She's flip flopping in what she says to different people. Something isn't quite right with her."

"We'll talk later and don't worry about stuff you can't change."

"I'm looking forward to seeing you after work." They hung up and she thought just four more hours and he would be with her. She had a bite to eat and then went into her computer. She was getting behind in her e-mails and she would try and catch up. The time passed faster than she realized. She heard his key in the door and saw that it was 10:30 on her computer. She closed it down and hurried to the living room.

"I'm so glad to see you," she told him as she rushed into his arms. "Would you like a beer or something else to drink?"

"I think just a soda tonight but I'll get them and you sit on the couch." She sat down and he soon joined her with two glasses of diet coke and ice. "Tonight at work I was thinking that we've never discussed the accident and I thought we should sometime."

"I think tonight would be a good time," she said. "I heard Ken say yesterday how upset you were that you couldn't get the door opened to get me out of the car. I didn't realize that was happening because I was unconscious."

"I was trying so hard to get help for you and it was frustrating. I did what I could but it wasn't enough. I let you down and it has bothered me."

"You didn't let me down at all and you need to stop thinking that way." She looked into his eyes and saw his tears. She leaned over and put the side of her head next to his and held him. She, also, couldn't stop her tears. "I never dreamed that you thought you had let me down because that has never crossed my mind."

"I remember not too long ago you told me that you always felt safe when you were with me."

"I still feel safe when I am with you. It's when we are apart that bothers me."

"You mean right now you feel safe?"

"I'm one hundred percent sure," she told him.

"You know I thought that you wouldn't feel that way since the accident."

"Joe, I can't believe you have been having these thoughts."

"I guess I don't know you as well as I thought I did," he said.

"Today I was thinking a lot about our relationship after Julie made her weird comments. Do you know what her problem is?"

"No, Pam, but there's one other thing that bothers me. You keep saying that Chris is a good friend so I feel that you tell him everything about us and I don't like that. He has such a big mouth and I don't think you should trust him."

"I would never tell him or anyone about intimate details of our relationship, if we ever get intimate again. You might tell Julie everything but I do not." Pam was instantly upset at his accusations. "Why is it okay for you confide in her but I can't do that with him?" She asked him in a very calm voice.

"I don't trust him at all. I really don't."

"You just said you assume I tell him everything. I'm the one you don't trust."

"The guy is gay and I don't like him. I can never deal with gays because it isn't a normal way to be. We don't like each other either and that'll never change. You never know what's going to come out of his mouth."

"You don't know that he is gay and so what if he is. I don't think it's catching. You have no reason to be bothered about him and me. My God, he's just a friend and nothing more."

"It may not be catching but it's irritating to me."

"Why does his sexual preference bother you? He would never be attracted to me and you should like that part. He's a friend of mine and he'll always be a friend of mine."

"Maybe you need to look at your friends and think things over."

"Jules is still carrying a torch for you and that's okay in your book. It must be a big case of flattery for you but it upsets me at times. I know you can't control what she thinks but don't encourage her actions either. She hugs you all the time and wants to be around you a lot. It's starting to bother me but I trust you."

"It'll never happen, if what you say is true," Joe told her.

"It'll never be that way with me and Chris either. You need to think about all the bullshit you just said to me." Pam walked into the bedroom and got ready for bed. Later on he climbed into bed but he did not hug her this night. She wished that he would. She had to trust him or their relationship would not last.

Chapter 10

The next morning she felt rested physically but mentally she was not doing very well. She was still upset with Joe but didn't want him to know it. She would do everything to try and keep their relationship intact. It would probably mean she would have to bite her tongue a few times. She looked over at him and felt so much love for him. He was so handsome even when he slept. His attitude about gays was the only thing that needed to be dealt with. Chris always got to him and she didn't understand why. She got up and went into the bathroom. It was a nice day with the sun shining brightly. She was looking forward to getting out for a few hours this evening. After her shower Joe was still sleeping so she decided to go and see her Nana. She fixed the coffee pot for him and left him a note about where she was going. She left the apartment. It felt good getting into her car and driving once more. This was her first time behind the wheel since the accident. It was something she needed to do on her own. She didn't realize it until she got into the neighborhood that she was headed for the intersection

where the crash took place. She saw the traffic signal up ahead and she had a red light. This is better she thought as she slowed her car down to stop. When the light turned green she carefully looked in both directions twice and then proceeded through the intersection. The tears filled her eyes and the perspiration stood out on her upper lip. She didn't realize her trip to the nursery would be so stressful. She would drive a different route going home. The nursery was situated on Main Street in what used to be the outskirts of the city. Now it was a good size oasis amongst the businesses that had sprung up in the past ten years. It was well kept and had plenty of parking in the front and to the sides of the main building. The entrance was through a roughly built building with checkout stands in the very front. Lee kept all of the garden tools, fertilizers, and bags of soil inside the building. There were two large doors that opened out onto the main nursery. All the plants that loved the shade were under an overhead screen just outside. Pam passed the screened area and came to the sun loving flowers. To one side of the area was a small shack full of exotic flowers and plants. On the other side stood small bird baths, fountains, and a small pond full of water lilies. Way in back of the nursery were trees and ceramics pots of all sizes and shapes. She noticed Boots her Nana's black cat curled up in a ball on a lounge chair near the angel bird bath. The cat was all black except for her four white paws. She sauntered into the nursery one day last year and she has been there ever since. Pam walked over and touched the cat's head and Boots looked up at Pam with only one eye open.

"Sorry for waking you up but I couldn't keep from touching your soft fur," Pam said to the cat. Boots gave her a little meow, closed her eye, and settled back into her nap. She knew where her Nana spent most of her time so she went to the shack. "Hi, Nana," she said as she came up behind her grandmother who appeared to be repotting ivy plants. "What are you up to?"

"What a nice surprise to see my granddaughter this fine July morning."

"I just thought I'd come over to visit and get myself out into the fresh air today. I have been cooped up too long inside."

"You never called and told me what the doctor said."

"I had to beg him but he agreed to let me work four hours a day starting Sunday.

I go back in two weeks for another check up. He wants me to take care of myself or he'll make me stay home."

"He sounds like a good doctor to me. You asked what I'm doing and I'm making up some small round planters for cute little gifts. I fill the pots with some small ferns, ivy, and I add a few little things in the pots such as flags for the Fourth of July. I do this all year and just change the extra items depending on what holiday is coming up. What doesn't sell for Halloween will be turned into Thanksgiving pots. Over Christmas, I sell the most."

"Sounds like a good idea and such a nice inexpensive gift."

"They are quite popular, Pam, I always thought you would follow in my footsteps and be interested in the nursery business."

"I love plants and flowers, Nana, and I have good luck growing things but I like my job very much. I can work and do something I like to do and visit you and still be around things that I like. I have the best of both worlds."

"Where is Joe fitting into the picture?"

"We've known each other for two months, we love each other, and I see us always together. I wish you could like him, Nana. Be patient and I know you will because he's the nicest guy."

"Pam, he may be the greatest guy in the world but you haven't been out in the real world for very long. You meet this guy the first day on the job and you think you're in love. Why don't you play the field and not settle for the first guy you meet? You might even find out that men aren't as great as you think they are. There's something that I do believe in and that is to live with the guy before you make a mistake of getting married. You cannot possible know someone unless you live with them. If I had lived with Tom first, there would not have been a marriage for me not with him anyway. The best thing that came out of it was your mom. I wasn't dumb enough to marry again and be stepped on a second time. I know you're living with Joe but it would be nicer, if you were engaged."

"I always think about what you tell me, Nana, but I have to live my life my own way. I just came by to say hello and I need to try and get some rest this afternoon." Pam left the shack and chatted with a couple of the ladies in the front of the building. They heard about her accident and expressed their condolences about the officer dying. She left feeling sad and made sure she avoided the crash intersection on her drive home.

She got home and Joe was not there and she didn't know where he was. She checked the closet to make sure his clothes were still there. The coffee pot was empty and his cup was in the sink. She decided to lie down on the couch to try and nap. She dozed off and the phone rang and woke her up.

"Pam, I'm over at Ken's playing tennis, in case you're wondering where I am."

"That's too bad because I wanted to make love this morning. It's nice of you to call and let me know."

"I'll have to take a rain check on the love making. You left me a note so calling is the least I can do. I don't want you worrying. I thought that since we're going out this evening to the Den that we could have dinner there around 8:30. We can stick around for the rest of the gang." Ken and Julie would like to have dinner too."

"Are you playing tennis with the two of them?"

"Yes, we're having a good time. You should try it some time. I'll be home in a little while."

"Have a good time, Joe." She put the receiver back down. So Julie is playing tennis with the two guys she thought. That must be quite a scene. She'll never have Joe and she needs to forget about him. Joe did not come home and she did not go to the Den for dinner. He was having such a good time that he must have forgotten about her. He made no more calls to her.

Later that evening she drove to the Den and secured their booth before 10. She sat down and the waitress came by for her drink order. "Honey, do you want to order now or wait for your friends?"

"I'll wait for one of them to show up."

"I saw your picture in the paper about the accident and I want to welcome you back. It was terrible about the officer but I'm glad you're okay."

"Thank you for your nice words. I know it's still hard for me." The tears welled up in her eyes.

"I'll be back when your friends arrive." She looked towards the entrance and saw Joe coming towards her. He sat down next to her.

"What's with the tears?"

"The waitress just ask me about the accident and it made me sad." He put his arm around her shoulder and it felt good.

"I guess it is going to be hard for you seeing people now and everyone mentioning Webb."

"It's something I'll have to get through. Did you forget your way home today?"

"We played tennis, got to talking after tennis, and Ken decided to feed us. We played more tennis because he has outside lights. I'm sorry I didn't even call you to cancel dinner."

"I knew better than to show up here when you didn't come home. Joe, I don't want you to think that you have to be in my face all the time. You've been single awhile and I don't want to be a weight on your shoulders."

"You're not a weight but I do lose track of time and I need to watch out for that."

Chris came wandering up to the booth and she was glad to see him. "How's everyone this fine evening?" He asked.

"I'm fine," Pam told him.

"Are you sure you're okay?" He asked. Chris noticed Joe's arm around her.

"Yes, the waitress brought up the accident and it made me a little sad."

The waitress returned and took their order. Pam asked for a diet coke. "Is Jules and Ken coming?"

"Yes, they're both suppose to be here," Joe told her. All three were looking towards the front went Suzy walked in. Pam felt a twinge of jealously upon seeing her. Chris and Joe hadn't even acknowledged one another. Soon Julie and Ken arrived and joined the others. Joe dropped his arm from Pam's shoulder. She didn't know why.

"I'm so glad you could make it Jules and you, too, Ken," Chris told them.

"This is my first time and I hope it won't be my last," Ken said. Julie gave Ken a great big smile.

"You missed out on some good fun today, Pam," Julie said.

"That's what I just heard."

"Oh, the town whore is here looking for a fix for the night maybe we should ask her to join us," Chris said. He glanced at Joe.

Pam told them about her trip to the nursery by way of the accident scene. "I came upon the intersection and it was so hard for me to drive through it but I did." She told them about her visit to the doctor and being released to go back to work. I need to get back to work in the worst way and four hours is better than none. I can have the same days off and I'll work 6 to 10 PM." They could all tell she was rearing to return. Ken and Joe talked mostly about their jobs and Ken was looking forward to being off training. Chris looked at Suzy and noticed she was glaring at them.

"Hey, Joe, your girlfriend isn't very happy sitting over there alone."

"I don't have a girlfriend."

"I wonder why that is? I stand corrected, your whore isn't happy sitting there alone." You could have heard a pin drop at the table. Chris knew he had struck a nerve and he didn't want to give up. "How could you be dating a beautiful intelligent woman like, Pam and decide to spend the night with that whore?" Everyone at the table was stunned to hear this coming out of Chris. "How would you feel, if you were Pam?"

"Chris, don't even pretend you're speaking for me. I didn't come out tonight to hear you ridicule Joe. If you'll all please excuse me, I'm going home," Pam said. She got up and they let her out. The tears were coming fast. She was hurrying and as she walked past Suzy's table, she called out to Pam.

"Look, bitch, he doesn't want you. He wants a real woman." Pam saw the glass of beer in front of Suzy and she poured it over her head. Joe was right behind Pam and heard the exchange. Suzy lunged for Pam and grabbed her arm. Pam twisted her arm away from her. She kept walking towards the door.

She got outside and could hardly see the way to her car for the tears. Joe took her arm as she got to her car door.

"I can't believe you told that little fag about my night with Suzy. I bet he's been waiting for a time like this when everyone was present to tell it."

"Joe, I never told him a thing. Why don't you ask your friend Julie? She's the only one who knew and you're the one who told her. You know, Joe, you have no respect for me and it has taken me a little while to discover it. To think I would tell Chris about your night with Suzy and the fact you spent the night with her shows you think nothing of me and my feelings. Chris probably knows this and he's trying to wake me up." She jumped into her car and drove away. She immediately got into the shower to wash her tears and her body. It felt so good. She got out and put on her robe. She came out of the bathroom and Joe was standing in the middle of the living room. "Why did you come home? You had such a good time with your friends today and now you are leaving them to come home."

"I wanted to make sure you were all right. I don't like you upset."

"You stood me up today and that was okay. What, if I had gone to the Den at 8:30 like you asked me? You couldn't pick up the phone and tell me you were eating with friends and I should fend for myself. Just one simple phone call to make things right."

"I apologize for being inconsiderate of your feelings, Pamela. I wouldn't like to be treated that way."

"Another thing, I don't like going to the Den and running into her and it appears she's always going to be there. It must be her second home. I would never say one thing to her but she couldn't keep her mouth shut to me. You must have heard what she said. She's probably right that I'm not woman enough for you. She must be thinking that because why would you go to her, if you were content with me. I couldn't take her mouth tonight so I let her have it. I love you so much, Joe." He pulled her into his arms and held her.

"I love you too and never more than I do right now." She pulled away from him and looked into his eyes. She was sure she could see his love for her. She gently kissed his mouth and he kissed her back. "Pam, I want you so much." She got up and stood in front of him and loosened the ties on her robe and opened it up.

"Please make love to me." He pulled her to him and kissed her breasts and she let out a little moan. With one swoop he lifted her into his arms and carried her to the bed. He lay her down and kissed her all over some more. She reached over and started undoing his pants as he was on his knees next to the bed. He helped her get them off and she grabbed his penis and squeezed it a little.

"Do you want that?"

"Yes, I do so very much."

He took off his shirt and took a condom from his pants. He put it on and he lay down beside her. She touched his penis again and stroked it. "Pam, I don't want to hurt you so if I do please let me know."

"I will, Joe, but you could never hurt me by making love to me." He kissed her more and she responded back. He nibbled and sucked on her nipples gently at first. She caressed his penis as he sucked her more.

"Are you still okay?" He asked her.

"I'm fine please don't stop." She rolled on top of him with his help and opened herself up to him. She rocked back and forth and asked, if he was ready. They intertwine their fingers as the thrusts turned into a burst of passion. Her body was rocked with ripples of pleasure. They lay quietly after the love making ended just enjoying each other's closeness. "I needed this so much, my Joe, you are always gentle and soft with me.

"Pam, if you feel anything like I do right now, you must know how much I care about you." She rolled off of him and gave him a grin. He gave her kiss and held her closely.

"I feel great and wonderful, Joe, at the moment. Ever since we first started making love, it's everything I imagined it would be. It'll be better when I can move a little more once again."

"Don't worry about pleasing me because let me tell you, it was great. I enjoy you whether you move around a lot or not. I know you want me so don't ever worry about that again." She kissed him and held him.

They talked for awhile before going off to sleep. He told her about his day playing tennis and she asked him quite a few questions. He wanted her to join them and have some fun. He would be glad to show her what he knows about the sport. It was Julie's first time and she needs a lot of training before she can hit the ball very well. Pam told him she would like to play with them sometime. He would hold her to that.

She was content as she cuddled in his arms and she was smiling as her eyes closed.

Chapter 11

Pam quietly sneaked out of bed and went into the shower. She enjoyed sleeping with him so much. She thought sleeping with someone might be a problem for her since she had slept alone her whole life. Being with him felt good and she was pleased. She went out to the patio to enjoy the warm day. She heard him stirring in the bedroom and looked up to see him coming out to join her. He bent over and put his arms around her and kissed the top of her head. "How's my girl this morning?"

"I'm just fine and very happy. Why don't you sit down and I'll get you a cup of coffee. It's nice sitting out here."

"Let me get into the shower first and then I'll be ready for one." She sat there very still thinking about last night and how glad she was they made love. Atticus, the crazy mockingbird, was squawking so she knew the cat must be nearby. Joe soon came out of the shower with just a towel wrapped around his mid section. "I couldn't just get dressed this morning after my shower."

"Do you mean you might want more because this is easy access for me?"

"Well, that's a possibility, if you feel up to it."

"It could be. Joe, I feel so good, so alive and so very happy. It's going to be quite warm today."

"It's sure going to be a nice day. Your eyes are shining this morning."

"You mean I'll walk into the Center and everyone will know how much in love I am. I could shout it from the tallest building."

"That's a good guess."

91

She gave him a smile that was full of love. "I'm looking forward to not using condoms again. I don't want us to use them forever."

"Pam, we have to for awhile and I went to the doctor myself to make sure Suzy didn't give me anything. It wouldn't be fair to you, if she did. He'll let me know, if there's a problem."

"I agree with that and let's not talk about the one night stand anymore. I wish we could get past it but if she is going to keep harassing me, it won't be happening. There's someone I must deal with and that is Chris. I'm sure Jules told him but he had no right to bring you and Suzy up in front of Ken." Joe nodded. She reached over and put her hand under the towel and on his knee. She started moving her fingers up the inside of his thigh until she felt him coming to life. She squeezed him lightly and smiled at him.

"What do you have in mind this beautiful morning?"

"I want the love of my life to make love to me again."

"I can arrange for that to happen." He reached over and put his hand inside her robe. He found her nipple and touched it ever so lightly. "You look like you want me as much as I want you." She smiled and got up from the chair and they both walked into the bedroom. They made love once more and cuddled in each other's arms when it was over.

"This was even better than last night, Joe. I want you to teach me to make love to you so you'll always feel good about being with me."

"Pam, you're just fine as you are. I already feel very comfortable when we make love. Don't worry about it so much that you don't enjoy it."

"I'm going to get up, get dressed, and fix you a breakfast that you so deserve. I want to wait on you a little to pay you back for being so nice to me."

"You don't have to pay me back but I would like something to eat." She made him a big omelet for breakfast and they were enjoying their time together very much. They were together all day. He helped her clean the apartment and they went grocery shopping together. They made love again in the evening. She would never get tired of him.

Sunday evening Pam entered the Center knowing she would be working with Julie and Dave. Chris was off on the weekends.

"Well, you're smiling so things must be okay in Hooterville." Chris said to her.

"I have some words for you, friend, and why are you working today?"

"Our good friend Jules is sick on her ass so I was asked to come in on my day off to work and what words do you have for me?"

"You know damn well what the words will be. It's your mouth, Chris, in case you haven't figured it out." She did not want to bring the conversation up in front of Dave and Chris knew exactly what she was talking about.

Later in the evening it was quiet and Dave took a break outside the Center. "You had no right to bring up Suzy and Joe in front of Ken. Our little group is family and Ken is still an outsider. You deliberately said it to upset Joe and when he's upset so am I. It was not appreciated and if we're to remain friends you need to accept him as my boyfriend. That means being respectful to him."

"Look every time I see the tramp and Joe in the same room it gets to me. I just had to let it out and I thought later on I shouldn't have done that."

"You're damn right you shouldn't have."

"I have no problem with that so let's get over it. What have you been up to since I saw you at the Den?" Dave came back into the center.

"I had a wonderful day off yesterday and I'm now back to work so life is great."

"You and Joe are still getting along, I take it?"

"We sure are and life is more than grand."

"I'm happy for you, if that is what you want. You're not walking very funny."

"What do you mean by that comment?"

"I figured there would be sex every hour on the hour, if you two ever started living together. You're athletic so it probably won't make a difference."

"Chris, you're something else."

"I just want you to know that I hope it works out for you but keep your guard up. An officer is an officer and they feel they're above the rules at times. A lot of married ones have problems and you know that yourself. Just be cautious until you get to know him better. That isn't too much to ask for from a good friend."

"I have never considered life as always being easy. We get along so far and we're very open with each other. Whatever comes up good or bad, we'll be able to deal with it and he'll be my life long partner."

"I wish you both the very best and I'll still tease you," he told her.

"I hope I won't be working the phones every night when I come to work at this funny hour," she said.

"You know I prefer the radio on the weekends, if I have to work, and the phones during the week," Chris said. Each dispatcher had his or her own preferences or quirks.

It wasn't long before Joe came in and stood next to Pam. He gave her a wink and asked how her shift was going.

"Well, Joe, how's it going with you?" Chris asked. "I need to apologize to you for my mouth last night. I got too carried away and I'll watch it from now on."

"I'm just fine, Chris, and I accept your apology. How come your working on the weekend?" Joe asked. "Where's Jules?"

"Well, she's sick and I get to work. I've had only one day off this week but I'm doing okay." The two guys heard Pam gasp as she answered the phone.

"What's wrong?" said Joe. He saw a look on her face that he didn't like. She hung up the phone and her face turned red.

"It was just a prank caller trying to be funny. Some people don't have anything to do except harass other people." She would tell him later that it was Suzy. It wasn't a very busy Sunday and Pam didn't mind at all. When she worked with Chris it was never a dull day. He could impersonate anyone and this he liked to do more than anything else, especially everyone's gestures and the way they walked. He would get up and perform and he was hilarious. They all knew he should have been a comedian.

Joe arrived home after Pam had taken a shower. She was a two shower a day person ever since she first started having sex with her first boyfriend. She could not be clean enough to suit herself. Joe usually took one at the office and wore regular clothes for the trip home. She gave him a big hug and she looked like she had something to say.

"What's on your mind?" He asked her. "You looked a little perturbed tonight."

"That prank call I received when you were in the Center was from Suzy. I didn't want the others to know what was going on."

"What in hell did she say?"

"She said that I shouldn't let you stay with me because I can't take care of you the way she can." Pam lowered her eyes and Joe took her in his arms. "I was hoping she wouldn't call me at work but it looks like she will. She has our address and phone number and we don't know what she has planned."

"This isn't good at all and I fear that all hell is starting to break loose with her and I don't know what it will take to get her to stop."

"She must be stalking one of us to know so much."

"I'm so sorry for all of this," he told Pam.

"We'll get through it because nothing she can say will turn me against you."

"Well, I don't trust her and she could come up with lies that may have you thinking differently."

"No way, my good man, I'm in this for the duration." She was letting him hug her when the phone rang. She jumped and he went to answer it. He said hello and whoever was on the line hung up.

"I guess she doesn't want to talk to me."

"Let me answer the phone here. She's probably checking on us and is wondering, if you're here for sure."

"She got her answer, I guess," Joe said. "We need to talk about this and decide what we're going to do. We could get restraining orders against her or wait and see what she's going to do next."

"I don't think the restraining orders are a good idea right now. I'm willing to wait until she does something else, if you don't mind holding off? Joe, do you know if she has a job and where it is?"

"She's a waitress at the Diner downtown." He saw a sad look in Pam's eyes. He knew he hurt the one woman who he really cares about by being stupid."

"I need to relieve some of my stress and I think I know the answer," she said to him. He looked into her eyes and saw a real sexy look. He knew she wanted him and he wanted her too.

"Take off your clothes and get real," she said. "You'll need a condom on, too."

"Now taking my clothes, may not necessarily result in me being able to put a condom on right away. I might need a little help in that department." She went to him and kissed him. She gave him her tongue and he gave his to her. She kissed him on his neck and around his ears while her hand was caressing between his legs. "What about you?" He asked as he started removing his clothes.

"I just have this thin robe on with nothing underneath. I may even keep it on because I want to treat you tonight." He finished taking off his clothes and was wondering what she had planned. He was already hard with anticipation so he slipped the condom on. She walked out of the bedroom and said she would be right back. She came back in a couple of minutes with something behind her back. He was already lying on the bed, naked and he couldn't wait.

"What do you have behind your back?"

"Something that I like and I hope it's a treat for you too." She swung a can of whipped cream from behind her back. She got on the bed and proceeded to spray him until his groin was covered with whipped cream. "I've heard about people doing this so I have always wondered how it would be."

"I'll tell you right now it is cold and I'm losing some stiffness as I speak." She bent over him and started licking. She was slowly licking him and swallowing at the same time.

"How does it feel?" She asked him.

"It's great so far." He once more became real hard. After the whipped cream was gone she softly nibbled and sucked until he made a slight groaning sound.

"Pam, this is so good and please keep going." She could feel him responding to her lips. "Oh, babe, I am so ready for this." He grabbed and held her head with both of his hands. She was moving her mouth and tongue until he couldn't move anymore. He held her head as his body shut down and his passion was waning. "That was so good," he said as she rose up and laid her head on his chest.

"Joe, it'll be better when you don't have to use a condom." He was lying on his back with his arms crossed over his forehead.

"You got cheated, young lady."

"Look the night is still young and we can talk and start it up again, if you feel like it."

"I like the way you think." The phone rang as he put his arm around her. Pam reached over to the headboard and picked the phone up.

"Hello," she said. In about half a minute, she told the caller, "don't call this number again. I'm not interested in anything you have to say." She hung up the phone and looked at Joe. "She told me that you liked to be fucked in the shower best of all." She lay back down in bed next to him."

"I have a feeling before this is all over with, I am going to know more than I need to know about your preference for sex." Joe got up on one elbow and looked at her.

"I have never been in the shower with that woman. She's making shit up. Do you want to know what I prefer? I prefer to go to bed and have sex with someone I love. I'm thinking that if I saw Suzy and told her face to face, that I don't want anything to do with her, she might realize I'm sincere."

"I don't mind, if you think it will help. If you talk with her and you feel it will not work, tell her you'll take out a restraining order against her and I will too."

"I'll call her tomorrow at the Diner and see, if I can meet her at the Den after work. I sure as hell don't want to meet her unless it's in a public place."

"I'll come home and wait for you while you have the meeting."

"Are you sure you can handle me meeting her?"

"I do trust you, Joe, and I know you love me." They spent some more time talking and Joe fell off to sleep.

The next morning Joe called Suzy at the Diner in front of Pam to see, if she would meet him later. Pam was glad he didn't do it behind her back.

"Suzy, I was wondering, if you could meet me at the Den after I get off work this evening?" He asked. Pam was looking gloomy as he spoke on the phone. It was best she couldn't hear what Suzy was saying to him. "I'll see you around 10:30."

"I'll bet she's glad to have a date with you?" Pam asked.

"Well, she agreed right away to see me but she'll soon find out it isn't a date. I feel bad about last night and you getting cheated. I don't like that at all and I apologize for falling to sleep on you."

"I'm not worried and you'll make it up to me, I'm sure." He was soon out the door.

During the shift Chris asked Pam, if she would like to go to the Den and have a couple of brews, after work. "You can even ask Peckerini to join us, now that you two are joined at the hip."

"I need to get out," Julie told him," so I'll go. I'll see, if Ken can join us."

"Let's do it tomorrow night instead," Pam told them. "I don't feel like going tonight." She could not believe Chris and Julie were making plans to go to the Den when Joe would be there meeting Suzy. They'll see it all and wonder what's going on. Chris would call her at home to give her a report. She knew her friend so well.

"We can go both nights, what else do we have to do after work."

"Can't go shopping at the mall, that's for sure," Julie chimed in. She tried to get word to Joe about Chris and Julie's plans but he was tied up going from call to call all evening. They would surely report back to her that Joe was stepping out on her. Since she couldn't get word to him, she decided to go to the Den after all. She and Joe could both talk to Suzy to try and get through to her. Chris was glad that she changed her mind and Julie pretended to be pleased, also.

The shift was moving along quite well when a call came in of a child being hit by a car. These calls always caused a lot of concern among the dispatchers. The sergeant asked Ken and Lopez to handle the accident for training purposes and Joe went to the scene to help them out. A five year old boy was learning to ride his bicycle with training wheels and rode out into the street. The car was unable avoid the child. Joe arrived at the scene first and Pam could tell in his voice that it was not good. He finally asked her to send the coroner and when he keyed his mike she could hear the sounds of a hysterical mother in the background. It tore her up inside and she wasn't even out there to see it. No officer ever wanted to handle an incident where a child was hurt or killed. Her heart went out to him.

Joe hadn't arrived at the office before she left so she wasn't able to tell him about the change in plans. She went by the apartment first because she didn't want to arrive there before Joe did. She knew, if she didn't go, she'd spend the rest of the evening wishing she had. She didn't know how long they would need to convince the bitch to leave them alone. She left after 10:30 and drove to the Den. Chris was waiting for her at the entrance.

"Where in hell have you been, Pam? You'll never guess what's happening inside right now? Your dear, sweet, wonderful boyfriend just came in and is sitting with the town tramp. They have their heads together so thought you should know what's going on. The shit will hit the fan for sure when you go walking in. Jules is holding our table so what do you plan on doing?"

"Thanks for telling me and I'll just go right in and join them."

"I didn't know you were a true blond. Wake up and smell the rat, for God's sake. This is beyond my imagination because I thought Joe really liked you but I'm having big doubts right now. Just remember I warned you when you end up kicking him out." Chris went back inside before Pam could say any more to him. She quietly walked inside and there was Joe and Suzy talking. Suzy had a big smile on her face but Joe was not happy. The two looked shocked when they saw Pam approaching their table. She sat down next to Joe.

"What are you doing here?" Suzy said angrily to her. "Joe and I are busy here and you need to leave us alone."

"Now, Suzy this is a public place and I have every right to be here. Joe and I need to talk to you about leaving us alone. Isn't that right, Joe?"

"Yes, that's why I made the call to you so we could talk to you. I need to get right to the point," he said as he turned to look at Suzy. "You need to leave Pam alone and I mean right away. She and I are seeing each other and living together. We love each other very much."

"Joe, I thought you wanted to see me tonight and let me give you some good sex."

"Look it was a mistake for me to see you that one night. I can't undo what happened but I'm not interested in you and you need to get on with your life."

"You listen to me," she told him, "you wanted me just as much as I wanted you and don't deny it," Suzy spat at him.

"That isn't true." He was trying to stay calm and not wanting to make a scene. "I was drunk and you badgered me into thinking I wanted you. There's a big difference between drunk and sober."

"You may have had too much to drink the first time we had sex but in the night you were half sober. Sex in the middle of the night was the best for me."

"Look, you performed oral sex on me once and that was it."

"That may be all that you remember but I remember both times. I even have proof that it happened."

"What do you mean you have proof?" Pam asked her.

"We didn't come here to discuss how many times," Joe interjected. "I came here to tell you to knock it off and stop calling Pam. If you keep calling her, I'll take a restraining order out on you and so will she. Do I make myself clear?" He whispered loudly to her. Pam was pleased at the way he was handling Suzy. All of a sudden Suzy got very calm.

"I do have proof for you two. I had a video camera all set up in my bedroom and I have the whole night of love on tape. I didn't think you'd believe me so someday when you least expect it, I'll mail you a copy of the tape. I won't send it to Joe because he would destroy it. I want you to see it, bitch, in living color. He can have sex with me anytime drunk or sober." Pam's mouth was half open as she couldn't believe what Suzy was saying.

"She's bluffing, Pam, because there was no second time for us." Pam got up and went to sit with Julie and Chris. She was in utter shock because why would Suzy say that if she didn't have proof. Joe sat a little longer arguing with Suzy and then he got up and left. Pam wanted to comfort him so she told her friends she was going home. Suzy followed Joe out through the entrance and over to his car. When Pam got to the entrance she heard him and Suzy. "Don't be following me and I don't want a thing to do with you," Joe yelled at Suzy. She started crying and was holding Joe's car door open. Pam looked out and saw Joe trying to get into his car with Suzy hanging onto the door. She finally let go, he slammed the door and took off. Suzy was crying loudly just standing in the middle of the parking lot. Pam started walking toward her car. Suzy ran over to her.

"I can tell you that your boyfriend lied to you. He told you he and I had sex once when he spent the night with me and that is a big fat lie. He doesn't remember having sex in the middle of the night when he was on me like a bee to honey. He did things to me that I never even imagined could be done. I'm sure you know what I'm talking about. I'll send that tape to you and you'll know that he lied to you. I'm sure he remembers but he doesn't want you to know what went on."

"I don't believe you, Suzy, Joe wouldn't lie."

"Before you walked in he wanted to make a deal that he would see me once a week, if I'd leave you alone. So what do you think about that?"

"I still don't believe you." Pam got into the car and drove away. She cried all the way home because she thought that Suzy could be right. She didn't want it to be true. She walked into the living room and Joe was waiting for her.

"You just couldn't stay away, could you? You upset her so that she'll never leave us alone. You've been crying so you must believe her."

"Chris and Julie made plans to go to the Den and I tried to talk them out of going. I didn't see you at work to warn you so I decided to go. I thought we both might be able to convince her to lay off. I thought you might like to be with me after handling the accident with the little boy."

"Why did you leave the table when she told you she had a tape? You really do believe her," Pam went over and put her arm around him.

"After you left she told me that before I got there you made a deal with her. You would see her once a week and not tell me, if she would leave me alone."

"Pam, I never said those words to her but she said them to me. Do you believe her or me?"

"I believe you, Joe, but if a tape shows up one of these days what then?"

"I thought you had an open mind and nothing she said could hurt the trust you have in me. She has a problem, Pam and it's her not being able to get over me."

"I'm confused but I still trust you. Maybe you were so drunk and you can't remember what happened in the middle of the night. Joe, stranger things have happened I won't leave you, if it turns out to be true, I promise you that."

"Pam, I'm sure I would remember. She has been trying to get you all riled up and tonight she succeeded. You let her get to you and I'll have to pay." He dropped his arms from around her and sat down on the couch. Pam immediately went into the bedroom. A little while later Joe came into the bedroom and crawled into bed. She was still awake. She turned toward him and put her arm around him as he was facing the other way.

"I do trust you and I didn't mean for her to get to me." Joe never said a word and she decided she was just talking to herself.

In the middle of the night Pam was still awake and hadn't slept at all. Joe was now turned facing her and she got her face next to his and gave him a soft and gentle kiss. She gave him another and he started stirring around. She nuzzled his neck and gave him more kisses. She was so ready and she was going to keep going. Joe stiffened a little as she grabbed him between the legs.

She wanted him really bad. She was wondering why he wasn't responding more to her but thought it was because he was upset when they went to bed. She kept fooling around with him and giving him more kisses. Suddenly Joe reared up in bed. "You have to stop this Suzy. I don't want you."

"I'm not Suzy," she yelled out and her love making mood was shattered with his words. "My God, Joe, do you have to dream about her?"

Joe groaned and realized he was awakened from a dream he was having. "I was asleep, Pam, what do you expect from me?"

"Is it possible you went to sleep and she fooled around with you like I was doing and you thought she was me and you did have sex with her?"

"I'm sure I'd remember, if it happened."

"Not necessarily, if you were sound asleep when it all started. You just called me Suzy. You could have thought she was me. Just remind me not to wake you up in the middle of the night again."

"Look, Pam, I guess anything is possible but I really don't think I had regular sex with her." She didn't want to argue anymore so she lay quietly next to him. "We're in for some hard times."

"Joe, we're in this mess together and I won't let you down again. I thought I had thick skin but I guess it wasn't thick enough this evening." He got up on one elbow and looked at her.

"You're sure we can get through this together?" He asked her.

"I'm positive, we can."

"It could get much worse, you know."

"She must want to be with you really bad, Joe, but not as much as I want to be with you." She rose up and kissed him and he kissed her back. They made love with more intensity than normal. They were both trying to prove to the other that they were in this relationship for the long haul. Afterward they held each and it felt so good. "Joe, I want to say something to you. I know you love me and you want to be with me. I know you feel nothing for her."

"I appreciate that Pam and it's another reason I love you so very much. I want this mess over with so we can plan for a nice future together."

"We can't control her actions. We can fight her but not control her. Let's talk about other things," she said. "You're so handsome and I love you dearly."

"We need to tell each other everyday our feelings," Joe told her. "When things are rough it's more important to communicate."

"I really like the way we just communicated," she told him with a giggle. "Lets do it more often and then we'll have less stress in our lives."

"You're something else, woman, and I'm so glad we found each other. From now on, I'll do everything in my power to make you proud of me."

"I'm already proud of you. I could kick myself everyday for not telling you that I cared about you sooner,"

"Pam, don't even say such a thing. I could have done the same thing and you know it. We both screwed it up but we'll get past it. Our love between us will prevail and we'll be stronger for it."

"I don't know if you really could have. Women are more emotional than men. We always cave in first when it comes to feelings because that's who we are. You have always given me attention but in a kinder and gentler way. I have never felt you undressing me when you were around me like other guys made me feel. I can feel the respect you have for me. You're kind and caring and you make a great police officer. I worry about you on the streets but I know you would never do anything stupid when you're out there." He held her closer and she got still for a few minutes. "I want you to know that you're my first true love and you'll be my last."

"I feel the same way. I've never been around a woman who made me feel as good as you do. I can see it all the time in those perfect big blue eyes." He kissed her and held her for a long time. She was enjoying the moment and he was too. Things had to work out between them because she loved him so much.

Chapter 12

They were starting to feel that Suzy may be giving up when a few days passed without any phone calls. Joe didn't get a restraining order because she had not made any more calls since they talked with her. They really hoped she believed he was serious and didn't want anything to do with her.

On Wednesday he left the apartment for work Pam was doing their laundry. Several minutes passed and he came back to the apartment looking angry.

"What's wrong?" Pam asked as he came back through the door.

"It seems we had a visitor in the night. All four of your tires have been slashed."

"Oh, no and they aren't that old either."

"You can take me to work and come back here and I'll have them send another officer for a report. You don't have to be to work until six and I'll get the new tires for you in the morning." She grabbed her purse and went with him.

"What are we going to do about Suzy and trying to keep things quiet? They're going to ask me, if I know someone who would do this to me and I have to tell them about her. Can't we just forget about a report and hope it doesn't happen again."

"You have to do this because it's the truth. I know it's no accident because your car was the only one targeted. This was a criminal attempt on her part. If we sit back and don't say a thing, she could do something worse the next time. I don't want a next time but she cannot be trusted."

"It won't look good for you, Joe."

"We're going to stop this bitch. She still doesn't have a clue about me not wanting to see her. Whoever takes a report can pay her a visit and that may be what it'll take to get through to her." Pam dropped him off at the office and returned to the apartment. Joe checked with his sergeant and they would send someone out for a report.

In about 30 minutes Ken showed up with Lopez to handle the incident. Lopez was a good foot and a half shorter than Ken, sporting a pencil thin mustache and small black eyes. They came to her door and she walked out to her car with them. Ken took out a clip board from the back seat of his vehicle and then got a sheet of paper out. He started asking her questions after looking at her driver's license. Lopez prompted him on asking if she had any idea who might want do this when Joe pulled in behind them in his patrol car. He got out and they exchanged greetings. He told Ken what he had found when he left for work and he figured Pam was targeted because no other vehicles had been vandalized.

"I was just asking her, if she knew anyone who might be responsible for this act."

"I have an acquaintance who we both feel is responsible and you must be familiar with Suzy who hangs out at the Den." He told Ken all about Suzy including the phone calls to Pam. "She wants to be with me and she's pulling no stops."

"Looks like you two are in a mess and that's too bad." Lopez told Ken to get Suzy's home address or where she works and they'll follow up with her. You know we can't prove anything unless a witness comes forward but it might scare the hell out of her. She might decide to leave you both alone after we talk with her. I'll catch you in the office at the end of our shift or see you on the street. I'll let you know, if we find anything out." Ken was handling himself quite well learning all aspects of his job.

"We'll appreciate whatever you can do to stop all this," Joe told his fellow officers. The two officers left and Joe stood next to her. "Are you okay?"

"Sure, this is all in a day's work, right? Will you call me after you see Ken?"

"I can't say too much to you over the taped phones at work but I'll call anyway. I wish I could give you a big hug right now. You look like you could use one."

"I sure could but I understand you can't be hugging your girlfriend on duty and in uniform. Whatever would the public think?"

"Follow me," he said. She walked toward the building right behind him. He motioned for her to go into the laundry room and he closed the door. He pulled her to him and put both arms around her. "No one can see us and I couldn't leave you without a hug." She gave him a big smile and kissed him on the lips.

"I do feel a little better. You have powerful arms, officer. I'll see what I can come up with later to make you feel good." They both left the little room smiling and he got into the patrol car and took off.

She decided to stop by the nursery on her way to work. She went into Lee's office and found her looking through invoices sitting at her desk.

"Oh, my God, an unexpected visit from my favorite granddaughter," Lee said to her.

"Well, I'm working just part time so I have more time to visit you." Boots was sitting on the couch licking her paws. Pam sat next to the cat and started scratching her head.

"You know Joe has never been here so you should bring him by some time."

"Would it be safe for me to do that? You weren't very nice to him when I was in the hospital. He was taking such good care of me and he only got your wrath."

"Things have calmed down a little since then and I know you care about him. I take it you're sleeping together since you're living with him?" Lee gave her a curious look.

"Nana, why would you ask something like that?"

"You must be sharing a bed unless he's on the couch because you have that look about you. That same look that a woman gets when she finds the guy she thinks she's looking for. It was called wide eyed and bushy tailed when I was young."

"Yes, we're sleeping together because I don't want you to keep asking me. He's the most wonderful guy in the world and what else would you like to know?"

"That's enough for now. I just hope you can both stay happy. I do want that because I don't want my precious, Pamela, to ever be unhappy."

"Thanks, Nana, and I love you, too." She gave her Nana a very happy smile. Boots was pushing against Pam's hand and purring really loud. "It's too bad you had Boots spayed. She'll never know the experience of being with a good tom cat." Lee grinned at her granddaughter and Pam told her goodbye. She left the nursery about 15 minutes before 6 PM.

Pam was only a few seconds into the Center when Mike bellowed out to her. "This is the first time I have had to work a little overtime so someone could have a little love in the afternoon."

"What are you talking about?" She asked him.

"You're at your apartment and Peckerini goes off the air there so what else should I think. He's on duty and you're late for work."

"You're working overtime to fill in for me who can only work half my shift. To tell you the truth, Mike, we had a foursome going. Two other officers were there, also, and it went much too quickly."

"I know you're scheduled to come in late but I was trying to get a rise out of you." She got serious and told him about her tires being slashed.

"It must be that woman that Joe was with last night at the Den," Chris said. "She was crying when he drove off."

"I thought we had a talk the other day about your mouth and Joe, Mr. Sylvester?"

"I don't see him anywhere in here so I can say what I want to. You have some explaining to do to your buddies because there's some serious stuff going on here that you're keeping to yourself." Julie nodded in agreement. Mike was anxious to leave and figured he would hear all the details sooner or later. Pam sat down at the radio and spoke just a few words when Joe keyed his mike and she heard a low whistle. She couldn't help but smile. It always made her feel good and so wanted.

"Gee, he must not be in very serious trouble, if you can still smile at him."

"Who said anyone was in trouble, Chris, the lady you saw last night is mad at us and she probably slashed my tires during the night."

"Why would she slash yours and not his?"

"She wants to be with him, she can't have him, and I must be the reason why. Don't you know that three's a crowd."

"What will she be doing next?" Julie asked.

"I don't have a clue but we're on alert. I know we're all friends here but some things are still very private to me."

"Well, Paula Harvey thanks for not filling your good friends in on the whole story. We'll just talk amongst ourselves and we'll eventually figure out what's going on."

"Chris, she has started calling and harassing me so you know as much as we know," Pam told them in an irritating sounding voice. The phones started ringing and they didn't get a chance to talk to one another for the rest of the shift. Joe called in during the evening only to tell her he would see her at home.

"I don't think so," she told him. "I'll wait for you after work and we drive home together."

"Oh, you're right I do remember now we both used the same car. We can talk driving home unless you keep sending me to complex incidents."

"I can't help it, if the nuts are all running wild on your beat. I'm just the messenger." She was still anxious to find out. The shift was passing quickly and before she knew it, they were driving out of the office parking lot.

"Ken and Lopez went to see her at the Diner and she was very surprised to see them. She denied everything, of course, but now she knows we're serious by making a report. Tomorrow we can still get the restraining orders and go from there." Pam was fighting hard to keep from crying. The whole mess was getting to her and not knowing what was going to happen next was taking its toll on her system. They got out of the car and she couldn't keep the tears back. She was hurrying to get into the apartment and into the shower before he noticed what was going on with her. "Are you going to a fire?" He asked. She ducked inside the apartment door. He grabbed her arm and she stopped dead in her tracks. He turned her around and then he saw the source of her actions. She was crying and trying to hide it from him.

"Joe, please don't get mad at me but I can't keep from being upset. I'm really trying but I'm failing miserably." He drew her into his arms and held her closely. "I'm afraid that next she'll turn on you and do something terrible." Her tears came faster.

"You mean, you're crying because she might get me but it's, okay if something happens to you."

"No, it's not okay but I have this awful feeling about her doing something to you. I don't know why but it's a terrible feeling."

"Look we're home safe and she can't get to us tonight in here. She knows I have guns and I can take care of you and myself."

"I'm not worried about a female Rambo situation, Joe, but she's conniving and it appears she'll do almost anything to get what she wants."

"Pam, try not to worry and things have to work out for us. We have each other, we have good jobs, and I want us to spend the rest of our lives happy together."

"I want that too, Joe, so very much. Since you didn't take a shower at the office, why don't you join me this evening?"

"I can't believe you would bring this up. I haven't heard from my doctor about the blood test results and you want to take a shower together?"

"I meant we could wash each other and I didn't say anything about having sex."

"I'm looking forward to a shower with you, Pam, real soon and it better include sex."

"I'll go first, if you don't mind." Pam was taking her shower and thinking what Suzy could do. She could cause so many bad things to happen to them and she had to trust Joe for now. She finished and he was standing naked outside the shower when she opened the door. She looked him up and down really good.

"You're an awful woman but I still love you."

"You look so good standing there naked and I'm so happy being with you." She cuffed his penis and went into the bedroom. It didn't take him long to shower and they were soon in bed loving one another. They both got quiet for a few minutes.

"I went to see Nana today and she asked me how come you have never been to the nursery. I reminded her about the way she treated you at the hospital. She has this darling cat that you need to meet. Do you like cats, Joe?"

"I always wanted a cat or dog when I was little but we never had any animals. They were too much trouble and I couldn't be trusted to take care of one."

"Every kid needs some kind of an animal to care for and love." She hugged him.

"Not with my mother, but someday I'll have a cat and a dog. I wouldn't even mind horses and cows either, but of course we'd have to live in the country."

"I wouldn't mind living in the country at all."

"Would you mind being a farmer's wife, my Pam?"

"As long as I'm with you, I'll be any kind of a wife you would like. We could make love in the barn on top of a pile of hay. As long as I'm with you, I won't mind the circumstances."

"You could really go for all of that?"

"Yes, my Joe, I'll be with you forever." He kissed her with a lot of love.

The three friends were working a couple of weeks later when the phone rang and Pam answered it. She was going to be released by the doctor to work full time starting on Sunday. She was so looking forward to it.

"I'm going to fix you really good," a female voice said to her. She thought it was Suzy but the female was trying to disguise her voice.

"Why are you calling?" Pam asked.

"You think you have stolen my boyfriend but I'm going to get him back real soon."

"If you're talking about Joe, he doesn't want you."

"He'll soon see me and he'll keep coming back to me because you aren't woman enough. He'll be getting rid of you real soon" The caller hung up and Pam was ticked off at what Suzy had just told her. She knew Joe wouldn't see Suzy so why was she making the phone calls she wondered.

"My God, you look like you just heard something really bad," Julie said to her. Chris was on his phone trying to get rid of a caller and he also noticed the look on Pam's face.

"What's going on?" He asked as he hung up his phone. "Who doesn't Joe want?"

"Nothing, Pam told him in a quiet voice.

"You know you can't fool us," Chris told her.

"Maybe I should tell Joe to call here, Julie said.

"No," Pam told her. "I'll tell him later at home."

"The only person who can call in and upset you so is the town tramp. It's Suzy Q the one he was with at the Den, isn't it? She's the same one, also, known as the 'Slasher' for doing a number on your tires."

"Look you guys, I think it was her but she was trying to disguise her voice." In a few minutes Joe told her he was coming into the back of the office so she let the other dispatchers know.

"I'll take your radio and you go and talk with him," Julie told her.

"The Sergeant is out of the office and no one else is around." Pam let Julie take her radio and she walked down the hallway. She went to the back door and saw him parked under the carport putting flares into his trunk. She opened the door and walked out to the patrol car.

"Oh, how nice greeting me like this." She went to him and gave him a hug.

"Don't worry you're the only one in the office." She hugged him a little longer.

"You do look like something is wrong."

"I just got a phone call from Suzy." Pam told him all that Suzy had told her.

"She's crazy. I saw her the one night and there won't be any more visits."

"She's desperate, she wants you, and we should have known she would keep making some kind of contact. She's just the type who would try something bad, Joe. I can see her getting vicious because you're with me and not her. She's already gotten my tires and now I have to worry about what will come next."

"Did you tell Chris and Julie, what she said?"

"God, no, they know someone called and they think it was Suzy but they have no idea what she said to me."

"I guess it can't get much worse than this, can it?"

"I have to get back to the radio and we can talk at home."

"You mean you still want to be with me? I hate putting you through this, Pam. You don't deserve what she keeps dishing out."

"I'll always want to be with you." She gave him a quick kiss and went back into the building. The tears started as she approached the Center's door. She didn't want to cry but she needed some release from what Suzy had told her. She stopped off in the kitchen and got a diet coke from the refrigerator. She wiped away her tears but it always took her awhile to get over just a few tears. Her fair skin made everything turn red when she was crying. When she walked back into the Center, the two dispatchers turned immediately and looked at her.

"You've been crying," Chris said to her. "Why can't you let your two best friends in the whole wide world know what's going on? We'll not tell a soul, if that is what you wish. We can't help you and be here for you, if you won't tell us."

"It's bullshit coming from her and it won't help to discuss it. Suzy keeps calling and trying to upset me and sometimes it gets to me." The phones started ringing and Chris told her to hold that thought. A quiet evening turned into a busy one with just a few phone calls. Pam would not give them any more details during the shift.

"Let's go to the Den after work and finish the story?" Chris asked the two of them.

"I'll go," Julie said.

"Tell Joe you won't be home right after work, and just come out for one beer," Chris said. "Maybe we can find an incident for him at the end of the shift and that'll take care of everything."

Pam grinned at Chris and said, "I'll think about it." Sure enough, Joe had to handle a big crash and would not be going home on time.

"Thank you, God," Chris said when Pam gave him the accident call. "We may hear the rest of the story after all."

The three friends left the Center and agreed to meet at the Den. One by one they arrived. They gave their orders to the waitress when all three were present. Pam told them that Suzy wants Joe and she's not giving up going after him. Chris wasn't happy that Pam wouldn't give more details. He thought it was more than Suzy chasing Joe and he was determined to find out. "I think the whore is now in the building," Chris said. Pam and Julie turned and saw her just as she sat down at the small booth.

"I need to leave," Pam told them. "You two have a good time but I don't want to be in the same room with her." She got up and told her friends goodbye and left the booth. Pam walked toward the front door and Chris and Julie saw Suzy get up and go in the same direction. Pam had no idea Suzy was behind her. Suzy called out to Pam after she got outside. She stopped and looked around. "I want to talk with you," Suzy said to her.

"You've done enough talking and I want to get away from you," Pam said. She noticed that Chris had arrived at the entrance and was watching the two women talking.

"Don't be a sore loser," Suzy said to her. "There are loads of guys at the police station who'll take care of you. I just want Joe and you can have the rest."

"I only want one guy and I already have him," Pam said to her.

"You may have him now but not for long. The night he told me that he didn't want to see me again, well, I talked him into seeing me without you knowing it."

"How dare you come up with a big lie like that. He's with me every single night and he doesn't have time to see you. He'll never see you again. Are you so desperate to have him that you have to make up all that shit?"

"We'll see who's telling lies me or him?" Suzy said to her. "We had great sex without a condom when he spent the first night. He'll be back for more because you can't give him great sex."

"Joe will never see you again. You're just a tramp who's desperate." Pam just got those words out when Suzy slapped her hard across the face. Chris left the entrance and ran to the two women. Before Pam knew what happened, he grabbed Suzy and pushed her away.

"Look, you whore, you better get back into the bar or you'd better leave," Chris said to Suzy. She left them and went immediately back inside. Pam's cheek was stinging from the slap.

"What in hell were you two talking about?" Chris asked. "Don't tell me, must have been about Peckerini?" "You need to leave his ass before something terrible happens to you. That woman is crazy and I'll have a talk with him, if you won't."

"She followed me outside; I didn't want anything to do with her."

"I know I saw everything and your cheek is bright red."

"I'm going home to try and pull myself together."

"Are you going to be okay?"

"Sure I will what else can go wrong?" She left the Den to head for home. She was certainly glad that Joe had gone to a doctor to be checked and he hadn't caught anything from Suzy. When she got into the apartment Joe had arrived a few minutes earlier. He looked up when she walked in the front door.

"What in hell did you run into?"

"Your friend, Suzy slapped the hell out of me."

"What were you doing with her and why did she slap you? You're pissing me off by calling her my friend."

"At the Den where else would it be?"

"I didn't know you were going there after work."

"After you got the crash call," Chris and Julie talked me into going out for just one beer so I agreed. I didn't know Suzy would be there. I should have guessed she would be because it has to be her home away from home."

"I take it you updated your friends with the latest accusations from Suzy while you were drinking the one beer."

"They only know what you have told Julie. Joe, all Suzy told me was that you made a secret deal to see her. She said you've been seeing her and I know that's a big lie because you're with me every night. You already told me that she was the one who wanted the secret meetings with you." Pam told him about their confrontation in the parking lot. "I left as soon as I could get away from her."

"Pam, don't tell Chris or Julie anymore stuff about me and Suzy, the whole office will know right away and soon the whole world. I hope you can keep a secret. I don't even want Julie to know since she blabbed to Chris about me spending the night with Suzy. That little faggot knows too much as it is."

"You shouldn't call him that. He's a friend of mine, Joe, whether you like it or not. Please try and understand that."

"Gee, I thought I was your number one friend."

"You know you are but you're taking this all a little bit too far. From the very beginning when you told me about spending the night with Suzy, I wouldn't dream of even telling Julie. You, Mr. Big Mouth, called her as soon as you got home from my place and spilled your guts out. If you hadn't been screwing around, you wouldn't need to have a secret now, would you?" She soon realized she had said the wrong thing. Joe gave her a hurt and disgusting look and sat down on the sofa without another word. She was not going to apologize because it was the truth and it was the way she felt. She went into the bathroom to shower and calm down some more. When she emerged from the bathroom, Joe was gone. He can go and be with Suzy she told herself as the tears filled her eyes. I'll never chase after him. If that is what he wants, he can have her. I don't even feel like fighting anymore. She went to bed and hoped that the one beer might relax her enough to get to sleep. She was very wrong. Pam knew she was used to sleeping with him and tonight she was not. It never dawned on her that sleeping alone would bother her. She made a pact with herself just before going off to sleep. I'll not ask him again to stay with me in my bed. I'm not someone he can visit once in awhile to satisfy his needs and then treat me like shit other times. It bothered her because she didn't know where he would go. Surely he wouldn't go to Suzy's but what about Julie. That would upset her a great deal, if she thought he was there. He could be in a motel or at a friend's house and not with anyone at all. She hoped one of those speculations would be the case and she would hear from him the next day. She spent most of the night tossing and turning. She managed to go off to sleep after looking at her bedside clock every half hour until 3:30 AM.

Chapter 13

The sun was high in the sky when she woke with a start. She felt around on the other side of her bed and Joe was not there. She, somehow was hoping during the night he would come back but that was just wishful thinking on her part. She could not believe what was happening to her and to their relationship. She was so sure that whatever problems would surface, they could endure. She felt Joe should have apologized to her for ragging on and on about Chris. He was her friend and Joe needed to get over it. Chris usually gives her pretty good advice and he has good common sense. She liked that he can give her the male point of view. It was already 10 when she took her shower. She felt like going out for a bite to eat and decided to call Julie. "Hey, Jules, would you like to get some food now or I can meet you on your way to work. I'm hungry and I don't feel like going alone.

"I'm still in bed so how about, if I meet you at noon at the New Horizons. That way I can have breakfast or lunch, whichever I feel like."

"I'll be there," Pam told her.

"Is Joe coming too?"

"I don't know Joe anymore. We had a fight and he left last night."

Pam and Julie arrived within a couple of minutes of each other. They were seated at a booth and gave their orders to the waitress. "How late were you and Chris out last night?" Pam asked.

"We left about midnight after three beers. He came in after you left and told me what had gone on in the parking lot. Your cheek is still pink today, by the way. Your eyes are sad and dark underneath too."

"My God, if you give me any more compliments, I just won't know how to act."

"Why did you two fight?"

"All about Chris being gay and being a good friend of mine. He can't be jealous of Chris in the male to female sense but he doesn't like him. He doesn't want me to be friends with him."

"Joe told you that?"

"No, he didn't come right out and forbid me to be friends with Chris but that's what he would like to happen. Just because Chris may be gay, the troops can't deal with it or him. He's a good guy and I like him."

"You don't think big macho men can like gay men do you?" Julie said. "It's against all the rules."

"I'm not fond of gay women but I treat them well and with respect," Pam said.

"I feel the same way but we must be comfortable with our sexuality and men are not."

"I would never tell Joe who he should pick as friends and he has no business telling me who I can choose."

"Aren't you upset that he wasn't with you last night?"

"My insides are completely torn up over him not being at my place. I never would ask him to leave, he just took off. It makes me think he's tired of me after spending a couple of weeks at my place. He may need his own space. I can't let it ruin my life and I refuse to whine all the time about my sorry life. Jules, most of the time I think Joe adores me but there are still times when I'm not so sure."

"Well, his track record sucks at the moment and I can't blame you for having some doubts. Don't see him for awhile and see what happens."

"No one is perfect, Jules, and I know for sure I'm not. How much trouble can happen to Joe and I keep looking the other way. I've accepted everything that has come our way but I may have reached a limit. Staying away from me all night is something I am having trouble accepting and he must know this. This is what started all of our problems to begin with."

"When Chris and I left at midnight the whore was still there but Joe didn't show up. After that I cannot say what might have happened. He may have come back and gone home with her again."

"No, Jules, he'll not do that again. I guess I'm making too big a deal about this but I thought we'd be together forever. The first night he spent at my place he gave me the impression that he would be there each night. I wanted to go out to lunch, in case, he comes back to see me. I didn't want to face him and listen to what he did or didn't do last night. He must know I may be thinking that he was with her so why would he even think about staying away."

"Well, Pam, if you ever talk with him again, I'm sure he'll tell you."

"It'll be hard just working with him and not having anything to do with him.

"I can work the police radio and that will piss him off because we all know he only wants you on the radio," Julie said to her. "Stay off it for a while and see how it goes."

"I think you have something there, Jules. I'll come in later and work the fire radio for awhile. You could probably use the break."

"It's a deal, Pam." She thought that Julie was way too eager to work the police radio.

"Have you and Ken being seeing each other much? I'm so wrapped up in my own problems I need to see how you're making out with him."

"I like him a lot and I think he likes me but it's too soon to tell just yet."

"Well, keep me posted and I mean that." They finished eating and Julie left for the office and Pam decided to go to the mall. She hated only working part time but that was soon to change.

Later she arrived at the office and it was still a little early to start her shift. Pam decided to stay outside in her car until it was time to go in. She knew he was working as she parked next to his car. She would listen to a CD and then go inside. She didn't want to have to run into him. After 10 minutes went by a patrol car drove in behind her car and she saw that it was Ken. He got out of the patrol car and walked over to her side window. "Hey, are you waiting for someone?"

"No, I'm not I just arrived a little early and didn't want to go right in."

"I had to get my cell phone out of my car so that's what I'm doing here. Are you doing okay because you look awfully sad?"

"I'll be all right but my life does suck at the moment."

"For what it's worth to you, Joe is sad lately and I have been talking to him about life in general."

"I need to get inside, Ken and it's nice seeing you again." She got out of her car and walked into the building. The hall was quiet as she entered the building. She saw Chris walking toward the Center. She called out to him. He turned and gave her a big smile. She caught up with him and glanced into the briefing room to see Sullivan doing reports. They stopped to talk in front of the Center's door.

"Hey, toots," Sullivan called out when he saw Pam and Chris.

"I wonder which one of us he would prefer?" Chris asked Pam. She couldn't keep from smiling at her friend.

"Pam, wait up a minute," Sullivan said. Chris walked into the Center and she stopped and waited for the officer. She was dreading this confrontation because Sullivan flirts with her whenever he gets a chance. He was a short, black haired guy who was proud of his good looks.

"I've been off the last two days but I just heard you and Joe had broken up."

"Did he tell you?" She asked.

"I just heard the talk going around so wanted to check with you."

"If what you said is true, I haven't been told yet. I'm not interested in men right now and I'm not feeling very well today, please excuse me while I go to work." He was not happy with Pam's reaction. She slowly walked into the Center wishing she didn't even have to work today.

"Joe just came into the office so he's around here somewhere," Julie said as Pam took the fire radio. She didn't really care. She was glad her radio was busy right from the get go. Time would fly and this is what she wanted. It wasn't long before Joe came in and he went to Julie and asked her for a printout. Pam didn't even look his way. Her eyes were filling up with tears and she was trying to keep a professional voice as her radio was almost nonstop. The others in the room could tell she was struggling with her voice. Joe still hung around after he got his printout and she couldn't take anymore.

"Would you mind leaving the Center," she said to Joe and they all knew she was now in tears. He never said a word but walked out the door.

"Pam, you need to get a grip and you need to not let him see you cry."

"Chris, you can just fuck off. If I was made of cement, I could just do that but I'm human and my world is crashing around me as I speak. Sometimes friends need to back off and not give out any advice." It was rather quiet for the rest of the shift. Just before 10 PM Pam answered the phone and knew immediately it was Suzy.

"Your boyfriend friend spent last night with me because you kicked him out. I told you he'd be seeing me." The phone went dead. Pam must have turned white but she answered another phone to keep the others from finding out about the call. He left my place last night but surely he wouldn't go to see Suzy.

The graveyards dispatchers came in one by one and relieved the swing shift crew. "Does anyone want to go out and drink?" Pam asked Chris and Julie as their relief dispatchers showed up.

"Sure I do," said Julie. "I'm off tomorrow." Chris agreed to go, also. The three friends left for the Den. She was glad she didn't see Joe on the way out. She was making all kinds of excuses not to have to face him again. She could use some alcohol to help her sleep. She arrived first and waited in her car until Chris pulled up. Julie was following him and all three went into the Den together. They ordered beer and right away Pam said to Chris, if I drink too much you take me home and don't let anyone else. I mean this, my friend."

"It's a deal," he told her. "Don't tell me this is your way of telling me that you and Joe have split the sheets? Why can't you just come out and say it."

"What about me?" Julie asked.

"Either one of you can take me home I'm not picky as long as it isn't Joe. I don't know that he'll even show up. If he should, he'll not be sitting with us and that's a promise. I'll leave before I'll sit with him again."

"I was wondering why you were so eager to go out for a beer. Since you hooked up with Joe you haven't wanted to do anything with your friends. Speaking of men, Peckerini just entered the building."

"I'm not going to look and please tell me he's not coming this way."

"No, he took a booth right near the bar, the one where the whore always sits."

"She could probably service him tonight," Julie said. This did not sit well with Pam but she didn't say a thing.

"He doesn't seem to be sad at all. He isn't sitting around moping like someone I know," Chris told her.

"Gosh, Chris, do you really want me to have a good time?"

"You know I do. Just pretend you don't have a care in the world and he'll soon start wondering why you're happy when you have just parted. The best thing you could do to get back at him is go out with Sullivan or any officer."

"I don't want him to have a heart attack."

"Pam, I think that would do it. He's jealous whenever Sullivan talks with you in the hallway," Julie told her. He would have a shit fit, if you went out on a date."

"Why would I want to go out with another man when I'm pissed at all men?"

"I don't understand your reasoning," Chris said. "You women will be pissed at one man and you get down on all men. Is there a reason for this?"

"When we're pissed, we put all men in the same group."

"That explains everything," he said as he rolled his eyes at the two of them. They were on their second beer when the tramp showed up. The three of them all waited to see, if she would sit with Joe. She was talking with him like she was trying to convince him to let her sit there. She was standing in front of the booth.

"I'm going to the restroom," Pam told them and she got up and started walking toward the small booth. She approached their table and Suzy looked up to see Pam.

"Isn't this past your bedtime?" Suzy said to her. She looked straight ahead and didn't say a word. When she returned, passing the table, Suzy was sitting with Joe. Pam could have sunk right into floor when she saw Suzy with him. She still didn't look their way and went back to her table.

"Jesus, what's that all about?" Chris asked her. She told them what Suzy said to her.

"Joe can't be making any points with you tonight?" Julie said. "I thought, if you stopped seeing him, he would straighten out but hell I was wrong."

"I just have to forget what is going on and not cry and carry on," Pam told her. They continued drinking beer and tried to keep Pam from feeling bad. She finished her sixth beer and she was feeling no pain. The tramp was still sitting with Joe.

"Why would Joe sit with her, if she's chasing him and he doesn't want her?" Chris asked the two women.

"Duh, Chris, to make someone in this room jealous but I don't want to play games."

"Your friends have advised you well on what you should do. Jules said to stay away from him and I told you to find another guy to date. You won't listen to your good friends so we're unable to help you. You're sitting here with us crying, pissing, and moaning. It'll get you no where and he's the one having the fun here."

"He doesn't look very amused to me, Chris."

"I just got a brainstorm. I'll go and ask Suzy to take me to her place for a blow job and see what she says. I'll ask her right in front of Joe."

"I think I've had enough. Chris, are you ready to leave or do you want me to call a taxi? I don't want to shorten your evening to baby sit me."

"I'm ready," he told her. Pam got up and her head was starting to reel a little. I guess five should be my limit," she told them and she smiled at the same time.

"Hey, at least you can still smile." Chris had his hand on her elbow as he walked with her toward the entrance. Julie was right behind them. When they got to Joe's booth, Suzy spoke to Pam.

"Bitch, can't you hold your booze, honey?" she said. Pam got pissed but kept her mouth shut.

"Goodnight, Joe," Julie said as she walked by and that made Pam mad. The three continued out the door. She and Chris said good bye to Julie.

"How can he even sit with her, if he cares about me?" She asked Chris and the tears were starting to fall.

"He's the only one who knows that answer. Don't have anything to do with him ever again. I'm with Julie on that one. If you allow him to keep treating you this way, it'll never stop."

"I'm trying not to have anything to do with him. I can't go away on a trip or hide in my apartment because I have a job and responsibilities."

"He has his hooks just far enough in you and you'll keep letting him pull this shit." Chris drove her home and walked her to her door. "Are you sure you'll be okay?" Chris asked her.

"Yes, I'll take a cold shower and be just fine." He grinned at her attempt at humor. "Thanks so much, Chris, and I'm glad you're such a good friend."

"Me, too and you need to try and sleep. Forget about all the bad things." She was starting to feel worse when she unlocked her door. She noticed her answering machine was blinking so she pushed the button. "Pam, this is Nana and I haven't heard from you lately. This usually means something is wrong so call me when you get this message." Her Nana would not appreciate a call at midnight. Maybe after taking a shower, it would make her feel a little better. She pinned her hair up on top of her head and took her clothes off. She immediately felt nauseous, headed for the toilet, and was throwing up big time. After a while she knew she had nothing more in her stomach. Pam got to her feet and stepped into the shower. The warm water felt good but she wasn't even in a mood to shower. She hurried washing up and then rinsed off. She was glad to be almost ready for bed. She practically toppled into the bed. Joe must be seeing, Suzy now she thought, as the alcohol took over and she fell asleep.

Chapter 14

In the morning the phone rang and woke her up. Her head felt like it was splitting in half. She grabbed the phone and said hello, barely able to get the words out. "We need to talk," Joe said to her. She didn't say anything as she opened her eyes and the sunlight made them hurt. "Did you hear me, Pam?"

"I don't think we have anything to talk about, Joe. Obviously, last night you were with the woman you wanted to be with and I can't figure you out. I did not tell you to leave my place the other night. You left entirely on your own."

"I felt that was what you wanted me to do."

"You don't know anything about me or how to read my mind. Is this the start of what our future is going to be like? We have a few not so nice words between us and you leave. Are you going to keep running out or was this a one time only act on your part? It's too much for me to have to deal with, Joe. It makes me feel that you don't even like me by letting her sit with you in the bar."

"I thought maybe we could get a bite to eat somewhere and I could take you to your car? I just want to talk to you."

"You give me an hour and I'll be ready." She hung up the phone and was dreading getting up. She remembered being sick the night before. She didn't even like to drink that much. If her problems didn't get fixed soon, she could very well turn into an alcoholic. She rolled over to the side of the bed and carefully put one foot on the floor. She did manage to get on her feet and walk slowly over to the bathroom. She jumped herself when she took a look into the mirror. My God, she looked like a complete wreck. She decided to pop two Excedrin before getting into the shower. They were the only things that would make her headaches go away. She showered and dressed and her headache seemed to be waning. She checked her dresser drawer that she had given Joe and he had taken most of his clothes with him. He must have come yesterday while she was having lunch with Julie. It's what he really must have wanted to do. She was feeling sadder by the minute. She needed to be strong and not cry in front of him like Chris told her. It'll be hard but who said life was easy. She was glad she had her job to get lost in. She called her Nana while she waited for Joe.

"Are you going to tell me what's wrong, Pam?"

"At the moment I have a little headache but other than that I'm all right."

"I don't believe you. I know your voice and you're unhappy for some reason that you won't tell me."

"I'm sorry, if I sound that way so you tell me what's wrong."

"It has to be that man you're with because you sound like you don't have a friend in the whole world."

"I'm waiting right now for him to pick me up to go out for lunch, we're fine."

"Why is he picking you up when he lives there?"

"He went to the store and we're going to lunch when he gets back."

"I'll let you go but I'm here, if you ever need me."

"Thanks, Nana, I'm a big girl and I can handle my life." She hung up the phone and started pacing back and forth when he rang the doorbell. She grabbed her purse and opened the door. They left and drove to the New Horizon's.

"I expected you to take me to the Diner," she said as she got out of his car.

"I hope that was a weak attempt at a joke." She noticed that he was looking at her and she knew she must look like hell.

"You don't have to look at me that way because I know I look bad."

"Pam, I keep making your life miserable and I don't want to. You never look bad."

"You made me miserable by running out on me. I just want to know why?"

"Pam, did you ever meet anyone that you thought should be alone for the rest of their life? I may be that person because I have so many problems."

"Suzy would be one that comes into my mind." The waitress came and they ordered their food. "Why do you still hang around her when you said you didn't want anything to do with her?"

"I still feel kind of sorry for her. Last night she begged me to let her sit down so I caved in."

"I take shit from her and you still get cozy with her? You're sending her the wrong kind of message by even talking to her." She looked at him hard and thought how good looking he is and he doesn't even realize it.

"What are you thinking right now?"

"It's nothing important or worth mentioning. I didn't know you had taken most of your clothes out until this morning. You must be really serious about breaking up with me." This was so hard for her to say and not break down crying. I'll be strong she kept telling herself.

"I told you I thought you wouldn't want me around."

"I took a shower and you just walked out." The waitress brought their food and she started eating right away. "Now that I have done most of the talking, why did you want to meet me to talk?"

"Why don't you finish eating and I will tell you." They both finished and Pam pushed her plate away.

"Okay, you can talk now."

"I have been doing a lot of thinking these past two days and I have come to a decision. I'll be staying over at Ken's house now. I should have been up front with you and not just walked out the other night. I have caused you too many problems and I don't want to cause you anymore."

"What happened to caring about me and loving me?" The tears formed in her eyes. "I can't believe you set me up today only to knock me down again. You're disgusting and I don't even want to be around you." She hurried out the door.

"Pam, wait for me." The tears were falling down her cheeks and she didn't quite know what she was doing. The restaurant was just a couple of blocks from the Den so she would walk to her car. She was stumbling, more than walking as the tears would not stop. It wasn't long before Joe came up beside her in his car.

"Get away from me. I don't need you for anything."

"It tears me up to see you like this."

"Oh, does it really? This is what you want and I'll never forget it. Get away from me, now," she yelled. A white car came up behind them and Joe stopped his car. Ken stepped out and asked him what was going on. Pam kept walking and crying.

"What's wrong with Pam?"

"She and I are having a little problem and she won't let me drive her to get her car."

"Wait here, Joe, I'll see what I can do." He hurried and caught up with Pam.

"Hey what's going on, I want to talk to you." She saw Ken and stopped walking.

"Did he hit you or do anything like that?"

"No, he would never hit me." She was trying to wipe the tears away with her hands. "He just broke up with me and I'm hurt. He dumped me, big time and I need to stop crying and get over it. I'm really okay and my car is right over there at the Den."

"You certainly do not look okay," Ken said to her.

"What in hell do you care how I look? You have no business even stopping me."

"I just meant you look very unhappy and I would like to help."

"I'll be all right and I don't work today so I'll be fine." Ken let her continue towards her car. He walked back to Joe and she got into her car and drove off. It embarrassed her to have Ken find them like this. He gets to see another officer and a dispatcher having a fight going down the street. She had stopped crying but she was still upset. He doesn't want anything to do with me so he'll get his wish. I will become the invisible woman as far as he is concerned. The sooner we forget each other the better off we both will be.

She decided to drive to the beach. It was her favorite place to take a walk and she didn't do it often enough. She drove past the yacht harbor and pulled into the beach parking lot. She liked walking out onto the jetty as well as along the shoreline. The sounds of the waves and the sea gulls were so peaceful to her. She needed to spend more time here while trying to get over the love of her life. Everything he said to her at lunch kept going over and over in her mind. Some of the choices she had made were not good either. She knew she should never hang out at the Den since that tramp is always there. That's asking for trouble. She first walked over the rocks to the end of the jetty and the waves were hitting the rocks and spraying all over. The cool mist from the breaking waves was soothing. She then ventured along the shoreline for quite a distance. It just felt good being out in the sea air and the nice sunshine. After a while she looked at her watch and discovered she had been there for a little over three hours. She still felt hung over so she made her way to the parking lot. She hoped she wouldn't run into him any where He still had her same days off but that could change anytime.

She drove into the complex and walked to her apartment. She had the key in her door when she heard his voice. "Pam, I need to see you." She hurriedly unlocked the door and without even looking toward him she went in and locked her door. She immediately went to the stereo and put on a CD. Her doorbell rang and she ignored it. She would not have anything to do with him. He could find someone else to mistreat because she didn't want any part of it. He knocked a few times and rang the bell again and then she guessed he had given up. She checked her telephone and saw the red light blinking. The first message was from her Nana who was still worried about her. She wanted to see Pam real soon. The second one was from Chris who asked how her hangover was coming along. He would be working at this hour and she was not going to call him. She decided to check e-mail and send a few since her friends up north must think she had vanished from the face of the earth. As soon as she went into AT&T, her e-mail server, she made up her mind to e-mail Joe. She told him that she wanted no contact from him whatsoever. If something awfully important came up, she would read his e-mail but not necessarily answer it. She told him it would be hard working with him and she would try and keep out of his way around the office. She wished him the best and she hoped he would truly have a safe and happy life. She turned the TV on at six because listening to her sad CD's was getting to her. She kept flipping through the channels and not finding much to watch. An hour later her stomach started growling but she didn't feel like eating much. She got out a half gallon of strawberry ice cream, took a spoon out of the drawer and ate the ice cream sitting on the couch. She couldn't eat much so she put it back in the freezer. She was watching a movie when the phone rang and she picked it up.

"Hey, I called and left a message for you to call me," Chris said to her. "I called in sick a little while after I called you. I have the shits really bad and don't know why."

"That's too bad, Chris."

"I figured you could use a friend to talk to after last night."

"I'm really not good company when I'm upset," she told him.

"What did you do today?"

"I had lunch with Joe and he dumped me big time."

"He actually dumped you? I can't believe this."

"He sure did so it's really over between us."

"How are you going to ever cope with being dumped?"

"Well, I went to the beach and walked for three hours and for dinner I ate some ice cream right out of the container in front of the TV."

"It sounds like you're a completely normal type of woman."

"Chris, I love him so much and this'll be the hardest thing for me to get through. I know he may have some issues but I love him for who he is and how he makes me feel."

"I know this thing with the tramp is hard to go through, Pam. I don't think he wants you to go through this mess so he's letting you go until the whole situation is resolved." You would have to be an idiot not to see that he does care about you. He doesn't think he is worthy enough to be with you. His self esteem is low and he thinks he's dragging you down with him. I don't even care for the guy but he cares about you."

"You sound like a psychologist."

"I have taken a few classes on the subject and people fascinate me. We look like we would be simple enough to figure out but inside our heads is a complex system that just boggles my mind thinking about it."

"It has been nice talking with you Chris and I'll get through this. I hope you get better soon and I'll check on you tomorrow. I'm feeling tired from my hangover last night and being dumped at noon. I need some sleep, if that's even possible. How's Julie taking us breaking up, Chris?"

"She seems real happy lately but I thought it might be Ken doll giving her some deep thrills each night. Do you suppose she's happy about you breaking up?"

"It's like this, Chris, Joe is staying at Ken's and she'll be able to see him more with me out of the picture. They all play tennis together so she should be thrilled beyond words. That's what I'm thinking whether it's true or not."

"It makes a lot of sense to me so you not only have to watch out for Suzy but Julie as well. I wouldn't wish this on anyone."

"I may be all wrong but I think she cares a lot for Joe. I need to hang up."

"I wish you sweet dreams and a good night's rest."

"Chris, you must get tired of hearing me feeling sorry for myself."

"No, I'm getting used to it," and he gave her a chuckle.

"Thanks for being a good friend and worrying about me. I bet you never guessed I would be a high maintenance kind of friend. I didn't think I would be either until I met Joe. I used to think that life was simple but I don't think that way anymore."

"He's most of your problems but if he was a regular kind of guy things would be better for you. I know you told me he had a rough life as a youngster but why bring that along with you through life. Get rid of it or it can eat you up. He drags it along with him and it affects everyone he has contact with."

"Chris, I never thought of it that way. I think letting go is extremely hard for most people. I'm no expert but I think it would be."

"We are what we think we are."

"I was suppose to hang up and we're still talking."

"Sometimes it's better to keep talking with a friend especially, if you think you won't be getting much sleep" They said goodbye and hung up.

It didn't take her long to shower, brush her teeth and get into bed. Her mind was jumping with thoughts of Joe and she was having a time trying to relax. Sleep would not come her way until the wee hours of the morning. She knew she would feel exhausted in the morning.

Sunday morning was good for her. She would be returning to work full time and not just show up for four hours. She wasn't fooling herself. She wanted so much to get to work and run into Joe. She had never missed anyone the way she was missing him. She had only talked with Chris since Joe dumped her. Julie had called but Pam didn't return her call. She was the last person Pam would want to confide in at the moment. She was the type who liked to be left alone when things were really bad in her life. If she could dig a hole and crawl into it, she would or that's how she felt. She left for work at 1330 thinking she would chat some with the day dispatchers and get caught up on what was going on with them. Julie and Dave would be working her shift as Chris was on a day off. She would rather not deal with Chris feeling as bad as she did. She wished there was another way she could reach the Communications Center instead of walking down the hallway. She reached the briefing room door and glanced in as she walked by. She caught a glimpse of Joe sitting at one of the tables. She kept walking. He did not come after her and maybe didn't see her. Pam walked through the door and immediately went into the Center to visit with the day crew. The whole office probably knew something was going on and if they ask, she will tell them the truth. My friends will understand and help me get through this. It'll be a cold day in hell before I look at another man she told herself. She came into the radio room and started chatting with the three dispatchers. There wasn't much going on and they talked about her returning today for a full shift. Soon Julie walked in as Pam was getting her headset out of her locker. She greeted Pam with a little hug. Pam didn't feel it was genuine. "I called yesterday and you didn't call me back."

"I know, Jules, I wasn't feeling very well so I kept to myself."

"Most people when they're not feeling well like to hear from their friends but I guess you're different."

"I'm sure you heard from Joe so why hear my version. He dumped me and there's nothing more to talk about. For two days I've done nothing but think about my shitty life and going over things that maybe I could have done better or handled a little differently. I'll get through it the best way I know how and try to have a decent life." The two women did not know that Joe was standing outside the kitchen listening to their conversation. Pam walked out and almost ran into him standing there. "Oh," she said and she jumped when she saw him. She kept walking toward the radios. The tears were falling as she walked. She took her sunglasses from the top of her head and put them over her eyes. She would not be working his radio and she knew he noticed. Joe and Julie were chatting in low voices on the other side of the room. She thought he didn't look good today. His eyes were sad but this is what he wanted and there was nothing she could do about it. Dave came in and asked to work the phones and Julie told him he could. Pam had already relieved the day dispatcher but there was nothing going on at the moment. Joe left the Center and Julie took the police radio. Pam stopped crying and put her sunglasses on top of her console. Hopefully, she would not need them for the rest of the shift.

Chris called in to speak with her. He wanted to go to the Den but she would not be going. "Since you two broke up you shouldn't stay home all alone. That's a bad thing to do. "Go out with your friends and have a good time."

"Chris, I can't right now and I don't know when I'll feel like going again."

"Look you probably had a bad hangover the other morning so just come and have a soda. Your friends would like to see you. I know it'll be hard to cheer you up but we don't mind trying."

"Okay I'll go one for one soda but that'll be it." She was glad she decided to go and not mope around for the rest of her life. She and Julie didn't say much during the shift.

When their shift was over they went to put their headsets away and were alone in the kitchen. "Jules, could you tell me in what part of the cemetery Webb is buried in? I haven't been there and I need to go." As they walked down the hallway, Julie gave her directions to his grave site.

"It'll be easy to find because of the fresh dirt piled high," Julie told her.

"I feel bad that I haven't gone sooner since it's just down the street from the office."

"I heard you talking with Chris so are you going to the Den?"

"I told him I would for a little while. He was being so persistent and it's easier to tell him yes than no."

"I know exactly what you mean. Is it okay, if I go too?"

"Sure, you can and I'll see you in a little while. He's probably already there in our booth holding down the fort."

They both met again in the Den parking lot and walked into the building. There was Chris sitting by himself and he greeted them both with a big smile. "Well, look what the night dragged in," he said to the women.

"Gee, Chris, I didn't know we were going to hear such nice compliments."

"I was here last night and nobody came in just me and Sam. You watch, tonight the place will be jumping with people we know. Pam, you don't look too bad by getting dumped so you must be getting over it."

"The number one rule tonight is we do not talk about my awful life. We need to find other things to discuss."

"I wanted to hear all the details of the dumping and you just ruled that out."

"Okay, Jules, what's Joe's version?" Chris asked her.

"If Pam says no, we'll not talk about anyone's details."

"Let's hear about Jules and Ken Doll and then Chris can tell us about himself. It doesn't always have to be about me and Joe. Jules, you start the conversation."

"I'm dating him, I like him a lot, and I think he likes me, too."

"Is it starting to get serious?" Chris asked.

"We haven't declared our love but it's coming I believe. He has lived here all his life. We all know his family owns a produce business."

"God, a local rich boy and you have him hooked?" Chris asked.

"Good luck on declaring your love, Jules, don't forget what happened with me and Joe. If I had it to do over, I would have waited until he said it first."

"You think I should wait, Pam?"

"Guys, take longer to know what they want and I should have waited for Joe.

You look like you are losing weight, Jules," Pam said to her.

"I have dropped 10 pounds and you're the first one to mention it. When you have a good guy interested in you, it's easy to exercise and not eat."

"I'm going to have to watch myself. I had strawberry ice cream for dinner last night. I do not want to waddle into work because I'm upset and living on junk food."

"Chris, it's your turn to expound on yourself and your life. We're friends here and we don't know much about you. What brought you to the PD as a dispatcher?"

"There's not much to tell. I was born, raised by my parents, had one sister, and joined the Navy the minute I graduated from high school".

"That's what Joe did too," she told them. "Sorry about that, I'm not supposed to be talking about him."

"If his childhood was a great as mine, that must have been the reason for him joining. I received a discharge and my working experience was in communications with the Navy on aircraft carriers. Mission Park was looking for dispatchers and I knew I could do the job so I applied five years ago. Sam was living here and told me about the job openings. Now you're up to date," he told her with a chuckle.

"Do you have a girlfriend? We need to know everything."

"I was jilted after joining the Navy and haven't found one I would be interested in since."

"You're so nice, Chris, there are plenty of girls who would like to date you. You're cute and so fun to be around," Pam added.

"I'm still not interested yet. Don't look now but the place is getting crowded." Pam glanced toward the entrance and saw the tramp enter and take the small booth.

"The only lost soul who's missing is Joe," Chris told them. Pam kicked him under the table. "Oh, I spoke too soon because the pecker head is now here. Let's take bets you two, which booth will he be drawn too, the town whore or his lost love?"

"Chris, you need to settle down," Pam told him.

"I just want to have a little fun and you're spoiling it. If you would have a beer instead of soda, you could loosen up some more." Joe passed Suzy and made his way to their booth. Chris and Julie greeted him and Pam said nothing. He sat on the end next to Pam. All she could do was to keep herself from touching him or leaning her head against his shoulder.

"I'd like to buy everyone a round if you'll let me," Joe said to the dispatchers.

"I'm fine," said Pam. Her glass of soda was half full. Chris and Julie said he could buy for them.

"It was kind of a quiet night for me how about you guys?" Joe asked.

"This was a slow Sunday night that's for sure," Julie volunteered.

"Pam, do you have any openings in your complex?" Chris asked. "My place is over run with kids. The little bastards holler outside my apartment and it drives me nuts. If I yelled like that when I was a kid, I'd be beaten and wouldn't be able to sit on my ass for a week. The parents must be deaf not to hear that shit. I hate the summers most of all when they're all out of school tearing up the place."

"The parents tell them to go somewhere else and yell so that's how it is handled," Julie said.

"They should only be allowed to yell, if they are dying. Kids shouldn't be allowed in apartments, "Chris added. "What kind of a life is that anyway?"

"It isn't just kids who are problems, Julie told them. "I have an old fart living next door who's deaf. His TV is always up so loud but I would hate to complain. I work swings so I only have to put up with it for two nights a week. He goes to bed early and that helps too."

"What about you, Pam?" "Do you have any lousy neighbors, Chris asked?"

"I used to have a roommate who was bad. Oh, I forgot he's sitting right next to me." Chris and Julie's eyes widen at her remark. "I'm just joking, you guys. This has been fun but I need to be going. Are you going to let me out?" she asked Joe.

"Only, if you can give me the secret password and then you can go."

She looked him right into the eyes and she spoke, "I miss you." The two friends gasped and Joe got up and let her out. She told them goodbye and headed for the entrance. Joe was right behind her and she didn't know it. She went flying past Suzy because she didn't want to hear any comments from her. She reached her car and he spoke to her.

"Please wait a minute and let me say something." She reeled around and he saw her tears. He took her into his arms and she let him. He held her tight and she was enjoying it. She didn't want him to let her go. "You may not want to hear what I have to say but I have to say it. The other day at lunch I wanted to tell you that I wanted to come back to you instead of move out. You started talking and I got the impression you may not want me around. I know, I should have said it and let you decide. Those few short days and nights we were together were the happiest ones of my life. I enjoy being with you and sleeping with you and I haven't even mentioned making love. I feel really good in your company."

"Joe, will you take me home and make love to me." She moved away from his arms and looked into his eyes.

"I would be happy to love you completely." She gave him the biggest smile.

"There's one thing I must say, Pellerini, I'm never going to let you leave me not ever again. I mean that, Joe. If you go out my door, I will follow you and make you stay with me." He nodded at her and gave her a nice smile. They got into their cars heading home.

They arrived at the apartment and he sat down on the couch in the living room. She hurried and pinned her hair on top of her head and got into the shower. She finished and stepped outside and threw her robe on. She walked out into the living room and he was sitting on her couch. She went over and sat on his lap and she kissed his mouth so gently. She found his tongue and sucked it slowly. She leaned back and looked into his eyes.

"We have something to celebrate tonight."

"What might that be?"

"We can get back to making love without a condom. I'm still on The Pill and I'm safe and you were checked by the doctor and you're okay." She found his tongue again. "Joe, I want to ravish you all over."

"Let's get started because I'm over ripe for you."

"I feel the same way so we can finish what we start in the morning." He reached inside her robe and found her soft nipples and caressed them gently. He kissed each one and they soon become hard. She got up and led him to her bed. Joe undressed with her help and she rubbed his chest all over with her hands. He got down on the bed and she took her robe off. She lay down beside him and kissed him all over.

"Pam, we need to slow down a little. We have the rest of the night and I don't want to spoil it for you. I know you want to go all over me but if I let you do that I will have no control. I've wanted you so much and thought about making love to you just as much. Let me hold you because your body is so soft and it feels wonderful next to mine. Please don't get upset with me."

"I'll never be upset with you again because I love you so much. I'm just anxious to feel you inside of me."

"I know and you will, I promise." He kissed and fondled her until she moaned. She wanted to caress him more but she didn't quite dare. She could tell he was more than ready as she felt his penis so hard against on her leg. He kissed her all over and entered her body. She matched his thrusts with her own.

"Oh, Joe, I'm so ready," she cried out and they came together. "Don't get off me because I want to feel you longer inside of me." He raised his head up and looked at her. She had the biggest smile on her face. He kissed her soft lips and looked at her some more. They loved each other so much.

"I don't think you know how beautiful you are. Making love makes you happy and your eyes sparkle with a lot of love."

"Well, I'm seeing a great looking guy myself. Most of the time, you look at me like I am something precious. It makes me feel so good." He rolled off her and she went into the bathroom. She came back to bed and they each lay on their sides face to face.

"Will you let me move back in with you tomorrow?" He asked. You don't have to answer that because the smile you gave me says yes."

"I'll help you, if I may and you'll make me the happiest woman in the universe. Joe, I know we'll be good for each other. I can see it in your eyes and you can see it in mine." She kissed him and turned over. He put his arms around her and held her.

Chapter 15

Pam helped Joe bring his stuff back to her place the next day and they settled into their new life together. He was glad he didn't have any furniture to deal with. They stayed away from the Den and any confrontations with Suzy. The office was buzzing about them back together and most of their friends were being very supportive. There were two problems hanging over them. Joe and Chris not liking each other and not knowing what Suzy would do next. Pam felt Julie was a lesser problem because Joe would never have her. The feud between the men didn't bother Pam as long as they were civil to each other when they all got together. She thought that Chris might be jealous of her time with Joe. They didn't hang out as much since Joe moved in. The couple were both still off on Fridays and Saturdays and it was a perfect schedule for the two of them.

On Friday she woke up in a frisky mood. She reached under the sheets and played with him until she woke him up. "Can't a guy get some sleep around here?" He asked with a grin on his face.

"I can't keep my hands off you and it's your fault."

"I didn't do a thing but sleep beside you."

"I know but I want to take a shower with you this morning. Afterwards, I want to sit on the patio, listen to Atticus, and enjoy the sun. I'll even cook you breakfast, if you're nice to me."

"What do I have to do to get breakfast?"

"You must love me all over in the shower."

"You're not a very demanding woman, my love. I guess that's why I love you and moved in with you."

"Joe, you don't have any regrets about moving in here, do you?"

"I would be nuts, if I did. You make me feel loved everyday and that's special to me. Remember I'm the one who got hit all the time for being a kid."

"I wish so much that I could take those awful memories away from you and replace them with nice ones."

"What's really hard was the fact she went to church everyday. I've always wondered if she confessed to the priest each day that she beat me. Did he give her absolution so she could do it all over again the next day?"

"Joe, maybe some day you should see her and ask her for your own peace of mind."

"I'll never see her again or even speak to her. She can take that bit of information to her grave." Pam hugged him and wasn't sure, if he still wanted to shower together. "I'm sorry I got off the track there. I shouldn't let it surface like that. You're probably tired of hearing it so much."

"Joe, have you ever talked about it to anyone because talking can be good?"

"What I've told you is the most I've told anyone."

"If you ever feel like talking about it let me know. I'll always be here for you." He pulled her close to him and kissed the top of her head.

"When I was living alone I used to dread waking up. You make it so nice for me. I never thought I'd find a woman who would wake up wanting me every day and you do. This makes up for all the terrible memories in my childhood." He kissed her softly and gently. "Hey, the last one in the shower is a rotten egg." He jumped out of bed with her right behind him. He made it into the shower first and they were laughing the whole way. She started by washing her hair. He was busy lathering up his arms and chest. He kept grabbing at her breasts as she had her hands busy in her hair.

"Don't wash your jewels, my love, it'll be my pleasure." He gave her a grin. She rinsed her hair and put conditioner on. He grabbed the soap and started with gentle motions around her breasts. She stood there enjoying his moves. She turned and he soaped up her back. She stood still as he washed her back. He gave her the soap and put both of his hands on her breasts from behind. He caressed her nipples with his thumbs and they stood at attention. "Joe, I can't wash you properly with my back to you."

"Let me enjoy this and then you can." She was already enjoying it as her nipples sprung to life. He turned her around and she lathered him up and felt him grow hard in her hands. He leaned over and gave her a gentle kiss. She gave one back with her tongue. Her hands were moving all over him.

"I didn't realize I could get so excited just watching you in the shower." He smiled and started nuzzling her neck. He took the soap and lathered up his hands and started rubbing up and down on her soft mound. One of his hands was between her legs and the other hand touching her breast. He turned her around facing the shower head and let the spray rinse her off. He got down on his knees in front of her and his tongue went crazy. She was so overcome with excitement she had to work to keep her balance. He was working on her with his tongue and she exploded with a pleasure she had not experienced before. She held his face in her hands until her body calmed itself. She wanted to pleasure him. She helped him up and with one hand she was gently stroking him. He closed his eyes as her movements got to him. She leaned over and put her mouth over the tip and barely nibbled all around. She went up and down his shaft with her mouth partly open and her tongue licking the sides. He let out a small groan. He grabbed her head and held it as she concentrated on him. Her mouth was all over him as her hands were grabbing his ass. His body trembled as she worked on him.

"Pam, don't stop," he called out to her. She kept her movements up until he let go of her head. She stood up and he grasped her with both of his arms. "This was the very best for me, it felt so good."

"I'm good because I love you and I enjoy making love to you. I want to feel the things I feel when you make love to me. I just need to rinse the conditioner out of my hair and I'm finished." He got out and she rinsed her hair. They dressed and she fixed him breakfast.

"These pancakes are good with the blueberries," he told her as he put two more onto his plate.

"I can't say that it's an old family recipe. I used bisquick and added some blueberries to the mixture. Blueberries are one of the best and healthiest fruits for us to eat. Do you have any plans for today?

"Not a thing, what about you?"

"I need to go to the cemetery since I have never been to see where Webb is buried. It will be hard but it's something I have to do. I thought I'd take a little bouquet of flowers and officially say goodbye to him."

"Do you want to do this alone or would you rather have some company."

"I would like so much for you to go with me but I would understand, if you said no. I wouldn't be gone too long."

"I think you need me to go with you and I will." He reached across the table and squeezed her hand a little. They both cleaned up the kitchen.

They set out for the florist shop where she bought a small bouquet of carnations before heading for the cemetery. They drove through the gates and she felt a bleakness at the sight of all the gravestones. Joe had been to the grave site after the funeral so he knew exactly where to go. He parked and they both got out. The fresh dirt with little blades of grass pushing up through would be hard to miss. She walked over and placed the small vase of flowers right next to his flat gravestone. The tears came as she thought about such a nice guy dying so very young. He was only 25, so full of life and loved his job so very much. Joe came over and stood next to her and she went into his arms.

"Joe, he had so much energy and even though, I didn't know him for very long, I still feel like I lost a good friend. You were his friend and it must be really hard for you."

"It is but you just have to keep telling yourself to get on with life. I can't help but remember being in the sergeant's office and trying so hard to convince the sergeant to let you ride with me. I talked for at least a half hour but he would not budge from his decision."

"Joe, you never told me this before. If you had taken me, I would be here visiting you right now." The tears came harder for her. "I would be here everyday telling you that I love you and I miss you so much." She looked into his eyes and the tears came for him too. They held each other for awhile until both their tears stopped. "Let's go home now," she told him. "It was hard but I'm glad I came."

They got back to the apartment and there were two messages on the answering machine. Marge, the Dispatch Supervisor, asked if she could work eight hours on swing shift because Chris called in sick. The second message told her to disregard the first message they found someone to work for him.

"Phew, I was called to work and then cancelled. I wonder why Chris has been sick recently. It isn't like him at all to take sick leave."

"He's a little on the puny side so maybe he doesn't take good care of himself. His boyfriends are probably wearing him out."

"Joe, we don't know that he's gay so I wish you wouldn't talk like that."

"I know he's your friend but I think he's gay. You told me you asked him about girlfriends and he hasn't had any since he was in the Navy. Trust me, at his age he should be dating women. He doesn't like girls so that's why he doesn't have a girlfriend. I'll bet you his roommate plays the feminine role in that relationship. Have you met ever met his roommate?"

"No, I have not but Chris said he works at a beauty salon."

"I rest my case, Pam. I bet he didn't join the Navy to see the world but to be surrounded by men that he adores. Then he applies for the PD where there's another chance for him to be around a lot of men. It makes sense to me,"

"Has he ever made a pass at you or anyone else in the office?" Pam asked.

"No, but that doesn't mean a damn thing."

"Joe, he's just a friend, he's funny, and I enjoy his company. How he lives his life has nothing to do with me. Let's get off this subject because I don't want this to be a problem between us."

The phone rang and Joe answered it. "Yes, she's right here." He handed her the phone and he told her, "it's Lee." She shrugged her shoulders.

"Hi, Nana, is everything okay?"

"Pam, you used to always come and visit me on one of your days off and I don't see you anymore. That man is taking up all your time."

"I'll come by in a little while and we'll talk."

"I hope so and don't disappoint me." The two women hung up.

"Go ahead and see her, Pam, I have stuff to do."

"I thought I would go and visit but I would like you to go, Joe. We need to let her see that you're a good guy and you only want what's best for me."

"God, she'll have me tarred and feathered, if I go."

"Joe, we're in this together. I never told her that you moved out so she thinks we're together without any problems between us."

"You really didn't tell her that I dumped you?"

"No, what we do is our business and I don't tell her very much."

"Okay I won't argue about that so let's go."

They drove to her grandmother's nursery. She grabbed his hand as they exited the car and walked to the building. A couple of the ladies working at the checkout stands called out to Pam. She stopped for a few minutes and introduced Joe to them. They continued through the building. They found Lee on her hands and knees checking out a potted fern under the shady screen. "Hi, Nana," Pam said and Joe said hello too.

"Oh, I wasn't expecting to see you Joe so how are you doing?"

"I'm fine and yourself?"

"I'm always in a good mood when I am kneeling down and have my hands in the dirt. It's the best therapy in the world." Joe nodded. "Pamela, you look a little sad today. Is anything wrong?"

"We just came from the cemetery and I went to Webb's gravesite. I didn't go after the funeral and I wanted to do that today." The older woman squinted up at Pam's face.

"That would be sad, my dear, and it was nice that Joe went with you."

"Lee, I need to say something to you and maybe we can clear the air up between us," Joe told her. "I love your granddaughter very much and I'm going to do everything I can to make her happy. I know you don't approve of me but I'm hoping over time that will change."

"It's not that I don't approve of you but she's too young to get tied down. She hasn't met or dated hardly anyone and she needs that experience."

"That's just it, Nana, I don't need to date anymore because Joe's the guy I want to be with forever."

"You're living together but I think you're moving a little fast. You, young people, want everything yesterday and you need to grow patience."

"We love each other and this is what we want." Pam removed her hand from Joe's and placed it on his back. She liked being close to him.

"I just hope you both know what you're doing. Living together is a big step and you two aren't even engaged are you?"

"No but give us time, Nana."

"You already know that I think couples should live together before they get married but not being engaged and not knowing each other very long is different."

"We know this is what we want to do," Pam said.

"Joe, are your intentions to marry Pam someday and have a family?"

"Yes, I plan on doing that but we need time for all those things to happen. I'll keep her safe and happy. Please don't worry about her happiness."

"I'm telling you something right now don't you dare hurt her. She's precious to me and she needs to be treated with respect. If I ever hear of you laying a finger on her, I will personally hunt you down and go up one side of you and down the other side. Do I make myself clear?"

"You're perfectly clear and I'll never hurt her physically or mentally."

"See that you don't and I think you should tell your folks, Pamela."

"Nana, please don't say anything just yet. In time I'll let them know but not now."

"If you love him as you say then I would think you would want the whole world to know. If you're ashamed of him or what you are doing, you would want to keep it quiet."

"I love him and I'm proud of him but it'll cause them to interfere with our lives and I don't want that."

"I'll stay quiet for now but I can't promise anything in the future." They chatted a little more and made their way up to the front of the nursery. Inside the building they came across Boots.

"Oh, there you are cat, I want you to meet my wonderful guy Joe." Pam swooped the cat up in her arms and presented her to Joe. "Joe, this is Boots who came to Nana out of the blue and now has the run of the nursery." Joe took the cat in his arms and patted her on the head. Boots was moving her head against Joe's hand and purring really loud.

"It's nice to meet you Boots," Joe said and he winked at Pam.

"It would be fun to have a cat or dog don't you think?"

"Someday we'll have our own home and we can have whatever you would like. Well, everything except maybe a tiger or lion."

"I'm going to hold you to that so don't forget." He grinned at her. She put Boots down on the floor and they continued out to Joe's car.

"That wasn't as bad as I thought it would be," Joe said to her as he backed the car out of the driveway."

"She wants everyone to cower in her presence and I stand up to her." She's had a rough life but she shouldn't assume I'll be going down that same path."

"We shouldn't be bragging until the problem with Suzy is resolved." They spent the rest of the day in a quiet manner listening to music and talking.

The next week started out happy for the couple. Pam had convinced herself that Joe had only seen Suzy the one time. She was not going to let a desperate woman get to her with false accusations. She was sure whatever loomed in the future the two of them could get through it all. She loved him and she knew he loved her just as much.

On Thursday Julie called while Pam was getting ready for work. "Pam, I'm worried about Chris because I think there is something really bad going on with him. He's called in sick a few times lately and it's all diarrhea related. In all the time I have been here, he has called in sick maybe once a year so that's why I think it's not good."

"I agree and he looks pale at times. He's small to begin with and he looks like he may be losing a little weight."

"Do you think one of us should ask him in private and see what he says?" Julie asked.

"I wouldn't mind asking but it might be better, if we were both involved. We're three good friends and he might tell us what's going on. What does Ken think of Chris?"

"We haven't really discussed him and I guess I should find out what he thinks."

"Joe is still adamant about his feelings and lets me know often. How can the three of us get together away from work to ask him?"

"We could have lunch tomorrow. Chris and I both work and you are off. Tell Joe he's not invited because it's a girl thing. Chris acts like a girlfriend to us. I'll call him right now and tell him our lunch plans so I'll see you then."

"I don't mind telling Joe I'm going to lunch with you two. Good bye, Jules, I hope we can find out and maybe help him." Joe came through the door as she hung up the phone.

"Who were you talking to because you have a guilty look on your face?"

"Just Jules who wants me and Chris to go to lunch with her tomorrow."

"Oh, the three girls are going out to lunch to gossip about the rest of us?"

"Yes, Joe, I told her you wouldn't mind not going."

"You've got that right but why just the three of you? Why don't you tell me why you're having lunch with Chris? Is there something you aren't telling me."

"Jules called and she thinks there's something wrong with Chris because he's been off sick lately. She feels, if we can talk to him in private he might tell us what the problem is. There's always a possibility he may not say anything."

"Joe, I don't want to piss you off so I don't know how to deal with this situation."

"I'm not going to tell you not to see Chris or not to be friends with him. Is that what you wanted me to say?"

"Yes, because I can't dump him as a friend and I love you so much that I don't want to lose you."

"I have to leave so I'll see you in a little bit at work."

"Can I have a big hug?" She went into his arms and he kissed her. "Joe, it feels so good when you hold me like this."

"I love you pretty blue eyes," he said. He gave her a big smile and left.

She arrived at work and saw Chris just outside the Center. She called out for him to wait up. "I hear we're doing lunch tomorrow so what happened to going to the Den?" He asked.

"Nothing, Jules thought lunch would be fun and so do I. We haven't been to Hop Sing's in a while. You know damn well why I don't want to hang out at the Den very much. Put yourself in my shoes, Chris, and she would irritate you, too."

"You're letting the town whore dictate whether you go out after work and have a few beers? We used to enjoy choir practice. Ever since Webb died and

Joe couldn't keep his pecker away from the tramp, the Den is practically off limits now. I'm having a problem with that but my feelings don't count."

"When do you want to go and we'll go?"

"Tonight can't be soon enough for me."

"Tonight it'll be. I'll try and look past Suzy and have a good time."

"Are you keeping something from me or did you break up with Joe?"

"Not at all, do I look like I'm unhappy today?"

"I figured when you hooked up with him, we could never do anything again."

"You're wrong." She saw Joe coming out of the locker room and motioned to him. "Chris, I want to talk with Joe for a minute alone, please."

"Sure I'll see you inside." He went into the Center and Joe approached Pam.

"Chris is whining because we haven't been to the Den in a while so could we go there after work?"

"You're seeing him tomorrow for lunch and now you want to see him after work. Should I be jealous or will this soon pass?"

"Joe, you know better than that, I'm inviting you."

"I have to get to briefing and I have to think about it." He quickly turned and walked down the hallway. She knew Chris was going to be a problem for them from now on.

"I called Jules about tonight but she wasn't home so I left a message on her machine. Can I assume you asked Peckerini?"

"Yes, but I'm not sure, if he feels like going."

"I still can't believe the tramp is doing this to you both. She sits in her own little booth while we're there so what's the fucking problem?" Pam couldn't very well tell her friend that he was part of the problem not just the tramp. She didn't know why life had to be so complicated. They got through the shift and at 10 hit the door. Pam had not heard from Joe at all during the shift. She had no idea, if he was going or not. Chris told her he would see her there. Joe was still out on the road. They had not heard back from Jules so it may just be the two of them.

She and Chris walked inside the Den together from the parking lot. Their booth was empty and he ordered them a beer. They were both looking around the room. "Well, so far no tramp to report but she usually shows up after Joe gets off. She must know his schedule by now. Is he coming or not?"

"He didn't say, Chris. This is my first venture out without him and it feels funny."

"I knew when you hooked up with him you'd be joined at the hip."

"Well, you have someone else to consider not just yourself when you're a couple. I could never be involved in one of those open marriages or open couple situations. Does it make me possessive feeling this way?"

"No, you just don't like to share."

"If you have a good thing going, who would want to share?" Pam asked.

"When are you two getting engaged?"

"That's his decision. I'll not do the asking so I guess I'm old fashioned."

"Don't you discuss these things?"

"He told Nana that he wants to be with me forever so we both know that marriage is definitely in our future. He told her that he would marry me and we would have a family someday. Chris, that surprised me so much when he told her that. Nana certainly wasn't shy asking him about his intentions."

"I'd like to meet the "battle axe" someday. She sounds like a kick in the ass. You knew she would want to know your fate. I don't blame her for asking him so did he squirm a little when she asked him?"

"Not at all and he replied quickly and gave the right answers."

"Well, when you're screwing the piglet you better be nice to the old sow. Oh, my God, Joe and the tramp are walking in together. They're taking the small booth." Pam looked toward them and her heart sank at seeing the two together.

"Chris, I can't believe he's doing this." The tears immediately filled her eyes. "I can't look anymore what are they doing?"

"The bitch is smiling and Joe doesn't look unhappy. Oh, he just smiled too. You're letting him get to you and fast. Why can't you pretend it doesn't bother you? This is a movie set and you're the leading lady and you have ice water in your veins."

"If I wanted to be an actress, I would be in Hollywood right now. I want to leave but I don't want him to see me leave."

"If he goes to the men's room, I'll let you know and you can leave then."

"Why is he pushing her into my face like this? I just don't understand his reasoning."

"Doesn't it make you wonder, if he hasn't had more to do with her than he's telling?"

"Yes, it does but I want to trust him."

"I wouldn't trust him at all and I'm not just saying this because I don't like him. I think he has an evil side and he enjoys you being miserable at times. Look at his past experience. He goes home with the tramp and tells you all about it. He sits with her in public and in front of you. He dumped you not too long ago and made you and everyone around you miserable. Wake up, Pam, and take a long look at this guy you're with. Something isn't right with him to do those things to you." Pam didn't say anything. "He is getting up and going to the men's room so when I say go you get up and leave. Okay, leave now and good luck. I'll call you in a bit." Pam was out of the booth and walking towards the entrance in a flash. She walked by the tramp.

"I told you he'd be mine," Suzy said to her as she passed by. Pam didn't say a word just kept walking. She went out the door and into her car. She heard a yell as she backed out of the parking spot. She glanced and saw Joe coming down the steps. He was waving at her. She turned her head and never looked back. He can have Suzy she told herself. I'm not playing anymore of these games. She took a left turn out of the parking lot to make it look like she wasn't going home. Pam drove a couple of blocks and turned around back towards the apartment complex. She didn't know what he was going to do. They were living together and they should spend their nights together. He had already run out on her so she was wondering, if he would do it again. She got inside and immediately took a shower to cool off and help her relax. She put her robe on and went into the living room. The phone rang as she turned on the TV to catch some news.

"Did the asshole come home?" Chris asked her.

"No, he hasn't and I haven't heard from him."

"He came out of the men's room to see you leaving and hurried after you. He never came back inside and the tramp wasn't too happy about that. I left a little after you and Joe's car was not in the parking lot. "Maybe he knows someone else he can visit. I wish you could see the other side of him. He cares about you long enough to have his way with you and then the bad stuff starts all over again."

"Chris, we love each other and he would have no reason to leave me again."

"Are you trying to convince me or yourself? The last time was probably just the beginning. How many times will it take for you to see he's not very stable?"

"Chris, friends try to help each other and you shouldn't try and degrade my choice in life. You don't have to like him but you should respect my decision to be with him. I wouldn't do that to you."

"You're absolutely right you have to live with him and I don't."

"I did think about going to Nana's for a few seconds but I wouldn't be able to take all the questions and innuendoes. We went over there the other day and told her how happy we were and we're in it for the duration. I can only imagine how she would take it, if I showed up and asked her, if I could spend the night."

"You mean she doesn't like good old Joe?"

"She hates all men. If he shaves his face and has balls, he can't be any good."

"She may not want me to visit in that case," Chris chuckled.

"I'll have to take you to her house someday because I think you'd like it. She's stuck in the fifties and her house is decorated the same way. Elvis is still the King and she has his stuff all over the place. She has an autographed black and white photo of him and the membership card when she joined his fan club in 1956. They're in a frame in her bedroom."

"I would love to see her house so let's plan a visit soon."

"She can give you a grand tour and she enjoys showing off her stuff. You wouldn't believe all the stories behind the junk."

"Pam, it may not be all junk and she may be a smart lady for saving it."

"How have you been feeling lately, Chris?"

"The doctor is trying out a new drug that seems to be helping."

"I'm so glad for you. Well, I'm getting tired so I'm going to hang up. I'll see you at lunch tomorrow."

"You need to try and sleep and not think wild thoughts about what he might be doing right now." She was all ready having those thoughts. Pam was going to bed too often thinking about where he was and what he might be doing. She fell asleep again thinking about him and wondering what tomorrow would bring.

Chapter 16

Pam woke up and knew that Joe was in bed with her. She vaguely remembered him coming home. She looked at him sleeping and was wishing that everyday could be great for them. The memories from the night before came back into her head. Pam couldn't understand why he was putting her through so much. She decided to shower, get dressed right away, and maybe go to the beach. She didn't have a clue what Joe was planning and she didn't want to face him just yet. She would make it difficult for him to make contact today. A cooling off period was needed. She was too upset to even cry. She told him she wouldn't let him not spend the night with her ever again. Maybe that sunk in and that's why he came home to her last night. He needed to get over her friendship with Chris. She would go to the beach until it was time to meet Chris and Julie for lunch. She might even help her Nana in the nursery later today to try and stay busy. She dried her hair and put it into a half-assed pony tail. Pam didn't have time to mess with it. She grabbed her purse and went out the door. She was driving out of the complex when she saw her Nana's car approaching. She did not feel like facing her right now. She just looked straight ahead and drove out onto the street. She looked into her rearview mirror to see, if Lee noticed her car but apparently she did not see Pam. She turned onto the next street and drove up an alley way to keep Lee from finding her. It worked because Pam didn't see her grandmother. She didn't like doing this but she would see her Nana later. She drove back onto the street again and headed for the beach. She had an hour and a half to kill.

The day was overcast but that didn't bother her. She loved the ocean under any conditions. Just seeing the waves and walking on the sand was enough for her enjoyment. There were only a few people out this Friday morning. A young guy with a Frisbee was playing catch with his dog. A large woman in a black bathing suit was lying on a beach towel and appeared to be sleeping. She had a large bag right next to her and enough junk around her to be spending the whole day. The seagulls were creeping closer to the fat lady looking for something to eat. Pam walked out onto the jetty and sat on some rocks to enjoy the waves. The tide was definitely going out slowly but surely. The movement of the waves was soothing. She was out there for quite awhile and checked her watch. It was time to leave for lunch. She walked in the loose sand back to her car. Pam kept a small towel in the back seat to wipe the sand from her feet and in between her toes. She looked in the rearview mirror and brushed her hair and put on a little lipstick. Her hair was a bit on the wild side but she couldn't calm it down. She drove to Hop Sing's and was the first one to arrive. She waited in her car for Chris or Julie to appear. It wasn't long before Chris showed up and flashed her that cute grin of his. He took a second look at her hair on his way to her car. "Jesus, did you piss into a light socket or something? I've never seen your hair so wild. You need some axel grease to tame it."

"I went to the beach with slightly damp hair and this is what I get."

"Follow me into the restaurant so you won't scare anyone away. Oh, Jules just showed up so we can go in together." Julie got out of her car and gave Pam a funny look. "Jules, this is Buckwheat in drag in case you're wondering." He nodded his head toward Pam. Julie smiled.

"I hope you're both having a great time at my expense."

"If we didn't love you, we wouldn't tease you," Chris said. The friends went inside and were seated by an Oriental lady in a Fuchsia colored silk kimono. She brought them tea and took their orders. "China Doll isn't bad looking," Chris said to the ladies. "Do you guys know how the Chinese name their children?" They both shook their heads. "They drop their silverware on the floor___ting, tang, and tung."

"Do you stay up all night thinking this shit up? Julie asked him. He grinned.

"How have you been feeling, Chris?" Pam asked.

"I've been fair the past couple of days."

"We've both been worrying about you because you never call in sick, and you have recently," Pam said.

"I think it was some bug I picked up when Sam and I went camping last month." The doctor thinks some parasite got into my intestines and I have to deal with it until it decides to leave me. It's called Giardia. You can't even go out into the wilderness anymore without bringing the creeping crud home."

The lady brought their food and they started eating.

"Now that we know Chris is okay, what's going on with you, Pamela?"

"I'm sure Joe called you already and told you what happened last night. There's nothing for me to add."

"He's real worried about you."

"That's so much bullshit and you know it. He walks into the Den with the tramp and sits with her. I'm supposed to let him do as he wishes and just forgive and forget all the time. I refuse to let him play games with me over her. If he wants her then he should tell me. I'll stay out of his way which is what I'm doing right now. I'll not stand for him being in her company not while we are together."

"He really does feel sorry for her. Joe spent the night at your place and that should have made you a little happy."

"He came home but not right away."

"Joe didn't think you went home last night. He went over to Ken's for a little while and then left. He said you left early so he didn't get a chance to talk to you and get things straightened out."

"I don't know why. He keeps this shit going and I'm not putting up with it. Did you tell him we were having lunch here today, Jules?"

"He tried to find out where we would be but I didn't tell him."

"I don't want anything to do with him until I can deal with some of my feelings."

"Pam, you know how I feel about the situation," Chris told her. "Dump his ass, find someone else, and he'll come around."

"You know, Pam, Chris may be right. Don't keep taking him back. You're having problems in your relationship so dump him."

"How can I erase him from my life when I'm head over heels in love with him? I can't turn this off. Someday I may get tired of going back and forth but not yet."

"Chris and I are just concerned and we're trying to help you," Jules told her.

"There is something else I need to tell you two since we're together," Chris said to them in a very serious voice. "You're probably not going to like this but I must tell you that I'm gay. I can't keep it quiet any longer and I hope we can all still be friends. Sam would like to join us sometimes at the Den and he wanted me to tell you about being gay." Chris looked at the two women expecting something drastic to take place.

"As long as you don't go after Joe, I can live with it," Pam told him.

"The same goes for me and Ken."

"You mean you can accept me as gay and it won't turn you away from me?"

"We're friends until the end, Christopher." Julie nodded too.

"What a weight that was just lifted from my shoulders. I knew you two were cool and you wouldn't kick my ass out of your lives." They could tell that Chris was so relieved and happy at the same time. The three friends finished eating and went outside the restaurant.

"You two have fun at work and we'll get together soon."

"We don't want you unhappy and feeling sad," Chris said. "Remember this is Friday the 13th so be careful what you do today."

"I'm fine and I'll see you on Sunday, Jules. Chris, I guess it'll be Monday for you. I'm always careful, Chris and thanks for reminding us what today was."

"If you need to talk anytime just call and we'll be there for you," Julie told her.

"I know you guys care and I'll be okay. I promise to call, if I get lonely."

Pam drove over to the nursery to see, if she could help her grandmother out. She arrived at the entrance and didn't see any of the clerks at the check out stands. She walked toward the outside nursery and saw two of them peeking out through the double doors. Pam told them hello and the women jumped. They smiled and went back to the front of the building. She didn't know what they were looking at as she didn't see anything under the screened area. She walked straight to the shack and stepped inside. She heard Joe's voice and her grandmother's arguing about something. Before she could turn and leave undetected, he saw her. She didn't say a word and neither did he.

"Pam, your friend is here accusing me of harboring you this morning. Would you like to tell me what's going on? You were both here the other day telling me how great and wonderful you were getting along."

"I'll take care of this, Nana." Pam moved away from the small building and he followed her.

"I want to talk with you, Pam."

"Julie already told me that you want to talk. She and Chris both told me to dump your ass today."

"I thought you didn't go home so I went to Ken's for a little while. I came home to you but I guess that didn't make you very happy. So what do you really want me to do. Come home to you or stay out all night?"

"You already know the answer, Joe. Does it make you feel like a real man to sit with her and make me feel awful? I thought we were committed to each other when you moved in. I took it seriously but I guess you didn't. I don't know what to do about it. I don't know why you keep seeing that tramp? I don't know why you flaunt her in my face? I don't know anything anymore." She looked hard at him and the tears filled her eyes. He put his hands to the sides of her face and wiped her tears away with his thumbs.

"Can't we go to the apartment and talk?"

"I'm going to be here for a few hours and then I'll be home." He gave her a wink and walked away from her. She loved him too much to keep him dangling. She walked back into the shack and her grandmother was looking her way.

"That was short and sweet. He came barging in here like he owned the place asking where he could find you. I told him I hadn't seen you so he was asking the wrong person. Are you ready to tell me what's going on or must I remain forever in the dark."

"It's something he and I will work out. We'll see each other later and talk. I came here to see, if I could help you with some things. I need to keep busy so this should be the place to start."

"Are you sure things are going to work out between you two?"

"I'm going to try. I love him very much."

"Just because a guy is great in bed doesn't mean he has what it takes for a good relationship. I'm an expert in that department. I have a new water feature over near the lily pond that I haven't had time to try and put together. You can to go over and take a look at it and see what you can do. It's in a box next to the angel bird bath. I'm putting out some new African violets that arrived this morning. When I'm done here, I'll come and help you."

"I'll go and see what I can do." Pam walked through a row of ferns and found the bird bath on the other side of the nursery. She found Boots asleep in the lounge chair and decided not to bother her. She opened the box, took out the directions, and was soon putting the waterfall together. Her Nana joined her as she finished the job.

"Hey, you're good, Pam. I think you were made for the nursery business."

"Nana, you have ladies working for you that have been here a long time. Do you ever take a vacation? You must be here 12 hours a day, seven days a week."

"I've taken a few days here and there."

"Why not plan a trip to Graceland and spend a week having a good time."

"It's funny you would mention that because Sharon my good friend in Phoenix has been trying to get me to do just that. We saw Elvis at the Phoenix Fairgrounds in 1956 and he just blew us away. I'll think about it. I have you living in Mission Park and if I left, you could keep an eye on things for me."

"Everything would be the same when you got back. I do want you to make plans and not just think about it. I'm going to leave now and have a talk with my Joe." She gave her Nana a hug and left for their apartment.

She went into the apartment and Joe was waiting for her. They both sat down on the couch. She was so drawn to him whenever they were in the same room together.

"I have been doing a lot of thinking since last night and we have three big problems in our relationship: Chris, Suzy, and your grandmother. I think we should discuss them one by one," he told her. She didn't say anything. "You don't agree that those three are our problems?"

"Yes, I agree so go ahead and start, Joe. First you need to begin by telling me why you were in Suzy's company last night?"

"I got out of my car at the Den and she had just arrived. She came running over to me so I saw a way to get back at you. I agreed to sit with her because you were with Chris. I know it wasn't the right thing to do but I can't take it back."

"He's not my boyfriend and I have not slept with him. He's just a friend. How can that even come close to you being with Suzy?"

"I just did it on impulse and she was never my girlfriend."

"I have to choose between you and Chris when you're not in the same category? I'll tell you something before you answer. He told Jules and me that he's gay at lunch today. So go ahead and tell me you were right and I was wrong." Joe shrugged his shoulders and looked disgusted. "Joe, I think we've both been honest with each other and I like that but how are we ever going to compromise?"

"I understand that you work with Chris and you can not avoid that but there are other ways you can. You had him over here for lunch and then you meet today for lunch so when will it end. You, also, see him at the Den. I can put up with work and the Den but not other cozy meals." Pam didn't say anything.

"Aren't you going to tell me what you want to happen?"

"You need to deal with Suzy and my grandmother now. I'll give my opinion when you have finished."

"As far as Suzy goes I'll not sit with her, speak to her, nor have anything to do with her from this day forth. Your grandmother is a most difficult subject for me to deal with. She is a blood relative of yours that you care about but she hates me so bad and I'm having a problem with that."

"She hates all men. I'm not trying to sugar coat her actions but she had a very abusive husband. It turned her against all men and I can't change that in her."

"My mother was abusive but I don't hate all women now."

"I talk to Nana all the time about being nicer to you. I told her that I love you with all my heart and you would always be in my life. I think she'll change over time."

"Are you going to tell me what you think?"

"I'll agree just to see Chris at work and the Den. I agree on your decision not to have anything to do with Suzy. I'll keep talking to Nana and will ask her to be nicer to you. Joe, I need to say something else too. When I walked out of the Den and you tried to get me to stop, I refused. I should not have done that. I want to apologize to you. If we're a couple and love each other then we both need to be home together every night. For the two of us to go off in opposite directions is not good."

"We need to think as a couple and things will work out," he told her. She walked over and sat on his lap. She squirmed a little and she could feel him.

"You probably shouldn't do that right now."

"Are you refusing my sexual advances, my Joe?" He got up, picked her up, and carried her into the bedroom. He stood her next to the bed. Joe pulled her into his arms and rubbed her backside with his hands. He held her close to him as his hands moved all around. She put her hand between his legs and caressed him. They kissed and undressed each other.

"Pam, you're the only woman I want and I hope I can prove it over time." They took turns ravishing each other's body with their hands and their mouths. She got on top of him and they became one as their bodies meshed and the passion exploded. "There's something I must say, Pam. I'll spend every night with you from now on. I'll never let you be alone, if I can help it." They spent a little time cuddling and talking.

"I don't know about you but I'm a little hungry right now."

"I could do with some pizza since I have my girl back for good." They ordered pizza and spent the evening watching the opening ceremonies of the summer Olympics from Athens.

Chapter 17

"Pam, have you been watching the Olympics?" Chris asked her when she arrived at work on Monday. They had driven into the parking lot of the PD at the same time.

"I sure have been when I haven't been working."

"I couldn't see the opening ceremonies but Sam taped it for me. I got to watch it this weekend and it was excellent. What did you think of Eros flying all over the place? He could move in with me anytime." Chris grinned at his own words.

"I liked his pretty blue color but the parade of countries was the best part. It was so vibrant with some of the countries and their real bright colors. All the participants seemed excited and so happy to be there."

"If you were from a country where you had a dirt floor in your home, you would be shocked to travel to Greece and stay in a nice room. Getting served three meals a day would put a smile on anyone's face."

"I know, Chris, give me the good old USA any day and I'll be happy." Both dispatchers went into the kitchen to retrieve their headsets from their lockers. Julie came flying through the door as they were deciding where they would sit. She had a look about her that was different today.

"Okay, Jules, spit it out because you have some news. It's showing all over your face and your feet are not touching the ground."

"I'm so happy because Ken told me last night that he loves me. I'm walking on air and you didn't notice, Chris."

"We can tell all right, did you get engaged?" He asked.

"It's too soon for that but it'll come later," she told her friends. "He took me to meet his folks and you should see their house. It's so big and has a beautiful swimming pool and two tennis courts. I've seen the house from the outside and of course played tennis but I got a grand tour of the inside. They have a full time maid and a cook too. He was born with a tennis racket in his hands."

"Don't you mean a silver spoon in his mouth, my dear?" Chris said teasingly.

"I would like him the same, if he was poor." Jules told her friends.

"Chris, you can hardly fault someone for being born rich. Ken had no control of that.

"He seems like a down to earth kind of guy, Chris told her. Pam didn't notice that Joe had walked into the Center.

"Nana always says you can love a rich man just as well as you can a poor man. I've only been looking for a good man much to her despair." Pam looked up and saw Joe. "I have the best man of them all," she said and she smiled at him. He smiled back.

"I know Joe is good but Ken is to me so you can't say Joe is the best."

"I just did and it is true," Pam said back to her.

"Joe, Ken and I are an official couple so we should all go to the Den tonight and celebrate."

"Did you get engaged?" Joe asked.

"Not yet but we love each other and we want to tell the world." Julie was looking intently at Joe, as if she expected some kind of a reaction.

"I guess we can go out for a few beers," Joe told her. "Do you care to do that, Pam?"

"I can go for a little while," she said. He knew that she didn't like running into Suzy. Pam and Chris spent the whole shift listening to Julie expound on her feelings for Ken. They were happy for her but she was talking a little too much about his rich family. They were glad when the shift was over and they could leave. Pam saw Joe in the hallway and asked, if she should go home to wait for him or just drive over to the Den by herself. He didn't care. She told him she'd go home and wait since they didn't need to take both cars. Chris walked outside with her.

"I love Jules but I don't know, if I can take another few hours of her and Ken doll."

"We have to do this for her. She's just excited and she'll mellow out over time."

154

"I'm not so sure. I noticed a few dollar signs in her pupils when she was talking about him. Did you see them?"

"Chris, you notice everything but you may be right. She does seems to care about him and the money is just a bonus. She could be acting for Joe's benefit. If Joe would show an interest in her, she would dump Ken in a second. I truly believe this."

"She knew about his money before she started dating him."

"How do you know that?" Pam asked.

"I told her all about his family and their finances when he first started here."

"She went after him big time after that conversation. Hey, see you at the Den in a few," he told her as he got into his car.

She drove to the complex and waited outside for Joe to arrive. He soon drove up and they headed for the Den. She leaned back against the seat looking at him on the drive over. He gave her a wink before they got out of the car. They got out and she put her arm around his back and he put his arm across her shoulders. They walked to the entrance. They got inside and there the tramp was sitting in the small booth by herself. Pam stiffened as she saw Suzy and Joe removed his arm from her shoulders. She glanced at him and was upset at this move on his part. They walked passed Suzy and Pam dropped behind him. If he couldn't put his arm around her, she didn't want to walk next to him. The others were all waiting and sipping their first beer. She and Joe ordered after they sat down.

"Pam, you look like you lost your best friend between work and coming here."

"No, I'm still the same."

"Pam, you used to be so much fun but anymore you are dismal and never in a good mood. Why is that Joe?" Joe gave Chris a hard look.

"Chris, how's your boyfriend?" Joe shot right back at him.

"Sam's great, he went to the Russian River to frolic this week."

"Joe, why don't you come over Saturday and we can play some tennis?" Ken asked him. "You and I play about the same kind of a game."

"Sure, I would like that. I'm a little rusty but it shouldn't take me too long to put the heat on you."

"Ken is teaching me and I like playing a lot," Julie told them. "Have you ever played, Pam?"

"Yes, I did some in high school and college."

"You guys are way too upper class for me," Chris told them. "We had a basketball hoop over the garage door when I was a kid. That was as good as it got."

"My time in the Navy, Chris, was spent in San Diego playing tennis. I didn't care to frolic with the guys." Joe said to him. Pam nudged Joe with her knee under the table.

"Did you guys know that the ancient Olympic games were played in the nude? Can you see Big John doing the broad jump? He would get disqualified for tripping over his dingus in mid air." They all smiled including Joe.

"I have a question for everyone," Pam said. They all say how terrible it is that we have earthquakes here and Florida has the hurricanes. I don't think we're as bad off as they are. What do you guys think?"

"You want us to pick the lesser of two evils?" Chris asked.

"You do have a warning for a hurricane but not for an earthquake," Ken told them.

"I think earthquakes are much worse on the nervous system because they do hit with no warning." Pam asked. "They can be very humbling, if you ask me."

"I see the regulars are here this evening." Chris was looking at the tramp. "Since Sam is gone, I should ask her to take me home for a blow job."

"All right this is enough," Pam said angrily. "I don't want to hear anymore." Joe got up and walked away from the booth. He was heading for the men's room. Suzy saw him go in and got up to wait outside the door. They were all watching to see what was going to take place next. Joe walked out and Suzy grabbed his arm. She was talking a mile a minute. Joe kept walking and she was following him and still talking. "She must be trying to take him home again," Chris said. It looked serious to Pam because Joe stopped to talk to Suzy. He told her he would never do that again. She was wondering what they were saying. She didn't understand why Suzy couldn't leave them both alone. She could never have Joe. He talked for a few minutes and returned to the big booth. He looked upset but didn't say anything. They were drinking their second beer.

"Joe, did she try and make a date for later?" Chris asked him. "Oh, that's right you and Pam came in the same car. If you want to go with Suzy, I can take Pam home."

"Chris, you need to keep quiet," Julie said to him. "We're here to celebrate Ken and my happiness and you shouldn't talk that way to Joe."

"Oh, Joe now has three women to fight his own battles, it must be nice to be so popular. You have the town whore, the innocent dispatcher, and the rejected dispatcher all clamoring to be with you. You're such a lucky guy, Joseph." Julie's mouth dropped open as she knew she was included in Chris's list.

"What are you talking about, Christopher?" Julie asked. Pam was enjoying their exchange very much.

"Don't look so innocent around Ken doll. Joe was your first choice when you started working here. I remember those days all too well. You flirted in every possible way known to man. I saw more of your body parts during that period than I care to even think about. I guess it hurt you when Pam showed up and they started dating right away. Little quiet demur Pamela who didn't have to undress herself to try and get his attention. Still water runs deep, Jules, or did you never hear that expression before. You would have liked Pam to fail with her training but she was too good so now you pretend to be a good friend to her and Joe. You're quite cunning."

"You don't even know what you're talking about," Julie told him. Ken was quietly sitting and trying to take in all the bantering.

"Are you ready to go home, Ken?" Julie asked him. He nodded his head. "It's been a wonderful fucking evening you guys and I'll see you at work tomorrow." Ken followed Julie out of the bar. Pam looked at Joe and she knew he would like to leave.

"Well, Chris, now that you've pissed off all your friends, Pam and I'll leave you to cry in your beer," Joe said to him.

"Well, the truth always hurts, Joe, you should know that all too well." They walked out together passing Suzy.

"You better tell her, Joe, or I will the next time I see her," Suzy called out to him.

They kept moving and soon got out to the car.

On the way home Joe was still not saying anything. Pam knew he had to tell her something and she was very curious what it was all about. They got to the apartment and still no word out of him. She took her usual shower and then came out to the living room where he was sitting on the couch. He was watching baseball scores on TV. She sat down next to him. "Please tell me what you talked to Suzy about since this was not suppose to ever happen. It's so hard when I see you close to her."

"I wish I didn't have to but I would rather tell you than you hear it from her. She's two weeks late for her period so she said she must be pregnant. Of course, she says the baby is mine." Pam gasped but didn't say anything. She leaned back against the couch trying to take in what he had just revealed. This

157

was never going to end with Suzy she thought. She took his hand and held it in her own. He looked at her with sad eyes.

"I figured you would ask me leave," he confessed.

"You still don't know me very well, do you? I fell in love with you which includes your past, present, and future. As long as you love me, I can deal with almost anything. We'll get through this together." He put his arm around her.

"You're the best woman in the whole world. I can't believe that having oral sex could produce a child. I know that's impossible but she keeps saying that I had regular sex with her. I don't remember that at all."

"Maybe she was seeing someone else when you spent the night and she got pregnant by him. You're probably the better of the two so she's going after you."

"I appreciate you standing by me and someday this has to be resolved. I want a good life with you and I want nothing hanging over our heads."

"Joe, we can't give up and we can't cave in where that woman is concerned. There are DNA tests that can give the results in a day or two."

"I never dreamed in a million years that my night with her would turn into a pregnancy or so she says. I'm so stupid to ever have anything to do with her."

"Joe, this is not a perfect world we live in. I'll stand by you and we'll beat her."

"What did you think about Chris going after Jules?" Joe asked. "Ken didn't look too happy and it was really uncalled for."

"I had no idea she wanted you so badly back then. Did Chris exaggerate or did she act that way?"

"He was accurate but it's four years in the past. I don't think Chris wants you or Julie to have a man in your lives. I don't know what the deal is. He did describe you perfectly. You did look so innocent and those eyes showed you were too."

"You mean, if I had come on to you bold with my tits showing, you never would have looked at me."

"I can't really say one way or the other. I'm glad you weren't that way. I have to admit I'm glad you haven't been with a lot of guys. I would still love you but there would always be questions in my head about your past. I fell in love with you in the emergency room when you realized you were naked and wanted to be covered up. It wasn't because I was standing there as much as it was because of the other men there. You only wanted to share that moment with me. It was precious and one of the highlights of our relationship."

"You do have strong feelings for me, Joe. I do love you so very much." Pam snuggled up next to him and he held her closely. "I'll never fall out of love with you because you're the best guy in the whole world."

Chapter 18

The rest of August dragged by as the thought of Suzy carrying Joe's baby hung heavily over them. They tried to avoid the Den but missed the good times they had there before Suzy came into their lives. They were more tolerant of each other and their love making was keeping them from falling apart.

On Wednesday, September 1st Lee called Pam to ask her for a favor. "I want to know, if you could watch the nursery for me Friday and Saturday, while I go to LA? There's a garden show that I must go to for new ideas and new kinds of plants and flowers. I'll fly out of here Thursday evening and come back Sunday morning."

"You know I'll be happy to help you out. I'm glad you're going away for a few days. Try and have fun along with taking care of business, Nana."

"Did you know that Elvis wore a neck chain with TCB on it? Taking care of business was his motto."

"Nana, I didn't have a clue but I have now been informed. I always think I've had a successful day when I learn something new."

"Pam, you're so down to earth. I hope Joe appreciates you."

"Yes, he does and I do him."

"While I'm gone you don't have to do much just check on my girls and make sure everything is running smoothly. They know what to do but I want to give them your number in case of an emergency. This is the biggest show of the fall and I do want to catch it."

"You're not going to be gone very long so don't worry about anything."

"Pam, is everything okay with you because you have sounded down when I've talked with you recently. I don't want you to be sad. Is Joe really taking good care of you?"

"Yes, he is and he's the best, Nana. I'm fine."

"I want to invite you both over Monday for our annual Labor Day cookout. You can come over for a barbeque before you both go to work. This is my yearly get together for the crew. I let them take two hours off with pay to come to the house and eat. Half will come from 11 AM to 1 PM and the other half from 1 PM to 3 PM. Their families come too and they enjoy it."

"I bet they do, Nana, you're always nice to your employees."

"If I'm nice then they work hard for me and I appreciate that. Sorry I didn't give you much notice about this weekend but I just found out about this big show last night."

"Don't worry and you know my schedule so I can help out."

"I'll drop a set of nursery keys off for you. Dorothy will open and close for me on Friday, Saturday, and open up on Sunday. She has been with me since the beginning. If you need to know anything, ask her because I trust her."

"I'll come by the nursery tomorrow on my way to work and pick up the keys."

"Thanks, Pam, it'll save me some time." They hung up and she told Joe about her Nana's trip.

"I can't believe she's going for a couple of days. This must be one heck of a show for her to make these plans."

"You mean she'll be driving around LA alone? Do they know she's coming?"

"Very funny, Joe, she has driven more miles than any 10 people that you know. She doesn't care, if it's LA or out in the wilderness, she has no fear when driving is involved."

The next day Pam gave herself a little extra time to go to the nursery before she left for work. She wanted to talk with her Nana before she said goodbye and was given the keys. She was happy that her grandmother was getting away from her long days of working and never taking a break. She found Lee in the old shack checking on some orchids she was trying to propagate. "Hi, Nana what's up?"

"Oh, not much but my mind is elsewhere today and I wonder why?" She gave Pam a big grin.

"Are you sure you're going to LA for a garden show and not some tryst with a guy you have been hiding from me?"

"It's a good thing I do crossword puzzles as you keep throwing those college words at me. That'll be the day when a man gets me to drop everything to run to his bed."

"Don't you miss that, Nana? I can't imagine my life without my Joe."

"Yes, I miss it very much but I can't get pass the abuse. It's my cross to bear. Quite often I wish that I could start from age 18 and do it all over. It would be a completely different life for me."

"How would you have changed your life?"

"I would have gone to college for four years and studied journalism. I would have worked for the news department for a large newspaper and then changed to TV when computers came into existence. I would have met a man who respected me. We would have gotten married and I still would have had your mom. I would write books in my spare time and tend to my flowers in my estate gardens."

"Those dreams sound grand and I wish you could have had that life."

"I still have your mom and now you so I'm very happy the way things are. My philosophy is, be true to yourself and never give up on your dreams. It doesn't matter which way you go through life as long as that's your choice and you're happy." The tears came to Pam's eyes as she pondered the words of her grandmother. "Look at you, where did those tears come from, young lady?"

"I was just thinking about what you said and how true it is. I must get to work and I hope you have a safe trip. Don't worry about the nursery, I'll take good care of it."

"I know you will and here are the keys." She had labeled the front door and other keys to make it easier for Pam. They hugged and Pam left for work.

Early Sunday morning the phone rang at 2 AM and woke Pam up with a start.

She picked up the phone from the nightstand.

"Pam, this is Dorothy, I hate to tell you this but the nursery is on fire and the fire department just called me."

"Oh my God, no," Pam said in a loud voice. "I'll be right there." Joe woke up and she told him about the phone call. She was already dressing as he jumped out of bed and grabbed his jeans.

"I can't believe this, Joe, she leaves for a couple of days and this happens." They both flew out the door in record time. They didn't waste anytime getting to the nursery and three fire engines were blocking the entrance. They couldn't see any fire. They parked on the street and ran to the firemen.

"I'm Pam and my grandmother owns the nursery where's the fire?" The Captain told her the fire was out and it had burned part of the fence only.

"We got here in time to save the buildings and most everything else."

"I am so glad for that." She explained to the Captain that her grandmother was in LA for a show and she was in charge. He asked some questions about her whereabouts before the fire broke out. Joe and Pam showed him their police department ID cards.

"The fire was deliberately set," the Captain told them.

"Who would want to do that to my Nana? She's known by everyone and is very respected in this city."

"Come over here and I'll show you what we found." The Captain took them to the fence where the most damage occurred. There was an empty red plastic gasoline container and several charred rags used to start the blaze. Pam just shook her head and couldn't believe what she saw.

"The fence is old and this is our dry season so it could have been a lot worse."

"Who reported the fire?" Pam asked.

"A guy who works for Sentry Security who happened to drive by and saw the fire just beginning. He noticed an older car driving away from the alley so he was nosey and drove up the alley. He saw the fire and called 9-1-1 on his cell phone. He said he would have followed the car for a license plate, if he had known there was a fire."

"We thank you so much for saving the place and I'd like his information to give to my grandmother. I know she'll want to thank him." Pam walked away from the scene and the tears started to fall. Joe took her into his arms. "Who would do such an awful thing? She leaves me in charge because she trusts me and the place almost burns down."

"Look, this was out of your hands. There are pyromaniacs living everywhere who love to do this stuff. They get their jollies seeing the fire department respond and work their asses off. They're sick and we can't control it."

"I wouldn't be surprised, if Suzy had done this. She hates me and she'll do anything to have you."

"She wouldn't have the brains to mastermind something like this."

"My God, Joe, she just needed gasoline and some old rags. I don't think you know what a woman scorned can do. They don't think straight and she's capable of more than you think. When I first found out about her and all the things she has tried to do to split us up, I worried about you. I don't worry about you anymore because I'm her target and now my family. She doesn't want to harm you because she wants you. If I'm out of the picture than she thinks you will turn to her. She's one sick woman. What are we going to do about her?"

"If she ever hurts you in anyway, she'll pay for it dearly." He took Pam into his arms. "I don't even want to think about something bad happening."

"She's the type who could do away with me and be tried in court only to prove somehow that I was the one who did it. She's bad." Joe held her closer and they were both thinking about the wrath of Suzy. "I'm not going to be able to sleep so why don't you go back to the apartment. I'll go inside and make coffee in Nana's office and stand vigil. She'll be home around 10 and we'll know what to do about the fence. This is not a lovely thing to happen on the Labor Day weekend."

"I don't want to leave you here alone. We'll both wait and when daylight comes I'll see what I can do to fix it temporarily." They went inside and Pam found the coffee and made a pot.

"Would you mind going to the 7-11 and getting me some coffee creamer, hazelnut fat free. I could use some donuts or something sweet to keep me awake."

"You want fat free creamer to have with your fat loaded donuts?"

"Well, I try and cut calories where I can and you can't find fat free donuts or I have never found any. Why are you teasing me?" She gave him a nice smile.

"Okay, you don't need to watch your weight so I'll do it. I'll be right back and keep these doors locked while I'm gone." He gave her a nice kiss and pat on the head.

He returned and they drank some coffee. Pam ate a couple of donuts. The time was going by slowly. Her grandmother had a couch in her office and Joe laid down on that. "Why don't you come over and lie down with me and get some rest." She walked over to the couch and he scooted over to let her lay beside him. He wrapped his arms around her as she faced him.

"I want to tell you something, Pam. I'm not going to let Suzy hurt you and I promise you that." He stroked her hair as she laid quietly in his arms. He soon dozed off but she could not sleep. The excitement had been too much. She lay for awhile longer and then got up to watch the sunrise through the back double doors.

Dorothy arrived a little before 8 AM and they looked at the damage to the fence. Joe was out back looking for lumber he might be able to use for a makeshift fence. Three other employees and some customers started arriving. Joe found enough lumber to make it work. He grabbed a hammer, nails, and pieces of wood. Pam helped him carry the lumber. Joe finished the fence about 10:30 and Lee arrived shortly after. Pam explained the fire to her and showed her Joe's handiwork.

"I'm so glad it was just the fence and I do have good insurance. I have needed to replace the fence but I keep putting it off. I'm glad I did because instead of wood I'll install a chain link fence that won't burn." Pam apologized all over the place for the fire. If her Nana knew that she suspected Suzy, there would be hell to pay for Joe.

"My dear, it was out of your hands and I feel lucky that the damage was small You need to go home and rest." She thanked them for taking care of things and the couple left for home. Pam jumped into the shower and then lay down to take a nap. Joe woke her up just in time to get ready for work. She was still thinking about the fire and she knew Suzy was to blame. She'll never stop until she has Joe. Pam was sure of this and she would fight until the end to keep Joe with her. He made a mistake but she knew he loved her and wanted to be with her. They would both fight Suzy as long as they needed to. They will win.

They next day, being Labor Day, found them both stopping by Lee's on their way to work. They met the families of the employees and enjoyed a barbequed steak. The families were enjoying themselves and Pam saw all the respect they had for her Nana.

Chapter 19

There were big plans in the works to celebrate Ken's birthday at the Den on the 17th. He had been released from police training on the 1st so Julie wanted the party to be extra special. She was all excited about pulling it off as a surprise for him. She even invited his parents but they declined. Pam didn't figure that the Den would be one of their favorite haunts. Everyone was on day's off except for Chris who would join them after work. Chris and Julie hadn't been as close since he spouted off about her being after Joe. The revelation did not put a halt to her future plans with Ken. She told Pam they would eat dinner at 8 PM so she reserved a table for the four of them. She asked Pam and Joe to arrive there before 8 and she and Ken would be there on time. Joe was agreeable. There was nothing he could do about Chris joining them because he had no control over the arrangements. Pam wondered, if Joe ever called Julie to talk anymore.

Friday morning they went shopping together to see what they could get Ken for a little gift. They knew it wouldn't be an easy task. "Well, what do you get for a guy who has everything?" Joe asked Pam.

"I was going to ask you the same thing. Does he have any hobbies or does he need some equipment for work that the Department doesn't hand out?"

"I guess we can look around and figure something out."

"We had better since tonight is the night." They settled on a funny card and a gift certificate from a sporting goods store. He could buy what he needed. They knew with his money he probably didn't need much. They hadn't been to the Den since Suzy told them she was late for her period. Pam was trying to cope with that news.

They arrived at the Den 10 minutes before 8. When they went inside they saw Suzy right away. They had to pass her booth before they went into the dining area. She gave Joe a big smile. As they walked passed she called out to him. "I have to talk to you, I have some good news." Joe and Pam kept moving. Suzy was still smiling. They were escorted immediately to a table with a reserved sign on it. Pam knew exactly what the good news was. Suzy had confirmed she was pregnant and she wanted to tell him again, he must be the father. The mood was already set for the evening and it wasn't going to be a good one. Ken and Julie arrived and Ken was very surprised when he saw the others. He thought they were having dinner alone. They did their usual small talk and discussed how old Ken was. He told them he was 27. He liked the card and gift certificate. Pam and Joe were sitting facing Suzy in her booth and this didn't make the evening any better. Suzy kept staring at Joe so Pam was not very happy. They ordered steaks and tried to enjoy the evening.

A little later Joe excused himself to go to the men's room. Suzy got up after he went by her and followed him. Pam was watching her every move. She stood outside the restroom and when Joe came out she started talking to him. She told him something and he said words back to her. He returned to the table looking pale and unhappy. Suzy still had a smile on her face. Pam was dying to ask Joe what was said but didn't want to bring it up in front of Julie and Ken. She would have to wait until they were home to discuss their little chat.

After dinner they decided to move over to the large booth and wait for Chris to join them. Just before Chris arrived Sam joined the two couples which made Joe more ticked off that he was. Julie asked him some personal questions. Pam remembered Chris telling her that Sam was handsome but she wasn't seeing it. He had a long narrow nose that matched his long narrow chin. It wasn't long before Chris joined them and the party livened up a little.

"Well, all the important people are here tonight, I see," said Chris as he looked around the room. Pam gave him a warning look so he didn't dare mention Suzy. "Well, since we have two happy people here tonight and two unhappy people we should talk about politics. Who are we all voting for in November?" No one spoke right away. "You all must be democrats," Chris told them.

"It's none of your business how I'm going to vote," Joe said to him. "Shouldn't you be a democrat knowing your sexual preference?" Joe asked him.

"I feel strongly for our country and we need a strong army and the democrats don't take care of the military. They think we can build a white picket fence around this country and survive."

"I'm for Bush and proud of it," Pam told them.

"Good for you, Pamela, not afraid to talk about your political preferences in mixed company." Joe glared at Chris but said nothing.

"I have some cheap real estate I'm willing to sell," Chris told the group. No one was asking him where. "You guys are no fun tonight."

"I was talking about Florida after the hurricanes you numb nuts," he said.

"Only you would make jokes about bad hurricanes, Chris."

"Is that how you get your kicks?" Joe asked him.

"People make jokes all the time about catastrophes. It doesn't mean that I don't feel bad for the people in them. I'm just trying to keep the party going, Joseph, but I'm failing tonight. Why don't you take Mary home on your donkey so the rest of us can have a little fun. If you hadn't let Suzy Q. ride your donkey, we wouldn't be having these bad evenings at the Den." Pam was livid at Chris's remarks.

"You know, Chris, it's nice to know that you have never made one bad mistake in your whole life. It's easy to talk and make jokes about everyone else's mistakes." Chris was surprised at Pam's remarks. Joe nudged Pam under the table and she looked at him. He nodded his head towards the entrance. "We're going to leave you guys and Ken, I hope your birthday party hasn't been ruined," Pam told them. They all said their goodbyes and Pam and Joe left. She walked out next to Joe and was surprised that Suzy didn't say anything to them. They got out to the parking lot and was approaching the car when Suzy called to them.

"Joe, did you tell your girlfriend the good news?" Suzy asked. He didn't say anything as he unlocked the door. "Oh, do you want me to tell her?" Pam had walked over to the other door waiting to get in. "I'm going to have Joe's baby in March. I just found out from my doctor and I'm so happy." Pam turned white, even though, she already knew it was a possibility. She got into the car as Joe took Suzy by the arm and walked her towards the building. Pam couldn't hear what he was saying. The tears were already flooding her eyes and she turned her head towards the side window. He got into the car without saying a word and drove home. She wiped her tears away discreetly as they drove through the city streets. They walked into the apartment and she stopped just inside the door.

"Would you please give me a hug, Joe." He turned to face her and he looked surprised at her request. "You know the thing you do when you put your arms around my back and hold me really close to you." She went into his arms. He let out a big sigh as he held her. She pulled back from him a little. "You don't have to say anything. If it should turn out to be true, I'll still love you and I'll stand by you. I'll never let you down." She kissed his lips and found his tongue. She took her shower and they got into bed. She scooted over and hugged him.

"We do need to talk, Pam, although, it was nice of you to say we didn't have to discuss it. We don't even know that she's pregnant and I may not be the father, if she is. She's been with plenty of men, I'm sure."

"If she is, she can't hide it forever." As small as she is, she should start showing soon. She would be about two and a half months along counting from the date you were with her. Do you know of anyone else who has slept with her?"

"Being with her isn't something the guys would discuss at briefing."

"We could go on Montel's show and have your DNA checked after the baby is born."

"How can you talk like that?" he asked.

"What do you want me to do, Joe? I just said a little joke because I don't want it to ruin our life together. I guess I can mope around for seven and a half months wondering, if you are the father or not. Is that what you want? I don't want to do that because I want to be with you and laugh like we used to. The sadness and moping around is starting to get to me. Please tell me that you don't want that."

"No, I don't want that. I want to be happy, too."

"Let's not discuss it anymore tonight. I want to ravish your body until that wonderful feeling overtakes my whole being. Joe, I could never feel this way with another man, not in a million years." She reached over and touched his penis. He jumped as he felt her fingers. "Joe, just relax and let me love you."

"I don't know, Pam, I'm hardly in the mood after the big news."

"You don't have to talk just let me have my way with you." She quickly went under the covers and her mouth found him soft. He pushed her head away with his hands. She rose from under the sheet and sat upright in bed. She knew when she was defeated. She reached over and turned out the light. Pam turned away from him and stayed on her side of the bed. She was trying to take Suzy's news in stride and not make it a problem between them. He was making it a problem and she didn't know what to do about it. She lay there thinking about the situation and she was not sleepy at all. She thought about getting up and watching TV or reading awhile to help her drop off to sleep. It wasn't long before Joe moved over in bed and put his arm around her.

"I'm sorry that I'm an idiot and it looks like I don't appreciate you very much. I love you and I don't want some tramp coming between us."

"I'm trying not to let her come between us, Joe, because I love you, too." She turned over facing him and made sure her breasts were firmly against his chest. She wanted him so badly. He took his hand and started at the side of her breast and ran in down the side of her body. He lifted her leg over his body and he ran his hand further down her leg to her ankle. He moved his hand back up the length her body.

"Do you have any idea how much I want you right now?" he asked her. She kissed his lips and moved on top of him. He kept running his hands up and down the sides of her body as she kissed his face and neck. It didn't take her long to work him inside of her as she opened up to him.

Joe went to sleep and Pam still lay thinking that Suzy could be pregnant with Joe's baby. The thought really upset her. How could another woman be having his baby when they were so much in love. She thought about the situation for a long time and then made up her mind that she would have to do something on her own. Life is all about choices and she needed some kind of insurance from Joe that she would always be in his life. She drifted off to sleep with a smile on her face and a plan in her head.

It was hard to believe that this was the month of September and they had known each for almost five months. This was one of the nicest month's of the whole year in Pam's opinion. She would always love flowers and they were blooming everywhere. Her roses in their pots were beautiful. She and Joe were enjoying living together and they were becoming quite the domestic couple. They both pitched in to clean the apartment and do some laundry. Her Nana was getting a new fence installed today and Pam would go by later to have a look at it.

"We should buy a house and fix it up the way we would like," Joe said to her.

"How about today or tomorrow?" Pam said.

"I'm serious about this."

"I can get a VA Loan and my credit is good."

"I like the way you're thinking but don't you think we need to deal with Suzy and get that behind us before we move forward too much?"

"I guess you're right but I'm happy with us and I'd like to do something."

"You mean you really think you can put up with me for the rest of our lives?"

"That'll be the easiest thing I ever have to do," he told her. "You have never been a problem in our relationship. I'm the luckiest guy on earth to have you."

"You say the nicest things at times. Talking about having our own home sounds so good, Joe. I can't wait for that to happen."

"After we finish our housework, let's go out for lunch and then to the nursery."

"You have a deal." He gave her a funny grin. "There's a catch to taking you out for lunch, if you don't mind."

"What will the ultimatum be, my Joe? Whatever it is, I'll be dessert."

"Would you make me some of those delicious tacos tonight?"

"That's too easy and you know I will." She slapped him on the ass as he walked by her and he jumped a little. "You do have a nice ass, if I never told you before."

"You keep that up and lunch will be real late today." She went to him and started caressing the front of his jeans.

"I like late lunches, if it means spending quality time in bed with you." They both headed for the bedroom and got naked.

"Pam, your skin feels so good. I love rubbing you all over."

"You don't feel bad yourself because I like to feel my nipples wandering over your hairy chest. It tickles them and makes them come to life." They explored each other's bodies and he ended up on top of her with her legs wrapped around him. They matched each other's slow moving thrusts at first and built up to strong faster thrusts. They called out each other's name as they came together. He lay on top of her until she could catch her breath. "Please don't ever stop wanting me. It gives me such a high. I love you, my Joe and I always will."

"I love you too, Pam and you have just made me very hungry." They got dressed and left for the New Horizon's. They went out into the parking complex and Pam gasped when she saw her car. Her windshield was shattered. She turned and looked at Joe.

"I hate her so much. She's never going to quit." Pam was so angry the tears would not come. Joe took her into his arms.

"Let's go for lunch and I'll call the glass company to meet me here after we eat. I'll drop you off at the nursery and I'll come back over here while it's being fixed. I'll pick you up later. They'll come right out and do it on the spot so the car doesn't have to be towed or anything like that."

"I could deal with her when she was calling me on the phone but she's getting too physical and too brutal. She must be following me around when she isn't working."

"This does it as far as I'm concerned. I have a friend who was a cop. He quit and started a small detective agency and I'm going to him for help. I want pictures of her drinking at the Den and I want him to follow her to see, if she is following you. Anything I can get on her to bring up later will be good."

"I think that's a good idea, Joe. I'll feel better, if I know something is being done."

"I don't think you quite realize how precious you are to me and I'm going to prove it." They took off in Joe's car for the restaurant. Pam was still upset but managed to eat a little.

After lunch he dropped her off at the nursery. The fence was looking good. She walked into the building to find her grandmother. She chatted for a few minutes to the ladies and went outside still looking. She could see her Nana by the new fence telling the workers what to do. "Hi, Nana," Pam said, "are you learning the fence business?"

"Yes, I am and what do you think of the chain link idea?"

"You're right it won't burn and it looks fine."

"Where's Joe, today? You look very happy by the way."

"He just took me to lunch and dropped me off. He'll be back by later because he had some stuff to do." She did not want to tell her grandmother about her windshield.

"Let's go into the shack and talk some more. I have some wild looking new plants to show you. When is Joe going to make an honest woman out of you, Pam?"

"I don't have a clue and I'm not going to ask him to marry me."

"I figured in this day and age women did the asking," her grandmother added.

"I guess I'm not your typical woman then. I think men should always be the ones to do the asking. Most women are ready to commit and settle down before men are. That's why the man should do the asking when he's ready. Too many couples are getting married and then getting divorced."

"I agree with you on that but do you think he'll ask?" Boots came up to Pam and started rubbing her body against her leg. Pam picked her up.

"I'm positive he will but don't know when. He was telling me this morning that he would like to buy a home and fix it up nice. He does tell me often that he wants me to be with him for the rest of our lives. Joe had a very

172

abusive childhood and he wants to have a family unlike his childhood. He'll be an exceptional husband and a great dad."

"I truly hope so, Pam. If he should lay one finger on you, he'll get acquainted real fast with the wrath of Lee. In my day no one helped abusive women, you had to put up with it or leave the country."

"Nana, that's the last thing Joe would ever do to me is hit me. I have never worried about that nor will I ever have to. Just because he was abused himself doesn't mean he would do that to someone. How did you eventually get rid of Tom?"

"He came home one night really drunk and beat the hell out of me. I took a golf club to him when he went to sleep. It worked wonders and he agreed to a divorce real fast. I should have done it a lot sooner than I did."

"Good for you and I'll never have to go through that with Joe."

"Your children will be very nice looking, Pam. I can see you having a little girl with Joe's dark hair and your pale blue eyes. She'll be a knockout." Pam grinned at her grandmother's prediction. She helped Lee rearrange some of the shelves in the shack. She was enjoying working and talking with her Nana.

An hour later Joe showed up and Pam shook her head and nodded toward Lee. "Did you shop and get the taco fixings?" Pam asked and winked at him.

"Yes, I did and I can't wait for dinner."

"Joe, I asked Pam a while ago when were you going to make an honest woman out of her? She couldn't give me an answer."

"Nana, you're nosing into our business. Don't say anything, Joe, she's out of line." Lee shrugged her shoulders. "I mean it, Nana, please let us handle our own lives."

"I know you care about him, Pam, and I don't want to see you get hurt."

"I care about Pam, too, so when the time is right I'll propose. I don't want you to think that she's just a casual person in my life."

"Joe, that's all I need to know and I thank you for being honest with me," Lee said. Pam beamed with love and admiration. Joe put his arm around her and drew her close to him. Lee smiled at the two of them.

"Are you ready to go?" Joe asked her. They said goodbye to her Nana. Pam couldn't wait to get into the car and talk with him. "What's with not telling Lee about the windshield?"

"I never told her about the tires being slashed nor about thinking that Suzy set the fire. I was afraid, if I told her about the windshield she might put two and two together because she's a smart woman. I don't want her to be worried about her business and she would be, if I mention Suzy's possible connection."

"That's a good idea until we can prove some things."

"Did you call your friend about Suzy?" Pam asked as soon as they were driving towards the downtown.

"First of all, the windshield is brand new and looks good. I went to the store and bought a car alarm and hooked that up. If anyone just touches the car, the alarm will go off. I should have thought about the alarm before this."

"That's what I need and anything to stop her will be nice."

"I called Jake and he wants us both to come by so he can get all the information we have on her. He will start right away. He said he has access to different vehicles so he never drives the same one, two times in a row. This is part of how he handles his cases. He has listening devices, secret cameras, and all kinds of spy stuff as he calls it. We'll fight together and we'll win."

"Joe, it sounds so good. I want us to have a happy life and I don't think that's asking too much, do you?"

"As long as we're together, it's not asking too much." They stopped at Jake's office just a block from the Diner. The two went in and got comfortable. From the other room came this blond haired Adonis who did not look like a detective at all. There wasn't a flaw on his face nor one wavy strand of hair out of place. He looked like a rich playboy who swam or played tennis all the time. He asked them a lot of questions.

"Joe, if it's Suzy who works at the Diner, I go in there occasionally to eat and I know who you're talking about. She should be easy to tail." Jake glanced at Pam's sad look and said to them. "I guess tailing isn't the best word I could have used just now." Joe told him about her hanging out at the Den and her saying she's pregnant and still drinking like a fish. He, also, mentioned the slashed tires, the broken windshield, and the fire at the nursery. "Don't you two worry, I'll find out some stuff real soon and I'll call you." They thanked him and left.

"Joe, I feel good about doing this and I know it'll help us in getting rid of her. Is that what you think, too?"

"I think so but like you said, she was scorned and I don't think it'll be easy. Let's go by the store and get taco stuff. I'm going to enjoy eating tacos and loving my girl this evening." Pam smiled at his plans.

Chapter 20

Things were starting to move in the area they lived in but not with the business at hand. On September 28th a 6.0 earthquake rattled the central coast while Pam and Joe were eating breakfast. It was the longest rolling quake they had ever experienced before.

"My, God, it won't stop," Pam said as the chimes in the living room could be heard in the kitchen. Joe smiled and took her into his arms.

"Now, I know why you don't have any pictures on the wall over your bed."

"You're just figuring that out, Joe? If your smart and you live in California, you never put anything on the wall over the bed. It could be worse you know. We could be living at the foot of Mount St. Helens. "She's been rocking and rolling that area and is getting ready to do something."

They were getting a little anxious to hear from Jake when 10 days had passed with no word. Joe called him to see what was happening. He told Pam to listen in on the other phone. She picked it up as Jake answered. "I haven't called because I don't have much to report," Jake told him. "I got several pictures of her at the Den drinking but that's about it. I have a suggestion for you. I think you should go to the Den more often or set up an evening there soon. I've been trying to figure her out and I feel that she does the bad things after seeing you two together. I may not get anything on her unless you go out and are seen by her. This is what it takes with some women."

"Tonight Pam and I will be at the Den after work. Whatever it takes, we'll cooperate," Joe told him.

"She basically has a quiet life. She works 1 PM to 9 PM and usually works seven days a week. She does have other days off occasionally or gets off work earlier at times.

She goes home and does her thing. I find her leaving her place at 10:15 PM for the Den. You can almost set your watch by her. I'll be there tonight so please don't recognize me. We can arrange these outings every once in awhile and see, if anything happens."

"Jake, I appreciate this very much and we'll be at the Den tonight." Pam was not looking forward to seeing Suzy again. They talked about what Jake told them and the plans for the evening.

"I think he's right, Joe, about her seeing us together and it triggers her to do something bad. He sounds like one smart guy."

"He has a eye for nice looking women so I hope you aren't getting any ideas?"

"Joe, I'm sorry but you're stuck with me. You only turn me on. I only said he was smart not good looking."

"I hope it stays this way because I want to be stuck with you."

"Suzy may go after him and you'll be off the hook."

"You really must think he's good looking to make a comment like that."

"Joe, please don't think that way. You're the best looking guy that I have ever met. I don't mean that Jake's homely but there's no one on earth like you. You have my heart and I'll never change my mind about that."

They got ready for work and left the apartment. She was enjoying her first fall in Mission Park very much. The day time temperatures were in the 70's and the nights in the 50's. This was her kind of weather.

Chris was on her case as soon as she got to the Center. He was looking pale and she wondered if he was getting sick again. "We never go to the Den anymore, Pamela."

"Tonight you're getting your wish. Joe and I are going after work. You and Jules can join us. You still need to watch your mouth, Chris. I love Joe and you say bad things about him and Suzy. Just remember when you hurt him, you're hurting me, too."

"I'll try and be nice but I can't guarantee anything. I didn't think I would ever hear those words again that we're all going out to howl. Sam and I have been going but it isn't the same without the whole gang."

"We'll all be together tonight and I plan on being in a good mood too," Pam said.

"What happened to change your mind about the Den? I know, forget what

I just asked, you like to keep secrets from your friends." Julie came in and Chris told her about going to the Den. She, also, warned him about his mouth. She would tell Ken so they could join the group. The shift was busy for a Monday night and Pam thought that Joe would not be able to go. He ended the shift by getting caught up. She had ridden to work with him so they would only have one car to deal with.

Chris and Julie left to get the big booth and Pam waited for Joe. They were soon on their way. Ken was right behind them when they drove out of the office parking lot. "I hope this works out tonight," she told Joe. "I'm keeping my fingers crossed."

"Something is bound to happen soon. I may be paying money out for nothing, too. We're not positive she has done those things but we need to find out." They arrived and the gang was there holding the booth. Suzy was in her small booth and her face lit up when she saw Joe. Pam was trying to stay in a good mood. She thought she saw Jake on a bar stool looking the whole room over. He was wearing a Dodger baseball cap, jeans and a loose long sleeved shirt. He had a pair of gold rimmed glasses on and a blond mustache. He didn't look the same as he did when they met.

Chris started right in with his words directed towards Joe. "Well, Joe, I tried to keep you busy so you couldn't come but I failed."

"That's okay, Chris, I've missed you too."

"The tramp just stood up and she's either pregnant or she recently swallowed a cantaloupe whole," Chris told the group. They all looked towards the small booth. Pam looked at Suzy and then lowered her eyes. Joe did the same.

"She has definitely put on some weight recently, Julie said. It could be just fat, Chris. Some of us have sat in front of the TV, snacked, and put on weight."

"She only looks fat in the belly and most people gain over the whole body," Ken added.

"I wonder who the father could be or who would want to go to bed with her?" Chris asked and they all knew he had Joe on his mind. Pam was very uncomfortable but trying not to show it. She glanced where Jake was sitting and noticed he was now standing in front of Suzy's table. He must be taking pictures or trying to get information she thought. She looked at Joe and he was thinking the same thing.

"The bitch needs to stop drinking alcohol but I guess there's no law against it," Chris said. "They put up signs but a lot of good that does the fetus when the bitch can't read. If she'll drink while pregnant, think what she could do after the kid is born. It sure as hell won't have much of a chance with her for a mother. This is why I do not embrace religion. Why would a caring God let an idiot like her become pregnant and drink alcohol. It doesn't make sense to me and it never will."

"They should have child abuse laws to protect the fetus," Julie said.

"The fetus isn't recognized as a human so there are no laws," Ken told them.

"Hasn't the weather been great?" Pam asked her friends. No one wanted to talk about the weather. She could tell that Jake was still observing the room from his bar stool. Pam wasn't sure how long they were suppose to stay out for him to do his job. Joe excused himself to go to the men's room. Pam watched as Jake followed Joe inside. Suzy was looking around but didn't get up from her seat. Pam hoped Joe would give her a signal that they could leave. She had just finished her second beer and didn't want anymore.

Soon Joe came out of the restroom and stopped at Suzy's table and Pam was upset in an instant. Chris was taking it all in. "Joe is sniffing around the tramp and you shouldn't put up with that shit. He could be the father of her baby, in case, you can't count from the time he screwed her."

"Chris, you need to knock it off and now." Pam was angry at her friend for his mouth. Joe came back and sat down.

"Joe, did you ask her when the baby is due and if you're the father?" Chris asked sarcastically. Joe was hot.

"Look, you little faggot, you need to mind your own business. You don't even know what you're talking about."

"She would be a little over three months pregnant from the night you spent with her. I can count, Mr. Big Cop." Pam told them she was going to leave. Joe got up and they both walked out. She was shaking by the time they got outside. Suzy followed them.

"I need to talk to you, Joe," Suzy called out to him as Joe was unlocking the car door.

"Spit it out now," he told her.

"This is private and I don't want her to hear." Suzy pointed at Pam.

"Go ahead and talk, Joe, I'll sit in the car and wait." Joe walked over to the side of the building with Suzy. Jake had come out and was standing on the steps smoking a cigarette. In a few minutes Joe left Suzy and he got into the car. He was quiet. Pam decided not to ask him anything. She wanted to know, if he would volunteer to give her information without her asking. They drove home in silence. She went into the apartment and got into the shower. When she came into the living room he was sitting on the couch not doing a thing. She sat down next to him. "Joe, why do I always have to ask you what Suzy said to you?"

"I'm not in a good mood and I'm sorry."

"I'm not asking about your mood just what Jake said in the men's room and what Suzy said? I didn't think you would mind talking about it."

"He suggested that I talk with her for a few minutes and I did. It only makes her want to have more contact with me which is what happened tonight. I understand he needs certain things for the investigation but he may require more than what I care to give. He has some big ideas."

"My, God, what does he want you to do?"

"He wants me to be friendlier towards her and I don't like that. He said you should understand in order to get to the bottom of everything. He wants me to take her out and be wired for sound so we can get some of it on tape."

"Isn't that fucking wonderful. Who cares what it might do to me as long as the investigation can be done? You were so close with her and to throw you into her face again would hurt me. I don't trust her at all, Joe, but I do know you'll be sober this time."

"I never agreed to anything, Pamela, so don't get yourself in an uproar. I told him I'd talk it over with you and I would let him know." Pam immediately got up and went into the bedroom. She took off her robe and climbed into bed. She thought he'd follow her to bed but he did not. She tossed and turned for a long time and then Joe got into bed beside her. He was not moving. She moved over and put her arm around him. He turned towards her and took her into his arms.

"Thanks so much, my Joe, because I need a big hug right now." He never let go of her for the rest of the night.

The next week still revealed nothing new in the investigation. Suzy was leading a subdued existence and Jake was sure she didn't know he was following her. He had all kinds of disguises that he used around town. He even had dinner at the Diner two nights in a row and she didn't recognize him the second time. Jake still wanted them to be seen at the Den or go to the Diner to eat. He was after Joe to be wired and go out with Suzy. Joe didn't want to do it and neither did Pam. They were both hoping Suzy wouldn't try anything bad against Pam.

Ken invited them over to play tennis Saturday morning. The day was quite warm for an October morning. Joe tried to coax Pam into going but she had some cleaning and other things to do. "We don't care, if you're not very good at tennis. I'll teach you what I know. We just want to play doubles sometime and we need you for that. Jules is improving all the time. We could help you the same way we helped her."

"I'll go next time, I promise but not today." He kissed her softly and said he would be home later. She knew that he always missed her when they were apart. She liked that and she felt the same way about him. She kept herself busy in the apartment while he was gone to play tennis.

In the early afternoon he showed up with an aggravated look in his eyes. She walked over to him and put her arms around his neck.

"What's wrong, my Joe?"

"You'll never guess who I ran into at the car wash. I decided to put the car through for a quick wash and Suzy showed up pretending to be there to wash her car. I had just finished wiping the excess water off the car and she came running over to me. She must be stalking me or us."

"What did she say?"

"All the same old stuff about being with me and I need to get rid of you."

"I told her to keep away from us and she started crying and carrying on really bad." Pam hugged Joe and laid her head on his chest. "I left as soon as I could but there were other people around. Lee pulled in as Suzy was trying to keep my door open and I was trying to close it and leave. It must have looked bad to her and she gave me a look that could kill." Pam didn't make any comments but kept hugging him. "If you keep this up, I'll have to take you to bed."

"I guess I'll have to keep it up," she said as she hugged him tighter.

"Pam, I want you right now. I love you so much and you're such a nice person to put up with my mistakes." He pulled her close to him. She reached down and touched his crotch and kissed him on the lips.

"It's a good thing I haven't made the bed yet," she told him. She gave him a sexy smile as she pushed him towards the bedroom. "

Sunday morning she woke up in a pretty good mood. Joe was laying on his stomach with his face towards her. How she loved this guy next to her. She knew it had been hard for him to tell her about running into Suzy. It meant he trusted her love for him and that made her feel really good. She was determined not to be jealous of that slut and not let it ruin her relationship with him. He opened his eyes to find her looking at him.

"Do I look funny or something?" he asked with a grin.

"You're perfect to me. I was just admiring your good looks and thinking how happy I am right now. I'm with the guy that I love so very much." She moved closer to him and kissed his upper arm.

"There isn't any better way to wake up than with you beside me. I hope you never get tired of me or get so upset with me that you leave. I couldn't deal with my life without you and I mean that," he told her.

"I'll make it easy for you. I guarantee you'll never have me out of your life."

He put both his arms around her and hugged her. "How about some French toast this morning, if you'll let me shower first?"

"It's a deal and you make the best." She was busy mixing up the egg batter when the phone rang. It was Jake. Joe was just getting out of the shower so she took the phone into the bathroom for him. She handed him the phone and caressed his wet penis as he moved to get out of her reach. He couldn't help but smile at her. She went back into the kitchen while he talked. He soon came out dressed. "He wants us to go to the Den tonight after work and I told him we could do that. He, also, wants me to talk to Suzy so don't be upset, if I do."

"I don't like it but I know it's business so I have to put up with it." He sat down to eat and they talked some more about Joe taking Suzy out.

"I won't stand in your way, Joe, if Jake thinks this is necessary. I want this vendetta she has against me resolved so whatever it takes, I'll trust you."

"I'll let Jake know tonight that we can set it up." They finished breakfast and she reminded him that she was leaving early for work to stop by her Nana's. He understood and told her he didn't mind.

Around noon time she hugged and kissed him before taking off. She was soon at her Nana's who was waiting for her. "Pam, I'm so glad you dropped by because I don't see you enough. I know I say this a lot but it is true."

"Nana, do you forget that I work, too and there are just so many hours in a day."

"Did Joe tell you he saw me yesterday at the car wash?"

"Yes, he did."

"Well, that was a stupid question for me to ask because he would have to tell you. Did he tell you he was with another woman?" Pam proceeded to tell her grandmother that Suzy was someone they run into occasionally and she was after Joe. She would not tell her Nana any more than that.

"It looked more involved than someone with just a big crush on him. He was almost pushing her away from the car, in order, to leave."

"Nana, haven't you ever known a woman who wouldn't take no for an answer."

"As long as you know all about it which is the only reason I brought it up."

"I care about him more and more everyday and he feels the same way."

"I still wish you were engaged, young lady. It would make me feel like he really did care about you. Why buy the cow when the milk is free? Men used to have to work to get a woman. Now women are climbing into men's bed before they're even asked."

"It that what you think I did, Nana?"

"You were raised better than that. I do think Joe has respect for you which is something I admire. I'm sure he would never hit you and I believe he's taking good care of you."

"Nana, you have just made me so happy with what you just said. You'll grow to really like him over time."

"We shall see." Pam visited for a little while longer and then left for work.

During the shift Chris called in and said he and Sam were going to the Den would they all meet them. Pam told him that they were already planning to be there. Julie and Ken would, also, be going. Pam was not happy about going but she needed to get use to the fact that Suzy may be pregnant and it could be Joe's baby. She was even wondering what Joe's future plans would be, if it all turned out to be true.

She and Julie drove to the Den in their separate cars and met in the parking lot. Pam preferred to enter the building with someone else and maybe Suzy would keep her mouth shut. They walked in and didn't see Suzy at her booth but Chris and Sam were in their booth. The Den wasn't very busy and she thought the guy sitting at the bar was probably Jake in another disguise. He looked like a construction worker who hadn't made it home. The waitress took their orders and they saw Suzy come out of the rest room and go to her small booth. Joe entered the bar and he passed Suzy who called out to him but he didn't stop until he came to their booth. He sat next to Pam and she gave his hand a squeeze. They looked into each other's eyes. Ken showed up next and sat next to Julie. Chris and Sam were acting more like a couple than the others were. This was bothering Joe and he was disliking Chris more all the time. Pam nudged Joe under the table and nodded her head towards the bar. He looked and nodded back. They were both thinking it certainly was a good disguise. Chris got up out of the booth and went to the men's room. On his way back Suzy said something to him. The friends in the booth watched to see what was going to happen. Chris was talking to her and listening to what she had to say. He left her and returned to the booth.

"Joe, the tramp wants to see you so I told her I would give you the message." Pam was immediately upset but was trying not to show it. Joe just sat there and didn't say anything. It got even more quiet for the two of them. Pam and Joe were both watching Jake, who had been standing since he arrived, walk over to Suzy. The two exchanged a few words and he sat down with her. Pam guessed he was trying to get real close and personal with her. She and Joe looked at each other. Chris and Julie kept the group going with their conversation about some of their first days on the radio. All the times they dispatched and the errors that they made. Jake was still sitting with Suzy as the night wore on. Pam was not having a good time but didn't want to spoil everyone's fun. She wished she knew what Jake was finding out. Maybe he needed a companion for later and it could be he has slept with Suzy before. Joe told her that the officers all knew her.

A little while later Pam told the group she was ready to go home. Joe let her out and she started walking to the entrance. She paused once and looked back and Joe was not following her. She passed Suzy and Jake but nothing came out of Suzy's mouth. Pam never broke stride. She got to her car and a voice called out, "hey, wait up, I want to talk with you." She turned around to see Jake approaching her.

"How come you're leaving so early?"

"It's my bedtime and I'm not having a really good time."

"I came out here because you need to let Joe see Suzy so I can get some things on tape from her."

"He and I talked about this earlier today and I told him he could see her. He hasn't had a chance to talk with you about it yet."

"I was sure he would do it but only if you would give your okay and that is why I came out to talk to you right now. Thanks for letting him do it because he's the only one who can get her to say things."

"What's he suppose to do on this date?"

"Talk about her pregnancy and he could ask her some questions to try and trip her up. Since she works seven days a week this would have to be a late date at her place."

"Are you looking for her to try and get him into bed so don't sugar coat this for me?"

"That's part of it but he won't have to sleep with her just pretend he's going to and let her talk. She never seems to have a problem talking so it'll be easy for him to get some information."

"You can go ahead and set everything up, if I can listen to the tapes after the date."

"It's a deal and I'll talk with Joe tomorrow about when we can do it. I appreciate you letting us do this and it'll pay off." He went back into the Den and she got in her car. She couldn't believe that Joe would stay there without her. It could be Jake asked him to but she wasn't sure. She got home and took her usual shower. She was tired tonight and decided to go right to bed. She figured Suzy made her depressed and she needed more sleep. It would be hard to get any rest knowing Joe was going to take Suzy out.

Sometime later in the night she felt Joe climb into bed. She moved over in bed, put her arm around him, and hugged him. He lifted her hand to his lips and kissed it. She kissed him on his back and went off to sleep again. She did love him and she knew he loved her.

Chapter 21

They were eating breakfast just before noon the next day. She fixed him one of his favorite meals of pancakes and bacon. They weren't talking very much. Pam didn't feel much better than she had when she had gone to bed. She knew Jake was suppose to call Joe to set up the date with Suzy. Joe didn't even know that Jake had talked with her in the parking lot. They were cleaning up the dishes when the phone rang. Joe answered it and she knew it had to be Jake. "You want to see me right away?" Joe asked the caller. He listened for a little while longer and hung up the phone. "Jake wants to see me before I go to work. Maybe he found out some stuff from Suzy last night."

"It could be," she told him.

"I'll get ready for work and go to Jake's from here. I'll come back by here for a few minutes before work and catch you up." He went in the other room to get ready. She was not happy about him seeing Suzy and Pam didn't understand what breaking news she might be able to tell him. She knew Suzy would not confess to trying to hurt her.

Pam thought that maybe seeing her Nana would make her feel better. She drove to the nursery after Joe left for Jake's. The ladies told her that her Nana was in her office. "You don't look very happy today so what gives?"

"We went out with the group to the Den after work and I was up too late. My ass is dragging somewhat today."

"That must be it but you usually have this same look about you when Joe is the problem."

"You mean I have all different kinds of looks that I didn't know about."

"You sure do and remember I have known you your whole life. I want to see those big eyes sparkle everyday and I'm not seeing that. If you're so in love, where is the sparkle?"

"We have some issues just like all couples and we're working through them."

"I know that woman I saw Joe with at the car wash is part of your problems. You won't tell me anything so I can't help you."

"You're right, Nana, and we're getting through it. He's at the moment, taking care of a few things and we should be rid of her soon. It's been hard because she wants him and she'll stop at nothing to get her wish."

"I know how some women can be but I would still like to help, if I could. Let me tell you what I would do when I was younger and unhappy? I would go to the library and check out a book that had to do with someone worse off than I was. I would read that book and be thankful I didn't have to go through a situation more terrible than what I was already going through. This is what kept me going through the real bad times."

"You're right, Nana, instead of feeling sorry for myself and moping around, I should think of the people who are worse off than I am. You always know what to tell me to make me think more. Joe and I will get through it and thanks for the offer. I have to get to work. Thanks so much for caring about me but I'm fine. Joe and I love each other very much." There was another reason why Pam wanted to go to the nursery. Deep down she wanted to drive by Jake's office to see, if Joe had left yet. Not only had he left Jake's but his car was parked in front of the Diner. He must be asking her out she thought.

It wasn't long after she got home that he arrived at the apartment. "I don't have much time," he said as he hurried into the apartment.

"Did you make a date with Suzy?" He came out of the bedroom walking slowly.

"Why didn't you tell me you saw Jake in the parking lot last night?"

"Why didn't you come home with me and you would have seen him too? I just drove by Jake's office to see, if your car was still there and lo and behold it was parked at the Diner. You had to make a date in person, you couldn't do it over the phone?"

"It was his idea, to make it look more sincere, is the way he put it."

"She must be all excited about being with you. She's getting her wish to have you alone once more. I have to trust you, Joe, but she'll try to get you into her bed."

"I don't have time to discuss this now so we'll have to finish this conversation after work." He left and she started crying really hard. He hadn't even told her when the date was going to take place. It could even be tonight. She had trouble stopping her tears. She figured things were building up and she needed to cry to get some stress release.

Pam arrived at work wearing her sunglasses on her face to hide her crying eyes. Mike tried to make his usual sexist comments and she wouldn't talk. They all knew that things must not be good with her and Joe. She sat down at the service desk position, another move that was unlike her. She hated working the phones. Chris didn't know, if he should even try and talk to her since she was wearing the sunglasses. He couldn't resist. "How is the world famous actress, Pamela Austin, doing this fine day? Is your limo waiting outside to whisk you to the spa when your shift is over with? Are you too high and mighty today to even say good day to your friends?"

"Knock it off, Chris. I'm just fine today but I have a little headache."

"Don't you mean you have a pain in the ass named Joe, who's your problem?"

"I don't recall saying that I had any problems today. You assume way to much, Christopher and you do it all the time."

Joe came around the corner and must have heard their comments. "Well, Peckerini, what have you done this time to make her cry?" Chris asked him in contemptible way. Joe glared at Chris and looked at Pam. She had definitely been crying.

"Pam and I are fine, Mr. Sylvester, you always look for something to be wrong."

Julie came in and caught Joe's remark. "Gee, you're always having problems, Joe, and the sunglasses usually confirms it, Julie added.

"Who in hell asked you to comment?" Joe asked her. Julie wasn't expecting Joe

to say that to her. Chris rolled his eyes at Julie. Joe left without trying to talk with Pam and the others remained quiet. Pam removed her glasses later in the shift but Chris and Julie were only talking to each other. It was fine with her. It was even better when the shift ended and she practically sprinted out the door. She didn't want any conversation with them. Pam just wanted to see Joe but she didn't even know, if he was coming home. It could be the date night for all she knew. He didn't talk enough with her and that was a problem.

She got home and took her shower. She turned on the TV. He arrived later and sat with her on the couch. "I'm taking her out Friday night when she gets off work which is nine o'clock. I'll be going to her place, although, she wanted me to take her to the Den."

"How nice, a cozy little date where it all began. She'll be all over you as soon as you get through her door and how will you handle that? You don't have to worry about getting her pregnant."

"I'm not taking her to bed so get that out of your mind right now. I don't like that comment, Pam, you must be trying to piss me off."

"I can't see how you can pull this off without doing just that. You're going to have to tell her that you don't care about me, if you haven't told her already." Joe hung his head. "So you told her we were breaking up or had already broken up?"

"She asked me, if I was still with you and I said I needed a couple of days to let you down easy. After I dump you, I told her I would be with her." Pam wasn't expecting to hear of so much to be involved with one date. "Jake said you agreed to this and now have you changed your mind?"

"I was upset today because you didn't even tell me when the date was before you left for work. For all I knew, it could have been tonight."

"I was in a hurry to leave for work and I didn't realize how it was affecting you."

"It's bad enough running into her often but you going to her apartment is hard for me. How would you feel, if you had to go through me doing this to you?"

"I would trust you completely and support you to get this mess over with."

"I know how much she wants you and I don't trust her at all."

"She can't get my pants off without me knowing it and that won't happen."

"Promise me, you won't go to bed with her?"

"I promise and don't worry about anything." Pam put her head on his chest. He took the pins out of her hair and stroked her head. She kissed him on the neck and then all over his face. He found a breast with each hand and caressed her nipples with his thumbs. She unsnapped the front of his jeans and unzipped them. She felt him get hard as she stroked the front of his briefs. He helped her get his jeans and briefs off and he sat back down. She sat on his upper legs face to face and she rose up so that he could find her nipples with his mouth. He licked and nibbled on them as she stood on her knees before him. She soon bent over and put her lips over the end of his penis. She licked him and sucked him until he groaned. She rose up and opened herself to his penis and slid down over his moist and stiff erection. He grabbed her ass with both hands and she rode him until they burst into a climax. How good this felt to her and she knew he enjoyed it, too. She hated to break away from him.

Later they were in bed and he was holding her in his arms. "I'm sorry I made you cry today because I never want to do that."

"I got over it. I just felt left out of things and it wasn't a nice feeling. Guys may not understand but sometimes a good cry can leave a woman feeling a little better.

"You're always number one in my thoughts and feelings."

"I just need to hear it once in awhile or until this Suzy mess is behind us."

"I'll remember that and I'll let you know often. I want us to be happy and not have any problems," he assured her. "You're right about not making plans for the future until Suzy is out of our lives."

"The only problem with that is, it takes nine months to have a baby and we'll have to put our lives on hold." He didn't say anymore. She thought that she needed to take things into her own hands. It hurt her to think that Suzy could be carrying his child. She thought things over for a long time and dropped off to sleep.

The day Pam had dreaded all week had finally arrived. It was Friday and Joe would take Suzy out this evening. She had been trying to figure out for the past few days what she could do to take her mind off the inevitable. She couldn't bear staying home to wait for him to show up after the date. She decided to call her Nana and see what she was doing this evening. Maybe a movie would be something to do to pass the time away.

"Isn't Joe home on Fridays?" her grandmother asked.

"Yes, he is but he has things to do and I thought we could see a movie together."

"I close up at 8 PM on Fridays and the movies usually start about that time. Why don't you come to my place and we can visit, talk, and snack on some goodies. We can stand each other's company for a few hours."

"I'll be over so expect me around nine. Let's have one of those dip parties that we used to have when I was little. I'll bring a couple of dips and some chips. You furnish the ice cream and toppings."

"I had almost forgotten about those little parties, it'll be fun." The women hung up and Pam started thinking about which dips to take. Guacamole, onion dip, salsa, and chips should do the trick. She would do anything to keep her mind off Suzy. Joe was getting both cars washed this morning and trying to keep busy himself. He wasn't as nervous as she was over the impending date.

She was making the bed when the phone rang. It was Chris. "Hey, can you talk, Mary, or is Joseph hanging out in the stable this fine morning?" He asked her.

"I can talk because he's in the village washing the donkeys this morning."

"Hey, that was pretty good. I was wondering, if you would ever get your sense of humor back. I miss going back and forth with you. The reason I'm calling is I saw Joe a little earlier go into the Snoop Shop downtown. I actually saw him get out of his car and go inside."

"If you're talking about Jake's office, they're friends."

"That may be so but Jake is gay and I thought Joe was straight."

"You're joking, Chris, are you not?"

"If you think all gay men are plain looking and act like women, you're wrong. There are some good looking hunks in the gay world. Jake and I used to be a couple in fact. He was too good looking for my taste and very popular in the gay community."

"I can't believe this. I'm sure Joe has no clue about Jake."

"I was just wondering why Joe was going in there?"

"He has some legitimate business with Jake and I don't wish to discuss it."

"Jake was getting into trouble at the police department which is why he quit and started his own business," Chris told her in a very serious tone. "It was a very hush-hush situation. I've known him a long time and we were very close."

"I believe you but I don't know what to say."

"I know he does a lot of spying shit so is that why Joe is there?"

"I'm not saying anything, it's Joe's business."

"Why do I have to have a friend, Pamela, such as yourself, who won't ever tell me a damn thing?"

"I can talk about my business but not Joe's."

"You and Joe are together and you should have the same business."

"He tells Jules everything."

"What do you mean everything?"

"I know why he's seeing Jake because Jules told me. I was just trying to get it out of you. You wouldn't talk to me, if you were tortured first."

"So, Chris, tell me all about our business?"

"He's trying to get stuff on Suzy so if the baby is his, he can get it away from her. You two can raise it. I've got to hand to you, Pam, that's a noble thing to do. He should get on his hands and knees everyday and thank God he has you. You shouldn't have to raise his bastard child because he couldn't keep from screwing the town tramp."

"Why do you even ask me questions when you know everything?" Pam was getting ticked and it was showing in her voice.

"You chose to hook up with Joe and you've inherited all his problems. He has more baggage than the LA airport has on a Friday night. All it took was a wink from him and you got hooked. Is he the first guy who ever winked at you? No one would blame you, if you bowed out and left his ass. If you stick by him, your whole life will be nothing but a bumpy ride. He's the type of guy who'll always live on the very edge. You'll never have stability and the happy life you're looking for. You can't deny that you're looking for the good life."

"Chris, it's rare when the good life is handed to a person. Most things have to be earned and some things are worth waiting for. Are you happy with your life because you have such doubts about mine?"

"Not really but I have an excuse for just living from day to day."

"What's the excuse? Are you a private person yourself deep down? The same thing you accuse me of all the time?"

"I'm not ready to say but you'll know real soon. I'll let you go, Pamela, and just think about your life and your future. She, now, knew that Joe told Jules everything. He warned her about talking to Chris and Jules but it was okay, if he talked. She needed to keep busy. She made salsa and would make the onion dip and guacamole just before leaving for her Nana's. All that Chris revealed to her kept going over in her head.

Joe came back later and she pretended everything was fine. She didn't want to screw up any investigation or be accused of doing so. "Ken saw me at the car wash and stopped by to talk. He wants to play doubles tomorrow morning. You promised you would the next time."

"I'll go with you and I'm not responsible for the way I play."

"We'll help you and won't mind at all."

"Is Jake going to be outside of Suzy's listening to what's going on inside?"

"Yes, he has a van that he uses and he'll listen and record out on the street."

"When are you going to get wired?"

"He's coming by here to hook me up before I go to Suzy's."

"I guess you can't very well get naked or she'll see the wire."

"I told you I would not sleep with her."

"I hope that's true, Joe, because I refuse to share you with anyone. I was thinking we could have a late lunch or early dinner out somewhere, if you don't mind? Nana and I are having some chips and dip at her place at nine. I can't stay home wondering what you're doing all evening."

Later in the afternoon they went to the New Horizon's for their meal. Neither one was very talkative. They were both thinking about what the evening would bring.

Around eight she started making the dips to take to her grandmother's. As soon as she finished making one, he would have to taste test it. The doorbell rang and he let Jake into the apartment. He brought in the wire and explained the whole thing to Joe. He helped put the wire on him. She stayed in the kitchen but she could hear a little bit of what was going on. When she thought Jake was getting ready to leave she went into the living room and joined them. "I'll be by the office in the early afternoon to listen to the tape," Pam told him.

"It should be ready to listen to by then," Jake said. Joe said nothing. She went back into the kitchen and Joe walked over to her. She was putting the dip and chips into a box to take with her.

"I guess this is it," he told her. She nodded her head. "I don't know when I'll be home but I don't think it'll be more than a few hours." She lowered her eyes when he said how long he would be.

"I don't want you to be upset this evening. I'm nervous as hell but I want you to trust me and believe in me. I hope this will work and we can win in the long run." Pam went into his arms and hugged him tightly.

"You know I trust you but I don't trust her at all. She's had several days to plan her strategy for tonight and she won't go quietly." She kissed him and he kissed her long and hard. He told her again not to worry and he left the apartment. She was out the door practically on his heels with the box of goodies.

She was soon at her grandmother's door ringing the doorbell. "It's nice to see you, Pam, come in and let's eat. I've been waiting for you and I didn't eat any dinner."

"Joe and I ate a late lunch or an early dinner but I didn't eat too much." She spread the dips out on the coffee table and they started digging in.

"You make the best guacamole and what do you put in it?"

"Besides the mashed avocados, finely chopped sweet onions, tomatoes, chili's, a few shakes of garlic salt, and a little lemon juice. Keep the pit in the bowl and it won't turn dark."

"It's so delicious." They talked about the nursery business and Pam told her some stories on Chris and his antics at work.

"He sounds like a kick in the pants to work with, Lee said."

"Oh, he is and I don't know how he comes up with so much all the time."

He would love your house and the 50's memorabilia you have all around."

"You should bring him over sometime to meet me and look around." It was getting harder for Pam to make small talk because she was wondering about Joe. Her mind would not stop wondering about what he may or may not be doing. She looked at the clock and it was almost 11 PM.

"I'm ready for a little ice cream, Nana. I need vanilla ice cream with chocolate fudge syrup poured over it. Also, some nuts and cool whip over the top of it all."

"Okay, two grand sundaes coming up." Her grandmother went into the kitchen to fix the sundaes. She soon came back with two heaping bowls of calories.

"I'm going to try and eat this but I don't know, if I'll be able to." Pam dug in but only ate half and complained about being overstuffed. She helped her Nana clean up the food and told her she had to leave.

"We should do this another time, Pam, as I've enjoyed this time with you."

"Yes we can and I'll call you soon." Pam left and drove straight home. If she knew where Suzy lived, she'd drive by and see, if his car was still there. It was best she didn't know. She would probably break in on them and ruin everything.

Pam got home and took her nightly shower. She debated whether to stay up or go to bed and read. She decided to try reading, in order, to get sleepy. The sweet concoction she ate had her wired and she didn't know how long it would take her to relax. It was getting close to midnight when she reached over and turned out the light.

Later he came home and climbed into bed. She glanced at the digital clock and saw that the time was 1:30. It made her upset all the more but she didn't want to confront him about it tonight. Tomorrow she would listen to the tape and find out exactly what took place. She was now wondering, if that was the right thing for her to do. It didn't sound like she trusted him at all and she didn't like that thought.

Chapter 22

It was a real nice sunny day and perfect for tennis. This would only last for the daytime as the first rainfall of the season was scheduled to come into the area in the evening. She could get a good workout on the courts before listening to the tapes. They were suppose to be at Ken's at 9:30. This would be her first exposure to playing with her friends. Joe didn't get up until nine so he hurried to shower and get ready. She had dressed in white shorts and a white top waiting for him to finish getting ready. He came out of the bathroom and he looked surprised when he saw her. "You mean you own a tennis outfit?"

"I've had it for a long time so I might as well wear it." He looked to her like he may have been drinking last night and that didn't sit right with her either. He was, obviously, not going to start a conversation about the past evening. Her curiosity got the best of her on the drive over to Ken's. "Something must have happened last night so would you like to tell me about it?"

"Nothing happened and since you plan on listening to the tapes today, you can hear for yourself."

"I didn't get a good morning, how are you, or kiss my ass when I got up and we usually acknowledge each other's presence in the morning."

"Good morning, Pamela, how are you on this fine day?"

"You can kiss my ass, Joseph," she said wishing she had not even come with him. She was not going to talk with him nor acknowledge his smartass attitude.

They arrived at Ken's and started hitting the ball around some to loosen up. Joe started telling her about serving and keeping score. "You don't have to do this, Joe, I can play."

"I didn't think you could since you never join us."

"I was asked, if I could play and I said I played in high school and college. You were there and you heard me."

"I thought you meant you played occasionally so are you trying to tell us you've played on a team."

"Yes, I have been on teams before, would you like me to serve first?" She dazzled them with her performance. Ken couldn't even keep up with her. Her backhand was her strongest swing and she used it often. She felt invigorated when they finished playing. Ken had lunch served on a small round table under an umbrella. It was very nice. Julie had been rather quiet during the matches. Pam thought she might be a little jealous of her playing skills. She liked tennis, she was good, and they would have to accept that or not ask her to play anymore. Pam was still hurting from Joe talking to Julie about all their personal stuff. She would never do that to him. "Ken, did you know Jake when he worked for The Department?" Pam asked.

"No, he was before my time but I've heard some things about him."

"How do you know him Pam because he left before you started with the Department?" Julie asked her.

"I don't really know him but I've heard about him. He used to be Chris's boyfriend and he mentioned Jake to me the other day."

"No way," said Joe and Ken at the same time.

"It's true. The reason he quit being a cop was to avoid a big scandal over his sexual preferences."

"Pam's right, I heard the same thing from Chris," Julie told them. The two guys were stunned and didn't know what to say further.

"He told me not to expect all gays to be plain looking and feminine acting."

"Jake is certainly the opposite of that," Julie said, "what a waste for some young lady looking for love."

"Is that what you did, Jules when you first met Jake?" Pam asked. Julie was not happy at her question. Pam was in a vindictive mood and she couldn't help it.

"He wasn't my type because I was looking for someone like Ken."

"You went after Joe so I thought Jake might have been on your list too."

"I don't know what your problem is today, Pamela? You need to get off your high horse and be a little nicer to your friends." Ken was not looking too good knowing that Julie and Joe were friends and she had gone after Joe too.

"Chris told me a lot of things yesterday especially personal stuff on myself that I discuss with no one. I wonder how he found out so much? Could it be that my good friend, Jules, and my boyfriend, Joe, talk all the time about my personal stuff?"

"Is this correct, Jules, that you share everything with Chris?" Joe asked.

"I talk to him and he said he wouldn't tell anyone."

"Did you tell him not to tell me?" Pam asked. Julie didn't answer her. "Joe, are you ready to go because I am?" They took off after thanking Ken for the nice lunch.

Joe drove straight to Jake's office and they went in. Joe was a little on the cold side to Jake. He had the tape recorder all set up and handed her head phones to listen in private. She stayed in his inner office and they were out front in the waiting room. Suzy started in talking about Pam and had he gotten rid of her yet. He admitted he had. She asked him questions about where Pam was staying and things like that. It was hard for Pam to listen to him say so many lies but she knew that was part of the game. Suzy gave him a beer when they first got into her apartment. She hinted that she wanted to give him a blow job right away. He told her they had to talk things over first. It was getting harder to listen. He asked a lot of questions about her pregnancy, her due date, among other things. They each started drinking a second beer and Suzy again wanted sex with him. She was pleading really good and then Pam heard a blip like noise on the tape. She knew something had been erased. Pam would know that sound anywhere. She took the headphones off and walked into the waiting room. "This was fine and dandy but I want to listen to the original tape. This one has parts that were erased." Jake and Joe both looked startled that she would know that had happened. Joe nodded for Jake to fix it. "On the original tape just fast forward it to where she gave Joe a second beer and she was trying to get him into bed. I don't need to listen to the first part again." Joe was not looking good and she knew something did happen with him and Suzy. Jake was soon ready and she listened to the rest. Pam was right. Suzy lifted up her skirt and showed Joe her private parts and begged the hell out of him to have sex. She even groped him a couple of times and said he was hard and ready for her. Pam dumped the headset on the table and ran out of the room. The tears were falling fast and Joe grabbed her around the middle with one arm before she could get out the door. He held her as she cried. Jake went into his office and closed the door. She managed to get in control of herself as Joe tried to soothe her. She left his hold on her and they walked out together. They got into the car and he sat there for a few minutes.

"I did not have sex with her last night. I know she tried really hard but it didn't happen. She lifted up her skirt and I wouldn't even look at her. She did grabbed me a few times but I wasn't getting hard because of her. This may be difficult for you to understand but guys get hard real often. It happens throughout the day at any time. This is how we are made and we have no control over it."

They were soon home. Pam had read this about men and she knew he was right. They got inside the apartment and she went into his arms. They kissed for awhile and their tongues were both hot after each other. He found her nipples and she his penis. They went into the bedroom and he lifted her up onto the top of her low dresser. She removed her shorts and panties and he found her with his penis. He grabbed her ass and lifted her off the dresser and she held on with her legs wrapped around him. His thrusts were fast and she felt so good. It was a new experience and one they both enjoyed. She got dressed and they both went into the living room to talk. "I want you to know how much I do care about you, Pam. There's not another women on earth that I want to be with and I mean that."

"I know you feel that way and I do, too."

"I doubt, if you heard the very end of the tape when I told her off and good. I'm not going to have Jake investigate anymore as I don't care to do anymore business with him. He didn't find much on her so we'll have to wait until the baby is born to know anymore. Do you think you can stand by me for that long?"

"You know I will and beyond. I truly love you and I know you do me."

"I don't think I had sex with her and I think she's trying to trick me into being with her forever. What a horrible thought that is to me. About me and Jules, I had no idea she would tell this latest thing about investigating Suzy to Chris. When you talk with a good friend you don't think you have to tell them not to tell anyone else. It should be a natural thing. I won't be talking to her anymore. I have my girl and my best friend

here and I don't need anyone else." Pam gave him a big smile.

"I'll always want to be with you, my Joe." He hugged her once more. The rest of the day was nice for the couple. She cooked him a pot roast for dinner and they had a quiet evening together. They held each other on the couch while watching some TV. They heard the rain arrive as it hit the window pane just before they went to bed. "I guess we'll never know, if Suzy was the one who did those bad deeds."

"Jake couldn't find a thing to link her to any of them. I would think, if she was the culprit, he would have found something."

"It's hard to think it could be a friend of ours because I don't know anyone who would stoop so low. I hope nothing else happens. I'm afraid the further things go along and she doesn't get you, she may try something really bad."

"Let's not worry about it because it may be over with. I want to take care of you and I don't want anything to happen to you. Does that sound like I love you?"

"It sure does and I love you, too."

Halloween Eve morning Chris called Pam. "Come on, Pam, let's dress up. It'll be a kick in the ass. We're already planning a pot luck party at work to celebrate and we should dress appropriately. You're off today so go and pick something up and join in the fun. I'm willing to show up at work on my day off; you should agree to wear a costume. You know how bad that is so help me out."

"I don't know, Chris, I'm not exactly a flamboyant type of woman."

"You could do something simple like a hooker or come as Mary since I call you her so often. It might be hard to rent a donkey though. I wouldn't expect you to go as Lady Godiva or anything risqué like that. Jules and Dave are going to dress up so you'll be the only one not joining in on all the fun. We haven't even had a pot luck in ages."

"Okay, I'll come as someone other than myself. What are you suppose to be bringing for the pot luck?"

"I'm bringing some hot chili beans. I haven't made them before but a friend gave me the recipe. I can't wait for your enchilada casserole that's so good. Jules is bringing taco salad, salsa, and sodas. Dave is bringing guacamole, chips and a Halloween cake."

"It's a good thing you're giving me a one day notice to get a costume together."

"Pam, I knew you would come through for the old gang. We'll have a ball. We can go to the Den after work to dazzle all the customers."

"Do you have a costume, Chris?"

"It's a secret and no one is suppose to tell what they're wearing. We can all surprise each other."

"If you plan on dazzling people, it must be some kind of shiny costume."

"Do not look for me as J. Edgar Hoover or any other such person. I'm not saying anymore either or I may let it slip out."

"I'll be there in costume and you may not know me," she jokingly told him.

"Those eyes will give you away unless you're going to wear colored contacts."

"Well, I have to go to town to buy food and put together a costume so I'll see you tomorrow at work." Chris was all hyper about the big bash and she didn't mind joining in. She thought it could be fun. She didn't know what Joe would think about her wearing a costume.

She picked up the phone to call her Nana. "Nana, we're having a Halloween Party at work tomorrow and Chris is insisting I dress up like everyone else. Do you have any ideas for a costume for me.?"

"Do I ever and it's in my cedar chest. Did you ever see the movie "Sunset Boulevard?"

"No, Nana, I haven't."

"How about the old Carol Burnett Shows when she played the character Norma Desmond from that movie? She would come slinking down the staircase with her long cigarette holder and her eyes wide open looking like a wild thing."

"I do remember that and she was hilarious."

"I have a costume that includes the cigarette holder, cloche hat, and dress. You just need to paint around your eyes and use lots of red lipstick and red rouge or blush as you call it today."

"It sounds just what I need, I'll be over later to pick it up."

"I have a better idea. Come over tomorrow about an hour before you leave for work and I'll fix you up in it. I can do the make up and all of that for you. I want to see you in it and take some picture, too."

"I'll see you about 12:45 tomorrow, Nana. Thanks and goodbye."

Joe walked in as Pam was hanging up the phone. "You're looking a little excited," he told her.

"Chris called and is planning a costume party along with the pot luck tomorrow. I didn't want to join in but everyone else is so I agreed. I called Nana and she has a costume she wants me to wear so I'm going over there tomorrow before I go to work. She'll fix me all up. Chris wants us all to go to the Den after work, of course."

"I guess we can do that, Pam, if you won't mind going?"

"I have to go to the store and buy the ingredients for the enchilada casserole. I'll make a big one for work and a smaller one for us. Is there anything you would like?"

"Yes, I want you right now. I love you so much and it's hard for me to stay away from you." He pulled her close to him. She reached down and touched his crotch while she kissed him. She gave him a sexy smile as she pushed him towards the bedroom.

The next morning she was up bright and early to fix him breakfast and start making the casseroles. It was hard to believe it was Halloween and the last day of October. She remembered to put their clocks back an hour before going to bed. It would get dark an hour earlier this evening. She didn't like that. Pam preferred more daylight in the evening hours. She put the casserole together and planned on baking it off at work an hour before it was time to eat. Joe could enjoy the small one for lunch the next day. She left for her Nana's after giving him instructions to drop the casserole off at the Center and put it into the refrigerator.

Pam was soon at her grandmother's who was waiting for her. She had make up all over the dining room table and the costume draped over a chair. "You're looking rather happy today for someone who didn't want to dress up."

"Nana, you inspired me when you told me about this costume." Lee immediately started dressing Pam and putting make up on her face.

"How's Joseph treating you?"

"He's still great and I love him so much. I can see our love growing all the time."

"I won't be terribly happy for you until I see a ring on your finger. Do you ever talk about marriage?"

"We have a few times but why be in a big hurry. We're enjoying each other so much." She finished Pam's make up and held up a mirror for her to look into. Pam was amazed at the transformation. Lee got the long cigarette holder and proceeded to slink around the house showing Pam how to act like the Norma Desmond character. Pam took the holder and did the same slinking around movements and gestures. She made her grandmother laugh.

"Maybe you should have been a movie star, Pamela, because you're good. You definitely have a movie star type name. Pamela Austin sounds like you belong in Hollywood." Pam shook her head at her grandmother's words.

She left in full costume and arrived in the parking lot wondering, if she would run into anyone. She checked the gold cloche on her head in the car mirror and held the cigarette holder in one hand as she exited the vehicle. Pam entered the building and started walking down the hallway. The locker door opened and out came two officers. She made wild eye gestures and flicked the cigarette holder their way. They both laughed. She got to the briefing room and saw Joe sitting at a table. She slinked into the room right towards him. Her eyes were moving all around and she was flicking the cigarette holder. He grinned at her. She walked over to him pretending to take a big puff on the holder and with her other hand opened his uniform pocket and pretended to be flicking ashes into it. She then turned and slinked out of the room. The guys were all laughing at her. She was the first one to arrive at the Center and the day dispatchers were getting a kick out of her antics. Julie showed up dressed as the witch from the Wizard of Oz. Dave came as a hobo complete with a half burned cigar hanging from the corner of his mouth. They were all acting up. They finally sat down at their positions. Joe came in to visit before he went out on the road.

"You're good in that role, Pam. I saw Carol Burnett do it but you're great yourself."

"Well, thanks, you should have seen Nana showing me what to do. She was good herself. The old gal could really move around."

"I wonder what Chris will come as?" Julie asked.

"Probably a fruitcake," Joe said. Pam was not happy with his comment. Joe tried to make some more small talk but she wouldn't say anything.

"You're coming to the Den after work, aren't you, Joe?" Julie asked him. "The party is moving over there."

"I wouldn't miss it for the world," Joe told her. Chris told them he would be at the Center at 7:00 in time to eat. They were all curious about what costume he would choose. Pam put the casserole in the oven at 6 PM to cook slowly. Just before seven, Lucy and Ricky came wandering into the Center. Chris was Lucy and Sam was Ricky. Chris had a red headed wig on and was dressed to look exactly like Lucille Ball. He wore a black dress with white polka dots and heels. Sam had a Ricky mask on with a black suit and carrying bongo drums. He introduced Sam to Dave.

"Pam, I cannot believe you as Norma Desmond and you act just like her."

"My Nana had this costume and she fixed me up in it." Chris and Sam got the food set up on a table they moved in from the briefing room. They all pigged out and had a good time. Ken and Joe managed to come during the shift and enjoyed the food, too. The radio wasn't as bad as they thought it might be. It could be because Halloween was on a Sunday night this year.

After the shift was over they all headed for the Den. The night was balmy, misty, and warm. They wouldn't need a jacket to wear and cover up their costumes. How she was enjoying the Southern Coast of California. They agreed to meet in the parking lot and the group would walk in together. The Den wasn't very busy either and their booth was waiting for them. Pam didn't mind going there dressed in disguise. If Suzy was there, she would not recognize Pam. The four ordered beers and waited for Ken and Joe to show up. The waitress was trying to figure out who they all were. Suzy came out of the ladies room and headed for the small booth. Joe came through the entrance and Pam watched to see what he would do. He passed Suzy who called out to him but he didn't stop until he came to their booth. He sat next to Pam and she gave his hand a squeeze.

They looked into each other's eyes.

Ken showed up shortly after and sat next to Julie. "Jules, is this the dark side of you that I haven't seen before?" he asked her.

"Wait until midnight and we'll see what she turns into," Chris added. "I hope you won't sizzle down to nothing right in front of our eyes. I'll throw my glass of beer on you and see what happens." Chris got out of the booth and went to the rest room. On his way back Suzy said something to him. The friends were wondering what was going on. He came back to their table with a smug look on his face. "Your ex-girlfriend would like to see you, Joseph. She asked me to give you the message. I can't help it, if she keeps stopping me to give me messages directed at you." Joe glared at Chris but didn't say anything.

Pam was ready to go home as Suzy always did this to her. "Joe, I'm going home, if you don't mind."

"Do whatever you would like," he told her.

"I was hoping you would come too but it's okay." She didn't understand why he wanted to stay longer. She needed to talk this over with him as she didn't think it was right. Pam said goodbye to everyone and walked out. Suzy got up and followed her out the door as the friends watched. Joe then got up to go out and see what was going on.

"Hey, bitch hold on," Suzy said as Pam got outside. "Are you going to a fire or something?" Pam stopped and waited for Suzy to catch up to her. "I don't think you quite understand what's going on between myself and Joe. I told you I have a tape and now I will send it for sure. You think I'm full of bullshit but I have him on tape screwing me and I would like you to see it. So look for it real soon because it'll be coming in the mail." Suzy turned and walked back towards the building. Joe came out to see Pam getting into her car and he stopped to talk with Suzy. Pam knew he would never stop having contact with the tramp. Pam left as soon as she could. She got home and went through all her rituals and Joe did not show up.

Later on in bed while she was trying to sleep he came in. He got in but didn't offer to hug her and it hurt her. After she thought he was asleep, she moved over in bed and hugged him. He laid his hand on her arm that was around him and she knew he was loving her in his own way.

Chapter 23

Within the next week was the presidential election and Chris told her the country was heading in the right direction when Bush was elected President for a second term. He told her all about staying up all night to watch the returns only to find out, when he woke up on the couch the next morning, there was still no winner. Pam voted and was glad Bush won. Her personal life was taking its toll on her wellbeing.

Pam waited for the tape to come from Suzy but it didn't arrive. She figured Suzy had nothing to send. She wished the woman wouldn't keep bringing it up.

She decided to get her portrait done for Joe as one of her Christmas presents to him. She got Ken to make up an excuse to keep Joe busy the day she went for her sitting. He invited Joe over to look at a tool shed he was having built. He wanted Joe's advice, at least, that is what he told him. She had the pictures made and would have to wait a couple of weeks to pick out the best one.

Chris was getting sick more and more. She would call him at home from time to time. Joe did not know about the phone calls. They hadn't gone to the Den since Halloween. Not having to face Suzy was doing her some good. She knew he felt the same way. She figured Suzy was not going to give up on them. A week before Thanksgiving her Nana called to ask her again about plans for Thanksgiving. Lee had started putting pressure on them just after Halloween to have Thanksgiving with her. They both had to work the holiday and Lee would have everything ready to eat around noontime. Pam wanted to fix a dinner for Joe but hadn't made up her mind yet.

"We can go to your grandmother's on Thanksgiving. On Friday we're off and you can cook a small turkey for the two of us. I do like turkey and all the leftovers, if you don't mind doing the cooking," Joe said.

"You must be reading my mind because I've been thinking the same thing."

"So it is settled and we'll have two Thanksgivings."

"I'd like to invite Chris, Sam, Julie and Ken over on Friday to eat with us."

"Pam, I don't like entertaining fags over the holidays."

"They're human beings, Joe, and he's a good friend. Why can't you get past them being a couple?"

"I caught two guys going after each other in a bathroom once and it wasn't a pleasant thing to come across. It was disgusting then and it is now. We have an agreement about not being around them except for work and the Den."

"Jake was okay until you found out he's gay. The holidays aren't like regular days at all. Sam and Chris don't have relatives living here." Joe didn't say anything further and she dropped the subject.

She made two pecan pies and several loaves of pumpkin bread and froze them. She wouldn't have to be so busy on the holiday and could enjoy herself. They would be at Lee's on noon for the feast. Joe picked up a smaller turkey for them to cook the day after. She would also make a fruit salad with whipped cream and the turkey dressing the day before. She didn't want her Nana to have to do it all. She made a small loaf of pumpkin bread for Joe to enjoy "How come you never mentioned you were a good cook?" Joe asked after he had eaten a piece of pumpkin bread.

"I have to have some secrets from you." She grinned at him. "When you live amongst the giant redwood trees there isn't a lot one can do except fish, hunt, or cook. I hung out in the kitchen and even collected some good recipes. I think I got my cooking skills from Nana because mom didn't like to cook and it showed. I was hoping someday to meet a guy who I could love and cook for."

"I can't wait to taste that pecan pie and I hope you have found that guy. How come the first guy you were with didn't turn out to be the answer to your dreams? I can't imagine any guy not wanting to be with you."

"I thought he was when I first met him and I'm glad it didn't work out. I would never have left up there and I would never have found you."

"What did he do to turn you against him?" She didn't want to tell Joe the truth. "I'm just curious, Pam, he had to be the one to screw things up. You fell for the guy as a virgin and I can't imagine you cheating on him or doing something bad. Did he cheat on you?" She shrugged her shoulders. "Do you think, if you tell me, I'll be upset?"

"I don't know how you'll react?"

"I love you and nothing will stop me from loving you." The tears came as she stood looking at Joe.

"He came to my house and he'd been drinking. My family was out for the evening. We had words the day before because I saw him blatantly flirting with another female. On this particular day he told me he wanted sex and I told him no. He knocked me down and he had sex." Joe took her into his arms. She hugged Joe as if she would never let him go. "You're the only person who knows what happened, Joe."

"He should be in jail right now. That's why these guys are still out there doing their thing because you ladies won't press charges. I'm sorry I shouldn't be preaching."

"I didn't have a chance. His dad owned more than one business in town. Later when everyone found out we had broken up, I started hearing other stories about him. He really liked to go after virgins so I was probably a notch on his bed post. I took a long shower after he left and tried to forget that it happened. I knew when I met you that you would never do anything like that to me so I fell hard for you."

"You're so right, I'll never hurt you. You mean so much to me, Pam." They both got ready for work and left the apartment. She had to drop the turkey stuffing at her Nana's so she could start cooking the turkey early in the morning.

She arrived at the office the same time Chris did and they walked in together. They entered the Center and ran into Joe. He motioned for Pam to go into the kitchen. They both went into each other's arms, as if on cue.

"Pam, I was thinking on the way to work about your first guy and right now, I wish I could take you home, lay down with you, and love you all over."

"I would like that so much, too."

"We have a big date as soon as we get off." He kissed her gently and gave her a big wink. She slapped him on the ass as he walked away from her. He jumped a little and turned and shook his finger at her. They both had big smiles. She grabbed her headset and went in to work the radio. Mike gave her a big leering grin.

"I thought this wouldn't be a bad day to work but the locals have started out early drinking and beating on each other," Mike advised Pam. "We've had several domestic calls but no one has been killed yet."

"Oh, the blessed family is together for the holidays and they're at each other's throats," Chris said. "It sounds like the ones we had when I was little." Julie arrived and the swing shift was primed and ready to take care of the community. An hour into the shift, Chris received an urgent 9-1-1 call of shots fired. He got all the information he could from a neighbor in the area where the shots were heard. Pam gave the call to Joe and sent another unit to respond and back him up. She gave him all the information she had. Chris kept the neighbor on the line to try and get further reports if he could. These were the calls that Pam dreaded the most. The address was in a low income area and one of the red houses in the community. Red was used as a code to denote a residence where there was a history of drugs, weapons, or gang activity. She advised Joe and the other unit en route that it was a code red response. The two officers arrived at the scene and Pam's heart went up into her throat. Chris still had the neighbor on the line but no additional information had been forthcoming. The three dispatchers waited to hear a report from one of the officers. They were silent. Pam and Chris looked at each other and knew what each other was thinking. Someone keyed their mike and they heard rustling sounds over the air.

"Send a canine unit," Joe said to Pam. He was breathing heavy and she dispatched a dog unit to go to his location. They could hear bits and pieces of the radio traffic but not enough to know what was really going on. Joe came on the air and said, "Code four, Mission Park, we have one in custody." She repeated, his code four. The three dispatchers looked at each other and let out a sigh of relief. The rest of the shift was relatively quiet. She was hoping he would come into the office during the shift but it didn't happen. He knew she would be waiting for him out back when his shift was over.

The swing shift group was relieved for the day and she hurried out back to wait for Joe. A couple of patrol cars came in and it wasn't him. He soon pulled into the back and saw her standing there. She slowly walked over to his car and he got out. The tears had filled her eyes and he looked at her. He took her into his arms and comforted her. The sergeant pulled in and saw the two of them. Joe broke away from her and told her he'd be home real soon. She left and hoped she didn't get him into trouble. She got home, took her shower, and waited. He had time to come home but he was still not there.

An hour after she had arrived he was at the door. "Please tell me I didn't get you into trouble?"

"Yes, you did but I understand why you did it."

"It's not right that you got into trouble for something I did. Joe, it's so hard sending you to those calls and not being able to react. Can't cops be human beings and act like they are?"

"He's not going to write me up this time because you're on probation but he will next time."

"There won't be a next time. I'll just pretend I don't love you at work. I'll save my emotions up for the privacy of our home and fuck them all for having ice cubes in their hearts. The back of the office hardly qualifies as a public place. I would know better than to hug you where there were civilians."

"You can hug me now and no one will know or care." She flew into his arms.

"I know one thing, Pam, you're the calmest sounding dispatcher on the radio. It doesn't matter what's going down your voice stays smooth and professional. I knew you were upset but it never showed at all. You're so good." She kissed him on the mouth and around his neck. He responded the same way. She pulled away from him.

"I'm just glad that I have you here to kiss like this." She kissed him some more. They went into the bedroom and stood next to the bed. He untied her robe and his hands found her rear end. He squeezed and caressed her all over.

"You have the nicest skin all over your body." She was trying to get his shirt and pants off. "I'll help you," he said. He stood naked in front of her and she flung her robe off her shoulders. His hands were on her back holding her body next to his. She put her hands between their two bodies and caressed him until he was ready.

"I like feeling you come alive in my hands," she told him. They went down to the bed and finished their love making.

"Pam, this just gets better all the time."

"You know why, don't you?"

"Yes, because our love is growing all the time or that's how I feel."

"You're right and we're getting more comfortable with each other too."

"One more thing, I found out today that you're a good cook and that is a big plus."

"We've known each other for almost six months and I haven't cooked much for you and I'll try and do better. The biggest problem is, we always work swings and I can't cook dinner very often."

"Maybe we should try and work the day shift," he told her.

"You could work days, I'm sure but I have a long way to go before I have any seniority."

"Did you take the pecan pie out of the freezer this morning before we left for work?"

"I sure did and would you like a piece?"

"You don't even have to ask," he told her. "It's my favorite pie, if I never told you before. You can make one for me anytime." He gave her a big grin.

"I'll just do that if it'll make you happy and I get to see that sexy smile you just gave me. Let's raid the refrigerator. I would prefer some fruit salad. I didn't even snack at work this evening so no wonder I am hungry."

"I didn't eat either. Just think we'll have nice a dinner for two days in a row and plenty of leftovers." He put on his briefs and Pam donned her robe and out to the kitchen they went. They were so very happy with each other as they snacked on pecan pie and fruit salad. She did not want the good times together to ever end.

The next morning they had bagels and coffee on the patio. They were in full anticipation for the big meal at noon. It was a cool morning but not cool enough to keep them inside. It wouldn't take long for the coffee to warm them up. This was a sunshine filled Southern California day. They talked about the "shots fired" call some more. A call like that always caused the adrenalin to flow a little more and it would be the talk of the office for days.

After drinking coffee, Pam got into the shower. It wasn't long before Joe joined her. "How nice," she told him when he opened the door. They washed each other and got out and dried each other off.

"This is such a nice way to start the holiday," she told him as he found her nipples with his mouth. Her breasts were so sensitive and he knew just how much. She enjoyed

making love and being close to him often. She was hot in a hurry. She got on top of him and rode him back and forth until he groaned and then got quiet. They nestled for awhile longer in each other's arms as they enjoyed their closeness very much.

They got ready to leave for Lee's and packed up the pumpkin bread, pie, and fruit salad. They would leave from her grandmother's to go directly to work. Her Nana was cooking a rather large turkey just because she always did. She made a lot of different dishes with the leftover turkey meat. They could smell the turkey as they made it up the walkway to Lee's front door. "I'm so hungry already," Joe said to her.

"Me, too, and we'll be enjoying it before long."

"Can't I have a little piece of pie now?"

"What and spoil the looks of it for the grand meal? I don't think so, my Joe."

Her Nana greeted them and told Pam where to put her food. They passed the dining room table going into the kitchen and it was full of place settings. Pam looked at Joe and raised her eyebrows. "I thought we were your only guests, Nana?"

"I wanted to invite a few people over. Why spoil a holiday being alone when friends should be asked to join in." Pam thought it must be people from the nursery. There were seven settings so the guests would take up four seats. It wasn't long before Julie and Ken came up to the front door and Joe let them in.

"What a surprise? I didn't know you guys were coming."

"Lee called us the other day and thought you two might like to have some friends to share the meal with," Julie told him."

"Hey, that's great, the more the merrier."

"Jules and I get to have two meals today, Ken told him. My folks invited her to join them and we always eat in the evening."

"Oh, you get to spend time with Ken's family today, how nice?" Pam said.

"Yes, I do and they're so much like Ken and it should be fun," Julie said. They had brought a couple of bottles of wine for the dinner. Pam went into the kitchen to help her Nana. She promptly gave Pam an apron to put on.

"When the turkey is out and on the platter would you make the gravy, Pam? Your gravy is the best. You know that's the only reason I invited you," she said with a chuckle. "I can make it but not as good as you can."

"Sure I will, Nana, and I'll take the turkey out for you."

"Joe can do that dear. It's a 24 pound bird and he should be able to handle it. I took the cover off the roaster to brown the turkey a little more."

From the commotion in the living room it appeared someone else had joined the group. Lee went out to greet more guests and Pam was watching the vegetables cooking on top of the stove. Her Nana would mash potatoes while she made the gravy. The rolls would be browning in the oven. Joe came into the kitchen with a disgusted look on his face.

"What's wrong, Joe?"

"You know damn well what's wrong. She invited that fag and his fag girlfriend and you must have known about it."

"I knew nothing, Joe because she didn't share any of this with me. I thought it was just the three of us."

"All you would have to do is drop her a little hint to get them invited."

"Joe, I did not do that. Why would you accuse me of lying when the day started out so great?"

"Why would she do this, if she doesn't even know Chris?"

"I don't know, Joe, I'll try and find out what's going on. No one has said anything to me about being invited."

Lee came back into the kitchen. "Joe, you're just the guy I want to see. Would you take the turkey out of the oven and put it on the platter for me?" He got the turkey onto the platter and immediately left the kitchen. Pam couldn't stop her tears as she made the gravy. She didn't know the others were coming but he thought she did. She knew the holiday was fucked up before it barely got started. She could hear Chris expounding on all the 50's memorabilia hanging on the walls. Her Nana came back in and mashed the potatoes. Pam started putting food into bowls for the table. She almost forgot the rolls in the oven but caught them just in time. They were a golden brown and looked good. Pam started carrying food to the table.

"Oh, my God, who do we have here, Betty Crocker in all her glory?" Chris said to her. "I've never seen an Elvis apron before," he added.

"At Nana's you never know who you're going to run into," Pam said to the new arrivals. Sam was taller than she remembered and he had a feminine air about him. He stood with his hands on his hips the way a woman would stand. He gave her a faint sounding hello. Seeing him in costume the last time could make a difference. Pam figured that Chris never stopped talking so Sam never got a chance to say very much.

"I do have a homey side so now you know." She was hoping nobody would notice she had been crying. Chris followed her into the kitchen.

"This house is fantastic, Pam, it's like a 50's museum."

"Nana has more stuff but she doesn't have room to display it all. She has a huge 45 RPM record collection and still has her old phonograph to play them on."

"Those should be worth something."

"I knew you would like the house so go into the bedrooms and look around." He left and she continued taking food to the dining room table. She took her apron off and announced that dinner was ready. Joe was being quiet sitting in a recliner in a corner. He got up to join the group at the table. He sat at one end of the table and she took a seat near the other end right between Chris and Julie. Her Nana was slicing the turkey with an electric knife across from her. Pam started passing plates of food to the others. The meal was quite festive as Chris was on a roll with his comments about the house and the group in general. Her grandmother asked him many questions about his life and where his family was this holiday. Pam was quiet and so was Joe. She couldn't believe that their first Thanksgiving together would end up being awful

"Pamela, you are being so quiet today how come?" Chris asked her.

"Christopher, I'm always quiet, you just haven't noticed before."

"This meal is great but the gravy is to die for," Mrs. Duncan," Chris said.

"I can't take credit for that, Pam is the gravy maker in this family. She's been making it since she was quite young and it's always delicious."

"So, my friend, what is your secret?" Chris asked.

"I make it like everyone else. I just add a little love and it makes all the difference in the world." The tears came to her eyes and she couldn't stop them. She excused herself and left the room. Joe followed her into the spare bedroom. He took her into his arms.

"I'm sorry I didn't mean to ruin the day. I thought you had something to do with this since you wanted to invite them to our meal."

"I promised you I would do what you asked me to do."

"Here I stand in front of a huge poster of Marilyn Monroe trying to show her ass and I would rather have you in my arms then all the Monroe's of the world."

"You're just saying that to make me feel good."

"You're more beautiful, you have a better figure, and that's the truth." Joe kissed her gently and she felt good once more.

"It's nice of you to think I'm beautiful because you're the only who counts. Joe, I have never been so happy."

"That makes two of us. I wish we could make future plans because I feel you're being cheated." They went back into the dining room. Her Nana was clearing plates to make room for the pies. They had her pecan, two pumpkin, and a chocolate cream pie to pick from. Joe took a piece of pecan. He rolled his eyes at her and gave her a big yum

after his first bite. She would have to make them often.

"This is beyond delicious so did you add that little extra ingredient to the pie like you did the gravy?"

"I sure did." She gave him a smile and helped herself to pumpkin, her favorite pie. When the dessert was eaten, Pam jumped up to clear the dishes.

"No, you can't do that, Pam," her grandmother said to her. "Julie agreed to help me clean up after you all leave for work. Go into the living room and relax before you have to leave." She and Joe sat on the couch and he took her hand and held it. It made her feel so good. They all sat around for just a little while and Joe had to leave since his shift started earlier than the dispatchers. He gave Pam a kiss. He thanked Lee and gave her a little hug. This pleased Pam very much. She followed him to the door and told him to be careful on patrol. He ran his index finger down the length of her nose.

"It's nice to have a beautiful woman worry about me once in a while."

"I don't just worry once in awhile but all the time."

"I know and I appreciate it." She gave him a big smile. Chris and Sam were the next ones to leave.

"Mrs. Duncan, thanks so much for inviting us, letting us share your great meal, and giving us a chance to see your precious memorabilia." He hugged Lee. Pam left soon after the two guys. She said goodbye to Julie, Ken and her Nana. She was happy that the day turned out well. She was looking forward to fixing a turkey and all the trimmings tomorrow afternoon. They would have good leftovers for awhile.

Chapter 24

They got through the Thanksgiving holiday very happy and eating good leftovers. Pam surprised Joe with a large pan full of turkey enchiladas. He ate most of them. Chris called in sick for two days at the beginning of the week. It didn't appear his illness was getting any better. Julie and Pam were still worrying about him. Pam and Joe were getting along better all the time. Staying away from the Den was helping their relationship. They knew Suzy would still have to be dealt with.

On Wednesday, December 1, they were talking about Christmas and how they would celebrate. This would be Pam's first Christmas on her own. She had recently started buying tree ornaments and other holiday decorations for their apartment. She was in her glory. This was her favorite time of year and she had the man of her dreams to share it with. She wondered what his Christmas present would be to her. "Are you one of those women who like a one theme Christmas or do you like different kinds of decorations? Joe asked her.

"I like old fashion decorations and all different kinds."

"I feel the same way. We had religious decorations only in our house, although, we were allowed a small tree on a stand in the living room. Mother found plenty of angels to put on the tree."

"I have to have a large tree and I hope you'll agree. We have the perfect large window to put it in front of. I like lots of lights, some steady burning and some blinking on and off. It'll be so nice. If you think the Thanksgiving food was grand, wait until you see what I can do for Christmas."

"I can see that I'm going to have to join a gym, if we're going to be a couple forever."

"What do you mean, if we're going to be a couple? I thought it was a done deal."

"Pam, we certainly are going to be a couple forever."

"I have to ask you something and I don't want you to get mad at me. I need to know, if Suzy's baby turns out to be your baby, what will you do?"

"Do you have to bring this up?"

"Yes, I do because it'll affect my life too."

"Do you think I'll dump you, if it's true?"

"I'll be honest with you, it has crossed my mind."

"You don't have very much faith in my love for you."

"It isn't about your faith it's about what she's going to try and do to us. If it's your baby and she says that you can't see it unless you live with her, what will you do? There's a very good chance she'll do this. She wants you and she'll not stop at anything to get you. I just want to know what will you do?"

"I'll not be with her because I want to spend the rest of my life with you."

"Thanks, Joe, I just needed to hear that."

"When do you want to get a tree?" He asked.

"Two weeks before Christmas is fine but I want to decorate the apartment right away. I made a list of things to buy. I sent away for a balsam fir wreath for the door and I want to find a special topper for the tree. What do you want Santa to bring you?"

"I was thinking of asking you the same thing."

"Joe, on Christmas Eve you can put a big red bow around your lovely jewels and lie under the tree. It'll be a perfect gift."

"You already have them so I'll come up with something really good. The perfect gift for a special lady. I'm getting some money out of the bank today to help pay for some the decorations. We're a team because when you're happy, I'm happy."

"You're pretty smart for a guy," she giggled. She laid her hand on the front of his pants and squeezed a little.

"Oh, getting me all excited before I leave for work is not very smart."

"I can't help it, Joe. If I get within a foot of you, I want to touch you and not just between your legs either. You do this to me all the time and I have no control. You shouldn't be so handsome, sexy, or appealing to me."

"You sounded like you really meant what you just said."

"You know I did with all my heart." He took her into his arms.

"I have to get going and you do in a few."

"We can have some fun tonight right after work." He kissed her and left.

The phone rang as she was going through a Christmas catalog. "Hello, Pam I had to call you with some good news."

"What's up, Nana?"

"I just talked with your mother and they're thinking about coming down for Christmas. I thought you would be pleased."

"Oh, yes I am and I'm glad you called to let me know. Mom mentioned to me the other day that dad was trying to get a few days off to come down."

"I have room for them so that won't be a problem. I haven't told them about you living with Joe so you should give that some thought."

"I certainly will and I hate to hang up but I have to leave for work. I'm stopping at the studio on my way to choose the picture I want to give Joe for Christmas. I hope they turned out nice." They said goodbye. Pam knew she had to tell her folks about living with Joe. She wanted them to know before they showed up. She got her purse, grabbed a salad out of the refrigerator, and left for work.

Pame stopped for a few minutes at the studio. She saw the photographer and she was surprised at the results. She picked out her favorite one to have done up and he would like it, too.

Chris was walking up the hallway ahead of her when she entered the office. She couldn't whistle so she didn't try and get his attention. He turned when he got to the Center's door and saw her coming towards him.

"Well, Miss Pam, how in the hell are you?"

"I was going to ask you the same thing."

"I think my ass died and went to hell or it feels like it did."

"It's hard to believe the doctors can't give you something to help you get through this." They were still standing at the door when Joe came out of the locker room. He didn't say anything but gave her an odd look. She and Chris went into the Center. Marge came into the kitchen and told Chris she wanted to see him in her office before he sat down. Mike would stay over a little while. Chris looked at Pam and shrugged his shoulders.

"This place is starting to get to me and I haven't even begun my shift."

"Don't worry, Chris, everything will be okay." Mike was on the fire console so she took the police radio and Sara sat on the phones. It wasn't busy at the moment and she hoped Chris wasn't in some kind of trouble.

"Jesus, you all look like you'll be hung at dawn," Mike said to her.

"Chris may be in trouble and I don't like to see anyone in Marge's office."

"What can they do, fire him? He'll be okay; she couldn't supervise herself on a deserted island." Pam grinned at him.

"See you look much better when you smile and you get an A-plus for breathing. Hell, I've lost count how many times I've been in the Blue Room. She'll rant and rave for a long while and when you come out you won't remember what you went in for." Pam had not been in trouble since she started but almost got Joe in trouble for hugging him. She knew she had to act properly around him and forget they're a couple. Chris soon came out of Marge's office and relieved Mike.

"Chris, I see your ass is still in one piece," Mike said to him.

"She's such a bitch and I can't stand her." Mike left and it appeared Chris didn't want to reveal what Marge had said to him. He was not in a good mood for the rest of the evening.

When their shift was over, he wanted to go to the Den but Pam couldn't go. He called Sam to meet him there. They walked out to the parking lot together and as soon as they were outside Pam asked him what was going on.

"The battle axe was asking me about being sick so much and it is starting to interfere with my work. I told her I didn't like to call in sick but I couldn't control it. She has no compassion or any feelings for anyone."

"Chris, she can't fire you for being ill so don't worry about it, you have rights. We all know that you're not making this up." They talked for awhile longer and Pam saw Joe get into his car and leave. "I guess I need to be going and try not to let this get you down. Your friends are here for you."

"I know you are or at least you and Jules care about me."

"Of course we do." She gave him a hug and they both drove off.

She arrived at home to find Joe not looking very happy. "Don't say a word, Joe, because I don't want to hear anything about Chris from you."

"You're in his face for eight hours a day and you still have to talk outside when you get off."

"Yes, we do. Marge had him in her office today and was on his case about calling in sick so much. He's not playing games and he has been sick lately. Why do you make him a problem for us? I've never said Jules couldn't be your friend and I never would object.

"She and I talked long before you came here."

"You never told me she went after you when you both first started working here. Chris and I are strictly friends and you can't deal with it. I can't see any difference between a straight friend and a gay friend. Actually, if he was straight I might be able to see a reason for you not wanting me to be around him."

"Are you attracted to him?"

"Hell, no, I'm only attracted to you. Are you attracted to Jules?"

"I didn't fall for her so what do you think?"

"I know that I love you and I only want to be with you, Joe." He didn't say anything. She went into the bathroom to shower and he turned on the TV. After her shower she came out and sat next to him on the couch. She reached over and took his hand in her own. She brought it up to her lips and kissed the back of it. He put his arm around her and drew her closer to him. She put her head on his chest. "I like cuddling with you so much. I hate having problems between us."

"You always feel good in my arms, Pam."

Pam woke up thinking about Joe and Suzy. Since he was abused when he was young, she still felt he would want to be with Suzy, if the baby is his. He would not want Suzy raising his child alone. Pam had big doubts about it. If Suzy was having his baby, she knew it would change everything. Joe was still sleeping so she got up and took her shower. She and Jules would shop for Christmas things this morning. Joe and Ken were going to play tennis for some exercise. It was a cloudy Friday morning and the weather forecast was possible rain. There was a big storm in the area but it was predicted to only be skirting the south end of Mission Park. Ken and Jules showed up and they all had coffee and a bagel. The men left for the tennis courts and the women for the mall.

"Jules, you look like something good just happened to you so what's going on?" Pam asked as she drove them to the mall.

"Ken talked about getting married and our future last night and I'm so happy. Of course he didn't come right out and ask me to marry him but it's coming. I was beginning to feel that he might be taking his time and would not be making such moves this early. I care about him so much and fell so hard for him."

"I'm so happy for you both. He must feel the same way you do or he would never bring up any future plans."

"As soon as I met him, I felt different than I had about any other guy. I lost my appetite and joined 'Curves' in order to get my exercise in. I've lost 20 pounds and only have 10 more to go."

"I'm proud of you for doing that."

"I have to bring this up about you and Joe. Something is not right with you two so has anything happened that you haven't told me?"

"We're fine and we love each other very much."

"We never go to the Den and I miss that and so does Chris. Getting together with friends away from work is especially fun."

"Joe does not like to socialize with Chris and now Sam. I told you about this before. I can't change his mind about gays, even though, I have certainly tried."

"It's about you and Joe that something has changed. I know you don't like to publicize your life but friends need friends to talk to."

Pam pulled into a parking space. The women had a couple of hours to shop before they were going to meet the men for lunch at the New Horizons. The clouds appeared to be getting darker as they walked through the mall entrance. They found the new shop and Pam had a ball spending their money on Christmas decorations. She found the perfect topper for their Christmas tree. It was a hollowed out angel in a pretty blue dress that fit right over the tip of the tree. There was an outline of a star around her with tiny lights to brighten her up. "I don't know, Pam, she looks more like a hooker than an angel."

"Who said angels have to dress in faded colors? She's pretty and I like her." She found some old fashion tree ornaments. The women went into the candle shop and they both picked out all kinds of scented candles. "It would not be Christmas at all without nice smelling candles," Pam said. Julie looked at her watch and told Pam they had 15 minutes to meet the guys. They stepped outside the mall and it was starting to rain.

"Of course my umbrella is in the car," Pam said. They dashed down the row of cars. "We didn't get hit too bad and we can use my umbrella when we get to the restaurant."

The men were waiting for them at a table when they arrived. "Did you spend all of your money?" Joe asked Pam.

"Not really but I bought enough. I found a tree topper that I like." Julie cleared her throat and rolled her eyes for Joe to see.

"So what did you pick for the top of the tree?"

"Joe, it looks like a hooker?" Julie told them.

"It does not," Pam said. "I'll show you when we get home and you be the judge." Pam got quiet.

"I heard that the Den is having a little Christmas party on the 16th and we should go," Julie volunteered this information. "Ken and I are off so we could go early and secure our table. You guys could stop by after work. They're serving all kinds of appetizers free throughout the evening."

"We can meet you there," Joe told them. Pam nodded her head. They could tell from inside the restaurant that the wind was picking up outside.

They finished lunch and Julie got her packages out of Pam's car and took off with Ken. Joe offered to drive her car home. A city maintenance crew was out trying to clear the debris from the drainage ditches and sewer holes. They arrived at the apartment and both grabbed packages and darted into the building.

"The wind hasn't blown this hard here in a long time."

"I was wondering about that," Pam said. They took the packages into the kitchen and put them on the table.

"I noticed there was a message blinking on the answering machine. You get the topper out for me to see and I'll check the message." She checked a couple of bags and found the topper. He came back into the kitchen.

"Julie, was right, it does look like a hooker. I told you that mother had angels all over the tree every year and you buy one like this for ours?" She took the topper and smashed it down over the edge of the counter. It shattered into many small pieces.

"There you won't ever have to look at it. If you want a topper for our tree, Mr. Pellerini, you'll have to buy one. I'll never buy another one."

"Damn it, Pam, I get the point. Lee is having a problem at the nursery with the wind and wants you to come over and help her." Pam grabbed her purse and headed out the door. She could tell the wind was picking up more as she drove south and slowly through the streets. It was not raining very much. She arrived at the nursery to find all the ladies out back trying to protect the plants and trees.

"I'm so glad to see you, Pam, and I was hoping Joe would come to help."

"He's busy right now. What do you want done first, Nana?"

"All hanging planters have to be taken down and put on the ground. A couple of them fell already. Then we need to secure the trees. I thought we could place the empty pots around them to keep them from falling over." Pam and the two workers started taking the hanging pots down. They worked as fast as they could. They had to use step ladders to take them down and this took longer to do. Lee had been keeping an eye on the front of the store and she would now close it up. They got all the hanging plants on the ground and headed for the trees way out back. The wind was still blowing a lot and the rain was coming down harder. Pam only had a light jacket on and she was already quite wet. The three women went out to the very back of the nursery and started grabbing empty pots. Pam was glad the trees and empty containers were not too far from each other. Pam was pushing the trees as close together as she could get them and the two ladies were bringing Pam the empties. She heard a loud tinny noise and looked up to see Joe coming with an empty wagon. He went to the empty pots and started loading them onto the wagon. She was so glad to see him. He brought a load over to her and she gave him a big smile and a hug.

"Thanks so much for coming, Joe."

"I couldn't let you do this by yourself and if you get tired go on inside." She nodded. They both worked with the two ladies and got all the trees secured. When they were finished they walked to the building. Joe had his arm around Pam. "I didn't realized what a good worker you are. You must take after your grandmother." Lee thanked her two employees and told them to go home. She would pay them for working the whole day. Pam was standing and feeling her wet clothes sticking to herself. She was starting to shiver a little.

"You go home and get out of those wet clothes and I'll take Lee home."

Pam was soon home where she took a real warm shower. He came in after she got into some dry clothes. "I cleaned up the angel and decided to help. I'm sorry that I made fun of the topper. I do care about you and I don't always show it."

"We could start by making out a little and go from there." He kissed her softy on the lips. She opened her mouth and gave him her tongue and his hand went up under her blouse. They both started taking their clothes off and went down to the bed. "You're making me really warm," she told him. He was being extra gentle with her and it turned her on even more. He started kissing all around her breasts without touching her nipples and it was really getting to her. He entered her and she grasped his waist with her legs. He groaned as he came and she called out his name. They lay quietly for a little bit and he raised up and looked at her.

"It doesn't get any better than this, Pam." She gave him her biggest smile.

"You feel so good inside of me because you're so special to me. I like seeing your naked body because it turns me on so much." He kissed her and hugged her. They both got dressed.

They ate some hot soup for dinner and watched a little TV. The wind had let up some but the rain was coming down in buckets. They held each other on the couch and watched a movie.

Chapter 25

The next day was clear of wind and rain but the streets were strewn with debris. A couple of big trees had fallen during the night. They made their way over to the nursery in the mid morning to help Lee get her plants and trees back in order. "I can't tell you how much this means for you both to come back today to get me all straightened out."

"We're off and we don't mind, Lee," Joe told her.

"It won't take us long to undo what we did yesterday." She and Joe started by hanging the planters back up. He got on the step stool and she handed him the pots. They went out to the back and moved the heavy pots back to their area. They moved the trees out away from each other. This was harder today because the rain had soaked all the planters and they were much heavier. They, also, helped by sweeping up parts of flowers and leaves that had been whipped off the plants by the wind. It took them about three hours and everything looked much better when they finished.

"I'd like to take you out for lunch or even dinner, if you'll let me. I can't stress enough how much this means to me and it was hard work, too."

"Nana, we didn't do this for you to buy us a meal. We did it because you needed help and we love you."

"That's right, you would help us, if we needed it," Joe said

"Anytime I can do something just let me know." They said goodbye and left the nursery.

"Since we didn't have breakfast and I'm starving, let's get us a high calorie fast food meal. Burgers, French fries, coke or a milk shake sounds great."

"I agree," Pam told him. They drove through the drive-thru at McDonalds and took their order home to eat.

They were just finishing eating when the phone rang. Pam didn't even get to say hello before her grandmother lit into her. "I just had a visitor who said that Joe was the father of the baby she's carrying. She's the same women that I saw him with at the car wash. I knew there was something more to the story than you were telling me."

"You mean she just came into the nursery and blurted this all out to you?" Joe looked at Pam trying to figure out what her grandmother was telling her.

"She came up to me and asked me, if I was your grandmother. I said I was and she let it all out. Now I want to hear it from you, young lady?"

"Nana, it's a long story and we don't even know, if she's pregnant or just getting fat."

"She's definitely pregnant because you can't hide a protruding tummy."

"You need to calm down and I'll call you back this evening, I promise." Pam hung up the phone and closed her eyes. "I should have gotten that restraining order on Suzy a long time ago because she's following me and now she has involved my grandmother. She must be sick to want the whole world know about her baby. My parents are coming and she will probably go out of her way to contact them."

"What did she say to Lee?" Pam told him what her Nana had said. "Call Lee this evening and tell her Suzy is crazy and making accusations because she wants me. That's all we know for sure so we aren't making shit up."

"Of all the people to go to and say those things," Pam said. "I don't think she's going to stop at my grandmother so what are we going to do? I bet she's still following us everywhere. I'm going to make damn sure she isn't around when I'm driving in town. I'll look for that old ratty blue Dodge with the paint peeling off the hood. I just thought of something. We should turn the tables on her. We should start showing up at the Diner and the Den often and follow her everywhere. She might get the hint and leave us alone. Let's go to the Diner right now and have a piece of pie." Joe was not sure it would work. They both got into his car and headed for the Diner. Suzy's car was parked on the street in front of the small older restaurant.

"Let's go in and have that piece of pie."

"This may not turn out the way you have it all planned."

"Maybe, if we do something unexpected, she'll be thrown for a loop and she'll leave us alone. It's worth a try." He reluctantly followed Pam into the Diner. They seated themselves and a waitress came over and asked, if they wanted coffee.

"Joe, we haven't seen you in awhile, "the thin blond said to him.

"I don't eat out much anymore," he answered her. Pam now knew that he must have known Suzy before he took her to bed. She was not happy with this news.

"This was your hang out before you met me, I take it? Suzy was someone you didn't have anything to do before you met me?" Joe would not look at Pam and was unfolding his napkin.

"I came in here occasionally but that was it." They had not seen Suzy. The waitress came back with two cups of coffee and they both ordered a piece of pie. Suzy came out of the kitchen with two plates of food and stopped when she saw Joe and Pam. They stared her down. She continued with the plates walking past their booth.

"She's definitely putting on weight," Pam said to him. "How could you hang out in a dump like this? This is not your class of people, Joe." Pam picked at her plate but just wanted to leave. She got up and went out the door. She stood leaning against the car waiting for Joe. He did not come out in a few minutes so she started walking towards their apartment. It was five or six blocks but she could do it. She decided to take some side streets so he wouldn't see her walking. She never should have gone in there but now she knew more about Joe. It was his old hang out and no one even knew. He must have more secrets that he hasn't told her. She was walking along when someone tooted their horn. She turned to see Chris pulling up to the curb next to her. He rolled his car window all the way down.

"When did you become a street walker, Miss Pamela?" He asked her with a grin.

"Just today and I have been caught."

"So where did you leave Joe? I'm assuming you got pissed and started walking home, am I correct?"

"You know me better than anyone. I needed some fresh air and thought I would walk but in this place everyone knows your business. I'm taking the side streets because I don't want him to see me."

"Jump in and I'll give you a lift."

"I really would like to walk. I can clear my head at the same time I'm exercising."

"It's getting dark early now and cooling off so why not let me pick you up."

224

"It won't take me that long to walk unless I fall down and break a leg. What time do you have, Chris?"

"4:05, young lady and the sun sets soon."

"I'll be fine, if you'll stop talking and let me continue. We're going to the Den on the 16th, did you hear about it?"

"Sam and I will be there ready to howl."

"I'm glad because we're overdue for a night out." Chris pulled away from the curb and she kept walking. She had walked a few more blocks when a cruiser pulled over to the curb. She turned to see Ken smiling at her. She walked over to the car.

"You're the second person to stop me. A person can't even take a walk on a nice afternoon."

"I thought you might be lost since I never see you out walking."

"I need some exercise but thanks for checking on me."

"You can hop in and I can drop you off. I don't mind at all."

"I'm really fine and this is very refreshing for me. He drove away and she gave him a wave.

In about 10 minutes she was walking into her complex. She didn't see his car. He can visit with Suzy and the girls at the Diner, if that is what he wants she thought to herself. She took off her sweater and hung it in the closet. The answering machine light was flashing. It was a call from her Nana. She got off a little early today and wanted Pam to call her. She picked up the phone and dialed her grandmother's number.

"Where have you been, Pam?"

"I went for a walk and just got home."

"I wish you would tell me what's going on and have you told your folks about living with Joe?"

"I haven't told them yet but I will."

"The plot is getting thicker with that woman saying she's carrying Joe's baby. Do you know what's going to happen, if your folks find out? I'll tell you, young lady. There'll be two Austin's on both of our asses and it won't be fun."

"I understand, Grandmother, when I know something, I'll let you know."

"Do you mean it could be true? Who in hell have you gotten tangled up with? It's never too late to back out of a relationship."

"Don't worry about me; I can take care of myself."

"Will you promise me, if things don't work out you'll come and stay with me?"

"Yes, I'll do that but I'll first try and work things out. I love him and I can't just dump him. If things don't improve, I'll make some changes in my life." They both hung up. Pam was wondering where he was and if he was even going to come home. Why didn't he leave the Diner and why isn't he home? She watched some news and then the food network. It was almost 8 PM and still no Joe. If she was doing this to him, he would not like it. She started watching "Cops" and her stomach was growling. She took a package of pop corn out of the box and started it in the microwave. She took a diet coke out of the refrigerator. When the bag was popped she took it into the living room and ate it for dinner. By nine she was feeling really bad that Joe wasn't home. She didn't know what to do. Why was he staying out, she did not know? She heard his key in the door and looked up as he walked into the living room. He didn't look good at all. He went right passed her into the bathroom. She heard him in the shower. He got out of the shower and went into the bedroom. She was thinking that if she had done this to him what would he do if she came home hours later. She knew he must have gone to bed and was sleeping. She took her own shower and got ready for bed. She wasn't real sleepy but at least she didn't have to worry about where he was. He did come home to her and not spend the night somewhere else. She climbed into bed and turned out the light. He was facing the wall away from her side of the bed. She wanted to cuddle so much but wasn't sure if she could.

Sometime during the night they met in the middle of the bed. Joe put his arm around her and she hugged him closely. How could something so good between them be falling all apart? She was late for her period and she wondered, if her plan to always be connected to him was working. She would find out soon enough. She tossed and turned the night away and fell off to sleep in the wee hours of the morning.

Pam woke up after sleeping a couple of hours only. The sun was still an hour from coming up in the East and she couldn't stay in bed any longer. She got up and took another shower. She would go to her Nana's and take her out to breakfast before she had to open up the nursery. The Christmas trees had arrived late yesterday and she wanted to pick one out. She dried her hair and looked at the clock it was 6:30 AM. She got dressed and went out to her car.

Pam drove over to her Nana's and parked in front. She saw the kitchen light on so her Nana must be up already. Pam went up the walkway and rang the door bell. "Oh, my God, what a surprise," Lee said when she saw Pam. "Did something happen?"

"I thought you might like to go out for breakfast with me since I ate popcorn for dinner last night."

"Where is Joe?"

"He's still sleeping."

"I wanted to take you out for french toast or something good and then I want to pick our Christmas tree out, too."

"Let me get some clothes on and it won't take me long. This is really a nice surprise." The two women left for the New Horizon's chatting all the way. They got their coffee and ordered from the menu.

"I was thinking I could put the tree in a bucket of water and it would stay fresh until I take it home next Saturday. You'll let me use your pickup to transport it home I hope?"

"Pam, you don't even have to ask to use it. We can put the tree in the shack in a bucket so no one will choose it by mistake."

"That'll be great. I need to buy a tree stand unless you're selling them."

"I sure am and I'll give you a good one."

"I want to buy the tree and stand. You're not running a charity organization. Joe gave me a couple hundred dollars to spend on Christmas decorations. I still have some of his money left plus my own."

"How does it feel to be having Christmas out on your own and starting from scratch."

"It feels great. I'm enjoying buying nice things. Joe and I both want an old fashion type Christmas. I wanted to give him something special so I had my portrait done at a studio. The pictures came out better than I expected and I'll pick them up next Saturday."

"You're going to give me one, aren't you?"

"Nana, I sure am with a frame and all. It was going to be one of your Christmas presents but I'll give it to you next week."

"I can't wait to have it. You take a great picture and it definitely be special. If he truly cares about you, he'll cherish it forever."

"I'm picking him up some clothes and a new tennis racket. His old racket looks all worn out so I'll buy him a really nice one"

"Do you know what he's getting you?"

"No, and I don't want to know. Have you forgotten that if I know what I am getting, I don't want it."

"You're right. You only want a present, if it is a surprise."

They finished their breakfast and went over to the nursery. Lee had to do some things in the shack and Pam was heading for the freshly cut trees. She was checking them all out trying to find the perfect one.

"Do you mind, if I help you pick it out?" Joe said to her. She looked up to see him standing back a short ways from the trees.

"I don't mind at all." They settled on a 6 foot tall, thick fir. "I want a lot of good branches to fill up with ornaments," she told him.

"If I were you, Pam, I wouldn't be speaking to me right now."

"That's why we're different, Joe." He carried the tree to the shack and she carried a pail. She filled the bucket with water and he had to trim some lower small branches to fit the trunk into the pail.

"Hi, Joe, I didn't know you were here."

"Pam let me sleep in but I wanted to help pick out the tree."

"It looks good and has a perfect shape," Lee said to them. "You missed out on a good breakfast so next time get up and join us."

"I'll do that if a certain young lady will wake me up."

"Well, Nana, we have to be going and thanks for letting me keep our tree fresh."

"You're both welcome and come back when you can stay longer." The couple walked out to their vehicles.

"Are you coming home now?" She asked.

"If you'll let me, I want to."

"I let you in bed with me so that should be a clue."

"I'm going to stop and get a fast food breakfast because I haven't eaten since the pie at the Diner."

"I'll fix you an omelet and make some coffee."

"I don't expect you to do that."

"I would like to. I'll see you home in a few. She got into her car and drove off.

They met in the complex parking lot. She immediately got the coffee pot going and started putting his omelet together. He sat down at the table. They were both quiet. She was standing at the stove cooking the omelet when he got up and put his arms around her. He had his face in her neck and he started nuzzling her. The goose bumps were standing out on her neck. "Pam, I wanted to make love during the night but wasn't sure, if you would want that."

"I did want that as a matter of fact but I was upset with you. I have to get this out of the pan, if you'll hand me a plate from the cupboard. Do you want toast?"

"I can put the bread in the toaster." She put the plate on the table and poured him a cup of coffee. She sat down across from him after the toast was ready. "I take it you didn't tell Lee about what happened yesterday."

228

"I don't talk about my personal life to everyone."

"I appreciate you not making me look any worse than I already do in her eyes. I saw Ken at the office and he told me he stopped you out exercising. I knew you were almost home then. Apparently you didn't tell him either that you were upset."

"This is the way I look at life. I made the choice to live with you and I didn't expect life to be wonderful everyday. I know that we love each other and we could take on the world, if we need to. I don't mind a cooling off period between us but shutting each other out is never good. I felt shut out completely when you didn't come home."

"I finished my pie yesterday and Suzy came over to try and talk with me. It was the same old stuff about the baby being mine. I left and drove up and down some of the streets but didn't see you. I stopped in at the office to clean out my locker that was long over due. I needed to keep busy and think about our life in general. Emerson was getting off work and talked me into going over to the batting cages and hitting some baseballs so that's what I did in the evening. It wasn't right that I didn't call or let you know what I was doing."

"Joe, I know this thing with Suzy is hard for you but don't turn things around and make our life together difficult. If you need to talk about it then talk to me. I want to be here for you whether things are great for us or not so great. You don't have a hard time talking to me do you?"

"Not at all but I don't like bringing it up to remind you what an awful mistake I made. I know, I'm letting my ego get in the way of things. Men are suppose to take care of their women and I let you down in a big way."

"I forgave you for that mistake so quit dwelling on it. I do think about our future together a lot and you've never given me the assurance that I need. You tell me that you always want to be with me but if the baby turns out to be yours, you won't tell me your plans. It's really hard trying to live under these circumstances, Joe. It doesn't give me the hope that I need to keep going."

"I'm trying to be honest with you, Pam, but it isn't working. You want definite answers and I can't give you any."

"That hurts me because you told me that you love me and you want to spend the rest of your life with me. If she is pregnant and drinking beer every night, how can she take care of a child, your child, if it's true? She's hurting the baby now by doing alcohol."

"I know she is and it bothers me but I can't physically make her stop. I could talk from now on and she wouldn't listen. She's a druggie and an alcoholic."

"Please see, if I have this straight? You're willing to live with me and make love to me for the time being. In less than four months the baby will be here, if the baby is yours you could dump me?" Joe looked into her eyes and said nothing. "The longer we're together the closer I feel to you. How can I put up with getting closer to you, loving you more over time, and then getting dumped?" She didn't expect an answer from him She got up from the table and started clearing away his dishes. "When you decide what you're going to do with your life, let me know, please?" She went into the bedroom. What a day this was turning out to be. Last night she couldn't sleep and today her emotions are running wild. Her work day hadn't even started yet. How would she ever get through her shift intact? Why couldn't he give her a straight answer?

A little later he came into the bedroom and kneeled down next to the bed. She turned to face him. "Pam, I know that I love you with all my heart and I want to be with you forever. That's the only answer I can give you at this time. I can't make decisions when I don't even know what's true and what isn't. Please don't be upset with me anymore." She lifted her hand to his face and ran her index finger around his jaw line. How she loved him and wanted to be with him forever.

"You're so handsome, my Joe, and I love you so much." She raised up to meet his lips and kissed him gently. He gathered her into his arms and matched her kisses with his own. They were all over each other in no time. They did not stop until he was inside of her and their physical love intensified as one. Her body turned pink from her breasts to her cheeks as their lust for each other exploded and then abated. He raised up, looked at her face, and saw love and contentment.

"Why are you looking at me like that?" She asked him.

"Because I like to and you mean so much to me." These words from him would have to do for now. She didn't want to be a problem for him at this time. They had enough problems dealing with Suzy. She only wanted to give him peace. She turned her head to look at the clock.

"We do need to get ready for work, although, I wish we could stay home in bed. "Let's call in sick together and send the office into a tizzy. There isn't enough talk going around about us now."

"I wish that we could but we have the rest of our lives to enjoy one another," he told her. "I'll always try to be here for you." She wasn't so sure.

Chapter 26

This was supposedly going to be the start of an exciting week for them. She was glad when Saturday arrived and they could bring their Christmas tree home from the nursery. Joe was almost as excited as she was. He had not had a tree since he left home to join the Navy. This was their first Christmas together and she hoped it would be a nice one. She needed to pick up the pictures today and she got her wish when Ken called and asked him to play tennis. It gave her an excuse to get the pictures without him knowing anything about it. Joe would be out of the way. He tried to talk her into going with him to play but she kept giving him one excuse after another. It being the Christmas season was her main excuse that worked. She had already purchased a beautiful frame for his picture and two 5 X 7 frames for her folks and her Nana. It turned out to be a sunny but cool day and it felt like Christmas on the Southern California coast. She got busy cleaning the apartment and he went off to play tennis. She brought out all the tree ornaments she had recently purchased and laid them on the coffee table. She wanted everything to be ready for later. She would have to remind him again to get a tree topper. She was being stubborn she thought. The apartment was in order so she took off to pick up the all the pictures. She dropped a 5x7 off at the nursery for her Nana.

"Pam, this picture is just beautiful."

"You're prejudice, Nana, but thanks for saying so. I just want Joe to like it a lot."

"You don't have to worry, if he cares about you half as much as you say, he will love it. I'll take the big one, if he doesn't like it." She gave Pam a big grin. "This is my lucky day because I'll get to see you again later when you pick up your tree."

"I enjoy seeing you, also, and it'll be a double treat. Nana, you can't display my picture until after Christmas and don't forget. If he sees yours, mine won't be a surprise."

"I'll put it in my bedroom drawer until after Christmas, I promise. God forbid that I should spoil one of your Christmas surprises." She gave Lee a hug and told her she would see her later. As soon as Pam returned to the apartment, she wrapped his picture up and took it out to her car. She placed it carefully into the trunk. She wasn't taking any chances of him finding it.

Joe returned from tennis and she fixed them both some lunch. They were anxious to pick up the tree. They finished eating and hurried to the nursery. Lee met them at the front entrance. She pretended to be very happy to see Pam. The three walked to the shack together where the tree was still sitting in a pail of water.

"Oh, Nana, you have such beautiful Christmas cacti and I'll have to have one." The shack was full of the pretty plants. Pam picked out a bright pink one fully blossomed. They walked out to the front where Pam paid for the tree, a stand, and the cactus.

"Do you two have plans for Christmas because I would like you to come to my place?" Lee asked them.

"We haven't even discussed any plans but we will later and I'll let you know. We don't want you spending Christmas alone, Nana, so we'll work something out."

"If your folks don't come, I was going to fix a big ham for the three of us." There'll be plenty for you to take half of it home for leftovers. I hope you can join me." She loaned them the nursery pickup truck to transport the tree to their place. They helped each other set the tree up in the new tree stand right in front of the big window. He had to take the pickup back to Lee.

"You can't start decorating until I get back and I mean that," he told her.

"Well, don't take too long or I will." She started picking through the decorations when he was leaving. She would not dream of starting without him. She strung several light sets together while he was gone to make sure all the lights worked.

He returned shortly and they got started. "We should have bought some booze and planned a little tree trimming party," she told him.

"We can celebrate after the tree is trimmed. I want to sit on the couch this evening and look at the tree. We can enjoy it together." She smiled at his plans. They first strung the sets of lights and got each tiny light in its little place. He thought she was a little too fussy. They decorated, laughed, and had a good time. The tree was finished in about an hour except the bare spot at the very top. The tree needed a topper really bad.

"I guess we do need something at the top," he admitted.

"That's your problem now, I refuse to buy another one. I want to bring something up, if you don't mind. It's exactly two weeks before the holiday. If I leave and don't tell you where I'm going, you have to accept that. You can't be curious this time of year either. I'm not dumb enough to hide presents around here but I may have to be secretive and I don't want you to take it wrong."

"I accept that and the same goes for you. Pam, how come your mom doesn't call you very often?"

"That's easy to answer because I never tell her anything. She gets more out of Nana so why bother with me? She e-mails me all the time so we do communicate. Nana was right about them not coming down. It doesn't look like dad will be able to come and mom doesn't want to leave him alone."

"I'm sorry that you won't be able to spend the holiday with them."

"I consider you my family now since I don't live at home."

"It's real nice of you to say that, Pam. I've wanted my own family for a long time."

"You have me already and someday we'll have little Joey running around." She lowered her eyes and walked over to him. She put her arms around him and got real close. "Don't you think we should name him Joe Jr.?"

"I'm not sure but if that's what you want, I'll go along with it."

"I would like that very much," she told him with a big smile.

A little while later Pam went out to get the mail. She brought in a couple of Christmas cards and a package wrapped in brown paper. It was addressed to her and had no return address on it. She handed it to Joe who opened it up and there was a plain piece of paper inside with a VCR Tape. On the paper was written in red ink Merry Christmas. They both looked at each other and he saw the hurt look in her eyes. They knew this must be the tape Suzy had told them that she had made when Joe spent the night. This was apparently meant to be her Christmas present to them. "Will you look at this now and let me know what it is?" She walked into the bedroom and shut the door to wait. After about 10 minutes he called to Pam to come out. She knew from the look on his face that it was indeed the tape from Suzy.

"I did make love to her," he told Pam.

"You made love to her like you do to me and you didn't just have sex with her? Aren't you one fine fucking fellow!"

"No, I'm sorry that was a slip, I had sex with her."

"Well, now we know the truth and we know that she could very well be pregnant with your baby. Isn't this going to be a fine Christmas this year?"

"Just because I slept with her and she's pregnant doesn't mean that baby is mine."

"You're right, Joe, but the odds are in her favor that it's your baby, I would think. She enticed you to her place to have sex and it worked. Suzy's smarter than we give her credit for. She fell for you and she knew if she got pregnant she would really have her hooks in you. I guess having it on tape would be living proof. This started out by being such a nice day and it has gone completely to hell."

"Pam, I told you before I can't take back the night I spent with her. I wish I could but I can't."

"I don't know what to say, Joe. I don't want her to have your baby. I wanted to be the one. I feel like I'm on the outside of this situation looking in."

"You're on the inside with me and you always will be. Do you think I could be with her when I'm stone sober? I would have to have my head examined to want her."

"Those are nice words for you to say to me but if this baby is really yours, how are you going to feel? I keep asking and you don't want to be truthful to me. What does your heart say is all I want to know?"

"I don't know what my heart is saying because my mind is so confused. Haven't you ever been so mixed up that you can't make a decision? I regret giving her the time of day but it happened."

"You can do me a favor right now by getting this fucking tape out of our home. I don't want it in here for one minute more." Joe took the tape out of the VCR and went out the door. She was sick at heart over the whole mess. She knew she would always love him but it has been one problem after another.

He came back to the apartment later and she was sitting on the couch looking at the tree lights. He walked over and sat next to her. He took her hand and brought it up to his lips and kissed her palm. "I always want to be with you, Pam. I'm so in love with you and this is coming from my heart."

She leaned over and put her head on his chest. "I'll always love you, too and we have to get through this together. I cannot see myself without you."

On Thursday she was almost wishing the day away in order to go to the Den for the Christmas party. She fixed her hair nicer, wore a royal blue skirt, a lighter blue blouse, and heels to work. She definitely had a party to go to. Joe gave her some nice compliments before they left for work. She knew she should dress up more often. Pam wanted him to be proud of her. She told him she would meet him at the Den and she would like to walk inside with him. He said he would try and get over there as soon as he could.

At work Mike gave her a wolf whistle and Chris rolled his eyes in approval. She told him later about the portrait she had taken for Joe as one of his gifts. "Chris, do you think the portrait will be something he'll like?"

"I'm sure he will because he's with you and he loves you. You tell me often that he loves you so I have been brainwashed."

"Are you all right because you look tired and dragged out."

"I feel just the way you described me. The doctor keeps trying new drugs but nothing is working so far."

"I don't want you to feel so bad and I wish there was something I could do."

"They are bound to find something that works sooner or later. In the meantime, I'll look like my dog just died and someone shot my horse out from under me. It doesn't get much worse than that." She didn't know how he could look so bad and still have a sense of humor. She admired him a great deal.

"Jules, was telling me that you're quite the cook at Christmas. I'm dying for some goodies."

"I told her that I like to cook for the holidays but I'm not a great cook. I'll cook for you guys, I promise. On my days off I'm doing fudge and cookies so I won't leave you out."

When the shift was over Pam slowly took her time in leaving. Joe had come into the office but couldn't leave for 15 more minutes. She would drive to the Den and wait in her car until he arrived. The parking lot was full but someone pulled out as she drove in. She waited for Joe. Chris came along whacked her fender with his hand and jumped the hell out of her. "Are you trying to give me a heart attack, Christopher?" He laughed and stood next to her car. She rolled the window down.

"I saw you drive in as I had to park in the back 40 near the Shell Station. I thought I would have a little fun. Get out of the car and let's howl, woman."

"I'm going to wait for Joe. I want to walk in with him."

235

"Oh, you want this to feel like a real date?" She grinned and nodded. He waved and walked toward the entrance. In about 20 minutes Joe pulled in and got a spot not too far from her. She got out of her car as he was parking. He joined her and gave her a hug and kiss. She always felt good in his arms.

"You look really pretty, my love."

"Thanks so much and you're handsome as ever." She took his hand as they approached the door. It was quite crowded and the first person they saw was Suzy. Joe glanced at Pam and she bristled a little. He dropped her hand much to her disappointment. Pam stopped. "Why do you stop touching me whenever we come here and you see her? It pisses me off, Joe."

"I do it because I don't want her doing something else to hurt you. She's a jealous maniac and you know that." They continued on and Suzy gave him a big smile. Pam looked straight ahead. They turned and saw the others at their big booth. Pam was starting to feel bad and she was thinking she never should have agreed to go to this party. The others were drinking beer and seemed happy. Everyone scooted over as she and Joe approached the booth. Pam ended up next to Julie and Joe sat on the end. They had a small tray of appetizers in the middle of the table. Joe ordered a beer for the two of them.

"No, I just want 7-up," she told the waitress.

"How can you party by drinking soda?" Chris asked her.

"I don't have to be drunk to have a good time."

"Why did you stop after you got through door? We thought you were you going to turn around and leave." Chris asked Pam.

"I just stopped to ask Joe a question is all." Joe reached for her hand under the table but she moved hers away from him and wouldn't let him have it. Before Suzy, he didn't hide being affectionate towards her. Now he only touched her under the table.

"You should try and have a good time or pretend," Chris added. Sam looked like he had started drinking early in the evening and Julie was right behind him. Pam glanced at Joe as he looked toward Suzy.

"They really outdid themselves on all the little goodies," Julie said.

"Pam you missed the tramp's grand entrance. She's getting big in the belly and soon she won't fit into her little booth," Chris revealed. "When that happens we may have to accommodate her by letting her sit in our big booth." Pam kept her eyes down and didn't want to comment. "A guy would have to be awfully drunk to even want to screw her in the dark, even with a bag over her head." Joe was looking into his glass of beer. Pam gave Chris a look that could kill.

"She shouldn't be drinking at all and she should be locked up for doing so," Ken said. "She has a history of drug use so alcohol is milder than what she has been using."

"Did we come out here to discuss Suzy or to have a party?" Pam asked.

"Now, Pam, you know how dispatchers like to get together and gossip so we're just having some fun," Chris said.

"You guys that came late missed the crowds earlier. This place was really hopping and so loud you couldn't hear anyone," Julie told them." She and Ken were getting awfully cozy sitting next to each other. Julie kept looking at Joe as if she wanted him to notice her. "Pamela, Ken and I saw your picture in the San Francisco Chronicle last Sunday. It was quite a nice article about your dad and all the millions he makes in the computer industry."

"What are you guys talking about?" Pam asked.

"Don't play the dumb blond role, Pam, it's not very becoming to you. Your family is filthy rich so why did you come here to Mission Park?" Julie questioned. "Did you want to see how the 'have-nots' live out their lives?"

"What is this all about?" Joe asked Ken. Pam knew she had been caught. Ken was too nice to answer Joe.

"It's like this Joe, you're dating one of the richest debutante's in the country. Her dad is Lake Austin the computer magnate and this isn't the same story she told when she arrived here." Julie was enjoying relating Pam's history to the others.

"I didn't lie when I came here. I told you where I was from but I didn't tell you who my Dad was and how much money the family has."

"Do you want to tell me what's going on?" Joe asked Pam.

"It's true I was born into that life but I left because it wasn't me. I was so tired of it and I don't belong there. It's not fun at all being rich and I wanted to get out on my own and feel like a normal person."

"So it was okay for you to come down here and pretend you were just an ordinary person and trick us all?" Joe asked.

"My intent was not to trick but to fit in," Pam said.

"I can't believe this, Pamela, you're Miss Rich Bitch and you fooled us all," Chris said. "I have to hand it to you for being such a great actress. I'll practice bowing and scraping to you for our future encounters." Pam knew Joe was not taking this very well.

"I don't know what to say except to ask you, if this is the only secret you have kept to yourself?" Joe asked.

"You don't have to say anything, Joe, it shouldn't change anything, I'm the same person you met in May." Pam told him.

"If you think finding out that you're rich will not change anything then you aren't very smart. How long did you plan on pulling off this charade?" Joe asked.

"Forever, if I could because it isn't me."

"Now, Pam, you're not thinking properly when your trust fund is given to you at age 25 did you plan on throwing the money away or what was going to happen?" Julie asked.

"I would keep a little and decide what to do with the rest," Pam answered.

"I'm getting a headache," Joe said as he got up to leave. He left the booth and Pam was right behind him.

"Don't leave," said Chris, "we want to find out more about you."

"I think I made a mistake coming here, you guys, so I'm going home," Pam told them.

"Come on, Pam, don't let a bit of news spoil your evening. Joe should like you even more now." She walked down towards the bar and Joe was already through the entrance.

Suzy called out to her. "I need to talk to you." Pam kept walking towards the door. She got outside and took a deep breath. Someone grabbed her and swung her around. "I told you I wanted to talk to you, bitch."

"I want nothing to do with you, tramp."

"Did you enjoy the tape? I hope you did and now you must believe that the baby is his. Is that why you're not in a good mood this evening? I told you I would have him someday and you didn't believe me." Pam couldn't see Joe anywhere in the parking lot. She was near her car and was getting her keys out of her purse. "I want you to stay away from him because he's mine." Suzy swung her purse and took Pam right in the side of the face.

"Oh," Pam called out as she touched the side of her face. Joe stepped out of the shadows and grabbed Suzy's arm.

"You need to stop this," he said to Suzy. Pam's face was smarting from the hit and she turned to look at Joe. The scowl on his face was upsetting to her. "You'd better get back inside because I have some other business to tend to." Suzy hurried away from them as Joe's gruff voice cut through the air. I don't even know you anymore, Pam."

"How could you keep so much from me?" The tears started as he looked into her eyes searching for answers.

"This isn't about me and keeping my life from you. This is about you and that tramp. I'm so tired of her in our lives and causing chaos. You have to choose right now, me or her? I can't keep going through this. It should be a simple decision for you." The tears were streaming down Pam's face. "I want to know right now her or me? Tell me, now?"

"I can't do that and you know it," he told her.

"That's not good enough." Pam was devastated as she watched him turn and go back into the Den. Her tears turned to sobs and she slumped down to the ground. Her head was leaning against the car door as her heart was broken in two.

After awhile she got herself up and into her car. She sat there for a little while not really wanting to go to her Nana's. She could not face him tonight after this confrontation.

She drove to her grandmother's and rang the doorbell. Lee turned the outside light on and quickly opened the door. "Oh, my God, Pam, what's the matter?" Pam still had tears in her eyes and she looked terrible.

"Just the usual night out with Joe and getting dumped. He knows about my family and all the money. It didn't go over very well with him. I gave him an ultimatum and that didn't go over well either. I'm such a fucking loser."

"You shouldn't talk like that," Lee told her.

"I just want to be happy, Nana."

"Did he hit you because the side of your face is all red?"

"No, he would never do that but Suzy hit me hard with her purse."

"The three of you had a fight? Please explain what's going on." She escorted Pam over to the couch.

"I can't sit down because I was on the ground and it was wet." She had dirt caked to the back of her dress. Lee went in her bedroom and brought out a robe. Pam took her dress off and slipped the robe on. Lee draped the dress over a dining room chair. "Don't ask me to talk about what happened tonight. I feel bad and there's nothing to talk about."

"Talking helps, Pam, and I'm not going anywhere."

"Please go back to bed and I'll be okay. I just want to rest and look at the Christmas lights. Lee went over and turned on her Christmas tree lights. "Nana, I know where everything is and I'll be fine. We can talk tomorrow." Lee went back to bed. Later on she grabbed the throw that was draped over the back of the couch and dozed off.

Chapter 27

Her Nana was long gone when Pam woke up at 10 AM. She was glad that she wouldn't have to answer questions for awhile. Her most important task for the day would be to go by the apartment and get some things. She didn't want to face Joe either and maybe he hadn't spent the night there. Nothing would surprise her anymore.

She showered, ate a bagel, and hit the road. Her self dialogue kicked in while driving. She was not going to cry anymore. It would not help her situation to shed another tear. Her hunch was right, his car wasn't in the parking lot. She grabbed her suitcase and started emptying her dresser drawers. She got some things out of the bathroom and took the suitcase to her car. Pam came back and took her clothes on the hangers out of the closet. She wasn't going to hang around too long and be caught by him. She could get more stuff at another time. She stood in front of the Christmas tree and looked at all the ornaments she had picked out. Christmas would not be the same without Joe. She took the clothes and laid them across the backseat then came back for her computer. She took it apart and carried each component out to her car. She finished loading the car and drove away. That was easier than she thought it would be. She made a stop at the drug store to pick up a home pregnancy test. This would tell her what she needed to know. She then drove straight to her Nana's and unloaded everything.

It was almost noon when she finished putting her computer back together. The phone rang. Her Nana had Caller ID and she recognized the nursery phone number. "Hi, Nana, what can I do for you?"

"I called earlier but there was no answer so I didn't know, if you were still sleeping or had gone somewhere."

"I had some errands to do. I picked up some of my things and brought them to your place. I may be staying awhile but I'm not sure how long at this point."

"Pam, stay as long as you wish and I mean that. Your old Nana will love the company and I'll try not be a pest. What are you doing today?"

"I have to see Julie before she goes to work so I'll call her and then I'll probably come by the nursery."

"Well, come over when you can." Pam hung up from Lee and called Julie.

"Hi, Jules, I was wondering, if I could see you sometime today, have you had lunch?"

"No, I haven't."

"How about the New Horizon's? I'm just a few blocks away."

"Sure, I'll meet you there in 30 minutes." Pam knew she could usually depend on Jules to drop everything to see her. She hurriedly got the picture for Joe out of her trunk and opened it up. She took the picture out of it frame and tore it into many small pieces. She placed the pieces into a small box and wrapped the box in Christmas paper. Pam put a bow on the package and wrote to Joe from Santa on the tag. Julie had her other gifts from her to Joe and she could add this one to the pile. Before going to the restaurant there was something else she had to do. She took the box with the home pregnancy test and went into the bathroom. The test proved positive and she was elated. Now she was guaranteed a future with Joe. She would not tell a soul until the time was right. She didn't like going behind his back but she had to think about herself, too.

Pam drove over to the restaurant and went inside. She wasn't looking forward to being in Julie's company. "Joe called me this morning and filled me in," Julie said to her.

"That's good because I won't talk about him anymore. He can have the apartment and do whatever he wishes to do with his life. At least I got my answer last night."

"For someone who just left the love of her life, you don't look very unhappy. We're used to seeing you with red splotches and eyes but I'm not seeing that except for your cheek."

"It would have been nice, if you could have talked over some things with me before you revealed to the world about my real life. I don't think I'm too hard to talk to. You were so intent on letting everyone know about me."

"I didn't think Joe would be upset, but thought he would be happy to be dating someone rich."

"I don't think that it was me being rich that upset him. The fact that I kept it from him really bothered him. He must have told you about my ultimatum and that's the reason I left him. I know you and I have been friends but friends don't act the way you do, Miss Nichols. I'll be polite to you in the future but I won't be friends with you anymore. You have Joe as a friend and you don't need me. I'm getting more accustomed to my loser life. I've certainly had enough experience to learn a few things. As much as I would like to change Joe's thinking, I cannot do that. If he doesn't care enough about me then I'm in a losing battle and I have to try and get through life without him. Isn't this how you felt Jules when he wouldn't go out with you?"

"I got over that a long time ago." Pam didn't believe that for one minute.

"I asked to meet you because I have one last gift for Joe in my car. I thought you could add it to the others. This happens to be the most important one of them all. You have to promise not to tell Joe about the presents I got him. Just give them to him on the 24th or 25th. I don't want to take them back and he can consider them breaking up gifts."

"It's too bad that you don't want to be friends, Pam. I figured you'd be crying and carrying on about being away from him. You look like any minute you're going to completely fall apart."

"Not now but if I had stuck by him any longer, I would have."

"You may be fooling yourself but you don't have me fooled. You're hurting and you're hurting really bad."

"I truly do not ever want to talk about him. As of last night, he's in my past and he'll stay there. What do you think about, Chris? I talked with him at work yesterday and he's looking worse all the time."

"I'm getting more worried and I think it's more serious than he's telling us."

"They may not know what it is. Look at all the new stuff popping up all the time. West Nile virus for one and Mad Cow disease. I wonder, if he was checked for those."

"God, his doctors surely have done all the tests that they can do."

They finished their meal and walked outside. "Pam, I take it you're staying with your grandmother?"

"Yes, I am. I plan on helping her out at the nursery and keeping myself busy."

"I'm sorry you don't want to be friends, Pam, but I wish you the very best."

"I got some things from the apartment this morning but I need to make another trip to get the rest of my things. I'll figure something out I'm sure. Thanks, Jules, for meeting me. Do me a favor and don't try and get us back together, please. It's no fun being shit on all the time by some guy you thought truly loved you. He would rather be with the tramp than with me. I'll see you Sunday at work." Pam got his last gift out and handed it to Julie. They got into their cars and drove their separate ways. She knew that the last thing Julie would do was try and get them back together. She was so sure of it. She was glad lunch went well and Julie seemed glad to have their friendship over with. Pam certainly was. She would go to the nursery and see what she could do to help out.

She parked her car at her Nana's house and hiked over to the nursery. She walked through the entrance and greeted the ladies at the check-out stands. She passed the decorated Christmas trees and proceeded through the double doors out under the screened area. She saw her grandmother by the trees talking with a customer. There were poinsettias everywhere. All sizes and colors. She would buy one for herself and put it in her bedroom. She had already bought a Christmas cactus but it was now with Joe. She'd buy another one to enjoy at her Nana's. She picked one with bright orange blossoms. She grabbed a broom and started sweeping around some of the plants. She didn't notice her Nana coming towards her. "Well, young lady, I don't have to tell you what needs to be done. Did you get all your running around done?"

"Yes, I did and I have a picture of myself ready to send to my folks. I bought stuff to make the peanut butter fudge later so it'll be fresh to be shipped tomorrow. We have two boxes between us to be mailed."

"Do you have all your Christmas shopping done, Pam?"

"Not every little thing but I made a list and it helped me to stay focused this year."

"I have a few things left myself. You look like hell and I assume you aren't going to share with me what you are going through." Pam didn't say anything. "It's not good to keep everything inside. Look at me now a bitter sounding old hag. I talk bad about men all the time but deep down I know not all men are alike. I just happened to run into assholes throughout my life. If you ever feel like talking about Joe, let me know."

"All I can tell you is that Julie told him about me and my rich family. He didn't take it very well but we have other issues that are bothering me more so I just can't tell you everything now, Nana. I hurt so terribly that I try not to even think about him. What would you like me to do around here besides sweep?"

"I do want to put a couple of poinsettias at the end of each check-out stand. People sometimes grab things that are near the stands as a last minute gift idea."

"That's a good plan so I'll sweep and take some of them out front." Pam was actually enjoying working in the nursery. It beat sitting around thinking about her life.

"I'm going to put discount prices on some of our older plants. The holidays are a good time to do this to make room for new ones after the first of the year." Pam worked a few hours and then decided she had better leave to go and make the fudge. If she didn't send fudge to her dad, he would be very unhappy. Her mom had never cooked so it was the family cook, Marie who taught Pam how to make good fudge. She taught Pam other things to do as well. She enjoyed her little walk in the fresh air to her Nana's. It didn't take her long at all to mix up the fudge and cook it. While the fudge was cooling she threw a bag of pop corn into the microwave. She wasn't hungry enough for regular food but felt like snacking. She went into the living room and turned on the TV. She plugged in the Christmas tree lights and sat on the couch. Her Nana had a satellite and she would try to find a nice Christmas show to watch. The phone rang and she didn't recognize the incoming phone number. She picked up the phone and said, "Hello."

"Pam, I need to talk with you," Joe said. She returned the phone to the cradle and slowly walked back to the couch. She couldn't believe that he wanted to talk to her this soon. She guessed Julie couldn't wait to tell him where she was staying. He carried her Nana's number in his wallet since after the accident. Sunday at work would even be worse but she had to get through it all. There was no way she could talk to him now and she didn't know, if she would ever be able to. He can be with his tramp because he made that choice. Her Nana came in after 7 PM and had a piece of fudge right away.

"This is so good, Pam. You'll make some more for me won't you."

"Of course, my friends are already asking for some so I'll be cooking about everyday until Christmas."

"I need to ask you a thing or two. If he calls do you want to talk to him or how do you want me to handle it?"

"Funny you should ask because he called a little while ago and I hung up on him. He called from a strange number so I didn't know who it was. I'll not talk with him on the phone or in person. At work it'll be business only communicating for the two of us. I have to do it this way until I can get past it altogether."

"I understand and I'll handle it as you wish." They chatted for awhile about the nursery and her grandmother went to her room. She wanted to read some before going to sleep. Pam stayed on the couch watching TV and the tree lights as they blinked. She went to bed later after reading some of her book. She hadn't done much reading since Joe moved in with her. They had other things to take care of in bed. She was already missing being with him. She knew that over time it had to get better.

The next morning, Saturday, would become another day of unrest for her. It was the weekend before Christmas and it should be a festive time of year. Just being away from Joe was making it a sad time in her life. She rose out of bed and did her normal showering and drinking coffee. She packed the fudge in a plastic container to be shipped with other gifts to her folks. She was good at wrapping packages and soon she had two boxes ready to be taken to the post office. Her Nana was already at the nursery and she took off for the post office. She knew there would be a long line and it was expected with just a week away from the busiest time of the year. She didn't work today so she wasn't in a hurry. Pam parked a block down the street from the main entrance. She juggled the two boxes in front of her. They weren't very heavy just awkward to hang on to. As she neared the building she could see the line was all the way out the door. She got up to the last person in line and stopped. She put the boxes down on the cement next to her. Pam would keep kicking them along as the line moved. She got to the door and noticed Chris almost up to one of the counters. She wanted to get his attention but she didn't want to yell out. After several minutes he looked around and saw her. "God, Pam, you waited until the last minute like me." Everyone in line turned to look at her. She didn't say anything. He got waited on and then came over to talk with her. "I had to get up early to come here and I figure I can nap later, if I have to."

"I didn't want to ship these to my folks until after I made some fudge."

"You've already started making all those goodies for the holidays?"

"Yes, I started this morning. I'm going to make you and Sam some too."

"Oh, that'll be so nice. He can hardly boil water and I have just a few things that I cook so we eat out a lot."

"I guess you and Joe split the sheets the other night? I called you yesterday morning but didn't know you had moved out. I found out today that you kicked Julie out as well. Do you have any plans for getting rid of me too?"

"You're hardly in their class, Chris. I know you have a bad mouth at times but you I can tolerate. I do not want to talk about him and you probably know more about what happened than I do. Miss Nichols has never been a true friend of mine. Joe needs to tell her to get lost in the worst way."

"Well, Jules and I talked yesterday morning. For what it's worth, Joe did not sit with Suzy after you left. He came back and sat with us."

"You don't know what happened in the parking lot between us, Chris."

"I think I do. You gave him an ultimatum and he failed miserably."

"Jesus, so everyone knows what happened. I still don't want to talk about him."

"You can never give him up and you know it." She was now almost to the counter. I have to go, Pam, and could I have your grandmother's number in case I need a friend. This means we can hang out more at the Den and you won't have to get permission." He gave her his cute grin. "I'll call you later and see how you're doing. If you decide to get rid of my ass than give me a little warning. I've never had a rich friend before."

"You can call me anytime." She paid for sending the boxes and walked to her car.

She drove back to her Nana's to make more fudge and some cookies. There was a message on her answering machine and she listened to it. "Hi, Pam, it's Jules. Call me when you get a chance or we can talk at work tomorrow." I told her I didn't want her as a friend and she calls me, Pam was thinking. Joe probably want s to use Julie to get information from her but she won't cooperate. She would make some more fudge after she mixed up some dough to make her sugar cookies for later. The dough had to chill before she could roll it out to cut the cookies. She had a bell, star, tree, and a Santa. She made her own frosting from scratch and added food coloring to the icing for the different cookies. She could take some fudge and cookies to work tomorrow for her friends to enjoy.

Her Nana called and Pam told her the boxes had been sent. "Nana, if you don't need me at the nursery, I thought I'd spend the afternoon making fudge and cookies."

"What kind will you make?"

"A double batch of peanut butter fudge and a large batch of Christmas cutout cookies. Some for you and some for the gang at work. I'll be busy baking every day because I'll never be able to fill my friends up."

"It's nice that you share with them."

"I still have chocolate fudge to make and more kinds of cookies. I can't forget my special carrot cake for Christmas too."

"Joe, is going to miss out on a nice Christmas with you." The tears started and she knew she had to hang up.

"I have to go, Nana, and I'll see you when you get off."

"Goodbye, Pam and I hope I didn't make you sad just now." Of course I'm sad she told herself. Nana knows how sensitive I am so she shouldn't talk like that. She put the bowl of cookie dough in the refrigerator and got all the ingredients out for the fudge. Her Nana had some big old pots that were good for candy making. She mixed up part of the recipe and started boiling it on medium heat. She could tell by lifting the large metal spoon out of the pot when the candy had cooked long enough. She added the rest of the ingredients and poured the mixture into a pan to cool. Pam decided to sit in the living room for awhile before cutting out the cookies to bake. She would frost them in the morning. She was flipping through the satellite networks when she realized she had only eaten a bagel this morning. She hadn't had a decent meal in a few days. It would not be pop corn for dinner tonight. Pam called her Nana to see, if she would like her to pick something up for the two of them. Her Nana had eaten a sandwich and would indulge in fudge when she got home. Pam was on her own. There were plenty of fast food places but she wasn't in the mood for that either. She would call the Den and have them fix a steak and all the trimmings for her. She would go in and pick it up to bring home. Pam doubted, if anyone she knew would be there in the early evening. She called her order in and then got ready to pick it up. She would drive by the Diner to see, if Suzy's car was there to indicate she was working. Pam slowly drove passing the Diner and she saw Suzy's car. Thank God, she wouldn't be at the Den. She parked and went inside the Den and stood at the very end of the bar. She gave them her name and waited for them to return. She felt a hand on her arm and she jumped.

"I didn't mean to jump you," Chris said to her. She turned and saw him grinning. "I just ordered a steak so why don't you join me at my table over there. Sam's working late tonight at the Salon because the holiday rush is on."

"I was going to take my food home but I'll be happy to join you."

"We've never had dinner out before, Miss Rich Bitch."

"I won't be very good company this evening. Are you going to keep calling me that? It sounds awful."

"I like that name and you need to get used to it. You can't control who your parents are. Why couldn't I have been so lucky?"

"It was not great, Chris, I know that's hard to understand."

"Sure it is because everyone thinks that money is the answer to it all. Trust me our health is a lot more important." Pam took her take out meal to the table. His food had not yet arrived. The waitress brought her a plate and utensils when Chris's steak was ready.

"I'm surprised that you would move out just like that. You should make him move for all the problems he has caused you."

"I couldn't do that to him because I do have a place to go to and he does not."

"You're always thinking abut him and not yourself. Make it hard on him. You make it too easy for him to treat you like shit. I'm not trying to piss you off, Pam, but you don't handle him right. I know it was a shock for him to find out that your rich but that should make your relationship better instead of worse."

"I guess we think that way but he doesn't. I have gone over so many things so many times that my mind has gone crazy on me."

"You can't really think that he wants the tramp. It's a matter of him choosing between her and you. Whether the kid is his or not, he needs to choose. I can see him trying to get custody of it. With all of your money, he has a good chance of doing just that. After a cooling off period, he may come to his senses."

"I'm going to give him all the time that he needs. I hope you'll still be friends with me, Chris. I only have you and Nana on my side right now."

"You'll have to shoot me to get rid of me. I like rubbing elbows with the rich and famous." She smiled at her friend and they finished their steaks. "Are you going home to cry all evening?" Chris asked her.

"No, I have Christmas cookies to make. I'm doing everything to keep busy. Why don't you come over and help me cut them out?"

"I'm not very talented in the kitchen."

"I just have to roll out the dough, you use the cookie cutters, and they bake in the oven. It'll be fun."

"I've never made cookies before so I can come and try. You know I love your grandmother's house."

"I have a big pan of fudge already made so you can eat some sweets too." While Chris was waiting for his check, Pam felt someone hit her in the back.

"I see the bitch is out tonight without her other boyfriend," Suzy said to her.

"You need to stay away from her," Chris told Suzy.

"I just came over to say hello and I won't touch her again." Suzy left.

"Are you ready to leave, Chris?"

"Yes, I'll follow you over to your Nana's."

He arrived at the house after Pam. They walked up to the front door together. "Is Lee going to be here?"

"Yes she is and she'll be glad to see you." They went inside and Lee seemed really glad to see him.

"You haven't eaten all the fudge, have you, Nana?"

"Goodness no, but it sure is good. Chris, have a piece it's the best fudge in the world." She offered him a plate of fudge piled high. He took a bite and grinned.

"You're right about that, it's the best I have ever had." Pam smiled at him.

"We came to make cookies so I'll get started." She washed up and put flour all over the counter top and grabbed the rolling pin out of the drawer. She took the cookie dough out of the refrigerator and put a glob of it on the floured surface.

"When do I get to do something?" Chris asked.

"As soon as I roll this out you'll take the cookie cutters and cut us some cookies. We'll put the cookies on the cookie sheets and I'll put them in the oven to bake."

"It looks easy enough," he told her.

"I'm going into the living room to watch TV so don't make too much of a mess," Lee said to them both. Pam started rolling the dough out and Chris was watching her.

He put his finger into some flour and put it on the end of her nose. "Now you look like a cook." She rolled it out until it was flat enough and told him to use the bell first to make the cookies. She showed him how to put the cutter in flour and then into the dough. He was doing quite well for the first time. She put the cookies on the sheets. It took about an hour to bake the cookies off, two sheets at a time and then she cleaned up the kitchen. They sat down at the table to have a piece of fudge.

"Remember when you thought Joe enjoyed abusing you, do you still think that way?"

"I can't possibly know what's in his head. I felt that way at the time but so much more has happened."

"I need to get my ass down the road or Sam will worry."

"It was so nice having dinner and making cookies with you, Chris. I'll bring some to work after I frost them in the morning." She walked him to the door and he gave her a hug.

"Goodnight, Lee, and take care of Pam. She needs us now." Pam went over and sat on the couch with Lee.

"I guess you would rather have made cookies with Joe?" Lee asked her.

"Of course, but my life isn't good at the moment. It can only get better. I only have you and Chris and that's fine."

The doorbell rang as Pam's eyes saddened and filled with tears. Lee walked over and looked out. "It's Joe what do you want me to do."

"Just let him in and I'll see what he wants."

"Joe, you have balls coming over here now that you have Pam all upset."

"That's why I'm here, I just want to talk with her." He looked at Pam.

"You're crying and I haven't even said anything."

"I'm not terribly happy so what did you come here for?"

"I would like to speak with you in private."

"We can go into the kitchen. Excuse us, Nana, this won't take long."

"First off, I don't like hurting you or Suzy hurting you."

"Joe, she knows what she's doing so what's your excuse? You walked out on me at the Den because I have some money in my background. That upset me so I asked you to choose Suzy or me. You just left me in the parking lot like I didn't count for anything."

"Would you come home with me tonight?"

"I can't, Joe. You haven't convinced me that you'll choose me over her. I know we love each other but I don't know, if you love me enough. It wasn't easy for me to come here and stay with Nana. I didn't want to leave you but you gave me no choice."

"Do you want a sworn legal statement that I'll always stay with you?"

"You could break that at anytime. I can still see her making things so difficult for us. When that baby comes, if you find out it's yours, I'll be way at the bottom of your priorities. I know this in my heart right now. Women like her always seem to get their way. They can do bad things and come out smelling like a rose. She knows she has you in her back pocket. She's going to keep attacking me and making my life miserable. I have your love and she doesn't. It'll not stop her from trying to get you to be with her. She's crazy and she's not thinking like a normal person."

"It looks like you made up your mind some time ago. I'll leave now."

"Please take some fudge and I'll give you some cookies tomorrow at work."

"Nah, you want to give me crumbs in exchange for your love and I'm not interested. It's been nice knowing you and I won't be bothering you anymore." He left in a hurry. She tried but couldn't stop her tears.

"What happened in here that he left so fast?" Lee asked her. She then saw Pam's tears and took her granddaughter into her arms.

"He doesn't love me enough, Nana, so I have to stop seeing him."

"I don't believe that for one minute but you're not sharing everything with me either. I can't help you when you're so closed mouth."

"You're right, Nana, I haven't shared a thing with anyone and now I'm ready to talk about him." She spent the rest of the evening telling her grandmother everything that has happened. She started with the night Joe slept with Suzy and brought her all up to date. She cried a lot but managed to keep going until the story was all told.

"All I'm going to say is that you have had to put up with a lot in such a short time. How you live your life can only come from your own heart. I'll support whatever your decision is and I know you'll make the right choices. It's late and if you don't need me anymore I need to get my sleep."

"Thanks so much for just listening to me. I feel better by telling you everything. Sleep well and I'll stop at the nursery before I go to work tomorrow." Her Nana gave her a big hug. Pam still stayed on the couch for awhile longer to watch the tree lights do their thing. She loved him so much but she was tired of all the problems. She went to bed and sleep came right way.

Chapter 28

She woke up Sunday morning with a headache from hell. It didn't take her long to find two Excedrin to try and ease the pain. She didn't even feel like making coffee because the pain in her head made her stomach so upset. She would have to feel a lot better than she did to try and eat a thing. She went from her bed directly to the couch. She had to frost the cookies but would try to do so later. Maybe this is what a stress headache feels like she told herself. She wondered how Joe was feeling today. She would probably find out later at work. It was noontime before she felt like getting into the shower. It didn't make her feel any better when she was finished. She had to make the frosting so she got busy in the kitchen. She was sipping diet 7-up and eating some crackers while she frosted the tops of the cookies. It was a hard job to get through when you feet like shit. She put the dishes into the dishwasher and cleaned up the kitchen. She could call in sick but she didn't want to do that. Pam always felt, if she could get out of bed and walk around, she could damn well go to work. She got dressed and put the cookies and fudge into a large square plastic container to take to work. She knew the crew would like them. It bothered her a lot that Joe wouldn't take any fudge or cookies last night. He must have wanted some but she hurt his feelings too much. She did not want to hurt him but he was giving her no other choices. She quickly called her Nana to tell her she wasn't feeling well so wouldn't be going by the nursery. She had cookies for her to enjoy later. She grabbed her things and headed out the door. Chris was going to miss out today but she would make him some real soon. She wished he would get better.

Pam drove through the streets to the office. She made a right turn onto Rose Way just a few blocks from the office. All of a sudden she saw a car coming across the double yellow lines into her lane. She jerked her steering wheel to avoid the car and left the street. Her car went over the sidewalk into a chain link fence. She couldn't believe what just happened and she thought the other car looked like Suzy's. She wished she could have seen the driver but it happened too fast. She was shaken up and hoped she didn't have much damage. The owner of the house came out to check on her. "Are you okay?" a older woman wearing red pants called out to her. Pam nodded her head. She put both hands at the top of her steering wheel and laid her head against them. She thought her headache had left her but her head was throbbing again. The owner of the property came over to the driver's side of her car. "Are you sure you're not hurt?"

"I'm just upset and did you see the accident?"

"I sure did. That older blue car came right at you and you had no choice but get out of its way. I called the police and they're on their way."

"I'm sure glad you saw it because I can't believe this happened. Did you see the driver?"

"I saw it was a long dark haired female but didn't get a good look at her face." Pam was still sitting in the car when Joe drove up in a cruiser. He couldn't believe it when he saw Pam in the damaged car. He jumped out and ran over looking very worried.

"Are you okay? He asked. She nodded her head. He opened the car door and helped her out.

"Officer, I saw the accident and she's not at fault." The lady told Joe what had taken place and Pam just stood off to the side still shaken up. He took information from the witness and thanked her for her help. He called on his radio for a tow truck. He went back to Pam.

"I'm sorry I can't hold you right now because you look like you could use a hug."

"Would you tell dispatch that I won't be in to work today. I woke up with a horrible headache and it's now back so I won't be able to work." He talked to the dispatcher on a private radio line and told them Pam was in the accident. She would not be going to work. "Joe, we know who did this but I can't prove it? She's going to do away with me and I now have the proof." Joe didn't make any comments.

"When the tow truck pulls you out of the fence, the car may still be drivable. They can pull the fender away from the tire and you should be able to drive it." He took a camera out of his trunk and took a few pictures. "I take it she didn't hit your car just pretended she was going to."

"That's right, officer. She didn't want to hurt herself just me." Pam was trying to stay in control but she was starting to lose it. He won't even comment to me on this because he knows I'm right she thought. The tow truck arrived as Pam was giving Joe her driver's license number and her vehicle registration slip. He told the tow driver to remove the car from the fence and pull the fender from the tire. This was done and it was determined that Pam would be able to drive it home. Joe got the rest of her information and told her he would be by later to check on her.

"You don't have to do that," she told him. "I brought some goodies for the dispatchers so if you would take them to the office, I would appreciate it."

"Sure I'll do that but I want to make sure you're okay. You can give me some milk and cookies." The tears started as she thought about their situation and what Suzy was doing. Pam put her sunglasses on her face from the top of her head. She turned away from him hoping he would leave before she really started crying. She walked to her car and he reached it ahead of her to open the door. She got in and sat behind the wheel. He leaned over and rested his hands over the open window frame. "You know I don't have a case against Suzy because neither the witness nor yourself saw her face. I'm sorry that we can't do something. Under the law our hands are tied."

"If the lady could identify Suzy in a line up we would have a good case."

"You wouldn't want the mother of your baby being thrown in jail, would you?" She could not hide the tears. "It doesn't matter about your so-called special woman in your life. Hey, I'm still alive so we should be grateful the tramp didn't kill me. Thanks for nothing, officer. You're doing your job by turning your head the other way." Pam started her car and took off. She decided to go by the nursery and see her Nana.

"Oh, my God, you could have been hurt really bad." Her Nana walked outside with Pam to look at the damage to her car. "What do you mean they can't do anything to that tramp?" Pam explained the law to her grandmother. She just shook her head.

"I have to leave, Nana, because my head is just pounding. I'm going to lie down and see, if I can get some rest this afternoon."

"I'm glad you're not hurt but Joe needs to do something to protect you. I'll hire you a body guard, if I have to so she can't hurt you."

"We can talk about it when you get home and don't worry about me. I have a feeling Joe may keep a closer eye on me but I'm not sure. Actually living with him, I felt quite safe because she wouldn't want to hurt him. Now that I'm with you, I don't want to put you in any danger. I may have made the wrong decision last night by not going home with him. I'm so confused I don't know what to do anymore." Lee hugged her and she left for her Nana's home.

As soon as Pam was in the house she got a wash cloth out of the bathroom and ran it through the cold water. She took it with her to the couch, she lay down, and put the folded wash cloth over her forehead. The cool water felt good. She had to get passed this headache. She couldn't even think clearly. She was remembering the accident and how concerned Joe looked when he saw it was her in the crash.

She must have dozed off for a little while as the ring of the doorbell startled her. She got up slowly and walked to the door. The clock was showing 4 PM before she looked out and saw Joe standing in front of the door. She opened the door and stepped back for him to enter. She looked him in the eyes and neither one spoke. It was like he was looking at her for the first time. He walked towards her and kept looking directly into her eyes. He put his hand on the side of her face and he moved his face close to hers. He gently kissed her lips and she started responding. She pushed her body against him and she found his tongue. His hands found the sides of her breasts and she put her hand on the front of his pants. They wanted each other really bad. He pulled back from her with his hands still at the sides of her breasts. "Please be home tonight when I get off work."

"You mean you're not going to promise me the world, if I go to bed with you. I'm not going to hear that you love me and want to be with me. You're not going to promise me that if the baby is yours, you'll still be with me. And last but not least, if she refuses to let you see the baby unless you live with her, you'll still be with me."

"I just went by the Diner and talked with her. I took her outside and read her the riot act and told her she belonged in jail. It scared her some but I can't guarantee she won't try something else. I can't protect you over here and not home with me."

"I can't come home with you until you can convince me of all the things I just mentioned. You can't do that so I can't come home." Joe stepped away from her and wearily sat on the couch.

"I do have cookies and milk, if you would like some?"

"No, that's okay, I can go back to the Diner and have dinner."

"You do what you have to do." She was trying with all her being not to cry anymore. She walked over and turned on the Christmas tree lights as darkness was descending upon them. "You need to get a topper for our tree," she told him.

"I don't care about the tree anymore, if you aren't going to be with me over the holidays. The tree means nothing to me without you."

"You can only guarantee me four more months, Joe, and I can't agree to that. In four months I'll love you even more and it'll be harder for me. The System won't let you have the baby. They'll do everything they can to keep the baby with the mother, I know this. You'll have to be with her to be with the baby. If she succeeds in what she tried today, I may be out of the picture. She's so sick that deep down she thinks, if I'm gone you'll run right to her. You can't reason with a sick person."

"I have to be going because my lunch half hour is over with. You might be a little sore in the morning so take care of yourself. Do you mind, if I call tomorrow to see how you're doing?"

"I'm going to work but you can call, if you wish." He walked over to the door and turned to look at her. She stood next to the tree with the tears streaming down her face. "You can't do this to me," he told her. "I love you so much."

"I love you, too but I can't fight for you anymore. She's winning and she knows it." He opened the door and walked out. She ran into the bedroom and got on the bed. She cried this time out of control for her miserable life. She cried for a long time and thought about her life without him.

A couple of hours later she was still on her bed when she heard her grandmother come into the house. "Are you here, Pam?" she called out.

"Yes, Nana, I'll be out in a few." She went out to the kitchen to greet her Nana.

"You look awful. Have you been crying all afternoon?"

"Not the whole time but Joe came by and it started all over again." She filled her grandmother in on Joe's visit. Lee shook her head when Pam finished.

"I don't know what to tell you except you're right. He should decide and not keep you hanging. He must know that would be the right thing to do." They talked for quite awhile and both women went to bed earlier than usual. Pam's headache was gone but it had been replaced by the pain in her heart.

This was the week before Christmas and she kept busy baking cookies and making more fudge. The pain was still with her no matter how busy she kept herself. He came into the Center a few times but there was no interaction between them. Chris was very worried about her especially since the accident. He thought Suzy was capable of doing her great bodily harm. Chris wasn't shy in talking about it to Joe either.

On Tuesday Joe came into the Center and Julie offered him some goodies that Pam had brought in. He ate a piece of fudge and a couple of cookies. "These are really good, Pam, thanks for bringing them in."

"I was glad to do it," she told him. She couldn't look at him because she was close to tears. She could never in a million years get over him.

"Gee, I wonder if the tramp can cook like this?" Chris said to no one in particular. "She's probably home right now mixing up her brew of poison apples to give to Pam. Let's go to the Den tonight and get drunk, Pamela."

"You don't have to twist my arm, Chris, it's what I need to do." Joe was listening but he didn't say a word.

"Can I come too?" Julie asked.

"You don't have to ask because you're part of the 'IN' crowd." Joe soon left and they talked about Christmas. They were telling each other what gifts they were giving their significant others. It made Pam sadder to think about not being with Joe on Christmas. She wondered what he would do with the torn picture she had wrapped up. She was wishing that she had just given him the picture in its frame. If they ever got back together, she had a spare picture that he could have. The shift was passing really slow so they talked a lot more than usual.

She called her Nana during the evening to tell her not to wait up for her. She felt she should do this since she was staying in her home. It was soon time to leave and Pam told the others she would meet them at the Den. She knew Suzy would be there but she couldn't let the tramp run her life. Chris arrived first and got their booth. The two women walked in together. Of course, Suzy was there still drinking alcohol and still in the small booth. They walked past her and she yelled out, "Bitch" when she saw Pam. They ignored her. Chris was happy that they were all out together. Ken wasn't going to join them as he had to work overtime for a few hours.

"I can't believe "Los Tres Amigos are back together again." He hadn't called Sam to join them. Pam ordered 7-up to drink because she wasn't going to drink, if indeed she was pregnant.

"What's with you and 7-up, Pamela?"

"Alcohol doesn't agree with me anymore. I have enough problems without turning into a drunk." She was much more relaxed than she had been in a long time. It didn't even bother her so much that Suzy was there. At least she knew where she was and Suzy wasn't lurking around trying to hurt her. Pam wondered, if Joe would show up. He certainly heard them all talk about coming here. She didn't have to wait long to find out. He came through the front door as handsome as she had ever seen him. She watched him go over to Suzy and sit down. In just a few seconds her spirit was being shattered. The tears came as she didn't know how he could sit with the tramp, if he truly cared about her. He had a right to do as he wished but it broke her heart at the same time. Chris saw her tears and looked towards Suzy. He was disgusted at Joe for doing this to Pam.

"Remember I told you once there's no crying in bars." She nodded her head and closed her eyes.

"Pam, he doesn't care for her at all, he's hurt and trying to get back at you," Julie said.

"Well, Jules, it's working isn't it? He got his wish tonight." She got a tissue out of her purse and discreetly turned to wipe away her tears. She did not want Joe to know how his actions were affecting her.

"Can you believe only four more days until Christmas?" Chris asked.

"I believe it and I'll feel every second until it's here," Pam told them. She was wishing she could drink alcohol and feel numb but she didn't dare to. She glanced at Joe occasionally and he didn't appear to be having any fun. He could have sat with them she thought so he made his own choice.

"Pam, you're not drinking and Jules isn't drinking fast enough because this little party is running out of steam," Chris said berating the women. "We look like three lost souls standing at the gates of hell wondering what job we'll be doing when we get inside." Julie and Pam both smiled at his attempt to cheer them up. Pam was on her second 7-up and the others on their fourth beer."

"Are you going to drive us home tonight, Pam?" Chris asked her. "Jules and I couldn't find our asses with both hands right now."

"You know I will and return the favor."

"I'm not drunk, you guys," Julie said to her friends.

"Sure you are, you've had just enough to think you're fine. That always means that you're under the influence and you should listen to your friends. Pam, at least, you won't be going home with Pecker Head. He'd take you to his place and have his way with you."

"No, he wouldn't do that against my will."

"How long have you been away from each other? If it's been over three days, he would seduce you."

"It's been five days and feels like 50," she told them.

"He can always go home with Suzy. I can't believe he went home with her that first time."

"He must have been drunk on his ass."

"Chris, why don't you like him?"

"He doesn't treat you good enough. You deserve to be treated like royalty and all you get from him are sad days and bad nights. I'm going to tell you, I told you so."

"Jules, when are you going to give him my gifts?" Pam asked.

"I invited him over for Christmas Eve to have a few drinks with me and Ken. I will give them to him then. Knowing Joe, he'll probably wait until he's home before he opens them. You won't get to see him either day, will you, Pam?"

"No, not until Sunday." The tears came to her eyes again.

"He's getting just what he deserves by treating you like shit," Chris said.

"He did do something that surprised me, though, he bought a topper for your tree. It's one of the nicest ones that I've ever seen." Pam got even sadder with Julie's words.

"I think it's time for us to leave so if you two will join me, I'll drive you both home."

"Pam, this is nice of you to take us," Julie said.

"You both have had the same number of beers so I don't mind doing this at all. I only have to go to Nana's and watch the Christmas tree lights."

"A cab would be okay." Chris offered. Jules and I won't mind a cab.

"If you don't want to go with me then I'll call you one." Pam got up and went to the bartender and asked to use the phone. There was the number of a cab company on the wall next to the phone. She dialed the number and requested the taxi to come to the Den. She was told it would be there in 20 minutes. She looked at Joe and he was looking at her. He's trying to figure out what I am doing she thought. She went back to the booth and told her friends that the cab was on its way. All three took their drinks and would finish them sitting at the bar. This was the first time any of them had called a cab to take them home.

"Isn't this a novel idea going home in a cab?" Chris asked his friends.

"It sure is. I guess it means that we have driven home drunk too many times."

"Not really," said Julie. We usually only drink two beers over two hours so that made us safe." Joe was signaling with his hand.

"I think Joe wants you, Jules," Chris told her. "Go and see what His Highness wants." Julie walked over to his table. They talked for a few minutes and she returned.

"He was just wondering what we're doing. I told him you and I are drunk and we're taking a taxi home."

"I'm going outside now to wait," said Pam. "It'll be here shortly. I won't leave until I make sure the taxi is here." She left her two friends. The air outside was very cool and it was what she needed to wake up. She heard a noise near the entrance and turned to see Joe walking towards her.

"I don't mind taking you home but I don't have room for everyone. You could go with me and they could take the cab."

"I don't need a cab, Joe, because I didn't drink beer. I'm just waiting with them until the cab shows up. Why would you even offer to take me home?"

"I think we need to talk some more in private."

"You want to talk to me when you're sitting with that woman who just tried to kill me. I don't understand you at all. You're telling her and everyone else that you're interested in her."

"She means absolutely nothing to me and I was trying to hurt you tonight. I've been thinking a lot about what you said. I understand your concerns but I don't know why I have to make any major decisions right now. We don't even know, if that baby is mine. You're asking me to choose when nothing has been proven."

"I don't want any surprises or letdowns from you. I guess I'm trying to protect myself from being more hurt than I already am."

Chris and Julie walked out and joined them. It looked like their conversation was over. "You two don't mind taking the cab because if I had room I'd drive you home?"

"We don't mind taking the cab." Chris said.

"I could sit on your lap, Joe, and Chris could sit in the passenger seat," Julie told him. Pam was disgusted with Julie's remark and got into her car. She left with Joe driving right behind her. She would talk some more with him but that would be it. They both got to her Nana's and Pam got out her car and got in with Joe. As soon as her door was closed he took off.

"What do you think you doing?" She asked him as she grabbed the seat belt to belt herself in.

"I have something to show you this evening. I want to show you our tree topper and then I'll bring you back there. You have to see it before Christmas and this will be my only chance to show you." She was quiet the rest of the way.

They parked and walked toward the apartment. She felt a shiver go down her spine as the approached the door. "You have to stay outside the door for a minute. I want to put on the tree lights before you see it." He closed the door and went inside. In no time he let her in. She walked over and stood in front of the tree and saw the beautiful angel on the very top. She was similar to the one Pam had picked out. The tears came to her eyes as he stood behind her and put his arms around her. He rested his chin on her shoulder so they both could look. She put her hand on the side of his face, relishing the moment of closeness.

"It's really pretty."

"I found one that had your eyes so I had to buy it. She's only lacking the blue dress. I don't want you to cry."

"I'm crying because I want to be here with you so badly. You can't want me as much as I do you."

"How can you say that?" he asked.

"It's true. I would never tell you that I want to love you for a few more months but after that I can't guarantee anything." He stood up and dropped his hands.

"I have always tried to be honest with you but I guess it has come back to bite me. I'll take you home when you're ready."

"This is home, Joe, you can take me to Nana's."

The drive was quiet as was expected. He drove up to the walkway and stopped his car. "Thanks for showing me our tree. It's perfect now with the angel on top." He was gripping the steering wheel and she put one of her hands over his and squeezed it a little.

"Is that all I get before Christmas a little hand squeeze?" She put her hand to the side of his face and drew his face to hers. They kissed and found each other's tongues. He hugged her as best as he could in the small car. She did not want to stop kissing but finally did. "That's much better he told her." The tears were coming again. "I know you still want me and that gives me a little hope. Do you ever think about hope, Pam. I needed that kiss to keep the hope alive inside of me. It's in a little place in my heart because I want to be with you again. When people don't have any hope they give up and many die from the lack of it. Thanks for seeing our tree with me tonight."

"I love you so much, Joe. Don't ever forget that. I just can't be with you until our problems are all settled. I know this is a bad time of year to be apart but I can't help it. I'd give anything to be with you every day and night. I just can't let you keep hurting me so much." She got out of his car and walked to the door. She let herself in. He waited in the car to make sure she was inside. She flipped on the light switch just inside the door. She heard him drive off. She leaned back against the door and cried for him more than she had ever done before. Pam still didn't think he loved her quite enough. She wouldn't settle for a little part of his life but she wanted to be included in his whole life. Maybe the baby growing inside of her will change his mind. She was not sure, if he would want her to be pregnant.

Chapter 29

She woke up the next morning when she heard her Nana banging around in the kitchen. She decided to surprise her and get up. "Oh, my God, I wasn't expecting to see you out here."

"You just never know what I'm going to be doing."

"I'm guessing you didn't have a very good time last night. Your eyes are puffy like you cried yourself to sleep." She told her grandmother all about her evening.

"You're getting closer and closer to going to bed with him again."

"I'm determined not do that. I can't just stop loving him overnight."

"I know that, dear, but you're putting yourself into compromising situations. I'm sure part of you is saying I don't want him and the other is saying I do want him. You may go weak and let your emotions rule your actions. I know you must feel a strong bond with him to get involved in the first place. Taking you to the apartment to see the tree was him chiseling away at your heart. He's not going through the same emotions you are. He knows he has your love. He's not waiting for you to make a decision about being with him. Getting you to the apartment was his plan to be with you and take you to his bed. I'm glad you were strong last night, even after a few beers."

"I didn't drink anything except 7-up but if I had been drinking I still wouldn't have gone to bed with him. Being strong and being a loser is what I excel in. Didn't someone write a book once about *Nice Guys Finish* Last?"

"I should read it because it might help me to cope with my awful life."

"There are many books out about coping and they may help."

"I'll go Barnes and Noble on my way to work to try and find a good one." Her Nana went into her bedroom to get dressed for her day at the nursery. She came out and said goodbye to Pam. Her plans for the day were to start acting better and not be so sad. She thought that her friends were tired of her bad moods. She didn't want to bring the atmosphere down at work. This was suppose to be the happiest time of the year. She knew her friends liked her bringing in cookies and fudge. This morning she would make Joe a special box of goodies and give it to him after work. She didn't want him to miss out on this holiday. They wouldn't be together but she could still ply him with sweets. She took her shower and got busy. She had just finished a batch of cookies when the phone rang. "Well, you know I couldn't wait until you got to work to talk today," Chris told her. "Tell me all about your evening with the big guy."

"There is nothing to tell, Christopher."

"We know you left with him and we know how weak you are when you get around him. Did he stay with you at your Nana's?"

"You know me quite well but I did not succumb to Joe's charms last night. I don't think he would stay with me at her place. She would probably run him off."

"I'm very observant. I do know that you didn't spend the night with him so that is very remarkable, I must say."

"How do you know that?"

"You'd still be in bed with him this morning asking for more."

"Jules and I had a lovely ride home with Hadji. We could have been killed and it would be your fault. At one point I asked him, if I could drive the damn thing."

"What are you talking about? You went home in a taxi."

"He couldn't drive, Pamela. If I'd been really drunk, I wouldn't have noticed so much but he was terrible. She and I hung on to each other and prayed we'd get home in one piece. He liked to talk, looking at you in the back seat and not looking at the road. We tried not to talk but that didn't stop him."

"I'm sorry but I don't hire their drivers. He must have a driver's license."

"Yeah, he picked it up in Bombay. They don't even have cars over there but plenty of people. So you're not going to tell me what happened?"

"There's nothing to tell whatsoever. He showed me the tree topper he had picked out and that was it."

"Ah, he pulled the old tree topper trick did he?"

"I'm not going back with him unless he can tell me he won't dump me for Suzy later on. Isn't that what you're wanting me to tell you, Chris?"

"That's part of it but I don't think you can pull it off."

"He won't make a decision until the baby is born and he finds out, if he's the father or not. He still doesn't believe he is. I'm not saying anymore about the situation because that's all there is to tell. Don't call Jules and tell her anything either. Joe may have already told her."

"He told her all that you just told me and she's encouraging him to dump you."

"She told you she wants him to dump me?"

"Not in those exact words but that's what I feel now."

"I've felt this way for sometime. She must be thrilled that he's alone now. I feel sorry for Ken. She's using him to try and get Joe."

"I'm sure that's true and I hope to see you at work, Pam, but I'm feeling mighty bad right now."

"Please rest so you'll feel better. The shift without you is horrible." They hung up and she went back to baking.

Later on she had baked a nice selection of things to give him. She hoped he would be pleased. She got ready for work a little early to shop for a book. It didn't take her long to find the one she thought would be appropriate. She left the store and found herself a little early for work. Pam could chat with the day shift. She walked down the hallway and glanced into the briefing room. He was sitting there in uniform working on reports. She stopped and went in to see him.

"I didn't expect to see you like this today," he told her.

"I went by the bookstore and didn't spend much time there so I'm early for work. I was hoping to see you. I have a box of cookies and fudge in my car that I made for you. I thought after work I could meet you outside and give it to you."

"I would like that very much so you have been busy this morning?"

"It helps to stay busy." She looked him in the eyes and again they started filling with tears. She looked away from him.

"It hurts me when I see you cry."

"I'm really trying not to but I'm failing badly. I need to start acting better at work and not be so down. I'm failing at that too."

"It's a rough time of year to be alone and I'm going through the same thing," he said.

"I know you are. I had so many plans for us over the holidays and I feel like a big failure."

"It's not your fault, Pam, so stop thinking like that."

"I'll let you get back to your work and I'll see you at your car."

"I'll be there and you try and have a good shift."

"You, too, I always worry about you."

"Thanks, for worrying because you just gave me another little dose of hope." She gave him a smile and walked out of the room. She couldn't wait to get into the Center's bathroom. She cried some more and then got herself ready to face the others. Chris had called in sick after all. Sara would stay over and Rose would come in early to cover the shift. Pam hadn't worked with either one in awhile so it would be interesting. Julie was in a good mood for every shift nowadays. She changed completely when she met Ken. She used to be very moody when her life sucked. Pam smiled a little more this day and the crew noticed. The love of her life was just down the hall and how she wanted to be in his arms. The shift moved right along. Sara was happy for the overtime since she had spent too much on Christmas. Julie was being extra nice to Pam. She must feel good that Joe and I are no longer together. She has Ken who cares about her and she has Joe who she cares about. She's so happy and I'm so sad. She hoped Julie would get a ring for Christmas. Pam would be very happy, if she got engaged. An engagement ring would not stop Julie from still caring about Joe.

It got a little quiet and then the shift ended. She had enjoyed working with Chris's replacements but he would always be her favorite co-worker. She took her time leaving the Center because Joe couldn't leave for 15 more minutes. She chatted with the graveyard shift about what they were doing for Christmas. She put her headset away and said goodbye to everyone. She walked out the Center's door and Joe was just coming out of the locker room.

"I guess I can walk you to your car," he told her.

"Sure, you can." She gave him a big smile. They walked side by side and she wanted so much to take his hand into her own. They arrived at her vehicle and he looked at the damage again.

"You need to get this fixed soon."

"I'm actually working on it. The repair shops are busy right now and I have an appointment next week on Wednesday. I have to leave it for a few days but Nana will let me borrow her car and she'll use the nursery pick up."

"I wouldn't mind driving you around, if you need a ride sometime."

"I'll keep you in mind but I should be okay." She unlocked her door and reached in to get the box. She handed it to him. He had to open it right away.

His eyes got big.

"This is a lot. Are you sure you want to give me so much?"

"I wouldn't do this, if I didn't want to."

"You sure you won't come over and visit with me tonight?"

"No, Joe, I can't."

"Do you mind, if I keep asking you?"

"Not at all but you'll know the answer. I would like to give you a wine cake to enjoy for Christmas. I didn't have time to make one it today but I'll have time tomorrow."

"Well, you know that's my favorite cake and I would like one very much."

"I'll bring it to you and we can meet here tomorrow night. It'll keep good for days so don't worry about it spoiling or going bad."

"I still feel really close to you especially with you giving me these nice things to eat. You know I would rather have you than all the goodies in the world."

"I know, Joe, and I feel the same way. It helps for me to do nice things for you, even though, we're living apart."

"You have that same hope inside you like I do, don't you?" She nodded her head. He took his index finger and ran in down the length of her nose and put his finger in front of her lips. She kissed his finger and then he put it up to his own lips. "You're still so special to me." She was trying not to lose it again.

"Don't eat too much before you go to bed. You'll be wired all night."

"I know but I may not be able to stop myself. Sweet dreams to you, Pam."

"The same to you." She got into her car and drove away. She managed not to start crying until she was well on her way to her Nana's.

Pam turned out her light around midnight and nestled down into her bed. She heard her car alarm go off and she jumped out of bed. She ran to the front door in time to see a pair of taillights moving away in the distance. She couldn't see anything wrong with her car from the front door.

"Pam, what's wrong with your car."

"I was just getting settled in bed when the alarm went off but I can't see anything. Do you have a flashlight so I can go out and look it at?"

"Yes, I always keep one on top of the refrigerator and I'll get it for you." Pam went into the bedroom and put on her robe and shoes. Lee handed her the flashlight and she went outside to look around.

"Oh, no," Pam said when she got to her car. Someone had spray painted her windows red. There was a big red "Bitch" printed on the driver's side.

Pam was immediately in tears. Her Nana was still by the front door waiting for Pam to come back in. She reached the door and told Lee what she had just found.

"Who would do this to you?" her grandmother asked.

"I know it has to be that Suzy, the one who wants Joe. I thought she was through doing bad things to me."

"What has she been doing that you didn't tell me about?" Pam told her Nana about her tires, her windshield and the fire. She thought Suzy had done all of those things but she couldn't prove it.

"She probably knows you're staying here and this was a good chance to get your car again. She must be a terrible person and you must not feel very safe. I'm going to call Joe and tell him and he had better do something about her." Pam tried to keep her grandmother from calling him but she would not listen. Lee called Joe and he told her he would be right over. Pam was sitting on the couch when he arrived and he hurried over and took her into his arms.

"I know who did this Joe and so do you." Pam told him what happened. She was upset but she was trying not to show it. He held her close to him and kissed her on the forehead.

"Pam, you have to come home with me. I can't take care of you when you're here. I can watch you at home and they won't dare try anything over there. We'll do everything together including going to work and back. I won't let you out of my sight for one minute."

"Joe's right, you should be with him until you find out who is doing these things to you," Lee said. "I fear that you may be in danger."

"I'll sleep on the couch, if that's your problem," he told her. "I just want you near me so I can keep you safe."

"I have to get some things out of the bedroom and bathroom." She went into the other rooms and soon came out with a bag packed and a few clothes on hangers.

"You'll have to bring me back in the morning so I can make you a wine cake."

"You're worried about making me a cake in the morning?"

"Yes, I am because Christmas is almost here. Nana will you be okay alone."

"Sure, I will, we know you were targeted so I'll be all right. I keep a pistol next to my bed." She hugged her grandmother and left with Joe.

They drove quietly through the streets. The event was minor but it had not yet hit her. He drove into his parking space and went around to open the car door for Pam. She got out and went into his arms. The tears came fast. "Pam, I'm sorry you have been through so much and we have got to do something about Suzy. I'll not let her harm you or even try to again." He had one arm around her all the way to their apartment and her bag in his other hand. They went inside. She took the clothes on hangers into the closet and she came back out to sit on the couch.

"Would you put the tree lights on because I don't think I can go to sleep just yet?" He put them on and her face lit up. "I didn't think I'd be here to see the tree lights again before Christmas." He sat beside her with his face in his hands. She had her robe on and nightshirt as she didn't bother to get dressed for the trip over. She put her arm across his shoulders and laid her head against his upper arm. After a few minutes he straightened up and sat back against the couch. He took her hand into his, brought it up to his lips, and kissed the back of it.

"Pam, I don't want to lose you, it would kill me."

"I'm still here, I'll just have to watch my back." Thank God she was only after my car this time but she's capable of so much more. Joe, it's that look she gets in her eyes when she sees us together."

"I know and I'll watch your front and back because I have to keep you here with me." The box of candy she had given him was sitting on the coffee table. She leaned over and looked inside.

"You made quite a dent in this box, Joseph, you'll never sleep tonight."

"Everything was so good that I couldn't help myself." He gave her a big grin.

"I can make more, if it'll make you smile like that." They talked for awhile longer and she started relaxing a little more.

"Pam, do we have sheets for the couch because I don't know where they would be?"

"I was thinking that I would feel safer, if you would sleep in the bed with me. I'm not trying to throw myself at you, it would just make me feel better."

"It'll be fine with me so I'll turn out the lights. Your bag is in the bathroom." She went into the bathroom and got ready for bed. She came out and he was still in the other room. She took off her robe and laid it on a chair. She got into bed and how nice it felt. He soon came in and went into the bathroom. He was wearing his briefs when he entered the bedroom. He climbed into the other side of the bed. She reached over and turned out the light.

"This feels so good being in my own bed again." He didn't say a word and he was very quiet on his side of the bed. "What are you thinking about?" She asked him.

"About what just happened to your car and the other day when she ran you off the street. You could have been killed and I don't know what I'd do."

Pam moved over in the bed and put her arm around him. "Maybe I'm like a cat and I have nine lives."

"I have to say something and it can't wait. I promise that no matter what the outcome is with the baby, I'll always be there for you, I'll always want you by my side, and I'll love you forever."

"Joe, do you really mean that?"

"I sure do. I want my girl back and I want you back for good." They kissed and were all over each other in no time. Off came her nightshirt and his briefs. She ended up on top of him, one of her favorite positions to make love. They came together with a heightened passion they had not yet reached before. She slept the whole night in his arms.

The next morning she woke up with a big smile on her face. The love of her life was next to her in her own bed. She tried to quietly get up without waking him. "Where do you think you're going, young lady?" He pulled her back into his arms.

"I was thinking about getting up, taking a shower, and enjoying being back home with you. I'm so happy this morning. Christmas will be here in a few days and we can celebrate it together."

"So you think you're getting something nice under the tree, I take it?"

"I don't care about that as long as I'm with you. Being together is the best present I could have hope to get."

"Will you go with me over to Julie's for Christmas Eve?"

"Joe, I told her I didn't want to be friends but if I'm with you, it'll be okay."

"I know she'll be happy that we'll be there together."

"Of course I'll go. Nana wants us for Christmas Day and I want you to go with me. She's doing a huge ham and she'll give us half to bring home."

"Sure I want to go with you. I have to call the garage this morning about fixing the car windows. I'll get the car towed to the place that's doing the repairs and they can do the whole thing. You can be with me or borrow my car until yours is fixed." They got up and got ready for the day. Pam had all the ingredients for his wine cake at her Nana's so they left to take care of the cake and her car. Joe called the repair shop and they would be right out to tow her car. Pam was in the kitchen making the cake. She made coffee when they first got there to enjoy with a breakfast of cookies. Just as the cake came out of the oven, the tow truck arrived. It didn't him long to hook up the car and be on his way.

She was soon finished and they were on their way back to the apartment. They stopped at the store to pick up a few things. They were going through the check out line when they both saw Suzy at the same time come into the store. She looked like she had been through a rough night. Pam looked at Joe and then Suzy saw the couple. Her mouth fell open. Pam turned away from Suzy. "The look on her face doesn't surprise me, does it you, Joe? She must have thought I wouldn't be with you." Joe left Pam's side and went over to Suzy. He was saying things to her in a low voice and she was not happy. Pam got to the cashier and used her bank card to pay for the food. Joe was still talking. She took the bags out to the car and waited for him. He came out shortly.

"I didn't mean for you to pay for the groceries but I had to say something to her." Pam waited for him to continue. "I read her the riot act like I did before but this time I added a few more words. I told her that I loved you, I was going to be with you, and she would not be able to stop us from being together. She started with the tears. She was telling me the same old story about the baby being mine and she won't let me see it after it is born. I told her it wasn't mine and we would do a DNA test as soon as it was born. I told her that if she harms you in anyway or does anymore to your car, she would be dealing with me and it wouldn't be pleasant for her." Pam reached over and put her hand over his wrist and squeezed a little. They both smiled at each other and she thought about how much she loved him on their drive home.

"I'm so glad to be back with you and I feel so much safer." They did a few more things around the apartment before leaving for work. Pam had meant to call Chris this morning to see how he was doing. When she got to work, he had called in sick again. He had to be very sick to call in two days in a row. She didn't like this illness of his at all and she didn't understand why the doctors couldn't help him. She called him during the evening when the shift quieted down. He sounded weak in his voice and she knew it wasn't good. In the morning she would make him a wine cake and take some goodies over to him and Sam. Joe would just have to understand her need to do this since Chris was not at work to receive the sweets. He was her best friend and this was the holiday season. She knew Joe would not mind at all.

Chapter 30

Last night they had gone to bed as soon as they had gotten home in anticipation for all that was going to happen this day before Christmas. They were, also, anxious to make love again as they couldn't get enough of each other. She woke up at 7:00 and jumped right out of bed. She showered and went into the kitchen to start baking again. First she mixed up a wine cake for Chris and Sam. While the cake was baking she would make more peanut butter fudge. Her friends could not get enough of it. Julie and Ken had asked them to go to eat a nice dinner at the Den before going to Julie's for drinks. Pam even bought a royal blue dress with silver trim to wear for the occasion. She rarely dressed up any more. Her mind was going over so many things while she stirred the fudge in the pot. She told Julie to get rid of the torn up picture of herself because she had wrapped the other picture of her in the new frame. She heard Joe in the shower as the fudge was ready to be poured into a pan and cooled. He soon came out to see her.

"I can't believe you're still baking. We still have tons of fudge and cookies."

"Chris hasn't been to work and he is awfully sick so I have to drop some goodies off to him today. I had planned on giving him a box at work but he's been calling in sick."

Joe didn't have a nice look on his face. "We did have a deal you know."

"Yes, I do know but I can't help that he's sick and Christmas is tomorrow. Joe, please let me do this in the spirit of Christmas."

He walked over to her and took her into his arms. "You're a good woman and I'm so lucky to have found you."

"Do you know what lets me know all the time just how much you do care about me?" He shook his head. "Ever since we first started making love you have done this. When the moment of passion is over with, you always give me a kiss and you hug me for awhile. It makes me feel that you're so much in love with me. A lot of men just turn over in bed and go to sleep but you take the time to love me more."

"Is that what your first boyfriend did?"

"Yes, he did and he never loved me either." A look of disdain was on her face.

"I don't stop loving you when the love making is over with because I want to still be close to you. You make me want to hold you and never let you go." He kissed her softly and nestled his face into her neck.

"You're giving me goose bumps, my love, is that what you're trying to do?

"I have to make up for the days we lost when you weren't here."

"I like that idea." The phone rang as she kissed him back. It was her Nana.

"Pamela, I haven't heard from you since you went back to Joe so how is everything?"

"Nana, we're more than happy and I'm the happiest I have ever been in my life. I knew we'd see you tomorrow and I'm sorry I haven't called you. What time is dinner?"

"I figure around one but I'd like you over a little before that to open my present to you."

"We sure will be and I have a few little things for you too."

"I would like to bring something for the dinner to help you out."

"No, Christmas is my treat to you. You work a lot and it's not going to be a very fancy meal. You already have the carrot cake you made in the freezer and that'll be perfect for dessert."

"That's good because plain and simple is better so you can enjoy the holiday, too. We'll be there around noon, Nana, and I can't wait to see you." She hung up and went to get a Christmas box for Chris's goodies. She wrapped the cake in red plastic wrap for a festive touch. Joe had gone into the living room to look at the tree. She went out to join him.

"We never discussed when we're going to open up our presents and this tree is mighty bare underneath. I have ordered a gift that hasn't arrived and may not before Christmas. I was late shopping this year and I hope you'll understand."

"Of course I understand. You know your gifts from me are at Jules. We can bring them home and open them tonight or wait until in the morning. As a kid, I opened them in the morning because Santa had to come during the night. When did you open yours?"

"You don't think I got presents do you from someone who hated me and beat me? Being real young and believing in Santa she said it was because I was bad all the time. I used to watch my sisters open their presents Christmas morning and how I envied them. Uncle George brought us each a gift and he made mom let me have it. She didn't like him doing that but he liked me. He always got me something really special because he knew it was the only thing I would get. I got a train set one year and that was my best present ever. God, how I liked that train." The sadness crept into his eyes as he told her the story.

"How could she treat you like that, Joe? I hate her and I don't even know her." Pam held him and hoped this Christmas would make up for all his bad ones. Joe was going to play a little tennis with Ken while Pam was doing her running around. He left first after giving her a kiss and she followed soon after. She had one more present to buy.

She shopped and found what she was looking for and loaded it into the trunk. She then went over to the nursery to talk to her Nana. She agreed to help Pam out this evening while they were out for dinner.

Everything was set with her Nana so off to Chris's she flew. She hadn't even called to see, if he was home but figured he would be. She pulled up next to the curb in back of his gray Tracker. She would know the car anywhere with the decal of the American Flag on the bumper. She walked up to the older apartment house and went into the main entry way. She looked on the mail boxes to see which one Chris was in. She saw another small flag decal on one of the mailboxes and it was his mail box. He was on the first floor in number 105. She found the door and rang the bell. In a couple of minutes Sam opened the door and looked surprised seeing Pam. "I hope I'm not bothering you but I haven't seen Chris in a few days. I have some Christmas goodies for you guys."

"Come in," Sam told her. He called out to Chris to let him know he had company. Pam put the box and cake on the coffee table. She heard him shuffling as he walked to greet her. He looked really bad.

"My, God, Chris, you're worse. When will they do something for you?"

"I feel worse than I look but I did just manage to get out of bed so that's a good thing. It's just an over all bad day for me. Marge came by and I signed papers to resign from my job. It was so hard for me to do that."

"Oh, Chris, you just made me so unhappy. I loved working with you."

"I can't keep working under these conditions so it was best that I leave. Marge can hire someone else to take my place and you guys won't be shorthanded forever." She didn't stay very long because he needed to get back to his bed. He thanked her for all the sweets. He would have some later. She gave him a big hug and wished them a Merry Christmas. She left and felt so sad as she made it out to her car. It was past lunch time so she would check to see, if Joe was home. She called him on her cell phone from her car sitting in front of Chris's apartment house.

"How's my sweetie?" She asked him. "I was checking to see, if you were home and if you were hungry?"

"I don't want too much since we're going out to dinner."

"I feel the same way so how about a salad from McDonald's or something light?"

"A salad would be fine since I've been eating too many sweets the past few days."

"I'll be home real soon." She picked up the salads and went home. They ate and she told him how bad Chris looked. She was sad telling him that Chris had resigned. The place would not be the same without him. They spent the afternoon talking about many things. She noticed a few presents under the tree that she hadn't seen before. She didn't say a word. The only thing for him under the tree was her picture to him in the frame. They were going to meet Ken and Julie at six. Reservations had been made by Julie. She had picked up a gift for their friends and signed the card from Pam and Joe. How very nice this holiday was going to be for the two of them? It was time to get ready and Pam showered before putting on her dress. Joe liked it and gave her many compliments. He put on a suit so they were soon ready to leave for the Den. They arrived a few minutes before six to see Julie and Ken already seated. They looked special themselves. After they exchanged compliments, the waitress took their orders.

"I guess not too many people eat out on Christmas Eve," Julie offered.

"You would think they would since tomorrow is the holiday," Pam added. She and Joe were facing the entrance. The waitress brought their drinks and Suzy entered the bar.

"Damn," Pam said but not to anyone in particular." Ken and Julie both turned to see what she was looking at." Joe could see Suzy and was not very happy.

"It would be nice to come in here just once and not have to look at her,"

Pam told the others. Julie nodded in agreement. Joe put his hand over hers and gave her a little squeeze. She looked at him and smiled. They would not let that bitch spoil their evening. Suzy was glaring at them from the small booth. Pam was glad when the meal was over and they left for Julie's. Suzy tried to get Joe to stop and talk with her as they were leaving but it didn't work. Joe unlocked the car and they got inside. He leaned over and gave Pam a big kiss. "This is for putting up with me and my mistakes."

"I love you, too, Joe." They drove to Julie's and went inside. She had her apartment decorated almost as much as Pam. They got cozy sitting in front of the tree and having another drink. Julie had piled Joe's presents on a chair so they would not forget to take them home. She had the stereo on playing some soft Christmas music. All of a sudden. Ken got up and went down on one knee in front of Julie. He took a small box from his coat pocket and opened it up. "Julie, I love you so very much and will you marry me." She was so surprised and overcome at the same time. She didn't say anything. The tears came and she looked at him. He was not getting up until she said something.

"Hey, Jules, yes would be nice," Joe told her.

"I'm sorry, Ken, this was such a big surprise. Of course, I'll marry you." She went into his arms and they kissed. Pam's tears came as she was happy for her. She hugged Julie and so did Joe. Pam hugged Ken and wished him the best.

"I can't believe you, Jules, the man of your dreams asks you to marry him and you forget to say yes."

"It was too much of a surprise and I wasn't expecting this at all."

"Well, Pamela, if you ever get asked, you'll understand what it's like." Pam immediately felt bad. She couldn't believe Julie would make a statement like that. Joe glanced at Pam and knew what she was thinking. He took her hand and held it. They stayed a little while longer. Pam was anxious to leave to spend time alone with Joe. She looked at him and he signaled to leave. She couldn't wait for Joe to open his gifts.

When they got to the door of the apartment, she told him he had to stay outside for a minute. She went inside and turned on the tree lights and turned the train engine on. Her Nana had set up the train just perfectly to move along the track around and under the Christmas tree. She opened the door and let him and in and as he walked in the train emitted a little whistle. Joe could not believe his eyes. He looked at the little train moving around the tree and then he looked at Pam. She had tears in her eyes watching the expression on his face.

"This is the best present you could ever give me." She told him about running out this morning to buy the set. She asked her Nana to come by this evening and set it up. It was the perfect surprise for their first Christmas together. She gave him his other gifts and he was like a little kid. The tennis racquet was a hit and so were the clothes. She saved the picture for last. She told him it could break so he carefully took the paper off the picture. He was so overcome when he saw what it was.

"This is the nicest gift you can give me. I'll have it forever and buying the train was great too."

"Joe, did you think I would be spending a lot of money on you this Christmas. We haven't talked about my trust fund. When I came down here I only brought enough money to pay my rent and buy a few things until I got my first paycheck. I'm determined not to live off my dad's money. I just wanted you to know about my financial status at the moment. I'll be getting more money than I could ever dream of having when I turn 25."

"I didn't expected anything expensive, Pam. Just being together for the holiday is the best gift I could get."

"I thought that when I get my trust fund I would buy you some nice presents but most of the money I want to spend helping abused children. This has been going through my mind since I first met you. I would like it to be similar to The Make a Wish Foundation. Spend the money to make the dreams of children come true."

"I knew you were special when I first met you but to want to do something like this is just blowing me away. I love you so much, Pam."

"I love you, too. When you get tired of playing with the train you could put it away. Someday when we have a little guy you could give it to him." This was too much for him and he broke down in tears. She put her arms around him and cried too. Joe got her a gold ankle bracelet with his initials on a small rounded disk on the bracelet. She adored it. He gave her an Italian Cook Book so she could try some of the dishes he grew up eating. She was willing to try any recipe. He reminded her that the main gift was still on its way. She didn't mind that the gift was late she didn't like to know ahead of time. They sat on the couch admiring the tree and watching the little train for awhile. They went to bed and loved each other all over and slept peacefully.

Pam woke up face to face with Joe. She raised up on her elbow and looked at his sleeping face. She was so happy to be with him and he promised it would be forever. She kissed him softly on the chin and he opened his eyes. "What a beautiful vision I just woke up to," he told her. "Along with a beautiful smile that's perfect." It took her just a few minutes to be on top of him and lying down. His naked body against her own was wonderful. He started rubbing his hands over her buttocks and back. "Your soft skin always turns me on, my Pamela."

"I like the feel of yours too, my Joe, especially your soft penis rolling around between my legs right now. I like it soft and hard. It's just magic to me how it can be so limp one minute and so rigid the next. It's one of the better phenomena's of nature."

"Just give me a few minutes and I'll have nature working overtime, if that is what you would like."

"I can't think of a better way to wake up on this best holiday of the whole year." She raised up and kissed his neck and nibbled on his nipples.

"Hey, I'm suppose to do that to you," he told her.

"So why aren't you then?" He rolled her off him and found her nipples and caused a shiver to come over her body. "You do that so well," she told him. He held her arms against the bed with his hands and kissed all around her breasts. "That's cheating, Mr. Pellerini, but please don't stop." He soon entered her body and they came together.

"We should wake up this way every morning," Joe said. She nodded her head in agreement. She kissed him some more and he rolled off from her. She turned to get up and he gently swatted one cheek of her ass as she rolled out of bed. "Thanks for another great gift this morning, my dear. One of the reasons I love you so much is how much you like to make love. I'm such a lucky guy to have you. You love me so well."

"I thought that loving you and wanting you all the time was what it's all about. It all happened when you gave me that first wink and I'm still hooked on you."

"Please don't ever get unhooked or let me know, if you get tired of me." He had a very serious look on his face.

"I never want to get unhooked so you don't have to worry about that," she assured him. She blew him a kiss and went into the shower.

They had a light breakfast together and talked about Ken and Julie getting engaged. "Did you know he was going to ask her?" Pam asked Joe.

"Yes, he couldn't keep quiet about it to me. Some people like to get engaged in public and others in private."

"I guess it doesn't really matter where it happens as long as it does."

"Pam, she hurt your feelings and I don't know why she would want to do that?"

"She likes to try and hurt my feelings but I have one over her. I have the best guy in the world who loves me and she has her second choice man. I'm sure there were other women who wanted to be with you really bad so I feel extra special that you chose me to be in your life. You're good and kind. Being handsome is just the topper on the tree."

"You're right about the other women but you're the only one I fell in love with."

"I think she cares about Ken because he fell for her and he has money. She would dump him in a minute, if you would have her. That's tough for me to have to deal with all the time. I feel sorry for Ken because if he knew, he never would have proposed. I fell for you, Joe, the minute I laid eyes on you."

"I'm glad you wanted me and I hope you always do." They hugged and kissed before they left for her Nana's.

As usual the wonderful smells of a holiday meal cooking greeted them at Lee's front door. They got inside and settled onto the couch to open more presents. Pam had sent away for a special gift for her grandmother. Lee collected small hinged boxes and Pam found one of Elvis. It was small figurine of Elvis standing on a stage with a microphone in his hand. You open the hinged bottom of the dais he was standing on to find a pair of blue suede shoes inside. Lee was delighted. Lee got Joe a large box of tennis balls and Pam a special Christmas tree ornament with the year 2004 on it. They were sitting around drinking spiced tea when Joe got up and reached into his pocket. He pulled out a small box and opened it up. He got down on one knee and Pam's eyes got even bigger.

"I'm afraid I lied about your gift still being on its way. I bought this ring about a month ago and kept it hidden from you here at Lee's. Pamela Austin, would you agree to marry me and make me a very happy man on Christmas Day." She flew into his arms.

"Yes, Joseph Pellerini, I'll marry you and you've made me so happy." Of course, the tears started falling when he got down on his knee. Lee hugged them both and congratulated them. Pam was in Joe's arms and so excited. "I'll be in shock for a long time. I never would have guessed you were going to do this."

"I hope the ring is okay because I picked it out."

"I love it and I'm glad you picked it out for me. It means so much to me."

"I got Lee's permission to ask you since your folks aren't nearby."

"Nana, you've known about this for awhile?"

"Yes, and I'm good at keeping secrets." Pam wasn't sure she would even be able to eat dinner she was so full of joy.

Halfway through the meal she stopped and said, "I'm going to be Pamela Pellerini as your wife and it has a nice sound to it." He gave her a proud smile and she took his hand and put it to her lips and kiss his palm. He put her face in his hand and leaned over and kissed her softly and gently. She knew now they were a true couple and they would be together until the end of their time on earth. They finished eating and she and Lee washed the pots and pans while Joe had another piece of carrot cake. Pam took off her Elvis apron and hung it up. She walked out into the living room and stood in front of the tree. She could not believe how this day had turned out. Just last night she saw Julie getting engaged and never dreamed it would happen to her, too. Joe was sitting on the couch and noticed Pam's shoulders shaking a little. He walked over to her and saw the tears streaming down her face.

"God, Pam, what's wrong?"

"Nothing's wrong, the day has just caught up to me." He took her into his arms and held her closely. "I'm really fine, I just got overwhelmed because I never dreamed in a million years you would ask me to marry you today. These are tears of happiness, my Joe." They visited for a while longer and Lee loaded them up with food to take home. She had made double batches of everything to share with them. They left with a full stomach and a full heart. They got home and Joe noticed the phone answering machine blinking. He pushed the button to hear Sam say that Chris was in the hospital as of 3 PM.

"Joe, I have to go and see him," Pam said.

"We can both go and see what's going on." They left for the Mission Valley Hospital. It was located on a quiet tree lined city street. There was construction going on to make the buildings taller since there wasn't room to spread out very much. They had no problem finding a parking space. They went inside and asked for Chris's room number. They were directed up to the 4th floor to the rear of the building. They walked down and hallway and came to a large sign that read, "Quarantine—Unauthorized Visitors Keep Out," on the outside of his door. They stopped at the nurse's station to see, if they could see him and ask why the sign was on his door. They were told it was a precaution for Aids patients only. Pam gasped at the nurse's words and Joe was stunned too.

"Can I see him?" Pam asked. The nurse said she would check and see, if it was okay with Chris. Pam turned to look at Joe and shook her head.

"Are you sure you want to go in?" Joe asked.

"Joe, I have to see him and you can't get Aids through the air. You can wait out here for me, if he wants to see me." The nurse returned and said he would like to see Pam. She gave Joe's hand a squeeze and followed the nurse. She went into his room and saw him on the bed as white as the sheets he was lying on. He opened his eyes and gave her a little grin.

"Now you know what the problem is, Pam, I intended to tell you after Christmas."

"What do the doctors say?"

"You know doctors, I'll live a while or I may die soon. They cover all the bases and admit to nothing." She tried but she could not hold back the tears.

"I don't want you to die, my Chris, we have a lot of howling to do."

"If I should be going to heaven, I'll have to howl up there and I'll make sure you hear me do that once in awhile. I don't want you to cry but I do know it must be a shock to you. The doctors told me several months ago but I couldn't tell you and Jules."

"Joe asked me to marry him today at my Nana's, see my ring? It was such a surprise and Jules got engaged last night."

"Oh, my God, my friends are all getting hitched on me."

"How do you feel right now and how long will you be in here?"

"I should be home in a few days. This is just one of many setbacks, I'll have to endure until it's all over with. I wish I could work but don't think I can. I'll miss working with you most of all."

"It won't be any fun without you. It's not as boring when you are there. You make us laugh so much that we don't mind working. Chris, we can't mention the "D" word because it can't be happening to you."

"I'm not ready just yet. I just got real weak yesterday and the doctor told me to come to the hospital. It's a fine time of the year to be in here. Who knows maybe they'll find a cure soon and I'll be back with you. Have you heard from Jules today?" Sam left a message on her machine."

"I bet they went to see his parents this morning and she would be at work now."

"I didn't realize it was that late," Chris said.

"She probably didn't go by her place and went straight to work. I'll call her when I get home."

"I wish you would just so she knows I'm here."

"I don't want to tire you out so I'll be back tomorrow before I go to work. Is there anything I can bring you."

"I would like a frozen chocolate milkshake from Wendy's."

"I'll bring one in for you." She leaned over and kissed him on the cheek and patted his head. "Please take care of yourself. I'll most definitely pray for you."

She slowly walked out of the room and paused just outside his door. She had to grab the door frame to steady herself. Joe saw her and rushed over. She was out of control but crying softly so Chris wouldn't know. She could not believe her best friend has Aids. They walked out to the car and drove home.

When they got inside she immediately went to the phone and called Julie on the office private line. "Jules, Chris is in the hospital and he's dying of Aids. I know it is such a shock. We got home from Nana's and Sam had left a message. Joe and I just got back from the hospital and Chris wanted to make sure you knew. He said he'd be home in a few days but he'll keep having these setbacks until it's all over with. I'll talk with you tomorrow and I almost forgot, Joe asked me to marry him today and I'm so happy. Of course I said, yes, you numb nut. Goodnight." She went to Joe and hugged him dearly.

"Joe, how can I be so happy and so sad at the same time? I'll miss Chris so much."

"No one really said that life is wonderful, my love, only parts are good and parts are bad. It would be nice if it was all good."

Chapter 31

The next few days were upsetting as far as Chris was concerned. He stayed in the hospital a couple of days but he would never be going back to work. He didn't have the strength anymore to keep a job. She visited him each day and cooked some food so he could eat well when he got home. She felt so sorry for him and she felt helpless at the same time. Joe was being very understanding and she was glad of that.

On Wednesday Joe drove Pam in a driving rain and wind storm to the garage to pick up her car that was being repaired. They were happy with the outcome. In three days the new year would be upon them and they had no plans. Lee would have the nursery opened and she did a pretty good business on that day. They thought they might go out to eat since they had ingested so much food over Christmas. No leftovers might be a blessing. She was excited over her engagement and showed everyone her ring. Julie showed hers, too. She let everyone know that her stone was two carats. Pam loved her one carat and displayed it proudly. It upset Joe more than Pam to have Julie announce her larger stone. "Look, don't let her bother you. She's a shallow person by brandishing her ring around so much. This ring is perfect for me. Your love is more important than any ring could ever be."

"It's because you have so much class, Pam, and one of the many reasons I asked you to marry me. I would never have guessed you were born into big money."

"She can have her mansion on a hill, she keeps saying they'll have custom made. I would prefer an older home that we can fix up ourselves. Hell, even and old tent would make me happy as long as we're together. I know that's hard to believe that I feel this way but I do. You're worth more than all the money in the world to me."

"I feel the same way and we'll be happier than they are, also." Joe put his arm around her shoulders as they sat on the couch. She went over and turned the train on and they watched it circle the tree for awhile.

"It's fun getting ready for Christmas but not much fun putting everything away. I'll do it New Year's Day and you can help me my husband-to-be."

"You bet I will my future bride. We haven't even discussed wedding plans."

"I know, there's so much going on. What do you think about the date?"

"We both have the last week off in March," he told her.

"Isn't that when the baby is due?" Pam asked. He bowed his head.

"You're right about that and we need to take a few days for a little honeymoon."

"We can think about it for awhile and then make plans. I don't want a large wedding. I want it small and cozy. Julie is making plans for a huge one with all the frills. The wedding should be a celebration for the couple not a big show off party. Joe, I'm so glad I met you and happy you asked me to be your wife."

Pam decided to call Chris. It was hard to call him from work, there were too many interruptions. "Hi, Pam,. What's up?"

"I must say you sound a little better today, my Chris."

"Don't you know you can't keep a good man down. Isn't that awful about the big tsunami. So many people have died and they're expecting a lot more. I was over in that area with the Navy and there's a lot of islands to check for casualties."

"I can't imagine being in something like that. It's a horrible tragedy."

"I just got a call from Julie and she's going off the deep end. Every time she calls her wedding gets bigger. They'll have to rent Dodger Stadium to hold the crowd, the way it's going."

"That's what Julie wants but I'm just a quiet, simple, country girl, I guess. I'm looking forward to a small ceremony and my big celebration will be with my Joe when the wedding is over. If he was loaded, I would want the same small thing."

"Have you talked about a family?"

"Absolutely, a boy and a girl would be nice but two of the same sex would be too. You never know it might be more. It depends on what I have to go through with my pregnancies."

"I can't see Peckerini with too many kids."

"He's going to be a wonderful, daddy because of all the abuse he went through. We need to talk about you, Chris, what are the doctors saying?"

"I'll have good days and I'll have bad days and near the end they'll all be bad. That's my prognosis in a nutshell."

"If there is ever anything I can do to help you feel better, let me know."

"Sam is going back up to the Russian River next week and I might need you to take me to the grocery store or pick up stuff for me. He'll be gone for the week."

"I'll do that and I'll cook some stuff for you too."

"I'm losing weight so good fat and protein would help me out."

"Does Sam camp out at the river?"

"We have friends up there who are loaded and have a nice house. Some rich guys that live in San Francisco who are still in the closet. They have money, wives, kids, and they spend a few days when they can, playing with the boys."

"Chris, have you ever been with a woman?"

"Oh, yes, that was my first experience and I didn't like it. When I found men, it was the best. I know, you don't understand the attraction at all because you're straight."

"You're right I don't understand and I could never think the gay way."

"Is Joe being good to you?"

"He sure is and I'm truly happy?"

"I think he'll renege, if he finds out the baby is his. He'll leave you when she gives him an ultimatum. If he doesn't go with her, he'll never be happy. He'll wonder about the kid all the time and how she's treating it. I hope that doesn't happen, Pam, but I believe that is going to happen."

"I really don't think so, Chris. He loves me very much."

"I believe he does but the possibility of the kid getting abused will be his most concern. What will really be sad is, I won't be around to pick up the pieces. Julie will be in her rich world and you'll be crying all the time with a broken heart."

"Chris, I've been trying to be so positive since we made up and he proposed but you just threw me for a loop. Now I'll wonder all the time what will become of me."

"I don't want you to be hurt but I have to tell you like I see it."

"I have to hang up, Joe's at the door and we have to talk."

Joe came in and he noticed a quietness that had come over her. "Are you okay?"

"I'm just thinking about what Chris just told me and he made me sad."

"Pam, all you can do is be nice to him and hope he doesn't suffer too much."

"You told me this morning, Joe, that you had to talk some things over with me. Is it something real serious?"

"Yes, it is and I don't know how to handle it. When we were over at Julie's Christmas Eve and I went over to get my gifts to take home, her purse was laying in the chair. I noticed that there was bright red paint on the end of her purse. It was in a place that she probably wouldn't notice. It matched the spray paint that was used on your car."

"Oh, no, Joe, how could she do those things to me?"

"You said she wanted to be with me so maybe she was trying to ruin our relationship somehow. We kept blaming Suzy and it was really her. Jake said he couldn't find a thing that Suzy was doing against us."

"What should we do?"

"First, we'll have to see her face to face and ask her about it. I don't think we should bring it up in front of Ken until we know for sure. We can figure some way of having her over here without him. We cannot tell another soul until we confront her."

"I agree with handling it like that. If it isn't her then it could be embarrassing or could cost you a friend."

"I need to leave for work so be thinking what we can come up with to see her alone."

"I think I can figure it out if it is her. She knew we would think it was Suzy and she wanted to do the stuff to cause a lot of problems for us. She was hoping you would dump me. When we separated before Christmas, she told Chris that she was glad we had broken up. She's not a friend at all." Joe kissed Pam and said he would see her after work.

It was hard for Pam to think of anything else on her drive to the office. She was missing very much working with Chris but the news from Joe about the paint had thrown her into a tizzy. How would she even be able to face Julie without saying anything. Her wedding plans were consuming her and making her friends cringe. Pam thought, if this was the Queen's wedding there would be the same elaborate plans. Julie was now planning for a horse drawn carriage to take the couple from the church to the reception.

The carriage would be decorated as well as the groomsman and horse.

During the shift Pam asked Julie to come over Friday morning because she had some bride's books she wanted to show her. Julie said she would be there at 10. She did not want to have anything to do with her but they needed to talk with her. Pam was glad the shift went fast. She visited with the graveyard crew for a few before leaving the office.

They were soon home and in each other's arms. "Do you still want to make love, Pam?"

"I sure do, after I shower, you'd better be ready." She came out of the shower into the bedroom and he was laying on the sheet naked. "I have you so well trained," she said as she dove onto the bed and laid her head on his stomach. She gingerly touched his soft penis with her fingers. She stuck her tongue out and licked the end. That was all it took to start the thing puffing out.

"You know what I like and when I want it," he told her.

"I always want to please you because you do me." She kept rolling her tongue around the tip and nibbling as it grew. She got over him and put his penis between her breasts and smothered it. He touched her nipples and caressed them as she rocked him back in forth. She knew he was almost ready and she raised up and came down over the tip and buried him inside. She rocked harder and he exploded inside of her. They became one once more.

"Joe, you feel so wonderful inside of me. I hope our love making never gets tiring."

"I feel the same way and I'll always want you. I'll never want a woman the way I do you nor will I ever be with anyone else as long as you'll have me."

"I do feel the same way and I'm so happy right now." She lay down beside him and looked at her engagement ring. "Am I sparkling as much as the stone is in this ring?"

"More than the ring and you already have blue diamonds for eyes."

"I'm proud of my ring and I want you to know it's the perfect size for me. I don't like gaudy jewelry."

"I've never heard a big diamond ring as being called gaudy before until you said it."

"I'm not your normal woman, I guess. I must be the abnormal kind."

"You're the perfect woman in my book and I hope you never change." Before going to sleep she told Joe about inviting Julie over Friday morning. They could find out, if she was the culprit. They stopped talking and fell asleep.

On Friday morning, New Year's Eve, Julie was all excited when Pam answered the doorbell. Joe was cleaning up in the kitchen. "I'm glad you asked me to come over this morning because do I have some nice plans for us and I hope you'll go along with it." Joe came into the living room when he heard Julie at the door.

"You go right ahead and tell me, Jules."

"I was just talking with Chris and told him that we should all go to the Den this evening for a little celebration and he agreed. Sam went North yesterday and will be gone all week. I told Chris we could pick him up and he got all excited. Please, will you and Joe join us there." She looked at Joe.

"I don't mind, if it's okay with Pam," he told Julie. Joe looked over at her.

"Tell him it's okay and it'll be so much fun." Pam nodded her head.

"Chris is having some good days right now and of course he always wants to go to the Den. He'll want to do that the day he dies," Julie said. Pam wasn't happy with that comment.

"Julie, there's a reason Pam asked you to come by this morning and it wasn't to look at bride's books. We both want to talk to you about private stuff."

"God, Joe, you sound so serious what's going on?" Julie asked.

"Could I see your purse for a minute?" Joe put his hand out to take her purse.

"Yes, you can but I don't know why you would want to," Julie said. Pam decided to let Joe handle Julie. She handed it to him. Joe looked at the end of it and showed it to her. She had a puzzled look on her face.

"Do you see this red paint, Julie, it looks like the same paint that was used on Pam's car. I have a sample from her car so I can have this analyzed to see, if it's a match." Julie mouth dropped open. "Do you want to tell me, if it's the same paint or do you want me to get it checked out?"

"It's the same paint and I'm so sorry for all the things I did to Pam." The tears came as she knew she had been caught. "You can't tell Ken about this because I can't lose him now."

"Julie, do you mean that you slashed my tires, broke my windshield, sprayed the windows, and set fire to my grandmother's fence? You did all of this to me and for what reason?" Pam asked her.

"I've been wanting to be with Joe all this time, for the past four years. I fell head over heels for you, Joe, and I couldn't help it. When you wouldn't go out with me, I had to be happy talking with you over the phone and just being good friends. It was hard to pretend we were just friends so I'd sit home evenings and think about you and eat. That's when I started putting on the weight. When Suzy came into the picture, I thought up this plan to try and break you two up. I figured, if I kept doing things you would both blame Suzy and it would be easy for me to keep causing problems. Pam, I thought you would dump Joe, if there was too much trouble but I was wrong. It didn't matter what I did, it brought you both closer together. Even though, I met Ken and I care for him, he's not Joe to me. I never would have done any of this, if I knew how strongly you both felt about each other. Nothing that I did could destroy that."

"Do you have any idea what you have put me through?" Pam asked.

"Yes, I do know and I wish I hadn't done any of those things. If Ken finds out, I won't have anyone." Pam got up and walked over to Joe.

"We really owe Suzy a big apology for all that we accused her of and for hiring a detective to track her down. We went through a lot of money, Jules, so you could keep your hopes up, to someday have Joe. You know what bothers me the most? The fact you went after my grandmother for God's sake. A lady who has worked so hard to build her nursery business and you tried to burn it down." Pam walked over to the Christmas tree and started playing with one of the ornaments. They could see her shoulders move as the sobs overtook her body. Joe went over and put his arms around her and Julie sat still on the couch.

"I would like to say something," Joe said to the two women. "Even though, you caused us a lot of problems I don't want to ruin your life, Julie. I know Ken cares about you and you need to care about him and forget about me. I love Pam so very much and nothing will change the way I feel. I won't be calling you anymore, Jules, and I won't tell Ken about this. I do expect you to act properly when I'm around because Ken and I are good friends. We'll still be playing tennis and you need to forget about me. Do I make myself clear, Julie?"

"Joe, I can't thank you enough for not telling Ken and letting me get off so easily. I promise I'll never do anything bad or try to hurt Pam again." Julie got up and went out the door.

"Do you have a problem with how I handled it?" Joe asked.

"Yes, but I don't know of any other way to do it. I still feel sorry for Ken for getting tangled up with her. He'll be the loser in the end." They didn't mention it anymore for the rest of the day. They had a very good day together. A weight had been lifted from Pam's shoulders by finding out who had done all of those bad things.

For dinner she fixed him lasagna and he really liked it. She was trying to make some of the dishes from the Italian Cookbook he gave her for Christmas.

After their meal they started getting dressed for the Den. Pam decided to wear a black sheath she had in her closet for a couple of years. A little jewelry added and it would do in a pinch. Joe would wear a dark suit. They had made reservations to go to the New Horizon's for New Year's Day dinner. The holiday plans were all set for them.

They arrived at the Den and there weren't many people around. The evening celebration would start about 9 and extend to 1:45 AM. They didn't think they would even stay until midnight. The large booth was empty so they secured it for their friends. It was nice to walk in and not see Suzy. She was six months along and they hadn't seen her since before Christmas. Joe ordered a beer and Pam a 7-up.

"I can't believe you're not having a little drink on this night," Joe said to her.

"I don't like alcohol anymore and what it does to me."

It wasn't long before Ken and Julie arrived along with Chris. He was pale and looked much thinner but he gave Pam a big smile. "I'm glad you two could make it for my last New Year's celebration."

"We're glad we could be here, too," Pam told him. Joe nodded at Chris.

"Not too many here yet so we're lucky to get our old table," Ken added.

"Pam, Chris was blown away by my ring size," Julie said. She was obviously trying to act like everything was fine between them.

"We all were, Jules, it's very nice." Joe was pissed at Julie already. After a few beers, he could very well let her have it. Pam took his hand and held it on the seat between the two of them. She knew he was upset and she wanted him to know it was okay. He squeezed her hand as he knew what she was thinking.

"Has the tramp stopped coming here?" Chris asked.

"No one has been here since before Christmas," Julie told him. "We hope she has and is not drinking alcohol."

"Did I ever speak too soon," he said. "She's in the building and is as large as the building." They all looked her way. She had on an old coat and it wasn't covering anything. "She's as big as a good size watermelon now." Pam hung her head and Joe noticed. He put his hand to the side of her face and gave her a sweet kiss on the lips. It made her smile and feel better. "Well, she hasn't stopped drinking unless that's a glass of piss in front of her instead of a beer," Chris said. "She'll never learn." Joe immediately got up and went to see Suzy.

"Oh, he's going to his one night stand and I wonder why? He must be telling her to stop drinking but there's only one thing that will stop her. He'll have to live with her to get her to do anything."

"Chris, please don't carry on about Suzy and Joe tonight. I didn't come tonight to hear any of this," Pam told him.

"I'm trying to wake you up, woman."

"Pam, Chris is right on this one, I know he'll stick with Suzy, if the baby is his. He's just using you in bed until he finds out." Pam was not really shocked at Julie's words. She was bitter now because they caught her doing the bad deeds. How could she carry on like that when she was gently let off the hook today. Pam already knew that was a big mistake on Joe's part.

"I know we sound cruel to you but we know it's true," Chris said.

"Pam, I think they're both right," Ken offered. "He loves you but the baby may take over his heart, too."

"You guys ask us to meet you here so you can ridicule us for being a couple? I think our love for one another will withstand any problems that we are faced with."

"That's just it, Pam, you think you're a couple and he does not," Chris said. "We don't want you to feel bad but you need to know what lies ahead."

"You're wrong, Chris, he thinks we're a couple. He sure as hell doesn't want to be with her. He loves me and does not care for her at all. I know Joe and he won't be with her. I'm getting tired of you telling me he's going to be with her after the baby comes. You don't know that at all." Pam watched as Joe was still talking and Suzy sat there listening. Pam couldn't take anymore and walked towards the small booth.

"Are you talking to her all night or are you going to sit with me?" Joe spun around when he heard Pam's words.

"Look, bitch, you have him now but not for long. Where did you get the ring, buy it yourself?" Pam turned and walked towards the entrance. She would walk home and to hell with all of them. Joe came after her.

"You can't go without me," he told her when she reached the door. "I can damn well walk home and you just stay and have a good time with your main screw. You should have heard our so called friends and what they were just saying. They're all telling me that you're sleeping with me temporarily until you find out about the baby. If you find out the baby is yours, you'll leave me in a second and be with Suzy. Everyone said that to me including Ken. I must be the biggest fool around to believe in you. Please, go back to your girlfriend and leave me alone." Joe stopped following her and let her go. She was kicking herself for wearing skimpy high heels. She tried to look nice for him and this was payback now. There was no way she could walk the whole distance to their apartment so she went to the 7-11 Store and went inside. She asked if she could call for a taxi and they let her use the phone. Pam waited about 15 minutes and the cab showed up. She was soon home. She went inside and turned on just the tree lights. It was so relaxing as she sat on the couch thinking about her fucked up life. About a half hour later Joe came home and didn't even speak to her. He walked straight into the bedroom. She decided she would stay up until midnight after all. She took her shower and came back out to the living room. It was only one night a year and she would keep the tradition. She played some CD's, mostly Christmas music, real low so as not to disturb Joe. She spent some time reflecting on the past year and then time thinking about what the future would bring. Could it possibly be that her friends knew more about Joe than she did? Maybe he talked to them except for Chris and that's why they think he'll leave me. Christmas Day she felt so loved when he asked her to marry him and a week later she was back to having doubtful thoughts. It ticked her off that he would even have words with Suzy. She guessed she would have to die at Suzy hands before he'll believe that she's wicked. Pam wondered, if Suzy would try and hurt her again? He thinks she's safe because she's living with him but Pam is not so sure. She thought about her pregnancy and if it will make a difference with him. It didn't matter, she would have the baby regardless. In a few days she would be about two months along and she needed to call Dr. Cho to make an appointment. She wanted to take care of herself and the baby so it'll be healthy. She loves him enough to have his baby and she had the right to make the choice of getting pregnant. She was sort of happy again knowing she could do this and he wouldn't know a thing. If he decides to leave her, she may hold the ace card. It didn't sound very good to her but it was true. She was playing games and she did not like that.

Just after midnight she was getting tired so she went to bed. He was on his side of the bed. She would stay near the middle because she liked be close to him at night. She liked to reach out and feel him while they slept. She would really like to know what he said to Suzy. Pam would have to find out in the morning. He knows that it bothers me when he has anything to do with her so why does he do it? I'm too easy on him is the reason he doing these things. Most women would have left him ages ago but she kept trying to believe in him. She has always want to trust him because she loves him so much she thought. She was a little sleepy but was having a problem getting to sleep. Her mind would not let her relax enough and she knew it. She moved over next to him and cuddled with her head next to his chest. He put his arm around her. She felt much better in his arms.

Chapter 32

She bounded out of bed earlier than she thought she would to face the New Year and what it would bring. She showered and made some coffee. She got the boxes out to put the Christmas decorations away. She might as well start undoing the holidays while she drank her coffee. Joe came wandering out with a cup of coffee into the living room. "I thought we were going to do this together but you've already started."

"I got up wanting to keep busy so I started. What were you talking to Suzy about last night? I didn't appreciate you making contact with her in front of the whole world to see."

"I was telling her to stop drinking alcohol because of the baby."

"You must think the baby is yours to be so concerned."

"I don't at all but someone should try and get through to her. It doesn't matter who the baby belongs to, it's being abused by her."

"By going to her, what do you suppose your friends were saying to me. They all told me, you'll leave me, if the baby's yours. How do you think that made me feel?"

"They don't know anything about the way I think or feel. I think they talk like that to get you upset. You need to think about it, Pam. Chris is getting irritable because he's dying and Julie can't have me so she's not happy. They just want to keep this going about me and Suzy. They're so unhappy, they want you to be unhappy, also."

"Well, they succeeded, didn't they? I wish you had a little more concern for me than her. It really shows, Joe, especially out in public."

"There's no one I care about more than you, Pam. You're sensible so I don't have to talk to you about not doing terrible things. You would never drink while pregnant. How did you get home? You left too early for Chris's final night at the Den."

"He was talking against you and I couldn't take it anymore. He bad mouths you more and more all the time. I'm sure the disease is the reason but it still bothers me. I walked to the 7-11 and called for a cab. I couldn't walk home in those damn shoes."

"I'm sorry about that but you can be very stubborn, Pam. You didn't even say goodbye to our friends, you just walked out."

"At the moment Chris is my only friend or have you forgotten about Julie and the way she has been treating me. She'll never be a close friend of mine again. They dragged me out to begin with and they know what being in Suzy's company does to me. She always shows up and they know it but they don't care either, I believe. I'll leave the lights for you to remove."

"No, don't bother, I thought it would be a joint effort but you didn't feel that way." He left the room and went to take a shower. She sat on the couch and didn't wish to continue but she removed the lights. She dragged the tree outside and stood it up next to the door. She would borrow her Nana's pickup to take it away. Pam left the train in front of the window. She wasn't sure, if he wanted it put away. She picked up the phone and called her Nana.

"Happy New Year, Pamela, and it's nice to hear from you."

"The same to you, Nana. It has to be a better year than the last one."

"Don't lose that optimism you always have."

"I'm calling for a favor. Could I use the pickup to take our tree away?"

"Sure you can and just bring it over here because I'll use it for mulch."

"Oh, that's good because I wasn't sure how to dispose of it."

"I brought Elvis to show the girl's today and they got a kick out of him. Is that ring still shining on your finger?"

"It sure is and I really like it. I'll see you in a bit, Nana."

Joe came into the living and heard her last words. "Where are you going?"

"I asked grandmother, if I could borrow the pickup to get rid of the tree. She wants me to bring it over there to be made into mulch. I thought we could take it over and then go to dinner, if that's alright with you?"

"Sure it'll be fine."

"Aren't you going to give me a hug or kiss today? You did ask me to marry you and I still love you." He went to her and scooped her into his arms.

"I'd really like to do something else to bring in the New Year. The day is young and so are we." She kissed him hard and brought both of her hands down to his penis real fast. She stroked the sides of it as she kissed him some more. "You are fast on the draw, young lady, and I like it." She started unbuttoned his shirt and pulled it out of his pants. She unsnapped and unzipped his pants and reached in to stroke him. He took his own pants down and stepped out of them. Joe led her into the bedroom. He took her top off and slid her pants to the floor. Next he unhooked her bra and found her nipples with his tongue and lips. He quickly had her panties on the floor and he lowered her to the bed. He kissed her all over and she responded by taking his penis and caressing it gently but steadily. She put her own arms back against the bed and he kissed all around her breasts.

"Joe, this really turns me on when you do this to me." He kept kissing and avoiding her nipples and he had her squirming under him. He mounted her and slid his penis into her wet vagina until he could not go any deeper. She dug her hands into the cheeks of his butt. They matched each other's thrusts and she grasped his waist with her legs until the passion was over. "Please, don't ever stop making love like this, my Joe."

"Don't worry, I'm yours as long as you'll have me." They held each other for a short period of time and then got dressed. They would leave for the nursery as the noon hour was approaching.

The day was cool and overcast as they made their way outside to Joe's car. He drove the small truck and got the tree while she visited with her Nana. He was soon back and Lee showed him the mulch pile. He laid the tree to rest. Pam took him out to the back of the property to look at the trees. She showed him a potato plant that was like a vine and had formed into a tree. It had purple flowers on it year round and she wanted a small one to start in a pot. The bright purple flowers were nice and he agreed. Joe walked back to the middle of the nursery to see, if he could find a smaller potato plant in a smaller container. He looked up to see Pam fall over in a heap to the ground. He hurried and got to her and went down to his hands and knees. Pam was moving a little and he tried to find out what was wrong. He took her into his arms. "Lee," he yelled to her grandmother and she saw him on his knees with Pam in his arms. She ran to them as fast as she could.

"Joe, I don't know what happened I fell over and felt a little weak." He rocked her in his arms.

"I'll get some ice and a cloth," Lee told them as she hurried towards the building.

"I don't hurt or feel bad but it hit me all of a sudden whatever it is."

"We'll fix you up real quick." Lee returned with the ice in a cloth and Joe held it over her forehead. "I don't want you to get sick or be hurt in anyway."

"Well, you just said the right things to me, Joe."

"Let's get out of this yard and go into my office," Lee told them. The three walked inside and Joe sat with Pam on the couch. He held the ice to her forehead and she leaned onto his chest in his arms.

"I'm feeling much better, you two. I'm getting awfully hungry so maybe that's my problem."

"Did you drink too much last night?" Lee asked.

"I had 7-up only so that isn't it."

They visited awhile longer and drove to the New Horizon's Restaurant. They got seated and Pam decided to have a broiled salmon dinner with a baked potato and grilled vegetables. Joe settled on steak. Pam was seated facing the door and she looked up and let out a groan. "The tramp is here Joe so how can we relax and enjoy our meal? We can't go out for a nice dinner without running into her." Pam was determined not to let Suzy get her started with the tears. "She must be following us again. I wish you hadn't talked to her last night and get her going again. She has such a terrible life that she finds time to chase after us."

"I guess we could stay home until after her baby comes so we don't run into her." Suzy was seated close to Joe and Pam, at her request to the waitress. She had a clean shot of Joe's eyes. He got up when the waitress left and went to her table. He leaned over and berated her for a few minutes. Pam turned, looked, and motioned for him to get back to their table. He came back with a sad look on his face.

"Why don't you just stay away from her? She's doing this for the attention she gets from you. Think about it Joe. She'll attack me good either physically or with her mouth and you go flying over to her. You have to cut that out."

"I'm sorry, Pam, don't you know how it upsets me to see you hurt. I think you're right about her getting off on me talking to her. I promise no more contact and you have to stay at my side all the time. I'm supposed to protect you and I'm doing a lousy job of it."

"I'm just glad that you're with me and you do take care of me. What did you do earlier this morning? You took care of my needs and it put a smile on my face. It can't get better than that."

"I can't believe how positive you always try to be. I love putting smiles on your face and I hope to do it all the time." They finished their meal and left for home. Suzy glared at them as they walked past her table. They spent the rest of the day watching football on TV. She knew the New Year would bring her a baby to love and take care of. She was wishing Joe would be around to enjoy the baby.

Monday evening Chris had called Pam at work to see, if she would take him to the grocery store the next morning. She agreed.

Pam got up a little earlier than usual to get ready. She woke Joe up and she didn't mean to. He had not been happy about her doing it but he didn't protest either. They were making a big effort to get along. "I'm sorry, my Joe, I didn't mean to wake you up. Why don't you try to get some more sleep."

"I worry about you, Pam and the reason I'm not thrilled about you taking him is because Suzy is still on the loose. Chris is in no position to help, if she decides to do something."

"To tell you the truth I hadn't thought about that at all. I can't stay hiding all the time either. I won't be gone long because I miss you too much when we're apart." He gave her a smile and didn't say anymore. She kissed him goodbye and left the apartment.

She arrived over at Chris's and rang the doorbell. She rang it a second time. "Hold onto your horses," he yelled through the door. She jumped back at his voice. "I can't move around as fast as I used to, Pamela, so you're going to have to grow a little patience with me."

"You're right, Chris, I'll do better, I promise." He was all ready to go and they left for the store. He griped about everything on the way over. She let him rant and rave. She figured Sam was gone and he didn't have anyone to complain to. Nothing was right with him today. He complained about the road bumps in the parking lot and told her to slow down to drive over them. Him being jostled around, bothered his back. They got into the store and he grabbed a shopping cart and then slammed it into the wall hard because one wheel was shaky.

"Chris, when I get a cart like that it starts acting up after I'm on the other side of the store and it's half full of groceries. I get so mad to have to fight it the rest of the way."

"It wouldn't hurt the bastards to have the wheels fixed. They're taking most of our money. You have to eat and they know it so they screw you to death with high prices. If that old fart over there hits my cart one more time, I'm going to shove a watermelon up his ass and see how he likes it." Pam had never seen Chris so hateful. She knew the disease was getting to him and his days were numbered. It was so sad and she could do nothing except help him get through it. He was even irritated when he was at the check out stand, making sure the clerk didn't over charge him for his groceries.

They got back to his apartment and Pam was relieved the ordeal was over with. It would have been better, if she had shopped for him by herself. Next time she'll suggest it and see what happens. He put his groceries away and then asked Pam for a back rub. They went into his bedroom and he took his shirt off and lay down on his bed. She could not believe how thin he was. He had just a thin layer of skin over his bones. He looked like a kid in Somalia who was starving to death. He cautioned her to be careful because he had a lot pain. She gently rubbed him with the baby oil he had given her. It kept hurting him but he wanted her to continue. "Pamela, this seems like what the agony and the ecstasy is all about. I want you to rub but it hurts when you do."

"I'll try to do it softer, if I can."

"Pam, what would you do, if you were in my position.? I want the truth so don't say something to make me feel good."

"The truth is, I would try to find someone like Dr. Kevorkian to help me to die. If that didn't work, I'd fly to Oregon and have myself put to death. A lethal injection would do the trick so I've heard."

"Pam, I just can't do that."

"Chris, that's fine so don't worry about it. We're all different and we all want different things. Do you feel that the end is near, my Chris?"

"Not quite but I'll keep you posted." She could not stop the tears as she rubbed his back a little longer. He had tears, also.

"I want you to be at my wedding and to take part in so many things. I don't want you to die." She had to stop rubbing to try and get herself composed.

"Hey, I'll be there in spirit with you always. When the punch bowl is spiked that'll be me. When you're walking down the aisle and you trip that'll be me, too. You'll always know I'm around so watch out." He smiled at her and she returned the smile. "You're so kind hearted, Pamela, and I'll worry about you when I'm gone. Joe just isn't the one I'd pick out for you. I have a confession to make so please promise you won't be mad at me?"

"I won't be mad."

"I talk real bad about Joe at times but he's basically a good guy. If I wasn't gay, we would probably be friends. I still don't think he's right for you. I would pick out Ken doll for you and that's the truth. He's not only good looking but his family has money and you would get along better. I can see you in the mansion on the hill but not Jules. She and Webb should have gotten hooked up. I wanted you to leave Joe and then you went and got engaged."

"I'm so in love that I'll never leave him no matter what happens."

299

"That's just it, you won't be leaving him but he'll leave you."

"There's still the possibility the baby won't be his."

"Yeah right, Pamela, it wasn't the immaculate conception by any means. If he was positive the baby wasn't his, he wouldn't have a damn thing to do with her. He's still in her face from time to time so that proves my point."

"Pam, I know you have to go to work and thanks for helping me get the groceries. I hate asking Jules because she's too involved with moneybags."

"I'll help when I can and don't forget it." She gave him a big hug and left his apartment.

She cried all the way home for her good friend. She would miss him so much. She was still crying when she got home and told Joe why. "I know you're going to think I'm heartless but he made his own bed by screwing men in the ass. Condoms have been around for ages and should have been used."

"Men don't worry about getting pregnant so I can see why condoms could be overlooked."

"What happened to staying clean as a reason?"

"I don't know, Joe, let's talk about something else."

"There's a storm coming and of course, they don't know how strong. It makes a lot of work for us but life can't be easy all the time. Pam, after you visit Chris, you should wash your hands really good. They don't know for sure how Aids can or cannot be spread yet." She walked into the bathroom to please him and washed her hands. He made her feel unclean and this was bothering her. She came out and sat back down. She was not smiling and she was upset.

"What would you like for lunch?"

"A grilled cheese sandwich with onions and hot tomato soup."

"Just give me 10 minutes and it'll be ready." She went into the kitchen and made his lunch. She needed him to comfort her not criticize her for visiting a friend. Pam was so upset she couldn't even eat. She put his food on the table and excused herself.

"Why don't you eat with me?"

"I'm too upset, Joe, so I can't eat." She sat on the couch. Later he came out of the kitchen and joined her.

"We need to talk, Pam."

"I know but you don't understand about Chris or you won't try and understand."

"Look, he and I haven't liked each other since we first met. You want me to embrace him now that he's dying?"

"No, you don't have to do that at all. Just give me a little support. It's hard for me to see him like that and you don't help any after I visit him."

"You're right and I'll try and be supportive." He took her into his arms. She told Joe about Chris asking her what she would do, if she were in his shoes. Her whole time with him was upsetting. Joe listened and held her until she was finished. He kissed her gently and comforted her in his arms.

"You were right to get upset with me today. You feel you're going through this all alone and that's not right. I want to always be here for you so knock me in the head and let me have it, if I do this again."

"Joe, you know you're just about perfect in my eyes. I just may need to lean on you every once in awhile. You should lean on me, too."

It was time to get ready for work. He left and then she followed him shortly thereafter. She got to work and told them about her visit with Chris. Julie listened but lately she seemed preoccupied when Pam talked with her. When she finished Julie didn't have much to say. "Jules, Chris isn't going to be here much longer so I wish you could try and see him."

"Oh, I will, I'm so involved with planning the wedding but I'll take time and see him tomorrow on my day off."

"I hope that you can do that because he's awfully lonely especially with Sam gone."

"I'll even take him some milk shakes and goodies that he likes."

"Do you have a list of wedding guests and have you set the date?"

"Oh, June 11th is the date and about 200 guests at the present time. His mother still has more to add to his side of the family's list. What about you?"

"No date yet but we are off the last week in March together."

"Isn't that when his baby is due?"

"It's when Suzy's baby is due."

"Whatever, Pam, you should think of it as his because he thinks it might be."

"Did he tell you this?"

"Not recently but at first he told he so. Isn't it great that DNA makes it easier to find out now."

"Yes, it is and such an easy test, too,"

"I'll bet you're hoping Joe is not the father so he won't leave you."

"Did Joe ever tell you he was leaving me, if he's the father?"

"Not in those words but I feel he will. He doesn't want her abusing his baby. I'm surprised that he gave you a ring before he knows. It wouldn't be so hard on you, if you were just dating and not committed." Pam was getting riled up and having trouble not showing it. She didn't want to fight so she got quiet.

She had a headache, her stomach was growling, and she was very upset when she got home. She took a yogurt out of the refrigerator to calm her stomach down. Joe came home as she was sitting at the kitchen table. "Joe, I think you were much to easy on Jules. She still talks to me like you're great friends and she's still telling me you're leaving me for Suzy."

"I'm not having anything to do with her and I'll remind her as soon as I get a chance."

"She keeps telling me you're going to leave me after Suzy's baby is born. I've heard it way too many times lately. She thought you shouldn't have asked me to marry you until after the DNA was checked. I don't like her at all."

"She's wrong and you need to tune her out when she starts talking this way. I love you and I'll be with you." Pam flew into his arms and buried her face in his neck.

"I love you too and I want to be with you forever." They went to bed and made love. She was peaceful once more in his arms.

302

Chapter 33

Most of Pam's thoughts were about her doctor's appointment on Wednesday. She was approximately nine weeks along and she was anxious to start her vitamins and everything to do with her prenatal care. She had gone into the Internet to find out what she would be going through as the baby grew inside her body. It was too bad Joe couldn't be included in this important part of their life together. Then again, she may not be in his plans, and he'll miss out on most of her pregnancy. She often wondered how he will react when he finds out.

On Wednesday she told him her Nana needed help with some of her plants and she would be gone a couple of hours. He would take his car and get it washed and do some things around the apartment. The little train set was still in front of their big window. "While you're gone, I think I'll put the train away for our little boy to play with someday. It's just collecting dust out here and I want to keep it nice."

"That's a good idea, Joe, and I know our son will enjoy it very much. I can't wait to have a baby with you and I want him to look like you."

"What's wrong with your looks, my Pam? You need to pass those eyes onto one of our children at least."

"We'll see about that but I think it'll be out of our hands." She was glad she had gotten him the train for Christmas. She gave him a kiss and hug and took off.

Dr. Cho was very thorough in explaining what she would be going through and how important it was for her to take care of herself. She would have monthly appointments for now. She came out of the examination room with booklets and papers on prenatal care. He had loaded her up with good information. She stop at the receptionist to get her next month's appointment. They gave her a card for her second visit on February 9th one month away. She just turned around to leave the window when Suzy walked through the front door. The receptionist congratulated Pam on her pregnancy and Suzy heard this exchange. Her eyes got wide and angry at the same time. Pam was upset that she had been caught. She rushed passed Suzy out the door. Suzy came right after her. "You're pregnant, too, you bitch," Suzy called out to her. Pam stopped in her tracks.

"Look, I don't want any more problems from you. I have a favor to ask you. I don't want Joe to know about my baby. I just don't want him to know yet."

"It won't be a problem for me to keep quiet about that. Why don't you want him to know?"

"He has enough problems with you, Suzy, and he doesn't need any more from me." Suzy was delighted that Pam wanted to keep her baby a secret. That's the last thing she would want Joe to know. "I know you hate me but I do wish you well and I hope you have a healthy baby. Do you know, if it's a boy or girl?"

"It's a little girl and I'm glad you're not going to tell Joe about you being pregnant. You're not such a bad person after all." Suzy gave Pam a smile and went back into the office. Pam was shaking when she sat down behind the wheel. Of all the people to run into in this town she thought. Pam knew Suzy would never want Joe to know about her pregnancy. It wouldn't be a worry for her. She decided to get out of the car and put the baby pamphlets in her trunk. Pam would try to bring them in and hide them somewhere when Joe left for work. She was already feeling guilty about not telling him but she needed to know his future plans first.

Sam had gotten home from his trip and Chris was getting weaker all the time. He didn't like talking on the phone much so Pam felt that she was losing contact with him. Everything was irritating him and she knew the disease was taking over him completely.

She was working one evening when Sam called and told her Chris was in the hospital again. She didn't need to come right away but he wished she and Julie would visit the next day. Pam promised him they would be there. She called Julie and told her about the call from Sam. Julie would pick Pam up tomorrow at 10 to visit him. Joe would go to Ken's and play some tennis, if the weather was okay.

The next day the weather was fine so Joe took off and Julie picked up Pam. The two women were barely speaking to one another and they would never be as close as they once were. Pam was getting tired of Julie constantly reminding Pam that Joe was going to leave her. It wasn't very conducive to a lasting friendship. They arrived at the hospital and found Chris rearing to go somewhere. He was pale, weak, and tired but he was more sick of staying in bed.

"Would you guys take me in the wheelchair to the garden so I can get some fresh air?"

"Sure, we'll, Chris." Pam told him. They helped him into it and he directed them to the open air garden that was located in the middle of the hospital. Pam was pushing the wheelchair and Julie was walking next to it. They reached the garden after Chris complained several times about Pam's driving. He didn't like the way she handled the corners. The garden was nice. They sat with him but the people smoking cigarettes were getting on his nerves. He asked to be taken out the front door to the street. He longed to see cars passing by once more. They made their way down the elevator to the main floor and out through the front entrance. They got out to the street noises and he seemed more content. Pam was standing next to him talking and Julie was behind him. He reached up and took Pam's hand and held it. She looked at Julie and they both had tears in their eyes. They turned their heads the other way hoping he wouldn't notice their sadness. They stayed out there for awhile. The women were sitting on a bench and Chris was facing them in the chair. Their best friend was shrinking smaller and his eyes looked much bigger sitting in his sunken face. They hoped he wouldn't notice how they were feeling.

"Chris, how come Sam goes off doing his thing when you're so sick right now. He should be here with you and not cavorting with your friends."

"Pam, he has his own needs that I can't do much about so he needed a little break himself. Don't worry about it. You're thinking that he doesn't care about me very much but he does. He has his own issues."

After awhile he told them he was getting very tired. Pam pushed him back to his room. They hugged him goodbye and told him they would be back soon. They slowly walked out to the car. "Hey, Pam, let's go over and see our guys. They should still be playing tennis."

"That's okay with me." She didn't have anything else to do except cleaning and shopping. They arrived at Ken's and the guys were glad to see them. Julie wanted to join them on the courts but Pam didn't really feel like it.

"I'll watch from the sidelines and root for my Joe." He gave her a big grin. She needed to think about things in her life. Pam was thinking about running into Suzy at Dr. Cho's office. She hoped she wouldn't run into her again. Pam was sure Suzy would keep quiet. She didn't trust anyone to keep that a secret. They were now drinking decaf coffee and she would drink sodas with no caffeine. She didn't want the baby exposed to anything like that. The three played a while longer and decided to sit with Pam and rest. Julie told the men about their visit with Chris. Pam didn't feel like talking about it. It was a rather cool day and the wind was picking up a little. Julie complained of being chilly so she and Ken went inside. Joe and Pam left for home.

On the way home Pam started mocking Julie about her wedding plans. "My, dear Joe, we must start the guest list for our wedding. It'll be here before we know it and the invitations won't be sent. Do you think President and Mrs. Bush should be on our list?"

"I'm sure they would like to be with us, if his schedule permits. Whatever you wish, my Pamela, I don't have very many friends and relatives. It might be too short for you."

"Joseph, nothing of yours is too short for me."

"You're so funny today and I can't wait to get you home and give you a real short injection."

"An injection of what?"

"Hot sausage, isn't that what you requested?" Pam grinned at his joke.

"Why are you smiling? It isn't that funny is it?"

"Your shortcomings or your sausage, Joe, which are you talking about?" He reached over and put his hand to the side of her face.

"You're so beautiful and I'm happy to be with you."

"Do you really mean that, Joe?

"Of course I do. You always get these doubts about me when you're around Julie for very long. She and I may need another talk and see what her problem is. We let her off easy regarding all the things she did to you so you would think she would be nicer about other things."

They arrived home and the answering machine light was blinking. Her Nana wanted Pam to call. She picked up the phone and dialed the nursery number. "I'm so glad you're home. I was wondering, if I could borrow Joe for just a little while. I want to move a few of my trees and I thought he wouldn't mind helping." Pam put her hand over the receiver and asked, if he would go to the nursery to help her grandmother. He told her he would.

"He'll be over shortly, Nana, and I can do some grocery shopping while he's with you." She told Joe she would pick up some groceries while he was at the nursery. They both should be back in a hour. She grabbed her purse one more time and went to her vehicle. The store was only a few blocks away. She was inside filling up her basket when someone slammed into her cart. She turned around to be facing Suzy. "You had better stay away from me, if you know what is good for you," Pam told her.

"Oh, you think your big stuff because Joe's sleeping with you now. You're getting too big for you britches since he gave you a ring for Christmas. You'd better enjoy it because you won't have him for very long. I just hired a lawyer to take care of any business where the baby is concerned. I'll make him pay child support and my medical expenses too."

"You're bluffing because you don't even know yet, if he's the father. You're just looking for someone to blame and to give you money."

"He had sex with me and now you know it. He didn't want to upset you at first so he lied. He enjoyed it too and it was all on tape. He was so eager to screw me during the night and he really liked it." Pam was stunned at Suzy's graphic description of their night together. "Don't tell me you thought he wouldn't enjoy it? I bet you didn't count on a lowlife like me making a tape of us having sex. Well, you found out that I'm not so stupid. I can't wait for the DNA to be proven either." Pam hurried away from her and went to the check out counter. She was more than upset but was trying to hold it in. She got out of the store and to her car as fast as she could. Pam went home and put the groceries away. She fixed herself a caffeine free diet coke and sat down on the couch. Her brain was being overworked lately with so much going on. Her stomach was starting to hurt and the trace of a headache was beginning. She didn't want to take aspirin, in any case, she would suffer through it. Joe soon came home and joined her on the couch.

"Your grandmother is a strong lady for her age and she kept right up with me." Pam just sat there and didn't say a word. "Okay, am I having a conversation with myself or are you going to join in?" Pam told him about running into Suzy and what she had said.

"She's so full of herself and you believe her that I enjoyed it?"

"How can you have sex and not enjoy it, Joe? You ejaculated to get her pregnant so tell me how that can be done with no feelings coming from you?"

"I didn't even know where I was or who I was with that night."

"You may have enjoyed it very much then. Don't tell me you went there to be with her and you weren't going to enjoy it? The only reason you agreed to be with her was for the wonderful feeling you were going to have." He didn't know what else to say.

"I should have looked at the tape and then I could see for myself how much you didn't enjoy being with her."

"Just shut the fuck up, Pam. You're driving this into the ground and you can say all you want and nothing can be changed. I'm sick and tired of talking about it." Joe got up and went into the bedroom. You don't have to worry I won't ever bring it up again she said to herself. She meant it, too. She didn't care what happened she would not mention Suzy, the baby or anything else connected to that one night of sex. Pam knew, if there was a lot of stress it wouldn't be good for her either.

She woke up a week later with a queasy stomach and figured this was a good sign for being pregnant. She had heard her mother talk a lot about having morning sickness when she was carrying Pam. She hoped it wouldn't be too bad or Joe would suspect something. The couple had been civil to one another but Suzy was still hanging over their heads. She wasn't terribly happy about deceiving Joe by stooping so low and getting pregnant. The rules of the game had changed and she had to make different choices. Joe got up and needed to do some running around so she decided to call Chris to see how he was doing. "I'm just hunky dory don't you know."

"We had a fight with an old lady this morning in the parking lot. Sam and I went grocery shopping because I needed to get out of the house for a little while. A couple of months ago I got a handicapped placard because I really need it with this disease. Today I parked at the grocery store in a disabled spot and got out of the car. This old bag told me I had no business parking there, it was for old people. I told her I had Aids, really loud, and to mind her own damn business. She looked like she went into shock and got the hell away from me fast. She must have thought it was catching in the air."

"That's too bad that you have to go through such things."

"I don't expect people to embrace me with this crud but they could show a little respect. I have a good reason for calling you because I just talked with Jules. I'd like to go to the Den tonight. You both work and can meet me and Sam when you get off. I know you have a problem going there but do it for me. Jules said she would go."

"Of course I'll go and I'm glad you feel good enough to go out."

"Thanks, Pam, I'm going to take care of myself for the rest of the day so I can see you tonight. I can't wait to howl for one last time." She knew that Chris was grasping at straws in his quest not to die. He wanted to do so much with his friends because his days were numbered.

Pam was sad when she drove to work later on. She missed her Chris so much and she would never get to work with him again. A new dispatcher had been hired but Pam hadn't met her yet. Today she would be going through some orientation and they would all meet her. Her actual hands on training would be starting on Saturday with Julie. Pam got her headset from her locker and walked out to the radio room. The new dispatcher would sit with Julie for today and listen while she worked the fire and ambulance radio. Julie introduced Pam to Mandi. She was a little on the bold side and very good looking. She had long brown hair and a very nice figure. Pam figured the guys would all be traipsing through the Center this evening trying to get a look at her. Word would get around fast and the guys would show up sniffing. She was from Mississippi and the sounds of the South permeated the air every time she opened her mouth. Chris would have a ball mocking her accent. Pam took the police radio and settled in. When briefing was over the troops showed up. They all wanted to meet the new dispatcher. Mandi was eating it up too. This was obviously one of the reasons she applied for the job. All the men in uniform for her to pick and choose. It wasn't long before Joe joined the group. Pam was thinking how not too many months ago she had seen him for the first time.

"Joe come over here and meet Mandi, our new dispatcher," Julie said to him.

"It's nice to meet you, Joe. I'm looking forward to working with you." Pam was having trouble with Mandi's flirty ways. She wondered, if Joe would wink at her too.

"It's nice meeting you, Mandi, and welcome to the police department." They talked a little more and Pam couldn't stand the constant giggling that was coming from this newbie. Joe was probably eating it all up she told herself. Joe came over and stood next to Pam. He discreetly rubbed his fingers up and down her arm. She gave him a smile.

"Joe, we're all going to the Den tonight to meet Chris and initiate Mandi. We hope you can make it." Julie told him.

"I'll see about going, if Pam wants to," he looked at her for approval.

"It's fine with me," Pam told them. Joe left the room.

"Pam and Joe are engaged Mandi so he's a little off limits," Julie said to her.

"That's not entirely true, Julie, he's way off limits to any female," Pam told them. Ken came in and met the new dispatcher. Mandi was quite taken by Ken doll. Julie was getting a little pissed with her flirting. When he left Julie told her that she and Ken were engaged so he was off limits, too.

Pam was so glad when the shift was over with. Julie had talked on and on about her wedding since Mandi hadn't heard her plans before. Mandi mentioned how good looking most of the officers were. Pam and Julie glanced at each other and knew this new female was going to be a handful. She didn't mind because she knew Joe wouldn't fall for her. Pam thought she might even get to like her. She was fresh and it was amusing to listen to her prattle on. They all walked out together and got into their own cars to drive to the Den. Chris and Sam were there and their friend was looking a little better. Julie introduced Mandi to them and they all got into the booth. Pam made sure that she was on the end, in case, Joe showed up. It wasn't long before he did arrive and she scooted everyone over. Suzy was no where around.

"Mandi, are you any relation to the Steel Magnolia's," Chris asked.

"I don't think so did they live in Jackson?" They all looked at one another.

"I'm from the South but I've lost all of my accent," Chris told her.

"What part of the South?" Mandi asked.

"South Boston, if you really want to know." The others grinned and Mandi didn't say anything. She kept trying to engage Ken in conversation much to Julie's disgust. Pam was lapping it all up. Now it was Julie's time to be upset about another woman. She had put up with it too long with Suzy.

"I'm glad you could come," she whispered to Joe and he gave her a smile. She put her hand over his thigh and kept it there. He liked that too.

"Looks, like everyone is here tonight except the tramp," Chris said. Pam gave him an angry look.

"Who's the tramp?" Mandi asked.

"She's just someone who hangs around this place. She's large with child and comes here and still drinks alcohol," Chris informed the newcomer.

"Can't they make her stop drinking because that's terrible."

"There's no law against drinking, if you're pregnant, they just have to post signs up and the signs don't do a damn thing to stop the drinking," Chris said. Joe put his hand over Pam's and held it tightly. She leaned her head against his upper arm.

"What's with you, Pamela, only having 7-up?" Chris asked.

"I don't care that much for booze so I'll drink soda."

"We used to have some wild nights when you drank but you're not much fun anymore." Chris was serious.

"That's too damn bad, Christopher, I can enjoy myself without drinking, you should try it some time." Joe put his arm around Pam and she felt so good. She was having a better time than anyone.

"Pam, I have a favor to ask of you. I was wondering, if I could go to your grandmother's again and look at her 50's stuff. You said she had stuff in some boxes and I'd like to look at it."

"I don't see why not. I'll call her tomorrow and ask so when would you like to go over there?"

"I thought maybe Friday since you're off, if that's okay with you."

"I will call her and let you know tomorrow." Chris proceeded to tell the others of the things Pam's grandmother had collected over the years.

"It's like a fucking museum," Chris said. Julie was being very quiet and Pam didn't know why. Ken got up and went to the restroom.

"Is everything okay, Jules?" Chris asked.

"Ken and I had a little argument today which is why we're not talking much. He thinks I'm going a little overboard with the wedding plans. I just thought it was what he would want. I'm sure we'll work it all out."

"You can probably work it out by not talking about it so damn much," Chris told her. "Why don't you just rent out Dodger Stadium and have it done with."

"So you all must think that I have been planning a bit much?"

"It's your wedding, Jules, do what you want but you both need to agree." Joe gave Pam a kiss on the cheek and she looked at him. She couldn't believe how affectionate Joe was this evening. She was liking it very much. Maybe he was trying to show Mandi not to even try flirting.

"Pamela, you and Joe seem to be very happy tonight. Is it because the tramp isn't here?" Chris asked. Joe motioned towards the door.

"We're going home people and it's been nice meeting like this again," Pam said.

"You two are party poopers to leave so early and not even drink," Chris whined.

"I'll call you tomorrow and Mandi, glad you could join our little group."

"Thanks, I've really enjoyed it," she told Pam. They walked out hand in hand. The couple got outside and Pam turned to Joe.

"Julie sounded like it wasn't just a little fight but something big."

"She's planning their wedding and he should be involved. She has pushed everyone to the breaking point and Ken must hear it constantly." They stopped at their car and did not see Suzy getting out of her car and walking towards them.

"Oh, Joe, do you get aroused when you see me now, big with your baby?" Pam was not getting into this and neither was Joe. Suzy stuck her tongue out at Pam and walked into the Den. The drive home was very quiet.

They got home and Pam took her usual shower and Joe turned on the TV. She came out with her robe on and sat next to him. He put his arms around her and she snuggled close to him. "Please tell me, if the baby is yours, you'll still stay with me."

"I promise, Pam, I won't leave you for Suzy or anyone else." She kissed him, tongue and all, and he responded by untying her robe. He felt her nakedness right away and got up to carry her into the bedroom. He lay her on the bed and undressed himself. She watched his every move savoring his body with her eyes.

"I love your naked body, my Joe. You can turn me on fully dressed but when I see you naked I know you'll soon be inside of me. I love you inside of me." He got down next to her and found her nipples. He sucked her nipples good and then pinned her arms to the bed. He slowly kissed all around her breasts without touching her nipples with his mouth.

"This is so good, my Joe, you pleasure me so well." He soon mounted her and they climaxed together.

"It's easy to pleasure you because I love you so much," he told her.

"You say the nicest things and I love you with all my heart." They slept well.

Chapter 34

The next day Pam called her Nana at the nursery and asked, if she could bring Chris over on Friday. Lee was delighted he was coming and she would get the boxes out for him to look through. "What time do you plan on bringing him and I'll be there to tell my stories?"

"I was hoping you would say that. We should be there around 10 in the morning."

"I'll be waiting for you. How's Joe?"

"He's fine and we both are doing quite well."

"I'm so glad to hear that. I want you both to have a happy life."

"We want that too, Nana, so I'll see you tomorrow."

Pam didn't have much planned since it was a work day but she did call Chris.

"Sorry about last night, Chris, but we had things to take care of at home."

"It was obvious to everyone that you had other plans," he told her.

"We talked last night about so many things until it was real late."

"I'm so glad to hear that. I didn't think you and Joe would be so cozy last night after meeting Mandi."

"I know Joe loves me and won't be after her but no man is safe with her around. Julie needs to watch her with Ken. She has her eye on him, big time."

"You both need to watch her. Those rings on your fingers don't mean a damn thing to her. She'll pick Ken because of his money."

"Joe loves me enough to not go after her? I wouldn't wish her onto my worse enemy but if she goes after Ken it might do some good. Julie doesn't know what it's like to have someone after her man. She certainly has tried to take Joe from me. Pay back, by way of Mandi, might be fun to watch."

"Julie is her trainer and she can make it really rough on her, if she looks at Ken or starts drooling when he's around."

"Hopefully, she's here to learn the job but no man is safe around her kind." They talked for a little longer and hung up. Pam was still experiencing some nausea but no vomiting and she was glad of that. Joe will never guess her condition unless she gets really sick. Things were turning around for her or that is what she thought.

On Friday morning she picked up Chris just before 10. Joe was going to vacuum and wash the windows to help her out. She was so happy to be with him. He was a jewel in her book. It was like he was trying to make things nicer for her with so many problems up in the air with Suzy.

"I can't thank you enough, Pam, for taking me to your grandmother's," Chris said when she picked him up.

"I'm happy to do it and I'll enjoy it, too." They got to Lee's home and she was eagerly waiting for them. She gave Chris a big hug and Pam, also. She had two large boxes opened and some of her things were laid out on the dining room table. She offered them a cup of coffee, Chris accepted and Pam declined. Lee started taking more things out of the box. She told all kinds of stories along with showing him autographed pictures of movie stars she had sent away for when she was a young girl. He had a perpetual smile on his face all the time he was there.

"You mean you just wrote to the Stars and asked for an autographed picture?"

"Yes, that was all it took. I had a list of all the Stars at each studio and just sent my request to each one. It was so easy and it got me a lot of nice things." The two friends stayed for a couple of hours and she served them some pumpkin bread.

Pam drove him home and all he talked about was the memorabilia. He couldn't wait for Sam to get home so he could tell him. They were sitting in the car talking in front of Chris's apartment. He was in no hurry to go in."

"I hope you don't have many problems with my replacement."

"Chris, you can never be replaced. There could be a lot of problems coming from Mandi but I'm not sure. She needs to learn the job before she starts messing with the troops. I think her main reason for applying was the men in uniform."

"I think you're right but she was looking Ken doll all over, every chance she got last night."

"Yes, and Julie was not happy about that. She has it so nice that a little wrench thrown into her engine might wake her up."

"Don't you mean wench, my Pamela?"

"That is exactly what I meant, Christopher."

"Well, you know that Joe screwed Suzy so are you sure he won't look to Mandi?"

"You guys don't understand how much I mean to Joe. I'm not just saying it but I do. He slipped up with Suzy and he'll never do it again. I believe that with all my heart and soul."

"You need to look at the whole picture, Pam, and you're not doing that. The baby will mean a lot to him because of his bad childhood. He won't want his kid to be abused by her. I don't think you'll win in the end but I do not wish bad things for you. I truly want you to be happy and I mean that. I believe he loves you and he feels nothing for any other woman. When the baby arrives you will have to take the backseat."

"I'll getting tired of my friends telling me that I'm going to lose Joe when the baby comes. You guys don't know that at all, you're just guessing."

"We keep saying this because it's true and we don't want you to get hurt. You should dump his ass before he does it to you."

"I don't want to dump him. I love him and I want to be with him forever."

"I can't talk to you, Pam, where Joe is concerned, there's no reasoning with you."

"I have to go Chris because my sweetheart is washing windows and vacuuming for me." Pam was glad to leave Chris and his negative attitude where Joe was concerned.

She drove home and found Joe just finishing dusting furniture. She went into his arms and hugged him close. "Did something happen while you were gone?"

"Just my fucking friends telling me to leave you before you leave me."

"They never give up do they?"

"I care about Chris but he never stops talking against you. I don't expect him to like you but he should keep his mouth shut. Joe, please make love to me and tell me you'll never leave me again." He did as he was told and she was happy and reassured once more. Her friends did not have a clue where Joe was concerned.

Saturday came in with a breath of cool air but the sunshine made the coolness seem unimportant. She got him a nice breakfast of french toast and they went off to Ken's to play tennis. She hadn't been going with Joe lately and she knew she needed some exercise. Ken and Julie were ready when they arrived. Julie started in talking about Mandi and how all she did was flirt

"Jules, there isn't much we can do about it. We have to trust our men to be true to us and forget about her," Pam told her.

"Pam's exactly right," Ken said. "Her flirty ways doesn't do a thing to me."

"She doesn't get to me either," Joe said. "I wouldn't touch her with a ten foot pole."

"You, guys, wake up, she's not looking for ten feet just a few inches," Pam said.

"That was good, Pam, and you're so right," Julie said to them. The guys shook their heads. Ken served them lunch and they left for the trip home.

"Joe, before we go home, let's go to the beach and walk around for a little while."

"Pam, this is January and not beach weather at all."

"The sun is out and it'll be fun." Please, my Joe, do it for me."

"If you say it like that, I'll go for a little while." Quite often she felt drawn to the ocean but she didn't always go. They got out of the car and kicked their shoes off. There were a few people walking around but that didn't matter. She could get lost in a crowd at the shoreline. The ocean mesmerized her for some reason. They walked hand in hand feeling the coolness of the water and smelling the salty air. They first walked out onto the jetty and the tide was coming in. They kept getting sprayed by the waves hitting the rocks. It felt good to her like a cleansing of her soul. She thought about the tiny baby growing inside of her belly and she couldn't share it with him. It was kind of sad but something she had to do. She prayed that Suzy's baby wasn't Joe's and he would embrace her and be happy with their baby. If he didn't, it would be a lonely life without him. They must have spent a hour walking along the shoreline. They laughed, talked, and just enjoyed each other away from home and work. They went to the car, wiped the sand from between their toes, and drove home.

"Joe, thanks so much for going with me. I liked being there with you."

"I enjoyed it myself and we need to get out more and do things like that."

"Spending a day with you makes we feel real good. We never talked about you and Chris going to your grandmother's. How did he like the trip back to the 50's?"

"Joe, I don't bring him up too much because I know you don't like him."

"I feel sorry that he's dying and I do let you see him when you want to. I'm always interested in anything you do, Pam."

"I've been on that trip before but Chris really enjoyed it. He doesn't have very many good days left."

"Did he tell you to leave me again?"

"Yes, he did but I told him not to say anything because you would never leave me."

"So now you want me to sweep you up into my arms, take you into our bed, and tell you I'll never leave you once more."

"I don't want that at all, if you say it like that. I didn't know I was becoming a problem for you."

"I was demonstrating with words what you expect from me after you've been around your friends."

"I don't expect anything, Joe, I wouldn't want to put you out any. It would be grand, if you could love me for me and not bring any other elements into it. I often wonder what Jules is saying about us now. I feel she would still like us to separate.

She'll not let up on us or I should say me. She would have you in a minute."

"Ken always speaks highly of her, of course, he doesn't know all those things she did to you. I think she's happy with Ken or she seems to be. I hope so."

"She doesn't talk about him because she has him wrapped around her little finger. She would like us to split up so she can try for you again."

"I don't think I make enough money for Jules. I don't have any desire to be with her so it wouldn't do her any good." Pam was tired of bantering back and forth and going to the ocean was making her sleepy.

"I'm tired so I'm going to try and take a nap, if that's okay with you?"

"Go ahead, I don't mind." She went into the bedroom and lay down on the bed. She was just starting to doze when Joe came and lay down beside her. He put his arm around her and drew her to him. He kissed the top of her head and stroked her hair. It felt so good and she loved him so much.

February came in dreary and overcast. It had been raining for three days in a row. Pam was still having nausea but nothing more than that. Joe mentioned how pale she looked at times and she blamed the bad weather and no sun. She was thinking that Suzy was seven months along now and it wouldn't be much longer before the baby was here. Then her fate would be sealed or she felt it would. She still had doubts that Joe would stick around. She was even thinking about not telling him about her pregnancy at all, if he decides to leave. She would show up for work one day in a maternity top and word would get out. She would have to think about this tactic.

She needed to talk to her Nana so she decided to go to the nursery this Friday morning. Joe and Ken wanted to go to the indoor batting cages and hit a few balls. Tennis was definitely out of the question in the rain. They kissed and took off at the same time. She arrived at the nursery and found her Nana in her office. She was trying to catch up on some paperwork. She got up from her desk and went over and gave Pam a big hug. "I'm so glad to see you, my Pamela. You don't come by very often and I miss you. You need to make time for your old Nana."

"I miss you too and that's why I'm here this morning."

"How is Joseph and are you still very much in love?"

"He's great and we're very much in love."

"You just said it like you were trying to convince yourself."

"Well, Suzy is seven months along and I have a lot going through my mind."

"I take it you think the baby is his and you're gearing up for what might happen?"

"I try to believe differently but it isn't working. I still don't know if he'll stick with me or leave me. I wish I could get inside his head and find out."

"You came here today to find out what I feel about your situation or to give you some encouragement. It could even be both."

"I need encouragement and advice. It never hurts to find out what someone else would do in my case."

"Pam, you're the only one who can decide what you are going to do. I don't mind giving my opinion and you may not like it. I don't know how long you have known what you know but I wouldn't have accepted his proposal under the circumstances. I would have waited until after the baby was born. I know I was after you both to get engaged when he moved in with you but I didn't know about the other woman and a baby. You still could have lived together and played house. I'm sure he had good intentions by asking you to marry him and I believe he loves you. Neither one of you was looking at the big picture."

"I'm guilty, Nana, of letting my heart rule my whole being. I love Joe and I always will no matter what happens to us. Can you ever leave someone that you care about so much and find love with someone else?"

"You may never love as strongly but you can love again."

"I have never met a guy like him that I want to be with all the time. I don't like it when we're apart for just a little while. Maybe I'm not normal but that's how I feel."

"You're definitely in love and have you told him all of your feelings? Is this how he feels about you, too? It's good to talk and let each other in on what you think and feel. If you come up against a problem and you leave or he leaves, that's very immature."

"We have both been guilty of that but not anymore. How come I always feel better after we talk, Nana?"

"You just need assurance form an old gal who's been driven hard and put away wet a few times in my life. We can learn from others or do our own thing."

"I decided that I'm not very romantic and I guess he isn't either. I would love to get flowers sometime just for no reason. I'll stop on my way home at the florist shop and get him a nice bouquet. It might give him a hint to return the gesture someday. He never had a mother who could teach him things like that."

"That's a good idea. Men sometimes don't get it and a simple sign could put the thought in his mind."

"I have to go, my sweet Nana, but I'll be back soon. I'll try and call you more often because I miss our little talks a lot." They hugged and Pam was off to the flower shop. She picked out a simple arrangement of red and white carnations." She loved carnations because they smelled so nice. She thought he would like them, too. She got home and he was still gone. She got a pretty vase out of the cupboard and fixed the flowers in the vase.

Joe arrived just after she finished placing the vase on the coffee table. "Who sent flowers, Pam?" he had a quizzical look on his face.

"Read the card and you'll find out." He read the card, turned, and smiled at her.

"Am I really the true love of your life?"

"Of course, you are and you know it."

"It's just nice to see it written down and to hear it from you," he told her.

"I'll always say it to you." She went to him and kissed his face all over. "That's just a bonus to go along with the flowers. Do you really know my feelings for you? I hate being away from you for a short time. When we're together I don't want to take my eyes off of you for a minute. I have this big urge to touch you somewhere when we're in the same room. I guess I'm just consumed with you completely."

"I know you love me but I didn't realize you had those feelings and hearing you talk that way, makes me very happy. Would it make you feel good, if I told you I have the same feelings for you? I like being close to you and the touching is the same for me."

"Yes, it would. I know making love with you is great but I didn't think you knew what I felt when we weren't in bed. It isn't just sex, I love everything about you and I just had to tell you today."

"I love how much you love me," he admitted. "I love how kind and caring you are. I love it when you make me a delicious meal. I love the way you put me above yourself. You're going to make a great wife and an even greater mother. There's nothing not to love about you." She gave him the biggest smile and her eyes lit up. "Last but not least, I love those two blue diamonds you have for eyes. They light up the world when you're happy. This room is already much brighter with you in it." She put her head on his chest and started rubbing his chest with her hands. She put one hand between his legs. "You can, also, read my mind and you know what I want right now." She felt him come to life and it was nice. They automatically went into the bedroom and took their clothes off. He was savoring her breasts and she fondled his penis delicately yet firmly. She raised her head up and went down on him to find the end of his penis. She placed her mouth down over it much to his delight. She nibbled for a few minutes and then got on top of him. She slowly worked it inside of her. They intertwined each other's fingers and she rocked back and forth. He groaned and she followed his climax and once more she felt at peace. She lay on him for a few minutes enjoying him inside of her. "How could I ever leave you and this wonderful feeling that comes over me when we make love?" he asked her.

"That's what I would like to know," she told him with a big grin. "You might get tired of me and want a new feeling someday."

"No way is that going to happen. You're the best and I don't have to look for something better." He made her smile again. "What does Lee think of our situation? Is she ready to kick me out of the family?"

"She feels we should have waited to get engaged after the baby is born but she's on our side with everything else."

"I figured she would personally kick my ass out of the family when she found out Suzy was pregnant and it could be mine."

"She thinks we'll be able to work it out."

"You still have doubts, don't you? Please tell me the truth."

"Yes, I do because I think you would like to raise your own baby."

"Don't you think we'll have babies someday?"

"I do, but this one would be your first and no one thinks she'll be able to take care of an infant. My friends think you'll leave me and be with her just to take care of the baby. You keep telling me you won't leave me but I still have doubts."

"I know it looks like the baby is mine but it still could not be."

"You won't make a final decision until you find out? That means I could still be left behind in your dust." She got off Joe and went into the bathroom. She came out to find him dressed and in the living room. She soon joined him. "Since I got you flowers today, I would like to take you out to dinner this evening. I feel awfully generous for some reason."

"I should buy you dinner for bringing home the flowers."

"No, all or nothing and it'll give me a good feeling to be kind to you all day."

"I won't argue so I'll let you buy me dinner. Where would you like to go?"

"I'm craving steak, a baked potato with a salad on the side."

"We will go to the Den and celebrate you putting up with me for ten months."

"My, God, it has been that long and I'm not the least bit tired of you."

"Ditto, my Pam, I feel the same way. Would you wear that black dress you wore for New Year's Eve, it turns me on for some reason."

Later they dressed up for their ten month anniversary dinner and left for the Den. The evening was quite chilly and Pam wore a light weight black coat. She didn't have any heavy jackets or coats. In Southern California a London Fog raincoat was the coat for most days. You didn't even need to wear the lining of the raincoat in the mild coastal climate. It was a rather quiet Saturday for the Den. The weather was probably a factor in keeping people home. They were enjoying their night out. They gave the waiter their order and he came back with their drinks.

"How come you're into drinking 7-up lately and not the usual diet coke?" Joe asked.

"I'm trying to cut back on caffeine because I think it has been upsetting my stomach lately. I have coffee in the morning but I don't think having more than that is good for me. I have a little heart burn at times during the day and drinking less caffeine is helping."

"That sounds logical to me but you never complain so I didn't realize you had this problem."

"I don't think it's a big problem and let's face it you have more than your share of things to deal with."

"I never want to be too busy for you, Pam, if something is wrong you need to tell me."

"I will but it's just a minor thing with me."

"You look very pretty tonight."

"Thank you, it is nice to hear those words."

"I know I'm not good at words or bringing you little gifts that you deserve. You're always in my heart and always will be."

"Oh, so the beautiful people are out dining tonight are they?" Suzy appeared behind Pam at their table.

"You haven't been invited to our table so please leave," Joe told her.

"I won't be long but I just wanted to see how you both were this evening. Are you celebrating something special this evening?"

"It's none of your business why we're here," Pam said.

"You're such a cold bitch," Suzy spat at Pam. You should enjoy Joe while you have him because it won't be for much longer." Suzy pinched the upper arm of Pam and she let out a small cry.

"You had better leave me alone, " Pam said to her. "You know I won't hit you because you're with child but you better keep your hands off me." Pam was rubbing her arm where Suzy's fingernails went deep.

Joe jumped up out of his chair. "You get away from this table right now or I'll have you thrown out of here," Joe told her. Suzy pinched Pam's other arm really hard so Pam got up and went around the table. Joe signaled for the waiter. The waiter came over and Joe explained what was going on and they needed to throw Suzy out. Pam showed them Suzy's fingernail imprints in both upper arms that drew blood. The manager was summoned and Suzy was escorted to the door.

"Your arms don't look very good, Pam, I'm sorry she did this to you."

"As I said before, she does it because she can get away with it. I wish I could hit her and knock her on her ass. It would make me feel a little better." Joe put his arm around Pam and told her he was sorry. They finish their dinner and left for home. Pam took off her dress and Joe got out some antiseptic cream to put on the wounds.

"I'm surprised you didn't yell out loudly because she got both arms good."

"I felt like it but I didn't want her to know how badly it hurt." He held her in his arms while they watched TV.

Chapter 35

Pam's upper arms healed and things were going smoothly for them for this next week. The days were still rainy and overcast. It was typical February weather for the area. Work wasn't fun anymore. The new dispatcher was getting more acquainted with the officers than she was learning the job. It was noticeable to everyone how she changed when Ken came into the Center. Her attention was on him and nobody else. Julie was going to have to take her aside and have a chat with her. She would be in training for two months and then on her own. She should be further along in her training than she was.

Pam was on the phones when an urgent call came in from Sam. Chris had been taken to the hospital by ambulance and wasn't doing well. Pam told him she would stop by after she got off work. She got off the phone and told Julie what Sam had said. Julie would go with her. It was hard for any of them to concentrate after that call.

As soon as the shift was over Pam went to find Joe. She wanted him to know where she would be. She was out back when he drove into the yard. Ken had just driven in before Joe. She walked over to Joe and told them both that she and Julie were going to the hospital. While the three were talking Mandi came out with a paper in her hand. "Are you looking for someone?" Pam asked her.

"Yes, I wanted to give this to Ken before I left."

"You don't need to track down the officers for the printouts. There's a tray in the Center for them. You write the officer's name on the paper and he'll pick it up after his shift. I believe Julie went over this with you the other day."

"Now I remember," Mandi told her. She handed Ken the paper and left the area. She was wearing a tight fitted sweater that left nothing to the imagination

"If she hand carries anything more to you, guys, I'm going to personally stomp her ass. She knows we're all engaged and it doesn't faze her."

"She could run around here naked and I wouldn't touch her, Joe said. Ken agreed. She told him she would be home soon. "Joe, I wish I could give you a kiss except I might be arrested." He gave her a smile.

She and Julie met at their cars and drove to the hospital. Chris's room was dark except for a small night light. They both approached his bed from each side. Pam took his hand in her own and he stirred a little. Julie took his other one. "Chris, it's us, Pam and Julie."

"Sam called and said you were here so we had to come by after work. How are you feeling?"

"With my fingers what do you think. Thanks for coming." His voice was sounding hoarse and he looked tiny in his bed. "I just had a real bad day and now the doctor has me on another new so called wonder drug. They're probably using me as a guinea pig for Aids research. I'm getting real tired so I have to go to sleep now and thanks for coming by." They both gave him a hug and left.

On the way to their cars Pam told Julie about Mandi hand carrying the printout to Ken. "She and I will clash one of these days, Pam, and it won't be pleasant. She has her eye on Ken and she'll not give up. Saturday she and I will be talking about her training and I'll bring up a few things that she won't be happy about. I didn't want to do it today and spoil her days off but it will come." They talked for a few minutes about Chris and then went their separate ways.

She arrived home and Joe was not there. She took her shower and then waited for him to show up. She started watching Jay Leno when he came through the door. He was wet and dirty looking.

"What happened to you?"

"Ken's car broke down on the way home. He left a little bit before me. We have been working on it for over an hour and trying to figure out what it was. We ended up leaving it on the side of the road and I took him home." Joe went into the bedroom to get out of his wet clothes. He came out in just his briefs and tee shirt. "This is more like it," she told him. He sat down next to her.

"Pam, I hope tonight isn't going to be another session with you talking about Suzy and me. You keep doubting my intentions. I don't want to be with her."

"You did that night or you never would have taken her home."

"God damn it, I was drunk and didn't know what I was doing. She must have kept after me because it's not something I would do normally." Pam stayed quiet. She shouldn't provoke him but if he hadn't been with Suzy they would have a good life. She could lose him and she had no control over it. This bothered her a lot. She put her hand into his and held it. "I don't like having these conversations about Suzy and me in the past. You need to trust me, Pam. I know that may be hard for you but please try. I don't know how many times I have to tell you that I don't want another woman. I'm getting tired of saying it to you. I can't change the past and you can't get over what happened."

She let go of his hand. "You need to look at my side of things, Joe. Just for once, pretend you're me. I invited you over to tell you I was falling in love and you left before I could discuss it. That very night, you slept with another woman. She has harassed me, tried to hurt or maim me, sent the tape of you having sex, and every time she sees me she does something else. I've tried to look past everything but she's constantly thrown up into my face by her own actions. We find out she's pregnant and it's very likely your baby. My friends constantly tell me you'll leave me, if the baby is yours. My grandmother thinks they may be right. So you tell me how you want me to act and I'll do as you suggest." The tears were forming as she finished her little spiel.

"That's another thing, Pam, you keep crying to make me feel sorry for you but it isn't going to work this time. I don't like arguing and that's what we're doing most of the time." She wiped away her tears and vowed to herself never to cry in front of him again. She got up and went into the bedroom. Pam put her night shirt on and climbed into bed. She couldn't believe that he made fun of her genuine tears. She didn't know that he detested them so badly. Her new agenda was to be civil to him and not bring up Suzy or the baby ever again. It was something she had vowed before but it was hard to ignore it. She would pretend to trust him. She would just be his bedmate until he got tired of her. The way things were going that might not be far off. She stayed on her side of the bed when he came in later. He didn't come over to her and hold her like he normally did. Things were definitely changing between them and not for the better.

These next two days off were not pleasant for the engaged couple. The rain had stopped and he was going to play tennis on Saturday morning at

Ken's. Ken invited Pam but she declined. She would visit Chris in the hospital and grocery shop. She fixed him some pancakes when she heard him in the shower. She said her usual good morning but nothing more. While he ate she went into the living room and read the newspaper. He left without a hug or even a goodbye. Her life was miserable and it was getting worse.

She went to the hospital to find Chris doing better and talking about going home the next day. It appears the latest drugs were helping him for the time being. "Pamela, you look worse than I do, did your dog get run over or something? I called Jules and she said that Joe doesn't call her anymore. What is that all about?"

"You'll have to ask Joe." Pam did not tell Chris about all the things Julie did to her in order to break them up. She felt she should keep it to herself. "I'll tell you that he expects too much from me. I'm suppose to put up with all of his shit and just smile and pretend everything is fine. It's hard to do that so our relationship is failing. I guess he wants a puppet for a girlfriend. I'm not suppose to react to anything but be pleasant and nice to him all the time. Did Julie tell you that Mandi is after Ken so she has a lot of problems right now?"

"Yes, she did and it's hard to believe that a new dispatcher would go after her trainer's boyfriend. She must have a box of rocks for brains. She's a steel magnolia all right."

"She's full of southern hospitality, Chris, it's in her blood. Why not go after a good looking guy with money." Pam stayed a while longer and left to buy groceries. She got home a little before noon and Joe showed up just after her.

"What would you like for lunch, Joe?"

"You should know better than to ask me that. Ken thinks he should feed us. You should have gone because Julie invited Mandi. She can't even swing the racquet."

"Why would she invite a female who's after her own boyfriend? Could it be that she is hoping Mandi will go after you instead of Ken. I take it you played doubles with Mandi?"

"I was stuck with her because you weren't there. She's still flirting with Ken so this won't last very long. It backfired in Julie's face."

"I'm glad, she needs to handle it by not flaunting Mandi in his face. I bought stuff to make tacos tonight, if you would like to have some."

"You know I can't pass up tacos. Don't you think we have things to talk about?"

"I thought you didn't want things talked about so I was trying to get along with you. I'll be your little puppet, if that's what you wish because I'll never discuss Suzy or the baby again. I thought it pleased you that I was keeping my mouth shut. You tell me what you want me to say and how I should say it."

"You have to be a smart ass about everything, don't you?"

"Do you think I like being shut out of your life completely? We go to bed and we stay on our own side of the bed. I have on this ring that is suppose to mean something and we don't even communicate on any level. However, you want me to be, I'll be that way. It's called pulling the strings."

"Look, Pam, you at one time liked sex but now you don't seem to want anything to do with me. At least that's how you are coming across lately."

"I still like it but you made me feel like I was a big phony the other night. If you want sex just tell me and it will be given to you."

"I want it right now." She got up and went into the bed room and took her clothes off. She pulled the covers down to the bottom of the bed and she lay on the sheet waiting for him. He came in and took his clothes off and got in next to her. He started nuzzling her neck but she didn't respond. He nibbled on her breasts and her nipples stayed soft. The tears came and she rolled over onto her side. He put his arms around her and held her gently. "I'm not having sex without you so don't worry that I'll hurt you. I would never do that to you. I love you, Pam, you just turn me on so much." She turned around to face him and kissed his lips. She found his tongue and sucked it. He always turned her on and she would show him. She was on top of him and ravishing his body with her lips and tongue. He was responding by rubbing his hands over the length of her body. He rolled her off of him and kissed around her breasts but did not touch her nipples.

"Oh, my Joe, please keep it up. I have missed this so much." He kept it up until he entered her moist vagina and they became one being. This was heaven to her with him inside of her. She was so happy that they were back making love again. She could never stop caring about him.

Sunday Pam wasn't looking forward to facing Mandi or Julie at work. She would talk to Julie about her inviting Mandi to play tennis. For breakfast she fixed Joe his favorite Italian omelet and they went back to bed and made love. She loved him so much and wanted to keep him in her life. They got ready for work and she sent him off with a big hug and kiss and a pat on his ass. He enjoyed it.

When she arrived at the Center, Julie and Mandi were already there. The newcomer wasn't as bouncy today as she normally was. Pam knew that Julie had planned on talking with her yesterday about training issues. She must have been talked to. Pam would like to tell her a few things herself but wouldn't get involved. She was experiencing some nausea today but felt it wouldn't hinder her working ability. Julie and Mandi would be on the phones for a couple of weeks and then would advance to the radios. When that happens it will mean less time for Pam to work with Joe. She loved working the police radio and handling all the calls. She knew, if anything happened to him she could get him help fast and that would be important. The shift was moving slowly which meant they could banter more. Mandi was still not being very talkative but Julie was making up for her. Ken came into the Center to tell the crew he would be in the office on reports. He was standing beside Julie. Mandi all but lit up as soon as he entered the room. They all noticed it but no one said anything.

"Ken, I hope I wasn't too much trouble for you Saturday trying to learn tennis. I'm sure I'm holding everyone back by not knowing how to play, she said to him.

"Actually, Pam's the tennis Pro of our group but I don't know, if she cares to teach." Pam gave him a no way look. Joe came in and stood next to Pam. He put his hand down and was rubbing his fingers on the side of her arm. She was wishing she could reach over and grab his crotch and caress him.

"I did well to learn myself, Mandi, and I'm sure, if you practice the different swings you can do just fine yourself. It really is all about practicing."

"I plan on going every Saturday so I can be as good as the rest of you," Mandi said. Pam and Julie were not happy with that revelation. Joe soon left and told her he would see her later. He gave her that famous wink of his and she gave him back a big smile.

"You two are so lucky to have a guys like Ken and Joe," Mandi told them. "They're two of the nicest men I have ever met."

"It's not luck, we met and we liked each other immediately. We hit it off right away and I love him very much," Pam told her. Julie agreed with Pam. Mandi didn't say anything back to them but they knew what she was thinking.

Chris called before the shift was over to let them know he would be going home from the hospital in the morning. Pam was happy for him. He talked with her and Julie for a few minutes. The shift ended and Pam and Julie went out the door. Mandi was hanging around talking with the graveyard shift. Pam asked Julie how the talk with Mandi had gone. "She was stunned that I would tell her she wasn't doing very well. She has perked up a little today so I think part of what I said got through to her. Her main priority is the troops, especially Ken. That's not a surprise to anyone who has seen the two of them together."

"Why would you invite her to play tennis to begin with. You're pushing her right into Ken, if you don't realize it.

"You weren't going to play tennis, Pamela, so I thought I would invite her to even up the players. I, also, wanted to see how far she would go in flirting away from work. She will do anything to get him in bed."

"She's the type of woman who'll act so helpless around a guy. She'll carry on just to get him to notice her."

"I thought I should ask her and make her feel at home."

"You don't have to encourage her to go after Ken. She's doing fine on her own. You need to uninvite her or things will escalate really bad."

"I know Ken loves me and won't have anything to do with her."

"I don't think Joe would either but he went with Suzy. You can never know when something like that will happen."

"It's quite apparent that you don't trust Joe very much and that may ruin your relationship in the end. Trust is very important if you have made a lifelong commitment."

"I understand that, Jules, and I'm working on it everyday."

"I wonder where the little flirt is," said Julie as she turned and looked towards the Center's door. "I want to have a few words with her before I go home."

"She's probably waiting for the guys to leave so she can run into Ken accidentally," Pam said to Julie. "Let's talk to her together and make a big point."

"I think you're absolutely right. We can wait and fix her actions this fine night." The women wandered back towards the briefing room. They waited just outside the door and at exactly 10:15 Mandi came walking out of the Center. She had a surprised look on her face when she saw Pam and Julie standing at the briefing room. She walked a little faster and started to say goodnight to them.

"Let's all walk out to our cars together because we need to talk to you," Pam told her.

"Sure I'm all ready to leave," she answered. Joe and Ken came out of the locker room as the three women were walking by.

"I thought you'd be home by now?" Joe said to Pam.

"I've been yakking to everyone but I'm on my way now."

"Joe and Ken can walk out with us," Mandi said to the women.

"We have to see the sergeant about some reports so we can't leave just yet." Mandi looked very disappointed. The three continued out to their vehicles. Once outside, Julie talked to her about flirting with Ken.

"I know what's going on with you, Mandi, and I want it to stop. Ken and I happen to be engaged and we love each other very much. You need to back off and leave him alone. There are other men around who are single so you need to direct your attention to one of them. He's a nice guy, he's a loving person, and he's mine. Do you understand what I am telling you?"

"Yes, I understand but I'm not flirting with him."

"You flirt with him constantly and you won't be playing tennis with this group anymore either. You're over stepping the boundaries," Julie said.

"If I truly wanted Ken or any other guy, I could have him," Mandi told her. "You would have nothing to say about it. All is fair in love and war and I'm going to see what I can do to get him from you. I was trying to do it quietly but our guns are drawn and there are no rules for us to follow. You shouldn't be trying to threaten me." Joe and Ken walked outside and saw the three women talking.

"Hey, do you all love this place so much you can't leave?"

"We were just saying goodnight, Joe," Pam said.

"I'll see you at home in a few." They all got into their cars and drove away.

Pam was still pissed when they arrived at the apartment. She quickly told Joe about their conversation outside. "There's nothing you or Julie can do about her, Pamela, and telling her to back off could encourage her some more. It sounds like it has. Julie can tell her how to do the job but after hours she's on her own."

"She won't be playing tennis anymore so that'll put a little damper on her plans. She'll probably flirt with Ken more than ever to try to take him away from Julie.

"I'm glad she isn't after me. I'm not interested because I have the best woman in the world to love and who loves me."

"Joe, that could change any minute especially since Julie is her trainer. Are you happy with me in bed? I mean really happy or is there something I could do to make it better for you?"

"I love you, Pam, very much and you're perfect in bed. Another woman couldn't possibly make me feel any better than you do."

"Is that the most important thing you like about me?"

"Sex is high on my list but you have everything I'm looking for in a woman. It doesn't even cross my mind to seek out someone else. When you have the very best you want to hold onto it. You're the best and I always want you in my life."

"You're saying the right things tonight, Joe, and you're right." She went into his arms. "When you were standing next to me at work and touching my shoulder, I wanted to reach out and grab your crotch. It was all I could do to keep from doing that."

"Now, that would have caused a big ruckus in the radio room, I'm sure. I might have enjoyed it, too. I know I would have let you have your way with me."

"We both would have enjoyed it, my husband-to-be." She reached down and stroked the front of his pants.

"I've been wondering what you were waiting for now that we're home."

"Just the right moment to start ravishing your body one more time. I started in my head at work and my nipples are already hard."

"Come to me and don't hold anything back." She smiled as she hugged him harder and looked up and kissed him gently. They were soon in bed enjoying their love making and each other.

A little later she was snuggling in his arms and so happy to be with him. "Do you have any idea how happy I am right now?"

"If you're feeling like me it's great. It's why I keep telling you not to worry about other women. I think Julie is a little shit-stirer-upper, if you ask me. She gets off screwing around with other people's lives and I'm serious about that. I don't talk to her anymore and I feel better about that. I should have woken up a long time ago." Pam was enjoying his decision to not call Julie. She felt right along it was a problem for them but wanted him to make his own mind up. She snuggled closer to him.

"I love you so much, Joe, because you have a lot of understanding about people and situations."

"I love you, too," and he kissed her, held her close. "There's no other woman that I ever want to be with." They soon went off to sleep.

Chapter 36

Friday morning Pam woke up knowing she was off the next two days and would not have to deal with Mandi and Julie at work. Julie was now having trouble training and knowing that Mandi was after Ken. Pam would go today and see her grandmother. She didn't see her often enough. She tried to get Joe to go with her but he had other plans. He was going to polish his uniform brass and do a few things like that. She kissed him and took off just after breakfast. She arrived at the nursery and found her Nana in the little shack messing with the orchids. They were so beautiful and delicate and not easy to grow. "Nana, I would like a few orchids for my wedding so you need to get busy cultivating some more."

"Why do you think I'm in here working today? I've already planned on the flowers for your wedding but you will have the last word."

"What would you suggest?"

"That depends on the time of year you'll have the wedding. Roses are good for the summer months. I like white roses with a blush of pink on the blossoms for your bouquet. The rest of the flowers depends on the color of the gowns for your attendants. The flowers should never clash but should blend in with the dresses."

"I'm not planning a huge gala and I won't set the date until Suzy is dealt with."

They heard Boots meowing and carrying on at the door to the shack. Pam went to let her in. The cat looked up with a mouse hanging out of her mouth.

She was proud of her hunting trophy. "Boots you're not going to bring that dirty dead thing in here." The cat kept up her meowing and begging to be let in.

"Does she have another mouse?" Lee asked Pam.

"Yes, and she wants to show it off."

"Let her in and I'll put it in the garbage. She never eats them because she's full." Pam let Boots into the shack and her Nana took the mouse and patted Boots on the head.

"How has Chris been, Pamela? He's such a fine young man."

"He's in and out of the hospital and looking worse all the time. He has no fat and his skin is stretched to the max over his bones. I swear he shrinks some everyday. It's so pitiful and I wish I could do something. His replacement has turned into a big flirt who told us she's after Ken."

"You're kidding, right? How could that be happening?" Pam told her about the confrontation she and Julie had with Mandi and what was said. "I can't believe you have someone else in your life who is after men. If she can't get Ken, she may try for Joe so be aware. You don't need anymore problems right now."

"Joe and I talked it through and I have to trust him. He assures me all the time he is only interested in me. Julie is at the top of our shit list for inviting Mandi to play tennis last week. Julie wasn't thinking straight when she made that decision. She told her last night not to come anymore so that'll help a little. I don't like living like this."

"You do need to trust him or try to. He's not interested in anyone else but there are bad women out there. He does love you, Pam."

"Suzy's baby will be here before we know it. It'll either cause more problems or the problems will be solved. I hope everything is solved."

"So do I, Pamela, and I will pray that you come through this unscathed."

"Nana, is it okay, if I run into your office to use the phone. I'll just be a minute and I'll be right back. I just thought of something I needed to tell Joe." She came back to Lee in a few minutes.

"That was quick," Lee told her. "You're not making a date to go out with someone else are you?"

"No way, Joe is stuck with me for good. I just asked him to start the clothes in the washer. I put a load in there and got busy so it needs to be done."

"I hardly think he calls it stuck and how has he been to you?"

"We're doing just fine and I love him dearly. If we stay away from Suzy, we do great. I try real hard to avoid her."

"I'm sure that you do and that's wise."

"Are you ever going to plan that trip to Graceland that we talked about awhile ago?"

"Well, I do have plans in the works and it'll probably be the first of April. I'll drive to Phoenix and get Sharon and we'll take off for Memphis."

"I didn't think you would drive, Nana, but that might work better. You can see some of the country by sightseeing along the way."

"That's exactly why we're driving across the country. April should be a nice time to travel. It won't be too cold or too hot in most areas."

"I was afraid you might postpone going since your place almost burned down, under my supervision, when you went to LA."

"Good, God, no, I would never blame you for something like that. Bad things happen at times and we have no control over it."

"Well, Nana, I need to get back to my Joe. I miss him a lot when I'm away from him. He says he does me, too."

"You're in love in a normal way and you can't help yourself." She gave her Nana a big hug and left the nursery.

She hurried home to see what Joe was doing. He was vacuuming the living room and she startled him when she came up behind him and touched his back. He turned the machine off. "God, I thought I was all alone and you touch me out of the blue."

"I like touching you anytime I can."

"How's Lee?" Pam told him about her grandmother's plans to go to Memphis in April. "So she's finally going to take the big plunge and by car no less?"

"That's what I thought when she told me. They'll enjoy the trip I'm sure."

"Ken called and wants to play tennis in the morning. I told him I would check with you first and call him back."

"Joe you don't have to check with me."

"I wanted to know, if you would go, too, before I gave him an answer. You haven't gone with us very much and it'll be fun."

"You know I'll go with you because you ask me in such a nice way. Mandi won't be there so it might be a little boring for you."

"I can't believe she told Julie she was after Ken. What an idiot to tell her trainer."

"You twisted my arm and I'll be happy to go with you."

"Thank you, babe, Ken will have a rough time fighting her off at work but Jules will help him. I want to play with you. You can teach me some more

334

good moves." She gave him a smile and a big hug.

"Joe, let's go shopping later and then to Hop Sing's for dinner. I'll treat you for helping me today with the housework. I do have the best guy in the whole world."

They enjoyed some love in the afternoon and going over some bills they both shared.

The couple woke up Saturday morning to the sun but there were clouds in the sky and a possible chance of rain. They were getting a fair share of rainfall this month and they were looking forward to a little sunshine. She fixed him a good breakfast and then got into her white tennis outfit. They took off for Ken's. She knew getting outside in the fresh air along with the exercise would be good for her. Joe was being frisky when she got out of the car and he put the head of his tennis racquet between her legs.

"Oh, you're trying to trip me up are you? We'll see about that." She whacked him on the ass with her racquet and off they ran to the courts. They were out of breath but laughing when they joined the other two.

"Gee, you two are having fun before we even start," Julie told them.

"We came to have fun," Pam said. "Also, some exercise to keep us in shape."

"Ken, is this the way I'm suppose to hold my racquet?" Julie asked him talking in a deep southern accent. "I'll have to be the magnolia blossom today." Julie kept talking that way throughout the whole session. They were having a good time and Pam was the best player but Joe didn't seem to mind. It was bugging the hell out of Ken and Julie. Pam looked good in her outfit and she played as well as she looked. Joe stretched to use his back hand and Pam hit him on the ass with her racquet. He wiggled his racquet in her direction. He then gave her a mean look. She stuck her tongue out at him. As soon as he got a chance he let her have one too. He caught her off guard and down she went hard on her ass. She grabbed her belly as the jolt when through her.

"Are you okay, Pam, I didn't mean for you to fall?."

"I just landed harder than I thought I would but I'm fine." He helped her up and took her into his arms. It felt good being pampered in mixed company.

"Why don't we trade partners and make it a little more interesting?" Julie asked.

She went over to Joe's side of the net and Pam walked over to Ken. She didn't like doing this but was trying to be a good sport. They were just getting into playing when Julie saw her chance and hit Joe on the ass with her racquet.

"Excuse me," Pam called out from across the net. You just crossed the line so don't even think about doing that again."

"I'm just doing what you did," Julie said to her.

"He and I are engaged and we can do that to each other. Don't you have any regard for other people's feelings?"

"I just hit him with a piece of aluminum. I didn't use my hand. Pam, we're all friends here." Pam got silent and Joe didn't say a word. She felt he should have. The day was getting worse as the playing moved on. She was glad when they broke for good and Ken served them all lunch. Julie was acting like nothing was wrong with what she did. Pam was glad when they left for home. She was upset with Joe, too.

"I guess you liked Julie hitting you on the ass."

"No, but I wasn't going to make a big deal out of it."

"That's what I mean about you, Joe. By not saying anything you're telling her to keep it up. She does not need any encouragement to keep something like that going. If another guy did that to me, what you do?"

"I'd be pissed but I wouldn't say anything in front of everyone. I'd take him aside and tell him."

As soon as they got home from tennis, Sam called to tell Pam that Chris was getting worse and would like to see her. She told him she would be there shortly. She explained to Joe what was going on and kissed him goodbye. She wouldn't be gone very long but it could be her last chance to see Chris alive. She parked again in front of his Tracker with the flag on the bumper. She heard another familiar voice as Sam opened the door to let her inside. The sweet smell of marijuana wafted through the apartment and hit her as she stepped through the door. Mike was talking with Chris who was propped up on the couch with pillows. He looked weak and it hurt him when she gave him a little hug.

"Well, Chelsea, I see you made it just in time for our little marijuana party," Mike said to her. She saw a marijuana cigarette between Mike's fingers. He was giving Chris a few puffs at a time. He was enjoying the weed a lot. It was making Pam sick. She even started sneezing at the strong smell.

"Pam, I never dreamed that marijuana could make me feel so good since I hurt so bad," Chris said. She was glad her friend was getting some relief. "Here take a few drags," Mike said to her.

"Not me, no way, I'm driving and I've never tried it before. I don't care to try it either. I was so worried when Sam called."

"Jesus, Chelsea, I never knew you were raised under a rock. How could you have skipped smoking pot in high school?" Mike asked her.

"It was easy for me to just say no. It's amazing what a strong but tiny word that is." They all grinned at her and knew she was right but they all felt she was missing out on a good thing. They talked some more about work and she was glad she got to see her friend. Sam had called Julie but she wasn't home and he left a message on her answering machine. Pam was there for about an hour and then gave Chris an extra long hug."

"My, God, Chris, kiss me quick and give me Aids, if it will get me a hug from Pam," Mike said to his friend. The guys all laughed but she didn't. She left for home.

When she got to the apartment Joe was going over an accident report, sitting at the kitchen table. She leaned over him and gave him a nice hug. "For Christ's sakes, where have you been smoking marijuana?"

"I didn't smoke it but Chris was. He say it helps his pain."

"You're telling me that you all work for the Police Department and there's a marijuana party at Chris's? That'll look good, if your bosses find out."

"Joe, he's suffering terribly and the marijuana relieves a lot of the pain. We can't be worrying about The Department at a time like this."

"Your clothes are saturated with the smell so you'd better take a shower and change clothes. It's a wonder you aren't high right now." Pam went in to shower. She wasn't worried about herself but the baby was her main concern. Joe would be livid, if he knew she was pregnant right now. She took off her clothes and could still smell the stench because it was clinging to every hair fiber on her head. This would be reason enough to quit smoking any cigarette she thought to herself. She washed her hair and body and put all clean clothes back on. She went out to the kitchen, leaned over, and hugged him again. She was enjoying it.

"This is much better," he said as he turned his head to kiss her on the lips. She stayed leaning over him with her arms around his neck and her head against his. She noticed a check made out to his sister laying on the table. "Is there anything I can help you with? What's that check for $200.00 to your sister all about?"

"I send one to her every month to help out."

"You won't have anything to do with your mother but you send money?"

"They have to take care of her so I can send a little money."

"I think that's very nice, Joseph. I knew you had a good heart when I met you."

"I can't punish them because I don't want anything to do with her."

"You must be one of the best sons in the world and how she could have abused you is beyond me."

"She was sick but that's no excuse. If she didn't want me, she could have given me away to someone. My uncle tried to take me several times but she wouldn't let me go. Oh, how I wish she had. She wanted me around so she could take her own frustrations out on me."

"Our babies will never be abused, my Joe, I'll promise you that."

"I'm looking forward to having one with you, Pam. It'll mean so much to me. I can take real good care of you while you're pregnant and I'm looking forward to that." She kissed him again and went into the living room. She just realized how much he would like her to be pregnant but she still couldn't tell him.

Work was somewhat slow this Sunday evening. It gave her plenty of time to think about Chris and what he must be going through. Pam was sitting at the fire and ambulance radio and she never liked slow shifts. The busier it was the better she liked it and the time flew by, also. Julie picked up a phone line and it appeared the call was urgent. Julie asked Joe to call in to the radio for a message. She didn't even tell Pam what was going on. It was 9 PM with one more hour to go in their shift. Mandi was on the radio sounding like a bitch in heat whenever she dispatched a call. Another phone call came in from Joe to Dave who gave him to Julie.

"Joe, the hospital just called and Suzy is there in labor and there's a problem with the baby." Pam gasped as she heard what Julie was telling him. That was all that was said and Julie told him goodbye.

"How dare you keep this from me, Julie," Pam said to her. "You know what this event means to me and our future."

"What did you think you could do tonight since you're working and so is he?"

"Why did you tell him now and not at the end of the shift, if nothing can be done?" Pam was livid at Julie and it showed.

"Well, Mr. Pellerini is coming into the office so I guess he's going to the hospital and hold Suzy's hand. Does he plan on being there for the birth too? I didn't realize that was going to happen."

"Don't jump to conclusions, Julie until you know what's going down."

Joe came into the Center and hurried over to Pam. "Could I speak to you in the kitchen?" Dave took her position and she followed Joe. "I have to go to the hospital because there could be something wrong with the baby."

"No, you don't have to go but you want to be there."

"Pam, please don't give me any shit tonight. I have to do this."

"Do it, Joe, but don't expect me to be happy about you following the tramp to the hospital. I never dreamed you'd run off like this and you're going to be there for the delivery, too, aren't you? You should have talked this over with me beforehand instead of dropping a bomb on me. Why are you even asking for my permission? Just leave me to hell alone." He turned and walked away from her. She started crying and felt completely alone. She composed herself after several minutes and went back into the radio room. They all looked at her as she walked in. "Dave, would you mind staying on the radio for 30 minutes? I'm sorry but I'm a little upset right now."

"No problem, I'll be happy to get off the phones." Julie looked at her as if wishing she was suffering. Pam was glad that the shift was even more quiet for the final half hour. She hurried out like she was on fire when the graveyard crew came in. She would go home and keep vigil. Waiting to learn her fate could be rough for the next few days.

She got inside the apartment and the phone rang. Sam was at the hospital with Chris who had taken a big turn for the worse. She would be over right away. It didn't take her long to drive through the quiet city streets. She parked and hurried inside. The lady at the information desk told her what room Chris was in. She hurried to his room and found Sam sitting next to Chris holding his hand. She went to the other side of the bed and held his other hand. "Chris, it's Pam and I came to see you after work. I don't know, if you can hear me or not but I need to say some things to you. I want you to know how much I've enjoyed working with you and how much fun it was. You kept me laughing most of the time. You gave me advice and worried about me a lot. I just want you to know that I love you so very much, my best friend. I'm going to miss you terribly because I need you to steer me in the right direction most of the time." Pam was sure that Chris lightly squeezed her hand as she finished talking to him. His breathing seemed to even out and he would stir every once in awhile. He never opened his eyes for her.

A little later it appeared he wasn't going to get any worse this night. She said goodbye to Sam and asked him to call, if Chris got any worse. He said he would. She needed to leave the hospital for her own peace of mind. Somewhere inside these walls Joe would be taking care of Suzy as she endured her labor. The tears fell as she walked to the elevator and got on. She pushed the button for the lobby and it started down. It stopped at the next floor. Joe was standing next to a gurney holding Suzy's hand waiting to get on. Pam looked at their hands clasped and she looked into his eyes. The nurse pushed the gurney onto the elevator and Joe followed. Suzy looked over and saw Pam with her tears. "What are you doing here?" Suzy yelled at her. "Get her away from me," she yelled at the nurse. The tears were still rolling down Pam's cheeks. Joe was sick looking. The elevator stopped and the nurse pushed the gurney and took off with Suzy.

"What are you doing here?" he asked her angrily.

"Don't worry, Joe, I didn't come to bother you but Chris got worse and is now stabilized. I thought he was going to die tonight." Joe looked surprised and sorry at the same time. "Joe, please come home with me because I need you right now. Please don't make me go home alone. I need you so much." He hung his head and turned away from her to follow the gurney.

The next thing she remembered she was home and picking up the phone to call her Nana. She felt completely numb all over. "My, God, Pam, what's wrong?" Lee asked. Pam was still crying but trying to get in control of herself. She was so upset she could hardly even speak. It took her a few more minutes before she was able to talk coherently. She soon poured out to her Nana all the events starting with the phone call from the hospital. Lee did not say one word until Pam was finished. "He should be with you and not with her and I'm angry at him for that. He doesn't even know, if it's his baby and for him to act this way is deplorable. I guess you were right to feel the uncertainty in your relationship with him. You're losing your best friend and you get no support from him either. I don't like him at all now. He's hurting you so badly and he's selfish for doing this to you."

"Nana, I'm glad Chris didn't die but he would be better, if he had no pain now. He doesn't deserve to suffer the way he is. He's a good person and I'll miss him so much."

"What are you going to do now?"

"I'll try and rest tonight but I don't know how. I have no idea what Joe will do or if he'll even be home."

"Why don't you come here and spend the night? I don't want you to be alone. You can stay with me as long as you wish."

"Nana, you need to get some sleep. Don't worry because I'll be okay. Sam is suppose to call, if Chris gets worse and I need to be here."

"I'm so sorry, Pam, about Joe and almost losing Chris. We'll talk in the morning.

It'll be hard but you will get through this somehow."

She got ready for bed but knew that sleep would not be coming for awhile at least. She figured Joe was gone for good. It would be so hard to live without him. This tiny baby growing inside her may not know his Daddy at all. It made her start crying even more. She still couldn't tell him about his baby. Sometime later she fell into a fitful sleep but she moved around in bed more than she slept.

Pam woke up the next morning with a bad headache. She wouldn't take aspirin anymore because of the baby so she would just have to suffer. She fixed a pot of coffee and sat at the kitchen table. She wondered what Joe was doing and if the baby had been born. She would find out soon enough. She would take a shower and think some more.

After her shower her phone rang and she thought it might be Joe. "Hi, Pamela, I had to call this morning to see how you're doing," Lee said to her.

"I have an awful headache and I haven't heard from Joe. It doesn't get any better than this. I'm a big girl now and I need to take hold of my life, what there is left of it."

"It doesn't hurt to lean on a loved one at a time like this so that's why I'm calling." The tears came to Pam's eyes.

"Before you called I was just thinking that someday he may be sorry he treated me so bad at the hospital and it'll be too late."

"You sound like someone who has already made some decisions in her life."

"I think he'll move out and go with Suzy now so the decisions are being made for me. As soon as the DNA is determined I'll know for sure. I'll go to work as usual and stay out of his way. He gets to make all the choices and I get to stand aside and accept them."

"Please come and stay with me, if it gets too bad and I mean that."

"I know you do Nana. This day is going to be awfully long. I wish I was on a day off but I have to put my eight hours in, too and so does Joe."

"See, Pam, you're already starting to worry about him being up all night and working later. You never put yourself first." They said goodbye to each other.

She was still sitting at the kitchen table when she heard Joe's key in the door. He walked in looking very tired. She hoped he wouldn't talk to her. He didn't come into the kitchen but went straight to the bathroom. She soon heard the shower water running. She took her cup and went into the living room and sat on the couch. He came out of the bathroom and went into the kitchen. He joined her in the living room with a cup of coffee in his hand. "We do need to talk, Pam. I'm really sorry about last night and Chris taking a turn for the worse. I should have been here for you and I wasn't. Suzy needed me too because the baby's not doing well. She didn't take care of herself and the baby is only four pounds. They have her in the neo-natal unit and they're only giving her a 50-50 chance to live. We should know in 72 hours what's going to take place. When you ran into us we were on our way to surgery because she had to have a C-section. I wasn't with her when the baby was born. I felt I should stick around last night. I've been mostly with the baby keeping a watch on her. She's the tiniest thing you'd ever want to see as a human being." Pam could not stop the tears. She still did not say anything. "I do wish you would say something, just anything, Pam."

"There's nothing for me to say. You made your choices last night and I won't interfere with whatever you decide from now on."

"They'll do a DNA on her and they took saliva from me during the night. We should find out the results later today. You broke my heart when you asked me to come home with you. I'm so sorry I let you down."

"I didn't break your heart at all. You followed your heart when you followed her on the gurney. I'm just someone you ran into during your life and I mean nothing to you, obviously, I mean nothing at all." He didn't reply to her words.

"I'm going to lie down for awhile, if you don't mind. I'm going back to the hospital for a couple of hours before I go to work."

"I am interested in the DNA results so if you could get word to me about them I will appreciate it." Joe got up and went into the bedroom and she slumped over onto the couch and cried some more. She managed to fall off to sleep after she stopped crying.

She woke up startled when she heard a noise nearby. Joe was at the door getting ready to leave. "Sorry I woke you up but I'm leaving for the hospital" She couldn't even look at him. He left and she went into the bedroom to get dressed. She didn't want to go to work but she would be more miserable by not keeping busy. Her stomach was making terrible rumbling noises so she fixed herself two poached eggs on toast. A glass of skim milk and the eggs settled her stomach down. Her Nana called her again at noontime.

"I just wanted to check on you and see what was going on?" Pam told her about seeing Joe this morning. "He apologizes for not being there for you and you're suppose to forgive and forget."

"I asked to be told about the DNA as soon as he finds out later. I'll then know my fate."

"I don't know if I should wish you good luck or not. I don't think I want you staying hooked up with him or whatever you young people call it nowadays. You mustn't forget the promises he made to you about not leaving you, regardless."

"Don't worry, Nana, I won't forget."

"Please call me when you know about the DNA. I want to know your fate myself."

"I'll do that and don't worry about me. I made my own bed and I must lie in it. I've heard you say that to me enough times in my life."

"I love you, Pam, and keep your head held high." Pam held the phone after finishing with her grandmother and dialed Sam's number. It took awhile for him to answer and he sounded very groggy.

"Sam, it's Pam and I wanted to know, if there is any change in Chris?"

"I left about an hour after you did and I'm going over as soon as I get ready."

"Call me anytime and I'll see Chris real soon. You need to take care of yourself."

She sat on the couch again wondering what Joe would be doing. An idea flashed across her mind and she hurried to get ready for work. She left the apartment heading for the hospital. She checked with the information clerk as to the whereabouts of the nursery. She was directed to the 3rd floor. Pam could hear the babies crying when she stepped off the elevator. She made sure Suzy wasn't anywhere around. She got to the large glass window and looked in to see all the babies lined up. Over in the corner she saw Joe. He had a scrub smock on with one hand inside the incubator stroking the leg of a tiny baby. It immediately brought tears to her eyes. She was mesmerized at this scene in front of her. She knew she should leave but her feet turned to cement as she watched the love of her life bond with the infant. Joe turned and looked toward the window and saw her standing there. He removed his hand from the incubator and went in her direction. He held up his hand and told her to wait for him. She wasn't going anywhere. He came out the door without his smock on and took her into his arms. She started crying softly and so did he.

"They just told me that she's my daughter so now we know for sure." He was stroking Pam's back and trying to comfort her as he talked.

"I wish I could see her up close to see if she looks like you."

"She has my hair but I can't tell, if there's any other resemblance. The doctors don't think she'll make it. Her lungs are not developed enough because of her tiny size. It's too bad her mother abused her before she was born. I know you would never have done that, Pam. I have to leave for work now so would you walk out with me. I have to see Suzy for a second and I'll meet you over at the elevator." She walked to the elevators as he went down the hallway. In a couple of minutes he joined her but she was still fighting her tears. He put his arm around her as they rode down in silence. They walked out into the bright sunshine. As they got to his car, she went into his arms again and hugged him hard and he did the same. She did not want to let him go. He soon grabbed her upper arms gently and pushed her away from him. "I'm going to be late, if I don't leave now."

"Will you be home tonight?"

After I go to the hospital to see the baby, I would like to come home. Will you have it in your heart to let me in?"

"Of course, you're welcome." She gave him a half smile and got into her car. It was so hard leaving his arms but he would be home tonight. She rushed home to call her Nana before she had to leave for work.

Pam spoke to no one in the Center except what had to be said pertaining to the job. Julie and Mandi did not even try to have a conversation with her. She didn't even know, if Julie knew that Chris was bad off. She wasn't acting very sad. Pam knew Sam had called and left a message but she didn't know what the message was. Joe came into the Center in the middle of the shift.

Julie, it's too bad about Chris," he told her.

"What do you mean Joe, he was just taken to the hospital last evening."

"He's not doing very well."

"I got a message from Sam but I didn't have a chance to see him since I got home late last night. Why didn't you say something?" Julie asked Pam.

"Why didn't you call Sam and find out, I have no control over you returning someone's calls."

"You're a real bitch for not saying anything," Julie yelled at Pam.

"You better leave her alone, Jules. You should have called Sam or the hospital, if you were concerned." Mandi was looking around with wide eyes and an unbelievable expression on her face. Joe stayed for a little longer to make sure Julie was going to calm down. He gave Pam a wink and left. The rest of the shift was chaotic as the phones got busy and the officers sprinted from detail to detail.

Pam was so glad when the shift ended. Julie was coming right after her down the hallway. "Wait up you idiot, Pam, I'm not finished with you yet." Joe was in the briefing room and heard her demand. He walked into the hallway and stopped her.

"You're not going to do another thing to her, Jules. She's hurting more than you'll ever know." By now Pam was out the door and almost to her car.

She did not look back. She hurried home because she needed her shower really bad. Anything to help her relax would be welcomed. The shower relaxed her so much that she started to feel exhausted from all the stress. She needed to go to bed and try to sleep. It didn't take her long to drop off to sleep. Sometime later she felt Joe climb into bed. He stayed on his side. She moved over and put her arm around him. He was naked and so was she. He turned toward her and took her lovingly into his arms. He could feel her soft skin and he rubbed her body with his hands. She kissed his neck and nuzzled him even more. She reached down and stroked his penis gently at first until it grew in her hand. Oh, how she wanted him. She found his lips and he responded with his tongue. She kissed his face all over and he then found her nipples. He nibbled and sucked gently until she was as hard as he was. He lifted her on top of him and she lay with his hard penis against her vagina. She opened her legs and invited him in. He found her moistness and entered her body with gentle thrusts. She raised up and matched his thrusts and then she rocked back and forth. He grabbed her ass and dug his fingers gently into the soft flesh. She called out his name and he did hers and they were one all over again. She sunk down to his chest and relished the closeness of their bodies. She knew no other man on earth could ever make her feel the way he could. How could she ever let him go without a fight? "I can't tell you how much I've needed you," he told her.

"The feeling was mutual, my Joe. Please don't ever forget what we have meant to each other."

"How could I forget the best feeling in the world with my best gal." She didn't feel like talking anymore but she wanted to hold him. She rolled off him and told him not to go anywhere. She went into the bathroom to take care of herself. She soon came back out and slid into bed beside him and hugged him again. They fell asleep in each others arms and her face showed a look of contentment as she drifted off to sleep.

Chapter 37

The next morning she woke up first and jumped into the shower. She wanted to make him a real good breakfast. He was up when she came out of the bathroom. He gave her a very guilty look and then she realized what was going to happen. Joe was going to leave her this morning after a wonderful night last night. He didn't have to say anything, he had that look about him. "Go ahead and take a shower before you start packing. I'll get dressed and stay out of your way. You knew you were going to leave me last night but you couldn't tell me, am I right?" He nodded his head but did not speak. He grabbed some underwear out of the drawer and went into the bathroom. She had to steady herself by holding onto the knob of the bedroom door. She slowly put on a blouse and pair of pants and waited for him. She sat in a chair and stared off into space.

After his shower, he came into the bedroom and got dressed. "I guess it won't change your mind about leaving, if I plead and beg, will it? I want to run to you right now, hug you, and beg you not to leave me." The tears could not be stopped. He grabbed his travel bag and started packing his clothes that were in the dresser drawers. "Well, it was nice of you to give me one last screwing. I'll be forever grateful."

"Last night we made love, Pam, and it was the one of the best that we've ever shared. Please don't make it less than that in your thoughts."

"I don't know how you can do this to me but you must be enjoying it. Oh, don't worry because last night I made my last memory with you and it'll have

346

to be sufficient to last the rest of my life. Thanks for giving me the chance to be with you for 10 months at least. I'll never be able to find anyone to take your place. She's not going to love you like I love you."

"I know that already and I'm not doing this for her. I'll never love her and I'll never be with her in bed. I have to do this for the baby. She deserves a chance to live a good and safe life. Do you mind, if I come back another time for the rest of my stuff?"

"Not at all, you can keep my key as a souvenir." He closed his bag and stood there looking at her. He wanted to love her one last time, she could tell. He slowly walked over to her and looked into her eyes. "Joe, I've fought so hard for you for 10 months. Deep down I knew I would lose you just like my friends tried to tell me so many times. I'm begging you with every inch of my being for you not to leave me again."

"Pam, I'll always love you and don't you ever doubt that for one second. I wish that I could set a wedding date. I wish that you could give me a little boy to love. I had so many dreams for us and now I'm destroying someone who has meant everything to me. Please forgive me for making you sad, for running out on you, and for upsetting your life."

"Joe, I just want you to know that you'll not be in a small part of my heart but you'll occupy my whole heart as long as I live and breath. I'll never stop loving you." She hurried into his arms and she gave him one last kiss. He tried to wipe way her tears but they were coming too fast. He had tears, too. He left her arms and hurried out the door. She sat on the chair and cried harder.

She calmed down a little and knew she had to see her Nana. She grabbed her purse and went out to her car. She drove cautiously because she still could not stop the tears. She arrived at the nursery and walked past the front counters. The ladies said something to her but she didn't hear a thing. She checked her grandmother's office and she wasn't there. She ran to the shack and found Lee in the corner. Her grandmother looked shock when she got a glimpse of Pam.

"Oh, my God, he did leave you! Please let me hold you, my Pamela." She went into her Nana's arms. She soon calmed down and told Lee the whole story.

"He says he still loves you and he doesn't love her so he may still have hope." Lee was holding Pam's hand as she finished her sad story.

"I've run out of hope, Nana, I just can't keep it going."

"It's understandable for you to react that way. I feel so sad for you because you love him so much."

"I have something else to tell you and you must promise not to tell anyone."

"You have my word, Pam."

"In October I stopped taking The Pill and I'm almost four months pregnant. I couldn't tell Joe because I didn't want him to have to choose between two babies."

"Why are you holding so many things from me?" Her Nana looked exasperated.

"When I show up for work in a smock, he'll know right away. Don't you see I couldn't say anything now. I want him to come back to me on his own, not because I'm having his baby."

"I can see that but I don't know why you would want to do this."

"If I can't have him forever, I can have a apart of him to love and cherish. He wants a baby boy and I want to give him one. Nana, I'm so hungry right now because I haven't eaten today. Let's go somewhere and get a bite before I have to go to work. We can meet there and I can leave for work from the restaurant."

"How about 12:45 at New Horizon's?"

"I'll see you there in 30 minutes." She gave her grandmother a big hug and left the nursery.

Pam went by the apartment to get a few things and then she left for the restaurant. The two women arrived within five minutes of each other. They were seated and Pam ordered a taco salad and Lee wanted an Chinese chicken salad.

"You look a little better, my dear."

"It's amazing what scrubbing and putting on cream can do for your face. I just need to stop crying for more than a few minutes."

"You do have a little glow about you now that I get a chance to take a good look at you. When is this darling bundle of joy due?"

"August 4th, if he's on time," Pam told her.

"That's a nice time of year to have a baby. How have you been feeling?"

"I have a little nausea from time to time but nothing else."

"That's good because there's nothing worse than being sick the whole time."

"I feel bad for Joe. His baby is really struggling and what, if she dies? It'll be hard on him, even though, he wouldn't want a baby with Suzy."

"Tell him about your baby, it could improve your chances with him."

"I want Joe to be with me for me not because I'm going to have his baby.

This is so important to me. Suzy drank everyday that she was pregnant and why can't there be a law against that. He should file charges against her, if the baby dies. She should be dying not the baby."

"Now that he's with her, is he going to be a couple with her?"

"He doesn't even like her, it's solely for the baby." The ladies finished their meal and walked outside.

"Pam, I want you to take care of yourself and not do harm to your own child because of stress. When you're upset so is the baby."

"Things have been bad lately but it'll improve. Thanks so much for listening to me and meeting me for lunch."

"I always enjoy seeing you, Pamela, and I'll worry about you." They hugged and Pam took off for the office. She was wondering why all the bad stuff happened on the days she worked. She could use a couple of days off but that would not happen for a few more. The ocean was calling her again.

She arrived at the office and saw Joe's car in the parking lot. She wanted so much to be with him all the time. The bed would feel terribly empty tonight. She walked up the hallway and the building appeared more quiet than normal. The briefing room was even empty and briefing would start in five minutes. She walked into the Center and she heard a big commotion when she opened the door. She heard dispatchers and officers talking and making a lot of noise. She peeked into the radio room and there were several officers gathered around Mandi. She was talking loud and wearing one of her real tight sweaters. Pam went into the kitchen and got her headset out of her locker. She remembered that Marge was taking the day off. She went back into the radio room and relieved the fire and ambulance dispatcher. Mike was joking with Mandi and ogling her tits too. Pam was glad the attention was off herself. She figured Mandi would go all through the roster in a couple of months. Julie arrived and the officers dispersed to the briefing room.

"Mandi, were you having some kind of a party in here from all the noise I was hearing when I walked in?" Julie asked her.

"I was just talking with some of the guys and they did get a little loud." Julie looked at Pam but didn't say anything. Dave was off and Sara was filling in for Chris until the flirt could get trained. It would appear her training would take longer than normal. Pam was starting to get a headache but she would have to bear it. She was still worrying about Joe and how he was doing. The shift was going pretty fast for a change and she was glad of that.

In the middle of the shift Joe came in to get some information from a criminal history check. Pam ran the name and date of birth for him. He stood close to her but was very businesslike. Julie and Mandi were both keeping an eye on the couple. Pam asked to speak to Joe in the kitchen and Sara took over her radio. She stood in front of him.

"Joe, I forgot to give you something this morning. She slowly took off her engagement ring and handed it to him. I can't wear this when we're not together anymore. It wouldn't be right."

"I don't want it back so it's yours to keep."

"I just can't keep it because it meant so much to me and my hopes have now been shattered. You should take it back and get your money from it. You might need it for the baby." She was determined not to cry but she could not hold back the tears. "It means a lot that you asked me to marry you but I can't wear the ring now. I, also, have the train set in my trunk so whenever you want it, I'll give it to you." She turned and walked back into the radio room. It was hard getting through the rest of the shift but she made it. She kept looking at her empty ring finger. When the next crew arrived she slowly walked down the hallway to the entrance. She used to rush out the door for home when he was with her. There were so many changes in such a short time. She drove home and walked into the empty feeling apartment. She quickly took her shower and turned some news on the TV. She couldn't concentrate on anything so she decided to go to bed and read. Reading wasn't much better than watching TV. It took her quite awhile before she could fall off to sleep.

Pam was still in a daze like state of mind for the next two days. She saw Joe on Wednesday and his eyes were looking sadder as each day passed. She could still see love in his eyes for her and she wanted to hold him so badly. Her heart ached for him and the baby. She seriously thought about telling him about their baby. She wanted him to come to her on his own and not do it because she was having his baby.

On Thursday she arrived at work thankful this day was her Friday and she would have two days off to get hold of herself. She had been stopping by the hospital on her way to work to visit Chris and there was no change. She would be working with Dave and Sara and that suited her just fine. Mandi was getting on Pam's nerves as her pursuit of all men was in full force. If they noticed she was not wearing his ring anymore, they did not say.

The shift was moving right along when a phone call came into Pam's phone position from the hospital. They needed to contact Joe because Suzy could not be located. It was about the baby. She had the radio dispatcher tell Joe to come into the office for a message. He wasted no time in getting there. He hurried through the Center's door and ask who he had to call. Pam got up and took him into Marge's office to use the phone. She dialed the hospital number and gave him the phone. He wasn't on the phone long. He put the phone down and looked her in the eyes. "The baby's going downhill and they can't find Suzy. I'm sure she's at the Den getting drunk. I'll leave now and be with the baby." Pam could not help but give him a hug. "You'll never know how much I need this hug right now," he told her. He hurried out of the Center. Pam slowly made her way back to her position. She knew she had to be with him when her shift was over. He shouldn't be alone as his little daughter is dying.

When the clock struck 10 Pam was out the door in a hurry. She drove fast through the streets hoping she would not be stopped. She parked, flew into the hospital, and up the elevator to the neo-natal unit. It was deathly quiet this time of night. She looked hard into the nursery through the large window. She pressed her face against the glass and saw her Joe stroking his daughter's leg. She had to get in there but she didn't know how. The tears were falling as she stared at her man.

In a little while a nurse came out and saw Pam. She opened the door and asked, if she could be of help. "Excuse me but I have to get in there. My baby has taken a turn for the worse and I can't get through the door." The nurse motioned for her to enter as she held the door open for Pam. She ran over and gave him a big hug from behind. It jumped him and he turned to look at her. "Joe, I couldn't stay away another minute. I want to be with you now." He held her close to him as he still rubbed the baby's leg. The baby was not hooked up to the respirator any longer because it was causing the lungs to be damaged more. Pam looked over and saw a blanket nearby and she grabbed it and lifted up the top of the incubator.

"You need to hold your baby once, even if it's the last time." She gently put the baby in the blanket and wrapped it up. She carefully lifted the baby and put it in Joe's arms. The tears were running down his face. Pam moved a chair over to him and he sat down. She leaned over the back of the chair and put her arms around his upper shoulders. She kissed his head. "She does look like you Joe so she was bound to be pretty." He turned a little to look up at Pam and gave her a little grin.

"How did you get in here?"

"I told the nurse it was my baby and she let me right in."

"You're so nice to do this for me."

"Joe, you know I would do anything for you." They waited in silence for the baby's last breath. Soon the infant seemed to start struggling to live. Pam started softy singing *Amazing Grace* as she leaned over, still holding Joe. A nurse came in and heard Pam singing. She watched the couple with the dying infant and she got tears, too. In a few minutes the baby stopped breathing and lay still in his arms. He lifted her up to his face and kissed her. The tears were coming faster for the two of them. The nurse came over to take the baby from him. He shook his head.

"I'm so sorry that your baby didn't make it," the nurse told them.

"Thanks for taking good care of her," Joe told her. Pam nodded but couldn't speak. "I just want to hold her for a few more minutes and then I'll lay her down." The nurse left them alone. Pam kissed two of her fingers and touched them to the baby's head. Joe looked at Pam with love.

"I want to take you home tonight, Joe, and hold you all night. Please let me do this for you."

"If you'll let me hold you, too. I have to stop at the Den for a minute."

"Let me drive you and we can stop there, if you like." He gently laid the baby down, took Pam into his arms, and cried some more.

They walked out to her car and got in. It was a quiet drive to the Den. "I'll be out in a few." I can't believe I have to come to a bar to let her know her baby died. It could be best that the baby died and now it won't have her for a mother." It seemed like a long time before Joe reappeared in the doorway. He was hurrying to get to the car. Suzy was right after him. She was stumbling down the stairs and Pam didn't see any tears. Joe got into the car and Suzy hit the hood with her hand. She walked to the driver's side window.

"I'll get you for taking him home tonight. You haven't seen the last of me yet." Pam quickly backed out of the space and took off. Suzy was still screaming as they entered the street. Pam's head was throbbing as she drove home. They got to the apartment and went inside.

"Why don't you take a hot shower before me. You moved out with some of your underwear in the dirty clothes. I washed them and they're in your dresser drawer. He didn't have to be asked twice to get into the shower. She put his clean underwear on the bathroom counter as he stood under the sprayer. He came out and got into bed. She took her shower and then joined him in bed with her night shirt on. At the same time they moved toward each other in bed. It felt so good to have his arms around her. His head was right next to hers and they were enjoying each other.

"Pam, why do babies have to die? Don't you think that God would want them all to live? He needs to get rid of the bad people in the world and save the babies."

"I think he's letting us handle our own lives and so we have to deal with the good and the bad. He didn't want Suzy to have the baby so he had to let it die to save it. Even if, you stayed with her and helped you couldn't be there all the time. Look where she was tonight when the baby needed her."

"She wasn't happy last night when I slept on her couch. It would have been a fight every night, if the baby was healthy. Pam, I don't know how you can stand by me the way you have."

"Tonight when the call came in and you left for the hospital, I knew I had to go and be with you. I didn't know, if Suzy was going to be there or not. I just felt a force inside of me telling me to go and be with you." He held her closer as she talked.

"I don't know what I would have done, if you hadn't shown up. You have a nice voice and singing that particular song was what was needed to be done for the baby. It was sad and beautiful at the same time. I'll never forget this, Pam, as long as I live. Before you got to the hospital they asked me for a name for the baby. I told them Lee Pellerini and Suzy will be pissed when she finds out. I don't care, they had to have a name and I chose that one. A tiny baby should have a tiny name. Tomorrow I'll pick out a tiny casket and a small tombstone and make all those arrangements. It's the least I can do for her short life." Pam kissed him on the cheek and started moving her fingers lightly around his face.

"This feels so good to me and you're the just the best person in the whole world."

"Joe, someday when you have your little boy what'll you do with him? How will you treat him?"

"I have to wait until he's about five before I can give him the train set but at Christmas he'll get lots of toys. I'll have to be careful and not spoil him too much. That'll be hard for me, not to spoil him. I should start over because first of all I want him to be healthy. That's my number one priority and always will be. Pam, I have to say something to you right now. I'm sure you're thinking that because I came home with you that I'll just move back in here. I can't do that right now and I hope you'll understand. I need to be alone for awhile, think about my life, and straighten some things out."

"Joe, I didn't ask you to come here tonight because I expected you to move back in. I knew you needed to be close to someone and I wanted to be that person. Tomorrow you can start doing whatever you wish with your life. I don't expect a thing right now and there'll be no pressure on you from me."

"Pam, I should never have gotten tangled up with you in the first place.

You have been so nice and kind to me and I've not been good to you. You deserve a real man to take care of you and make you feel loved."

"I feel loved right now, Joe, or am I getting the wrong signals from you?"

"I do love you with all my heart but I have not been good for you." She kissed his cheek again and kept running her fingers around his face. He seemed to be relaxing a little more and his breathing got more evenly. She loved him so much and now he was going to leave her again. She couldn't stop her tears as she held him as if she would never let him go. He moved occasionally during the night but kept her in his arms. He kissed her once on the cheek and it made her feel so good. She said a silent prayer for her own well being. "Please, God, don't let him leave me for long. Bring him back to me soon so I can love him even more."

Chapter 38

Joe woke up first and he was still holding Pam. He gave her a big kiss and she stirred around and opened her eyes. She could only imagine what she must look like after last evening. His eyes were red rimmed and he still looked sad. "How are you feeling, my Joe? You look so sad."

"I just have a lot on my mind but I slept good because I was with you."

"I do want to fix you some breakfast, if you'll let me. I don't have to shower and I'll put the coffee pot on and cook away."

"That delicious French toast you make with the sausage would be great."

"It'll be coming right up." She got out of bed and went into the bathroom. She stopped at the closet and took some clothes in with her. It wasn't long before she was in the kitchen banging pots and pans. She was so happy that he spent the night. They would have a good breakfast and she would take him to his car. "I'm not trying to tell you what to do but you could check with the landlord here to see, if they have any vacant one bedrooms."

"No, I'll just find a room somewhere so that I don't have to buy anymore furniture. It just shows you how unstable I am with my life."

"Joe, it does not. You've had a lot of rough times in your life and you have changed since I have known you. You've gotten kinder and more tolerant of other people. Look how you were with Chris at first and then you accepted him and me as friends. I know that wasn't easy for you. It was a big step in our relationship and you handled it very well."

"This french toast is great. I guess I didn't eat much yesterday so I'm making up for it this morning."

"I have plenty of eggs, milk, and bread so if you want more it'll be ready soon."

"I could eat a couple more, if you don't mind." Pam got up and fixed him two more pieces of toast. After he finished eating they both cleaned up the kitchen. "This is like old times, isn't it," he said as he put some dishes in the dishwasher.

"It sure is," she said with sadness in her heart. They finished and he was ready to go and pick up his car.

They started driving away from the complex and he asked her to drive by Suzy's place before they went to the hospital. They arrived at her apartment to see all of his clothes strewn across the walkway. "I guess she moved me out last night," he said to Pam. "Will you let me put the stuff in your car. She's probably sleeping it off and won't even know I was here." Pam and Joe got out and started gathering his things. They could tell immediately that she didn't just throw them out. She had cut them into pieces with a knife or scissors.

"It's a good thing I left my uniforms and other things at your place. I would hate to have to replace them all at once." They finished and got back into her car. She drove around to the back of the building and he put his cut up clothes into the dumpster. "I'm just glad that I don't have to face her today and I'll never have to face her again. Pam, you need to watch out for your back. She'll still be after you and will blame you for everything. I was taking care of you by living with you and now I'm leaving you again. I'm such an idiot and you deserve so much more."

"I'll be sure and watch out for her."

They arrived at the hospital and he acted like he didn't want to get out of her car. He turned toward her in the seat and leaned over and kissed her on the lips. One of those soft but sweet kisses he gave her so well. He looked into her eyes for some kind of a sign. "I'll miss those blue diamonds a lot." The tears started as she didn't want him to leave. "Please don't cry, my Pam, you deserve a good guy who won't ever leave you. I'm just a flake who doesn't deserve anyone."

"Please don't talk like that. You know where I am, even if, you just need a friend." He ran his finger down the whole length of her nose. She smiled through her tears. He was soon in his car and he gave her a little wave as he went by her.

She drove straight to the nursery and walked into her grandmother's office. Pam cried and told her Nana all that had happened last evening and today.

"You need to tell him you're pregnant, Pamela. What do you get by not saying anything?"

"I don't want him to be with me because I'm having his baby. I want him to be with me because that's what his heart feels."

"I understand your feelings but what if he never comes back to you."

"Do you think I want him, if he doesn't want me? What kind of a fucking life would that be? I could just dye my hair black and you could call me Suzy."

"Let me tell him and I'll say that you asked me to keep it a secret but I couldn't."

"Nana, you can't break your promise to me. Just let things happen as they may. You have no idea how much I want to be with him right now but he has to want me, too. It won't work out any other way and I know this is right."

"Let me tell you something, young lady. You're not taking care of yourself by being strung out and your emotions draining you constantly. You need to think about your baby and taking care of him."

"I understand that, too. I only have to get through Chris's ordeal and that's just one more hurdle. I promise to devote myself to staying calm for the baby. I promise you, Nana, I'll do that."

"Just remember you promised me and I'll hold you to it. What are you doing the rest of the day?"

"I need to get some more rest after last evening so I'll take it easy for my two days off."

"You won't go around town trying to find him or wonder what he's doing?"

"I'll wonder a little but I won't go chasing around, if that is what you think."

"So go home right now and rest and I mean it."

"I have to shop for a few groceries and then I'm going straight home and lie down." She hugged her grandmother and left the nursery.

Pam was back in the apartment in an hour after stopping at the supermarket. She put the food away and went into her bedroom to lie down. She kept thinking about last night together and holding each other all night. She wanted that to be every night. Her biggest fear was he would never come back. How could he love her so much and not want to be with her? Maybe he doesn't love me like I thought he did. It'll be so hard at work. Seeing him everyday and not being with him after work. Mandi could jump on that right away, if she knows we have parted. What if he falls for her and she has to see them together. How could she even think he would be that dumb to go after Mandi? Her mind was so full of things that she was failing at trying to rest. She finally willed her mind to stop and rest. It didn't take her long to fell asleep.

Later the phone rang and it woke her abruptly. She reached over to her nightstand to pick it up. She said, "hello."

"I hope I'm not bothering you but I have a place to live and was wondering, if I could get some of my things now?"

"Sure, anytime, I'll be here."

"I'll be right over." She leaped out of bed and straightened the covers before going to the bathroom and freshening up. She brushed her teeth, tousled her hair some, and put on a little lipstick.

He was soon ringing her doorbell. She let him in. "You're looking a little better now," she told him.

"Thanks, I feel a little better. I talked with Ken and he wants me to move in with him for the time being until I decide what I really want."

"Julie, will like you being there every day."

"I don't want Julie."

"You don't want me either so maybe someday you'll find someone who you can love. You need to find love, Joe, to be truly happy."

"Why would you say something like this when you know I love you?"

"Why don't you want to be with me? It's hard for me to understand that you love me but you can't be with me."

"I've screwed up your life already and you should be so tired of that from me."

"I'm not so you should let me decide what and who I want. Let's just stop this. I don't want to have these words with you. You can get your things and I won't say anything more."

"I'd like you to come tomorrow for tennis, if you would. You said we could be friends and I would like that for now."

"I'll be there, if that's what you want."

"It's what I want very much and every Saturday, if you'll accept."

"I promise every Saturday for exercise and fresh air."

"You mean just for that and not to see me?"

"Of course, to see you, too."

"I don't know what it is but you have this look about you lately that's coming from inside you. It's nice to take in."

"As long as it's pleasant it's okay."

"Is there anything I can get you before I pack up and leave?"

"Not a thing, I just bought a few groceries and I'm fine." She was trying so hard to keep the tears away. He grabbed a bag he had brought in with him and headed for the closet. How could he leave her when she needed him so much? He came out a short time later to find her looking out the large window. He couldn't see her face but he knew she was sad.

"I gathered up my things and if I overlooked anything just bring it to the office.

Here is your key." She was still standing quietly looking out the window. He laid the key on the coffee table. She couldn't turn around to say goodbye again. He opened the door and went out. He looked at the window and saw the most pitiful sight he had ever seen in his life. She was crying so hard but so quietly and he felt like an idiot. She raised one hand and gave him a little wave. He turned and almost ran to his car.

A while later she went into the bedroom to see the empty spaces in the closet. She noticed something shining on her pillow. He had left her ring behind. She slipped it on her finger and it felt good that she had it again. She managed to get through the rest of the day and she had a horribly restless night. The pain in her heart wouldn't leave her.

Saturday morning she woke up tired and hungry. She had not eaten dinner last night. She knew as soon as she woke up that she couldn't see him today. He probably would not even miss her. Sunday would be soon enough to face him. Her Nana called in the evening to tell her that Joe had just called her. Pam had not shown up for tennis and he was worried about her. "He knows where I live, Nana. If he was so worried, he could come by here."

"I thought you were going to take better care of yourself now."

"It was a little setback but I'll be okay. It can't get any worse for me. What else did he have to say?"

"He told me how you looked when he left you and there was a catch in his voice when he described you."

"Now, this is upsetting me, Nana, so you need to stop talking about him. Someone is trying to call me so I'm hanging up." It was Sam calling about Chris. He told her that Chris was bad and could she come to the hospital. She hurried over there. Sam had called Julie and left a message on her machine.

She drove into the hospital parking lot thinking about the night the baby died and how Joe let her take him home to love. She was missing him so very much. Pam made her way to Chris's room and Sam was on one side of the bed holding his hand. She went over to the other side and took his other hand. His skin was mottled looking as she put his hand in her own. His breathing was very heavy and he did not move. They sat there to wait for as long as it took. Every hour the nurse would come in to take his vital signs and shake her head. After midnight his breathing was even heavier and he let out a gasp and there was no more breathing. She looked at Sam and they both burst into tears at the same time. Her beloved Chris was gone and she had no friends left. She rang for the nurse and told her he died. She went over and tried to comfort Sam. They placed his death at 12:45 March 6, 2005. She and Sam both walked out to the parking lot and said goodbye. She wondered why Julie never showed up. She was too busy to be bothered by a good friend dying. Pam would have no one to comfort her this night and she knew it was something she would have to get used to.

She drove silently through the quiet streets. She approached the Den and knew she had to stop for a few minutes. She looked in the parking lot for any familiar vehicles and there were none. She parked, got out, and went inside. There weren't too many patrons inside as she made her way to their large empty booth. She slid over in the seat. The waitress came over and asked what she would like to have. She ordered a beer and a 7-up. She sat there for a little while sipping the 7-up and wishing Chris was there to enjoy his beer. This was the least she could do for him on his last night on earth. How he loved to come out and howl with the old gang. He wouldn't make her laugh anymore or even tick her off with his negative comments about Joe and the tramp. Those days were gone forever. She finished her 7-up and left the bar.

She woke up late Sunday not feeling very rested at all. She should feel glad she was alive after being with Chris last night. Maybe the worst was over with, even though, Joe had left her. She didn't want her Nana to tell him about the baby. She would have to keep reminding her not to say anything. She had to tell someone and her grandmother was the only person she could trust right now. In one month Lee would be leaving for Memphis and Pam wouldn't have to worry about it while she was gone. This particular morning she was wondering how long it would be before her belly would grow larger. She was four months along and she didn't notice much difference in her belly. She would probably get big overnight and everyone would know. Most of all she wondered how he'll react to the baby. She couldn't wait to see, if it was a boy or girl and who the baby would look like. She hoped for a little boy who looked just like Joe. It would be her dream come true. She had recently felt tiny movements inside her belly and she knew her baby was alive for sure.

Pam went into the kitchen to start the coffee pot before she went into the shower. She noticed in the bathroom mirror that her eyes were dark around them and her skin was paler than normal. She would fix herself and the baby some scrambled eggs and toast this morning. She would, also, have some mixed fruit that she bought at the store. It would be a grand and healthy breakfast. She ate slowly and enjoyed it very much.

About a half hour after she ate the nausea hit her full in the face. She vaulted for the bathroom and barely made it. So this is what morning sickness is all about she told herself. What a waste of food so why did I eat? She didn't feel any better after throwing up. It would not go away. She finally drank some 7-up. She called her Nana to ask her what she should do.

"The 7-up is good and some saltine crackers will help settle the stomach. I'm sorry that you're feeling so poorly. It could be a little bug you picked up or the fact that so much is going on in your life. I wouldn't call it morning sickness that should have started before this.

"Whatever it is, it isn't good. Maybe the fruit I ate for breakfast was contaminated or that's my guess. I think the past few days had something to do with it."

"You may not suffer much at all and it may just flare up occasionally. Every woman is different that's for sure."

"Thanks for the tips, Nana, and I need to get ready for work."

"Are you sure you'll feel up to going to work?"

"Yes, unless it gets worse and then I'll come home." She said goodbye to Lee. She wasn't sure what to take to eat later for her dinner. She would take crackers and maybe have some soup. She gathered up her stuff and headed for the door. She wanted to leave a little early to call Marge and let her know about Chris. Pam didn't have her number at home with her. She didn't want to run into Joe before the shift started. It would be better that way for her.

She walked up the hallway and made it into the Center without seeing anyone. She said hello to the day crew and went into Marge's office. She checked the roster and found her number and dialed. Marge answered the phone. "Hello, Marge, this is Pam and I'm calling to tell you that Chris died last night. I was with him at the hospital and I didn't want to wake you up." The tears started to form in hers eyes. "I know he's better off now but it's still hard to think about. I'll be okay and I'll see you tomorrow. Goodbye, Marge." Pam jumped as a pair of arms came around her waist from behind.

"I'm so sorry about Chris," Joe said to her. She turned and looked into his eyes.

"I wanted so much to see you last night or even talk to you. It was almost one when I left the hospital and I figured you'd be sleeping."

"Look you can contact me anytime and I would have liked to have seen you."

"I don't have Ken's phone number and I thought ringing the doorbell in the middle of the night wouldn't be right."

"Don't ever think that again. I thought we were still friends and we could talk to each other." She told him about going to the Den and ordering the beer and 7-up. He wrote Ken's number on a business card and handed it to her.

"Keep this card in your purse and don't hesitate to use it anytime night or day."

"Thanks, Joe, I will next time. I don't think Julie knows so would you tell her. I can hear her in the Center now." He nodded. They walked out of Marge's office together and Julie looked at Pam and her tears. Ken was in the Center, also. Joe asked Julie and Ken to step into the kitchen. In a few minutes they all heard Julie crying and carrying on. Mandi had just entered the Center and didn't know what was going on. Pam whispered to Dave about Chris. Joe and Ken had to go to briefing so Pam went into the kitchen to see Julie. Pam tried to calm her down and finally succeeded by telling her that Chris wouldn't want them crying very much. It was going to be a very bad shift for them all. They took over the radio and phone positions in a very somber atmosphere. Pam was on the fire and ambulance radio with Julie and Mandi on the police radio. Mandi started off by flirting. She didn't pay enough attention to the emergencies that transpired.

"Pam, you look really sick today, are you feeling okay?" Dave asked her. The two women looked at her but didn't say anything.

"I'm feeling a little sick but not too bad. It could have been something I ate this morning." An hour into their shift they got a report of something suspicious at an apartment house. A woman was reporting that she heard her neighbor come home during the night but had not heard anything since. He always got up and showered in the mid morning but today he had not. They sent an officer to check it out.

"Isn't that Chris's apartment house?" Pam asked Julie.

"I think it is but I don't know what apartment they are talking about. When the officer gets there, he'll tell us which one it is for the report." It seemed like ages before the officer told the radio anything.

"Send the coroner to apartment 105, it appears to be a suicide."

"Oh, my God, it must be Sam because that's their apartment." Pam was in shock. Joe responded to help the officer secure the scene for the coroner. She quickly asked Dave to take over because she was going to be sick. Pam ran out to the bathroom and was sick once more. She was in there longer than she wanted to be and came out looking much worse.

"Pam, stay on the phones because you look like you're very sick," Dave said to her. She thanked him for taking the radio and she sat down to answer phones. She had to run in about every ten minutes to vomit. She drank water and 7-up because she didn't want to get dehydrated. Joe told Mandi he would be at the office in a few minutes. Unknown to Pam, Dave called Rose to see, if she would come in to let Pam go home. She came back from the bathroom and Joe was in the Center. Mandi was trying to flirt with him but he wasn't falling for it. He and Julie talked about tennis yesterday. Pam quietly took her position. Joe looked at her but she did not acknowledge him. He walked over to her.

"I've come in to take you home and you look really bad," he told her.

"Pam, Rose is coming in soon so you can go home now," Dave told her.

"You'd better get a plastic bag out and give it to me, this won't stop." She thanked Dave and followed Joe out the door. They got to the patrol car and he belted her in.

"I think I can do this, Joe."

"I just want to make sure you're nice and safe." He handed her a medium size plastic bag to use, if she needed to.

"This should be big enough for the trip home," she told him. They just got out of the city parking lot when she had to use the bag. She felt awful. She wished she could lay down.

"Maybe I should take you to the emergency room because this isn't good. You may have food poisoning or something worse."

"I just need to get home and lie down, if you wouldn't mind hurrying." She leaned her head back against the seat and held the bag tightly in her hand. When was it going to stop she wondered?

They arrived at the apartment and he helped her out of the car and held her arm as they walked to the door. They got inside and he took the bag from her and threw in the garbage. The perspiration was standing out on her upper lip and forehead. She lean against him because she was getting weak. She let him hold her close. They walked into the bedroom and he helped her lay her down on the bed. He got a cold wash cloth from the other room to put on her forehead. He brought the plastic waste basket from the bathroom to put next to the bed.

"I'm going to call Lee to come and stay with you. I have to get back to work or I would stick around.

"Please don't call her just let me rest. I have to get better soon. She's still at the nursery and I'll call her, if I'm not better in a little while "

"I don't believe you, Pam. You'll stay here and suffer by yourself and you need someone here."

"I've been suffering by myself, Joe, and I'm trying to get through it."

"I won't call her but keep the phone close to you so I can check up on you. I'll try and come by on my break to see how you're doing."

"That's fine, I'll be okay." He patted her head and got up to leave.

"You have my cell phone number so call, if you get worse and I mean that." She nodded her head. He went in and ran cold water over the wash cloth and put it back over her forehead."

"Thanks, Joe, don't worry about me."

It wasn't long before her phone rang. Joe had put it next to her on the bed so she just had to lift it up. "Sweetie, Joe just called and told me how sick you are. I'll come over in a little bit."

"I don't want you to do that, Nana, it's too early to close the nursery and I'm fine."

"I can let Dorothy close, she knows what to do. You need to tell him about the baby because he'll take care of you."

"I told you no and the reason why. I just need to rest so let me hang up. I think rest with sleep will help me."

"I'll check on you later, if you don't call me."

"Give me a few hours and I'll call you, I promise." They hung up.

Joe called after a while and she told him she hadn't thrown up anymore. He would still keep calling. She unplugged the phone so she could get some sleep.

She was sleeping soundly when she heard someone banging at the door. She slowly got up and walked into the living room. Pam was bumping into furniture as darkness had fallen. She turned on the outside light and saw Joe through the peephole. She opened the door with a guilty look on her face.

"I hurried like a bat out of hell over here what happened?"

"I unplugged the phone because you and Nana wouldn't let me sleep any."

"That's a fine way to thank us for being concerned."

"I'm sorry, I needed a little nap and I feel a little better." She walked over and sat on the couch.

"If you have anything to eat, I can spend my lunch time with you?"

"I shopped yesterday so help yourself."

"Can I fix something for you?"

"No, but I need to brush my teeth and use the bathroom." She headed for the bathroom and he went into the kitchen. She came out in a few minutes to join him. "Just don't eat the fruit because I think that's what made me sick." He took the plastic bowl and dumped the fruit down the garbage disposal. Would you get me a peach yogurt and a spoon? He gave them to her. He made himself a grilled cheese sandwich with ham and onions. "I have a new toothbrush in the bathroom drawer you can use before you go back to work."

"You mean I shouldn't work with onion breath?"

"Everyone would know especially Mandi and Julie."

"Why do you keep mentioning them?"

"I don't know, I'm just jealous I guess."

"Why didn't you show up for tennis yesterday? I was really looking forward to seeing you and was really disappointed when you didn't come."

"It would hurt me too much to see you."

"I can understand that."

"I don't think you do understand, Joe."

"I noticed you put my ring back on and it makes me feel good. Why did you put it on may I ask?"

"You know why. Didn't you tell me one time about hope and what it means to you? This is my small token of hope. Even though, you left me you gave me a little hope, too." She looked at her finger and brought the ring up to her lips and kissed the stone. The tears were falling again from her eyes.

"You see what I do to you. I can't be around you for a few minutes when you're crying and feeling sad. I keep telling you that you don't deserve this." She wiped her tears away and composed herself. She didn't want to drive him away. He finished his sandwich and told her he had to go back to work. He went into the bathroom to use the new toothbrush. She got up and walked him to the door.

"Thanks for everything and I mean that. I don't mean to be a burden for you."

"You have never been a burden and you know it. Will you be okay now?"

"I'll take a shower and try to eat something in a bit." He gave her a little hug and left. She immediately called her grandmother to tell her she was better.

"I tried calling a couple of times but there was no answer," Lee said.

"I had to unplug the phone to take a nap and I'm better now. I won't need any more follow up calls and I'll give you a jingle in the morning."

Chapter 39

As the next few days passed she was getting better physically but emotionally she still felt drained most of the time. She saw Joe at work everyday but he showed no changes toward her. She took that as not being a good sign. Maybe he had fallen out of love with her she wondered. Maybe he was attracted to Mandi deep down. She would give him his space.

It turned out Sam had Aids, too, and he couldn't cope with Chris being gone. It was such a sad situation. She would have no closure on Chris because there would be no true memorial service now.

Wednesday night she stayed over and talked with the graveyard crew for a little while. When she left the office she found Joe and Mandi in the parking lot talking and they seemed to be having a good time. She walked past them towards her car. Mandi said nothing to her and Joe told her goodnight. She said nothing to him in return. She drove away and the tears came as they frequently seemed to do. Pam drove into the complex parking lot and stopped the car. She put her arms across the steering wheel and laid her head against them. She would finished crying in the car. The next thing she knew someone was knocking on her car window and she looked up to see Joe. She wiped her tears and open her door. "Do you cry often now?" He asked her.

"Don't fret about me, I'm a big girl. I'm trying to get used to coming home to an empty apartment. It's going to take me awhile."

"I don't like to see you like this and I do still care about you. Could I come in for a little while and talk. I'm not very tired unless you are."

"No, I'm not sleepy yet." She walked to the apartment with him. They went inside and sat on the couch. "Could I get you something to drink?"

"Do you have any beer because I could use one tonight?"

"Yes, I do." She went into the kitchen and returned with a beer for him and diet caffeine free coke for her.

"Have you stopped drinking now?"

"Just about and I don't miss it. I don't know that my stomach could take alcohol this evening."

"I just wanted to tell you that the baby was buried today. It's just a tiny plot with a good size headstone. I thought that maybe sometime we could go and see the site together. I haven't seen it yet and I need to do that."

"When would you like to go? I don't have any plans on my days off."

"I was thinking about Friday morning. I could pick you up around 10."

"I would like to go with you. I'm glad I got to see her before she died."

"She couldn't have had a better send off with you singing *Amazing Grace* to her. You did a beautiful job and it meant a lot to me." Pam put her hand over his for just a few seconds. He gave her a little grin.

"I'm glad you liked it and I wanted to be with you very much that night."

"You are a good person to put up with so much from me."

"That's what friends are suppose to do. You try to be there for the good and the bad." He finished his beer and sat way back in the couch. "Would you like another beer, my Joe?" He shook his head but didn't say anything.

"I guess I should be going because I'm upsetting your little routine."

"Not really, the night is still young." He got up and looked into her in the eyes. "Why are you looking at me like that?"

"Just checking to see, if you still care about me."

"And what did you find?"

"You still do very much." She walked over to the door with him. "Thanks for the beer and for saying you'll go with me Friday. It would be hard for me to go alone."

"I don't mind going and I'll see you at work tomorrow." He raised his hand and touched her cheek lightly. She took hold of his hand and brought it up to her lips. She kissed it softly. They smiled at each other. He left. She wanted so much to go into his arms but she couldn't bring herself to do it.

Friday morning found herself rising bright and early. She wanted to run out and get some flowers before he arrived to pick her up. She showered, ate yogurt, and left for the floral shop. She picked out a few pink carnations and baby's breath for the grave. She, also, got one long stem red rose for

Cannonball's gravesite. He should not be forgotten.

Joe arrived right on time and was touched with the flowers. "You never miss a thing, do you?" She gave him a smile and they left.

They entered the cemetery gate and it always got to her. It was always a sad experience. They drove first to Webb's gave and she placed the rose on his headstone. Joe had directions to the baby's grave and they were soon in the area. They got out and started looking for a small fresh grave. It wasn't long before they found the site with several small headstones in a row. The headstone read: To Our Fallen Angel—Lee Pellerini born February 28, 2005 died March 3, 2005. The tears immediately started to form in her eyes. The headstone had a reservoir built in to hold water and flowers. She placed the carnations in the hole and added water from her bottle she always carried. She stood up and put her arm through his and they both cried softly. She turned to face him and hug him some more. It felt so good and this is where she belonged. She only wished that he knew it. They stayed for a little while and got back into the car.

"I haven't eaten today so would you like to join me for an early lunch or late breakfast? You can have either one at the New Horizon's."

"I would like that very much." They drove in silence to the restaurant. He got out and opened her door and that always made her feel special. "Are you still going to be doing this when I'm real old?" She asked him. "Sorry about saying that because it means I'm jumping to conclusions."

"I'll always treat you like a lady, Pamela." They walked in and were seated right away. She ordered a salad and he french toast. "This french toast isn't nearly as good as yours but it'll do in a pinch." His comment made her sad. "Did I say something to offend you?" He asked.

"No, I liked making breakfast for you very much." They talked about work and he brought up getting a good workout from playing tennis.

"Please, can't you take time to play a little tennis tomorrow?" He asked her. "It isn't the same without you. The last time you said you would go and you didn't show up."

"I promise tomorrow I'll show up. I need a good workout, too." She was thinking she needed sex more than tennis but would not comment on something like that. The meal went way too fast for her and he was feeling the same way.

"Is Lee getting all excited about her trip to Elvis Land?"

"That's all she talks about and you would think she was planning a world tour. I, at least, know that the place won't burn down while she's gone. She would fire me for sure, if that should happen."

"Maybe I should go over there some night and see what I can do."

"Please don't, she still trusts me and if that happens, she'll never again leave me in charge. She probably has taken out extra insurance, if the truth was known."

They finished the meal and drove back to Pam's apartment. "Joe, this was sad but nice of you to ask me to go. I wish that things had worked out for you better."

"Do you really mean that, even though, I left you?"

"I didn't want you to leave but I would rather the baby had lived. She was such a cute little thing. I could have loved her as if she were my own." Again she couldn't stop her tears. He moved towards her and took her face into his hands.

"You're such a jewel and I know you meant everything you just said." He kissed her one cheek and then the other. He kissed her lips as if it was the first kiss between them.

"Thank you for lunch," she whispered to him. He got out of the car and went around to open her door.

"Do you mind if I call you sometime? I get lonely and I would like to hear your voice."

"You may call anytime or drop by, too, if you wish. Remember, friends are there for each other." The rest of her day dragged on and she was missing him terribly.

Saturday arrived and she was anxious to play tennis and see Joe. She was hoping being around him would make him come back to her. She was feeling quite good and hadn't experienced any nausea for several days. Pam wanted to enjoy the rest of her pregnancy. She wore pants and a loose blouse, not tucked in. She was gaining a little weight in her waist and belly. She arrived at Ken's before Julie. Nothing like being over anxious she told herself. Joe answered the door and let her in. He had a big smile on his face for her.

"I told you I'd be here today and I should have bet you," she told him.

"I'm not a betting man."

"There's other things to bet besides money."

"You're right, I never thought of that."

"How have you been since we last talked? You don't look as sad today," She asked.

"That's because you showed up and I wasn't sure, if you would."

Ken came into the living room and greeted Pam. "My, God, you made it and none of us thought you would. I'm sure glad Mandi isn't coming anymore. She gave me the creeps."

"Oh, isn't that too bad," Pam said with a big grin. "I know it's rough having a female after you all the time. It can just wear a guy out."

"You women are vicious creatures," Joe said.

"Where is Jules, I hope she'll be here?" Pam said.

"She slept in but she'll be here any minute." They sat around the living room waiting for Julie. Pam was not terribly comfortable because her pants were a little tight around the waist. She stood up to take the pressure off her midsection.

"Are you a little antsy today, Pam?" Ken asked.

"Just a little, I guess but I haven't been exercising in awhile." The doorbell rang and Ken went to let Julie in.

"Hey, I went to the courts and no one was there so I came to the house," Julie said. "There's a strange looking car parked a short distance down the driveway and I didn't see anyone inside."

"That happens here all the time," said Ken, "some drunk on their way home pulls into our driveway to sleep it off. It's all about living in the boondocks."

"There was no one parked there when I came in," Pam told them.

"Let's hit the courts," Ken said and they followed him outside to the side of the house. There were tall old Eucalyptus trees surrounding the courts with Acacia bushes in between the tall trees. The two couples paired off and started volleying back and forth.

It wasn't long before Joe saw his chance and hit Pam on the ass with his racquet.

"You're cheating, officer, and that isn't in our rules." She had to laugh at his attempt to make it appear it was an accident.

"Pam, you look like you're putting on a little weight," Julie said to her. "Is it too many lonely nights eating ice dream for dinner or something else?"

"I guess it's not eating right." Pam answered her. Joe looked at Pam but didn't say anything. Pam was starting to serve the ball when Julie and Ken both stopped and were looking wide eyed at something behind her and Joe.

"Stop, everyone," a loud female voice said from behind them. Pam stopped but turned to look at Suzy. She was standing with a handgun pointed at Pam. She had a crazed look about her and Pam knew something terrible was about to happen. "Get over here in front of me, you bitch." Suzy said to Pam.

"Suzy, drop that gun and stop this right now," Joe said.

"I'm not stopping anything but I'm going to start something big. I'm going to steal your girlfriend and get rid of her so she won't cause us anymore problems." Pam was getting sick to her stomach but she had to hang in there. "We're going to take a little walk to your car, bitch, so start walking and don't try anything. This gun is loaded and I know how to use it. Where are your car keys?"

"They're in the house in my purse," Pam answered. Suzy looked at Julie.

"Okay, other bitch, you'd better hurry into that house and grab her purse. I'll give you one minute to get back out here or I'll kill her on the spot." Julie ran like crazy and was soon out with Pam's purse in hand.

"Drop the purse on the ground and then back away." Julie did as she was told. "Bitch, you go over and pick up the purse and take your keys out slowly." Pam walked to her purse and slowly took out her keys. "Drop the purse and start walking towards your car fast. The rest of you had better not move an inch or I'll shoot her on the spot."

Pam turned and looked at Joe. "Please help, Joe, don't let her hurt me."

"I told you to go to the car or I'll shoot you right here. The two women walked fast to her car. The others didn't dare say anything or make any moves. "If you get in my way, I'll kill her before your eyes." Joe was devastated and Pam looked at him so scared. They were soon at her car. Pam got behind the wheel and Suzy got into the backseat. "Just start driving and I'll tell you where to go and when to stop. I'm serious so don't try to fight me. I hate your guts and I'm going to kill you the way you deserve to be killed." Suzy directed her downtown to the top of one of the three overpasses that traverses the city. She told Pam to park the car sideways to block traffic across both lanes. Suzy told her to get out of the car, to put her hands on top of her head, and not try anything. In the meantime, Joe, Ken and Julie were following them in Ken's car and they stopped at the entrance to the overpass. Ken had already called on his cell phone to the police when they left his house. Everyone was now alerted. Joe was sick because he knew how much Suzy hated Pam. It wasn't long before the Command Center was established where Ken had parked his car. Other police cars and CHP vehicles responded to the freeway onramps to stop traffic and keep cars from moving in either direction. Suzy was still holding a gun on Pam who was trying to stay calm, not knowing what Suzy would do next. "I want you to step over the railing and stand right over the street below so everyone can get a good look at you. You're going to make a big splash in Mission Park today and I'm not talking about just in the newspapers." Pam, now, knew that Suzy was going to cause her to fall to her death from the top of the overpass. She wondered, if Joe was going to be able to help her. Pam carefully stepped over the railing and held on the best that she could. There wasn't much room on the narrow ledge. She was scared to death at what was about to happen. She started shaking a little and she was trying to control it. Joe saw Pam stepping over the railing and he was in a panic. He had to get to her before Suzy could do anything. Ken was holding Julie as they both watched in horror. Joe ran over to the Chief and begged him to let him try and talk to Suzy. He briefly explained the situation but the Chief wanted to wait a little longer. He was trying to get the swat team organized to respond to the scene. Suzy was moving closer to Pam still waving the gun and calling her a bitch every few minutes. "Do you see what happens to bitches when you interfere in other people's lives. Joe and I could have been happy but you just couldn't give him up."

"I don't know what you're talking about because he left me to be with you. He's not living with me now. You're the one who should have treated him better and taken care of yourself. The baby died because you couldn't stop drinking."

"How dare you stand there and tell me what I did wrong. You're going to pay for all of this with your own life and your baby's. If I can't have Joe, you and your baby won't have him either."

"Suzy, he doesn't want me either or he would be living with me now. You're doing all of this for nothing." A huge crowd was gathering all around the overpass. Pam was starting to get dizzy from the height and standing close to the edge. She didn't like standing on the edge with so little to hang on to. One little slip and she would be gone. Joe was still talking with the Chief and watching Pam at the same time. He was begging him for permission to go to Suzy to try and talk with her. The Chief finally let him go. Joe slowly walked toward the two women and Suzy didn't notice him at first.

He was making his way when Suzy spotted him and turned the gun on him. "I told you to stay away from us or I would kill her right away." Pam turned her head slightly and saw Joe standing about 50 feet from her. She knew she had to be strong and she knew he would figure something out.

"Suzy, I just want to talk with you for a few minutes. I don't know why you're doing this."

"You stayed with me after the baby was born and then you dumped me as soon as the baby died. It's because of her that you did this. I'm going to take care of her so she'll never be a problem for us."

"Suzy, I'm not with her now. I'm staying with a friend. You can't do this because I'm not with her. You're doing this for nothing."

"She knows why I'm doing this so, bitch, why don't you tell him. Just tell Joe why you deserve to die. It wouldn't be nice, if he found you after you were dead, now would it?" Pam could not stop the tears. She had to tell Joe about his baby.

"Joe, she's doing this because I'm going to have your baby." He could not believe what Pam was saying.

"You're really pregnant with my baby?" he asked her.

"You know, bitch, I have to hand it to you. I thought you had already told Joe but I guess you haven't by the look on his face. This is as good a place as any to find it out. She wouldn't leave you alone, Joe, even after she found out I was pregnant. She kept a tight hold on you and now I am going to get rid of that hold she has. She's going to die and so is your baby with her. Now, bitch, I have one more word for you, jump and do it now." Pam just stood there shaking. "If you don't jump yourself, I'm going to shoot you so you'll fall anyway. Do us a favor and jump." Pam still stood tall. A shot rang out and just missed Pam. She was trying desperately to hold onto the railing. Joe saw his chance and rushed Suzy. He was so fast she didn't know what hit her. The gun went flying and so did Suzy. She ended up close to the railing. In a few seconds she crawled over the railing and fell to the street below. Pam was still standing outside the railing when Joe got to her and grabbed her with both of his arms. He lifted her over the railing and onto the overpass sidewalk. They both looked over the side at Suzy sprawled in a funny position on the street below.

"I have to get away from here, Joe. I have to get away." She turned and started running away from him. "I have to get away from here," she repeated. She was running faster. He kept up with her and steered her in the direction of a patrol car. The press was running towards them. All she could see was getting into the car and being safe. She got to the passenger door, opened it and jumped in. The news cameras and reporters surrounded the car taking pictures and shouting out questions. She locked all the doors. Joe couldn't even get to her. She lay down in the seat and covered her head with her hands. Joe ran over to the Chief to see, if he could get a key to the patrol vehicle. The officer that the car was assigned to was doing traffic control. Joe ran to him and told him he needed the key. He ran back towards the car pushed his way passed the reporter's. He slid in behind the wheel and started the car. Pam was still lying in the seat trying to hide. He slowly moved the car forward until the press dispersed and he was able to get up some speed. She sat up in the backseat as he moved along the streets. She was still shaking. "Joe, take me to the police station right away. I don't want to go anywhere with you."

"The Chief said I could take you home and they would send someone to talk to you later."

"I'll talk now to someone. I don't want to be with you." He drove her to the office. "You take the car back to the officer and tell them I'm here and ready to make a statement. If someone could drive my car here that would be nice. The keys are in it and it was blocking the overpass."

"You don't want me around at all?"

"No, I don't, Joe, you had many chances to stay with me but you chose to leave me and this is what happens. I want to be alone and deal with my life."

"What about the baby?"

"You can go to court and have visitation rights but I won't let you give me any support for the baby. I made the decision to have this baby and you chose to be with Suzy. When Suzy's baby died you still chose to be away from me. I can only take so much rejection from you. Now it has finally sunk in that you really don't want to be with me and I have to deal with that." She walked into the building and went to a pay phone to call her Nana. Joe did not follow her. She told her Nana what had happened and that she would be over when she was through at the police station. After a detective asked her questions he handed her the car keys and told her that her car was parked outside.

She left and drove to the nursery. "Oh, Pamela, I'm so glad you're safe," her Nana said as she hugged her. "You look so upset and where's Joe?" They walked inside the nursery to her office. Pam told her grandmother all that had happened and what she told Joe. "This is such a tragedy and to think you were almost killed. I'm glad Suzy is gone and out of your life for good. Is Joe really out of your life for good? You love him so much."

"Something snapped inside me when I looked over the railing and saw Suzy in a heap. I've been trying so hard to get him to be with me for so long and I need to give that up. I told you before I wanted him to be with me for me and not because I was carrying his baby. Now, I'll never know how much he wants to be with me because he knows about the baby. He'll find someone else to love him. I'll never find a guy I care about as much as I do him but I'll have my baby to love me. Lately, he's keeps telling me that he isn't good enough for me and all that bullshit. What he means is that I should get lost because he doesn't want me."

"He loves you and I know it hasn't been grand being with him. You need to think about what all he has been through. It's easy to focus on yourself and what you're having to deal with. There's always two sides to every story. It takes a caring person to look at both sides."

"I should be going, Nana, and thanks for listening to me."

"You're welcome to stay here if you feel like some company."

"I need to get a bite to eat and then I'm going to shop for maternity clothes. These pants are getting a little tight on me."

"Pam, I don't think that all you have been through has hit you yet so please take it easy."

"If I keep busy, I'll be fine and that's what I'll do. Don't worry about me because I have a baby to think about and not just myself all the time."

Chapter 40

The next week was harder to get though than she thought it would be. She planned to wear a maternity outfit to work on Monday for the very first time. Everyone would know. She didn't know, if Joe had told Ken and Julie about the baby. Julie called her a couple of times and left messages for her but she didn't answer her calls. She had no true friends and that was probably for the best.

She drove to the office and the first thing she saw was Joe's car. She got out of her car and walked towards the building. Pam stepped up to the door, held her head high, and walked through the entrance. She walked steadily and never faltered as she made her way down the long hallway. One of the clerks was walking towards her and said hello but her eyes were on Pam's stomach. She continued walking past the briefing room and a couple of guys stuck their heads out when she walked by. She was definitely being noticed and it did make her feel a little uncomfortable. After a few days when everyone knew about her condition, it would be a piece of cake. Pam went into the Center and stopped in the kitchen. She took a deep breath before taking out her headset. She could tell the place was buzzing about her, Suzy, and Joe. When she walked into the radio room they all looked and then their mouths dropped as they saw her in her maternity clothes. It would take a little while for them to get used to it. No one knew what to say to her so they didn't talk very much. She knew Mike would have something to say so she braced herself. She walked over to the radios and decided to work the fire radio for a change. She would be relieving Mike. "Oh, my God, Pamela, have you been doing the dirty deed?" He asked her. She didn't answer him. "What secrets you have been keeping from your friends but babies you just can't hide, now can you?" She still wouldn't say anything. "Chelsea, you can't sit here just yet because Marge ask me to work over for a little while. Julie and Mandi are in her office having a conference.

"I'll take the police radio then." Pam told him. Dave would be on the phones. He sent Pam a message and told her that Mandi was getting fired. For 30 minutes all was quiet and then Julie came out of Marge's office not looking very well. She got out her headset and relieved Mike and told him to go home. Julie noticed Pam's maternity outfit and kept staring at her. Dave and Pam both expected Julie to say something to them but she did not. The tension was building in the Center and then Ken walked in.

"Is something wrong because you all act like someone just died?" No one said a word and they all heard a commotion coming from Marge's office. Mandi's voice could be heard and Marge was trying to calm her down. "What's that all about?" Ken asked.

"Mandi is getting fired right now so be prepared for almost anything," Julie said.

"Fuck you, Marge," Mandi said to her boss. "You're all alike around here." She was walking towards the dispatchers. "Oh, are we having a party here? It must be a farewell party for me. Julie, this is all your fault. You're so insecure and afraid I was going to take Ken away from you that you filled Marge's head full of bull shit. I saw the way he looked at me playing tennis. He wanted me and he wanted me bad."

"You can't do the job so you're blaming everyone else," Julie told her.

"You can all go to hell and I'll never be back." Out the door Mandi fled and Marge came huffing and puffing out of her office.

"You guys get back to work and I'll be back tomorrow," Marge said to the group. Ken gave Julie a pat on the head and he left. It didn't take Julie long to start commenting on Pam being pregnant.

"You know Dave, we didn't even know that we have been working with a slut, did we?" Julie said as she glanced at Dave. "You planned this didn't you, Pam, to get your claws deeper and deeper into Joe. I hope he sees right through you and this plan to ruin his life."

None of them realized that Joe had walked in and was listening. "Julie, leave her alone and I mean right now." All three dispatchers turned to look at him. "You mind your own business as this is between Pam and myself. You need to pay attention to your own life and leave ours alone. You've never seen me mad before but if you keep this up you will." He turned and walked out of the Center. Pam was glad he heard what Julie had said. She wouldn't worry about what they said as long as he was defending her. She didn't think that Julie would stop going after Joe. Her being pregnant would not deter Julie for one nanosecond. It would probably speed up her pursuit of him.

A little while later into the shift Julie started in on Pam once more. "Joe's not going to stop me from talking about you or to you, Pam. He'll wake up someday and see how worthless you are to him. How could you get pregnant after what he went through with Suzy? I thought you were the most intelligent person around here but I was so wrong about you and your high and mighty ways. "

"Joe's right, Julie, Pam doesn't have to answer to you," Dave said to her.

"You men are all alike," Julie said. "Getting a woman pregnant is a plus for you guys. It makes you feel more manly but it's stupid to think that way."

"You don't know everything about men or Pam," Dave said to her.

"Go ahead and take up for her, Dave, she needs at least one friend in this world. I bet that Joe kicked you out when you told him you were pregnant. You're a silent drama queen, Miss Pamela. Usually they're very vocal but you are taking the other route. Did it make you feel real good strutting in here today in your maternity clothes? Did you get a real high from that?" Pam was wishing it would get busy so Julie would have to shut up. She didn't want to confront her while working so she would just have to listen to her anger. Pam would get her turn to get back at her one of these days. When they told Julie that they would keep the bad things a secret that she did, in trying to break up her and Joe a secret, it was a big mistake. Pam wasn't so sure that they should. Maybe she could convince Ken to dump her. He was too nice of a guy to be stuck with Julie for the rest of his life. Pam wondered why he couldn't see through Julie and her vendetta to go after Joe. Maybe he can see it but he chooses to look the other way. It looked like her wish was coming true when the phones and radio started getting busy all of a sudden. The rain was falling and the accidents were happening. It appeared no one could slow down when driving in the rain.

As Pam opened her locker to put her headset away, she saw the card propped up inside It was an expectant mother's congratulation's card from Joe. She opened the beautiful card and read that he hoped she would give him a healthy baby. He signed it, All My Love, Joe. How she loved him.

On Wednesday morning she was getting ready for her doctor's

appointment when the phone rang. She picked it up and it was Joe. "Lee told me that you had an appointment for a baby check up today and I was wondering, if I could go with you?"

"If you wish to go, you may. I have to be there at 10:30. It's Dr. Cho's office, do you know where that is?"

"Could I pick you up and you could show me?"

"No, I'll meet you in 45 minutes at his office."

"I'll be there on time." She was almost ready when he called and she figured he would be there early. She was so right. He arrived at 10:15 at the doctor's office.

"I should have called you to thank you for the beautiful card. It was nice of you to give that to me. I should have done the same for you." Pam checked in at the receptionist window. She then joined Joe in the waiting room. "Am I making you nervous today because you seem that way?"

"I'm a little nervous. I'll ask the doctor to let you hear the baby's heartbeat today. I've heard it before but I think you would like to."

"Hey, that's great, I didn't expect anything like this." The nurse opened the door and called Pam's name. She got up and Joe sat still. Pam turned and motioned for him to follow her. They both followed the nurse into an small examination room. There were charts of a fetus' growth for the whole nine months. Joe was fascinated with the diagrams of each stage. He pointed out to her the fourth month picture. She nodded her head. She was sitting at the end of the table when the Doctor came in to the room. Pam introduced Joe to Dr. Cho as the baby's daddy. It made Joe feel good to hear her say the word. The doctor helped her lay down on the table and he lifted her blouse and pulled her pants down. He pushed all around her abdomen, checking the size of the fetus and asking Pam questions. He got another gadget out and rolled it around on her midsection. They soon heard the distinctive fast beats of the baby's heart rate. Joe smiled big and so did Pam. They both knew the baby was alive and well. The doctor fixed her clothes back in place and helped her to sit up. He told her everything appeared fine and he would see her in one month.

"Dr. Cho can you tell from the heartbeat, if it's a boy or girl?" Pam asked.

"We can only guess at this point. A faster beat usually means a female and a slower beat is male. Your baby's beat is slower but it's only a guess. We can do an ultrasound for your next visit and find out for sure." The tears came to Pam's eyes just hearing his guess. The doctor left the room. Pam was wiping her tears when Joe got up and took her into his arms. She moved away from him.

"I'm sorry I just got carried away from hearing the baby." She enjoyed the hug but didn't tell him so. They were both happy but she was keeping it to herself. They left the office and walked outside.

"I know you don't want anything to do with me but I really would like to know how Suzy knew about the baby?" Pam told him all about running into her at this office.

"Thanks for telling me because it has boggled my mind about how Suzy knew. I guess you wouldn't be interested in celebrating me hearing the heartbeat. I would like to take you to lunch, if you would let me. We could meet at the New Horizon's at 12:15. We can leave for work from there." She agreed to meet him for lunch. She had an hour and half to kill so she would go to her Nana's before she met Joe.

She arrived at the nursery but couldn't find her grandmother. She gave up looking and asked Dorothy where she could find her. She was told Lee was at home and Pam thought this was strange. Her Nana was always at the nursery during the day. She hurried over to her house. Pam rang the doorbell and Lee was surprised to see her.

"Nana, I was worried when Dorothy said you were home."

"Well, don't be because I'm getting a few things ready for my trip. I only have nine days left."

"Why did you tell Joe about my baby check up?"

"He needs to be included, Pamela, and you know it."

"I wanted him to ask me to go and not have you prompt him."

"Men don't know what women have to go through so I just helped him along." Pam told her about the heartbeat and it could be a boy. Lee was happy for them both. "I wish you could be a couple again because when the baby comes, what then? The baby needs you both for nurturing in the same living quarters, young lady."

"If he asks to come back with me, I'll think he's only doing it for the baby. I want him to come back because he loves me and wants to be with me. Is that too much to ask for?"

"Yes and no. How will he be able to convince you of his feelings now that he knows about the baby? Use your woman's intuition to figure it out. Swallow your pride for once and do it for the baby."

"I'm meeting him for lunch and so I'm not a heartless person." They talked for awhile longer and Pam had to leave to meet him. She hugged her Nana and said goodbye. She was so anxious to see him and she wanted to be with him so badly.

She waited in her car until he drove into the parking lot. She got out of her car and she saw a new look about him. They approached each other and she saw more love in his eyes then she could ever imagine. He gave her a smile that lit up his whole face. They were seated and the waitress took their orders. "Pam, you're so beautiful. The baby makes you shine and those blue diamonds are dancing." She knew he was trying to be nice so she would take him back. She wanted him back so badly but not under the present circumstances.

"I went to the mall after the doctor's visit to look at baby stuff. They have so many nice things. I would like to buy the baby some stuff but I wanted to ask you first. I really don't want to piss you off."

"You didn't have a clue I was pregnant because you knew I was on The Pill. I made the decision to stop The Pill so I should be responsible for what I did. If it was a mutual thing then I would let you help me out."

"There's another reason I asked you to lunch. I want us to live together again. I have to explain something before you say anything. If I had known about your baby, I never would have gone with Suzy and I mean that. We all knew she was drinking every night and doing all she could to hurt the baby. I left because I felt it was the right thing to do at the time. I knew, if the baby died I would get far away from her and I did leave her right away. I didn't feel it was fair to you for me to go from her place back into yours. I wanted to do that but I couldn't."

"Joe, you have known right along I have wanted you to be with me. You went to be with Suzy while the baby was in the hospital. That didn't make any sense to me. I could see you doing it, if the baby was brought home but she was still in the hospital."

"You think I slept with Suzy when I went there. She just had a baby and I wouldn't have done that under any circumstances. I still felt sorry for her because the baby was so bad off. I was, also, afraid she could do something to you and hurt you. This is not going anywhere and I'm sorry I asked you to come back. I know when I'm not wanted and I'll just have to live with it."

"So now it is going to be my fault that we don't get back together. This is not my fault but the lousy choices you have made, Joe. Don't point any fingers at me. I have this baby to think about and I don't need any shit from you. I'm sorry I ruined your little party here."

"It's all right, I thought I saw a lot of love in your eyes but maybe I'm wrong."

"Why are you being this way with me?" Pam was feeling bad.

"I don't like to waste your time by asking you to be with me again."

Pam was very angry. "You listen to me and you listen good. You asked me to marry you and I took it very serious. When you left me I gave you the ring back and you left it on my pillow. I put it back on because it was the only hope I had to be with you again. I have always tried to be there for you. When I was on the overpass just standing on the edge I knew I was going to die and our baby would, too. I was praying that you could do something to save me and our tiny baby. You were standing there trying to talk with Suzy and trying to be my super hero. You were so close yet you were so far away. I have a question for you now. Am I wasting your time because you want to come home with me and I won't let you? Am I wasting your fucking time because I can't take you home and jump into bed immediately?"

"I don't want to be with you just to jump into bed. I want to be close to you and take care of you the right way. I've wasted enough of our time. I didn't mean to upset you by asking to live with you."

They finished the meal in silence. They walked outside together and stopped when they got to Pam's car. She felt bad for him because he was trying to make things right and she was being hard headed. "I'm sorry, Joe, that lunch turned out bad for us. When I saw Suzy lying on the street below in a heap it did something to me. It's like something snapped inside me and I had to make changes or my life would be terrible. Every time we have had problems and made up, other bad things happen and we never seem to stay together. I don't know about you but I'm tired of living that way. I want to be happy all the time because I deserve it. I simply can't take breaking up all the time. Maybe it doesn't bother you but it does me. We can't bring a baby into this world in chaos because I refuse to do that." He never said another word but walked over to his car and got in. She left, also, and got to the office too early. She sat in her car and thought about Chris. She was wondering what he would be saying to her now. The tears started falling and they turned into sobs. Pam held her belly with both hands as she cried even more. She didn't want to be alone but she didn't want the chaos either.

She walked down the hallway with her sunglasses on her face. She knew they would know she had been crying. She didn't care. He came into the Center after briefing and knew she had been crying, also. The shift dragged as she figured it would. It always dragged when things were bad and went swiftly when she was happy. Julie had her on ignore and that was fine with her. She thought that Julie was a little jealous that she was pregnant but she wasn't sure. Julie would be the one who would have the good life. She and

Ken would never any have problems because he couldn't see through her. Pam thought Julie must be greedy to want a good life with a man she was not in love with. She never thought it was greed before but it could be.

Soon the shift ended and she got to leave. She went home, took her shower, and went to bed all alone. This was her destiny from now on for all the choices she had made so far in her life. She had made one good choice and that choice would be linked to him forever. The tiny baby growing inside her belly would be good for her. She would teach him all about a good life. The one she never got to experience. She would teach him to love, to be happy, and to always make good choices. She reached over and turned out the light. Pam fell asleep wishing she had a good life.

This was the saddest period for Pam in a very long time. The more she was away from him the lonelier she felt. She was not looking forward to her days off anymore. She wished she could go to work each day and not think about her life so much. It was hard for her at work when she saw him yet it was easier because she could keep busier. She needed to have a more meaningful life. Ken was asking her to go to lunch or play tennis with them and she would decline. Joe still had some of his stuff at her place and she sent him an e-mail asking when he was going to pick it up. Seeing his clothes in her closet made her cry at times. He said he would be by Friday morning to get it all.

Friday came and she bounded out of bed wanting to be showered and dressed before he arrived. Soon the doorbell rang and she let him in. He immediately leaned over and kissed her belly before she could do anything. "Sorry, but I had to do that and I hope you didn't mind. It's the only contact I can have with my boy right now." He was not making it easy for her. She offered him a cup of coffee and he accepted. "You look very nice today," he told her.

"Thank you but I feel a little on the large size today. I guess I'll have to get used to carrying the baby around. It's quite an experience."

"What does it feel like when the baby moves?" He asked her.

"Oh, just little tiny sensations inside of me and it feels so good. It means the baby is alive and moving. I get a good feeling all over me when it happens."

"It must really be something to experience. You look so nice just telling me how it feels. He is one lucky baby to have you as his mother."

"I know I'll love this baby so much and he'll never feel lost or abused. I'm sorry that you didn't have that with your mother, Joe. She should have been proud of you instead of treating you awful."

"I didn't expect her at all to be proud of me. If she had just tucked me in bed for one night or patted me on the head one time without saying one word, I would have been so happy." The tears came to Pam's eyes. She turned her head so he couldn't see but she couldn't fool him. "I'm sorry, I don't want to make you cry. I shouldn't be talking this way but thinking about the baby has gotten to me."

"Joe, you shouldn't say the baby but our baby because this baby is as much yours as it is mine. I'll let you be part of his life as much of it as you would like to be. I could never keep you from him or keep you from sharing in his life. If I did that it would be abuse on my part."

"That's so nice to hear, Pam, and you've just made me so happy. I'll get my stuff and get out of your way."

"Take your time because I don't have any plans for the day." He went into the bedroom and started carrying his things to his car. When he was finished he came back into the apartment to say goodbye.

"I guess that does it for me. If you find something, I've overlooked then let me know or bring it to the office." She nodded. "There's one other thing, we're still playing tennis on Saturdays so if you should feel like joining us, you're welcome to do so. "Ken wanted to make sure that I asked you."

"Thank him for me and I'll think about it."

"I guess I'll see you for sure on Sunday and thanks again for including me with the baby. It'll mean so much to be part of his life." She was trying to get in control of herself and not cry anymore in front of him. He took his finger and ran it down the length of her nose and rested it on her lips. She kissed his finger and he brought it up to his own lips. He turned and walked out the door. He immediately turned back around and smiled at her.

"By the way, there's something in the parking lot that I would like to show you, if you will just walk out with me." Pam was curious as she walked out with him. Sitting in his old parking spot was a brand new teal colored van. Her eyes got big as she took a good look at it. "I just got rid of my little tin can of a car. I'm tired of not being able to use it, if there are more than two people in our group. This one sits six and it is a beauty." She smiled for him.

"Joe, it's so neat and will you let me test drive one time, if I'm careful?"

"Anytime you want to. I wanted it mainly because it would be safer for the baby, I mean our baby, to travel in. I have to think about him now and not just myself. Look at all the extras that came with it. It's the top of the line luxury van."

"This is so pretty, Joe. I love the color and the new smell is great."

"Go on and sit behind the wheel and get a feel of it." He helped her up and showed her where the handle was that she could use to get into it on her own.

"This feels so comfortable and look at all the gadgets."

"You can drive down the road and see what the outside temperature is at all times and dozens of little things like that." He was beaming at his new toy.

"I'm happy for you, Joe"

"I'll buy our baby the top of the line car seat and I'll show you the proper way to belt him in."

"I'm sure he'll be safer in here and it's so very nice." She felt the soft material with her hand and he showed her how to adjust the seat and mirrors. She was enjoying being with him.

"I'm taking up your time so I'll get out and let you leave. Joe, do you think that some night after work we could go to the Den. You could have a beer and I could have a 7-up. It wouldn't be like the old times but it's something I would like to do."

"I, too, would like that very much. How about Sunday right after work?"

"I'll look forward to it." She smiled and he did, also, and she watched him drive away in his new van that he bought just for their baby.

She needed to visit her Nana so she left right away for the nursery. She just walked into the building and Boots came running over to her. Pam picked her up and rubbed under the cat's chin. "Boots, you're so cute, have you caught any more mice?" The cat purred as she walked into Lee's office.

"Oh, I see you found a friend on the way in," Lee said to her. Lee was pleased to see Pam walk through her office door. She looked past her as if she was looking for Joe to be with her. "I was hoping you were coming by today to make me real happy. You're not smiling so I guess there have been no changes in your life."

"Joe just came by and got the rest of his stuff from my apartment. It was hard to see him but I did make him happy. I told him that he could be part of the baby's life, if that's what he wanted. His eyes just shone after I said that."

"I'm glad you're including him and you won't be sorry. Think of all the unmarried females who have to go it all alone. You've heard about the deadbeat dads. I was afraid I was going to Memphis and have to worry about you a lot while I was gone. Knowing that you're being civil to Joe will make me feel better."

"I wouldn't want to ruin your trip and I'm sure it'll be wonderful."

"What will mean more to me than going on my trip is that great grandson you will be giving me in August. I can't wait to spoil the "little devil.""

385

"No, I'm not going to name him Elvis, Nana, I have to draw the line."

"Pam, it would be such a cute name and such a famous one."

"How can you think like that? He'll be Joe Jr. or Joey will be acceptable."

"Did you tell Joe that you're using his name?"

"Not recently but we talked about it some time ago."

"Things have changed so you need to get permission to use his name, I would think.

"You're right about that so many things have changed between us."

"Your baby will be perfect and we all know it. I have more news to tell you. Your mother is flying in tomorrow at 2 PM and will stay with me for a few days."

"Nana, please tell me you are teasing. It has to be a joke."

"She called and she has her tickets. I know why she's coming, too. I told you to keep the lines of communication open between you two or this would happen."

"I have just gone through so much and I haven't had time to keep in touch."

"Pam, you should be happy to see your mother and we knew she would visit someday.

"You can tell her about her grandchild that's due and not living with Joe."

"I have no choice but to tell her since he won't be with me when she's here."

"She was not pleased with you living with Joe and you weren't even engaged at the time. Now, you're pregnant by him and not even with him anymore. It'll not go over well with her."

"I'll be a dead woman by tomorrow night. I'm expecting her grandchild and she'll go ape shit over that. I can hear her now ranting and raving about being too young to be a grandmother."

"Oh, Pamela, you're so right. I hadn't even thought of that. She's so vain and that'll put her into a real bad mood.

"Nana, I can't have her coming down here. Can't you make her cancel her plans. If you do this one thing for me, I promise I'll go up there and visit them. I'll show them I'm pregnant when you get back from Memphis."

"She's demanding that I take her straight to you when she arrives. She knows you're on a day off and wants to see you immediately," Lee told her. "I didn't tell her a thing about breaking up with Joe so she thinks you're still together unless you said something."

"No, I never tell her anything about my private life. If you can't persuade her not to come, take her to your house and I'll be over there when she arrives. She would start snooping around my apartment. She would see his clothes are gone and ask a million questions."

"You could always tell her, he has gone to Reno to visit his family and she wouldn't know the difference."

"Hold that thought, Nana. I'll see what kind of a mood she's in when she gets here. It would be an easy explanation that he's out of town and a big lie."

"Did you and Joe ever make any kind of wedding plans?"

"No, we talked a little about one. With Suzy around we wanted to wait until after the baby was born to make the actual plans."

"I envisioned such a nice wedding," Lee told her. "I had all kinds of plans in my head for you and him."

"If I don't marry Joe, there won't be anymore wedding plans for me."

"You sound like there could be a chance that you'll get back with him."

"I love him so much but I can't have him leaving me all the time." She told her grandmother about Joe buying the new van because of the baby. "I need to get going, Nana, thanks as usual for talking with me and being so kind to me."

"The pleasure is all mine and I like you coming by. Take care of yourself and the baby." Pam gave her a big grin and left the nursery.

There was something she needed to do today and that was go to the cemetery and take some flowers. Cannonball and baby Lee should always have flowers around them. She stopped by the florist shop and got a bunch of carnations to disperse at the gravesites. She made that sad little trip through the gates of the cemetery thinking about the ride she had with Webb. She got out of the car at his grave and walked slowly towards his headstone. Pam got down on her knees and wiped blades of dead grass from his headstone with her hand. She laid the carnations along the side of the stone. She wondered, if Webb and Chris were seeing each other in heaven. She then walked to where the baby was buried and she removed dead flowers from the reservoir. She added the carnations with fresh water. She was remembering the night the baby died in Joe's arms and how much she looked like him. She was glad she got to share that moment and to sing to the baby. The tears came to her eyes as she thought of Joe's tears for his innocent dying baby. She slowly walked back to her car and then drove home.

During the evening she thought about spending her life without Joe and it was not going to be easy. She would have to see him from time to time. She wondered, if he would find someone else and if he would want that woman to be part of the baby's life. It would kill her to share the baby with another woman. She shouldn't expect Joe to be single for the rest of his life. This was her choice but it would not be his. She was sure of that. She wondered, if Julie had her hopes up again that she could end up with Joe. That would kill Pam even more.

Chapter 41

As soon as she woke up Saturday morning she knew what she wanted to do. She got herself ready and drove to Ken's to play tennis. If they wanted her to play then she would play. She drove into his driveway and parked outside one of the three garages. She took her racquet out of the car and headed for the front door. She was wearing pants and a long sleeve blouse in this cool morning air. Pam rang the doorbell and Ken answered the door. He was very surprised to see her. He gave her a little hug and showed her into the living room. He went down the hallway to get Joe who was in his bedroom. When Joe came out and saw her, he got a big smile on his face. "I can't believe that you showed up today but we're glad that you did." He walked over and gave her belly a kiss much to her surprise. She liked him doing this.

"I still need to get out and exercise some so I thought I would try and keep up with you guys."

"Julie is a little late as usual so if you two will excuse me, I'm going to finish getting ready," Ken said to them. She looked at Joe again and liked seeing his handsome face.

"Here have a seat on the couch. I was going to call you later. I went to the cemetery late yesterday and saw flowers on both graves. I can only assume you put them there."

"Yes, I did because I thought they should both always have flowers."

"You're such a nice person to do that."

"Do you go there often?" She asked him.

389

"Just a couple of times recently. It makes me think about how precious life is and we all take it for granted. We're both on vacation this next week and we had originally planned to get married, do you remember? I cancelled my week off. I can't see taking the time to do nothing. We can't even be together and it would be a waste."

"Yes I do remember we talked about it but then Suzy was due to have the baby. We put everything on hold for her. I told Marge I would work, also. I would hate to stay home and not do anything.

The doorbell rang and Joe let Julie in. She gave him a hug and then saw Pam sitting on the couch. She went way overboard with the hug. "Oh, how nice to see you, Pam. I didn't think you would ever be back here."

"It's not easy to come since the last time I was here it didn't go very well for me. They say, if you fall off a horse, you should get right back on it again. I decided to do that today."

"We're glad you did and we should be all ready to go out to the courts," Joe said as Ken came into the living room. He gave Julie a quick kiss and she didn't give him a hug at all. Pam noticed she was wearing a tight blouse and shorts but this was no tennis outfit. Julie had lost about 30 pounds and she wanted everyone to notice. They started hitting the ball and every time Julie leaned over she showed the cheeks of her ass. Pam knew it was all for Joe's benefit. She couldn't very well say anything since she wasn't seeing Joe anymore. Joe was being very nice to Pam and she was being very receptive to him. Later they stopped playing and headed for the tables where lunch would be served. Julie hit Joe on the ass with her racquet just before he sat down. It upset Pam but she pretended it didn't bother her.

"Pam, how come you're still wearing Joe's ring?" Julie asked. This question was so unexpected and it threw Pam off guard.

"I like it and being pregnant are the main reasons."

"Julie, it was a gift to her and I didn't want it back, Joe said. He knew that the question was out of line. "How's Lee doing these days?" Joe asked.

"She's fine and getting excited about going to Memphis. She dropped a bomb on me yesterday by telling me that mom would be here at 2 PM today."

"Does she know about the baby?" Julie asked.

"No she doesn't. I've kept so much from her so it should be quite a visit."

"You mean she's coming here thinking you and Joe are still together and now you're pregnant and have split up?"

"That's exactly what she's going to find out," Pam told them.

"Pam, why not head for Mexico and not even be here?" Ken asked. "You don't even need a passport." She grinned at his attempt to humor her.

"Well, she's my mother and I have to face her sooner or later."

"I'm sorry that you have to go through that alone," Joe said.

"Nana wants to take us out to dinner at the New Horizons after I give mother all of my upsetting news. It should be quite a dinner."

"How did Lee think you should handle it?"

"If you want the truth, she thinks I should pretend you and I are still together. I should tell mom that you've gone to Reno to visit your family." Nana feels it will be worse, if mom knows I'm pregnant without you than if she thinks we're still together."

"I wouldn't care to be in your shoes," Julie told her.

"It's been real nice you guys but I have to be going to prepare myself for the wrath of Anne."

"I'll walk you out to your car," Joe told her. It felt good being with him. They got outside and he stopped when they got to her car.

"I'm sorry that you have to go through this with your mom under the circumstances. She's going to be too rough on you. It's not good to get all upset. I have an idea and I want to know what you think. Why not let me go to Lee's with you and pretend we're still together. Your mom wouldn't know the difference and Lee wouldn't mind, I'm sure."

"I don't know, Joe, do you think we could pull it off? Do you mind going to dinner with us?"

"Sure we can do it and dinner will be okay. She'll think we're still planning on getting married."

"If you think it'll work, I'm willing to try anything."

"What time do you have to be at Lee's?"

"I'll be there at 3 PM and you should be at my place to pick me up at 2:45."

"I don't have a thing to do today and I'll be happy to help you out."

"Thanks so much and I hope it does work. You always make me feel like we could conquer the world, if we stick together." She said goodbye to him and said she would see him at her place in about an hour.

As soon as she got back to her apartment she called her Nana to tell her what their plans were. Her Nana was delighted to know what they were going to do. She thought it would appease her mother for the time being. She was looking forward to seeing Joe again. Pam was quite happy that she was going to pull it off. She freshened herself up a little and it wasn't long before Joe rang the doorbell.

They arrived at Lee's and let themselves in with Pam's key. Her grandmother had not returned from the airport. They both settled on the couch to wait. Joe was making small talk and asking questions about her family. He seemed genuinely interested in getting to know them.

"I'm getting nervous now," she admitted to him. "She's soon to find out that I'm not the perfect daughter."

"Stop beating up on yourself, you're perfect in my book," he told her. She smiled at his attempt to make her feel more comfortable. They heard her Nana's car and they both stood up. Lee parked out front because she would take them to the restaurant in her car. Anne hurried into the house and grabbed her daughter around the neck. She was built the same as Lee with shorter blond hair and gray eyes. She was dressed in black silk pants and a white silk blouse. She looked like she just stepped out of a fashion magazine. "It has been so long since I saw you and you're looking fat my child. What's going on here? Is this a smock you're wearing?" Anne didn't even get a chance to greet Joe.

"Yes, it is mother, we're expecting in August."

"What have you done to my daughter, Mr. Big Cop? You can't marry her but you can knock her up?"

"The baby wasn't exactly planned for right now so it was s surprise to us both.

We're very happy and we'll eventually get married," Joe said to her. He put his arm around Pam and held her close. It felt good to her. Lee hadn't said one word and it didn't look like she would get a chance to. Joe and Pam sat down on the couch and Anne took a chair next to the couch. Lee just stood in the background.

"I can't believe you would let yourself get pregnant. You're an intelligent woman, Pamela, and this isn't what someone in your class should be doing."

"Are you trying to tell me that you don't want to be a grandmother? It would spoil your standing within the rich community."

"I don't know of anyone else in my age group who's a grandmother. Their daughters are going to college and planning for a rewarding career. These are the same plans I had for you." It was obvious to them all she did not want Pam to have the baby.

"What are you suggesting, Mother, that I have an abortion? It'll never happen so get that thought out of your head right now," Pam told her. "This is my life and I'm making my own decisions and choices."

"I agree," Joe said, "Pam would never get rid of the baby to please you, Anne. This is our precious baby and he'll be allowed to be born."

"When do you plan on marrying my daughter and making this so called union legal? There'll be no bastard children coming into our family. I won't stand for it."

"For you information this baby has a mother and dad and it'll not be a bastard child and I don't want to ever hear that come out of your mouth again." Pam was instantly livid. "This baby will have so much love in its life. A lot more than you ever thought of giving to me. Joe and I love each other very much and the baby will know this and will thrive on it." Pam stopped when she realized what had just come out of her mouth. Joe leaned over, kissed her cheek, and put his hand on her back. She leaned against his hand as she knew how much he still meant to her.

All of a sudden Anne grabbed a newspaper from under the coffee table and pulled it out to look at it. "What's this?" She asked when she saw Pam standing on the edge of the overpass on the front page. "Oh, my God, the woman was going to kill you and you never called and told me anything."

"That's why you haven't heard from me, Mom, we've been busy lately."

"I have all day tell me what happened." Pam proceeded to give her mother an abbreviated version of the events that day.

"Why would she want to kidnap and kill you, this story does not make sense?"

"She was someone that we both knew and she had a big crush on me," Joe told Anne. "She wanted Pam out of the way because she thought she could be with me. She was on drugs and real crazy acting that day. It was ugly and Pam was lucky to survive." He grabbed Pam's hand and held it.

"Is that what policemen and dispatchers do on their time off around here? If something like this ever happens again, Miss Austin, you'd better let me know."

"I will, it was all over in about an hour and everything turned out fine."

"I don't know about everyone else but I'm starving," Lee said to the group. They all nodded and followed her out to the car.

"Joe you sit in front with Lee, I have to sit next to Pamela." Pam knew that would happen. Her mother always had to be in charge of everything within her reach.

They were soon at the restaurant and Anne requested the table where she wanted them to sit at. "Joe, tell me about your family because I would like to meet them or will I have to wait for the wedding for that to happen?" He told her where his mother and sisters were living. "Pamela, you're looking better since I last saw you. Make sure you get enough exercise and you should eat healthier." Pam briefly looked at Joe.

"She's really perfect," Joe said. "She takes care of herself, too."

"Anne, why don't you stop picking Pam apart," Lee said. "There's nothing wrong with her and she looks just fine." Pam was so glad when the meal was over with. They said goodbye and Pam and Joe were expected to be back at Lee's in the early evening. Pam would have to come up with some excuse. She was so relieved when her mom and grandmother drove away from the restaurant.

Joe drove Pam to her apartment and she invited him in. "This has been quite a day and I want to thank you for helping me out, Joe."

"Pam, you sounded like you meant it when you said that we loved each other very much. Were you play acting or did you mean it?"

"I meant it for myself but I'm not sure, if you feel that way."

"I want to be with you and I don't know what I can possibly do to convince you. If you could just give me a hint, what it would take for me to be with you."

"How many times before Suzy's baby was born did you tell me you would never leave me, no matter what? You left the minute you found out her baby was yours. It's called rejection, Joe, for your information."

"I swear to you on my dead daughter's grave, if I'd known you were pregnant, I never would have left you. I know I hurt you something awful and I told you I still loved you when I left."

"You could have stayed with me and fought to get custody of your daughter and I would have helped you do that."

"I made a big mistake and I'm sorry. Don't keep me from being with you while you're pregnant with our son. I want to make things right with you and be with you. I let you down and I wish I could take it back. I would do anything you ask of me just to hold you again." Pam looked at him and she never expected to hear those words.

"Are you serious, Joe, please tell me you're not saying this to make me feel better?"

"Pam, I love you with all my heart and I want you to take me back. I'll do anything you want to feel you in my arms again."

"Joe, I still need some more time, I want to believe you but I still need to be able to trust you."

"The last thing I want to do is push you into making a decision you're not sure of. I'll give you more time just don't take a long time, please."

"I promise to let you know in the next couple of weeks, if you can be patient with me, Joe. We talked about this before but I wanted to hear it again, would it be okay, if I name the baby after you? I would like the baby to have your name because I want you in the baby's life. Would you let me name him Joseph Jr., please?"

"It would make me very proud for him to have my name. I'm going now and I'll give you time to let you think. I hope Anne doesn't give you anymore lip about being pregnant. I'm glad you're not like her at all." He gave her a smile.

"Thanks for helping me out today. You didn't have to do this but you're kind to for doing it. I'll be in touch with you."

"Is it okay, if I kiss the baby?" She nodded. He bent over, gave her belly a long kiss and it made her feel great. "I can't wait for him to be born and to hold him. I'll be so proud to be his dad. Won't we be surprised, if it turns out to be a little girl. I will love her, too.

Pam was going to spend several hours this Friday morning with Lee. Her mother had left Mission Park on Monday morning, still upset over becoming a grandmother and over Pam not being married. Tomorrow her grandmother was due to leave for Phoenix to pick up her friend Sharon. Off to Memphis they would travel together to see Graceland and say their goodbyes to Elvis. Pam needed to talk with Lee over any shipments due or any major transactions that would take place while Lee was gone. Her Nana asked Pam, if it was okay if Joe joined them this evening for dinner at the Den. Pam agreed. They could both say their farewells to her this evening and wish her a safe trip. Pam got up and left for the nursery. Her grandmother was not there and this puzzled Pam. It was not like her. Dorothy told her that Lee was home packing and would check on them later. She went to Lee's house and rang the doorbell. It took Lee a few minutes to answer the door. "I wasn't expected you this early, Pam, and I'm starting to do some packing." Her grandmother seemed to happy about making the trip. She may have been lying down instead of packing.

"I can come back a little later, if you're busy, Nana."

"No, we'll sit at the dining room table and I'll go over some things. I have a list of people to call, if there are any problems." Lee was very thorough with Pam and gave her all kinds of information.

"I think you've covered it all and I don't think there'll be any problems," Pam told her. "I'll ask the graveyard officers to drive by when they're not busy and keep an eye out for anything suspicious."

"That's nice of you to do that, Pam. I asked Joe to be available, if anything goes wrong and I didn't think you would mind."

"That's fine, Nana, something could go amok."

"Pam, I want you to work on your problems with Joe. You need to be together. I know you love him and he loves you, you can see it in his eyes whenever he looks at you. Don't let your pride get in the way of having a happy life. I strongly feel you'll make it as a couple and the baby will be a wonderful bonus."

"Nana, are you feeling all right because you don't quite look like your old self?"

"I'm fine and I had a headache earlier but I got rid of it. I'm looking forward to this trip. I'm glad you have been pushing me into going. Have you heard from your mother since she went home?"

"Yes, she sent an e-mail Tuesday. She seemed glad, if you can put it that way that she met Joe. She's not pleased with our situation but glad that I'm not hiding him from the family. What was she like, Nana, did she ever date much?"

"She always did like the men and I had to rein her in several times when she was a teenager."

"You mean she chased the guys?"

"She sure did until she met your dad and he tamed her down. Actually his money helped calm her. I thought she would end up having to get married but that didn't happen."

"Nana, tell me again about seeing Elvis in person. I never get tired of hearing that story."

"Well, it was the month of June in 1956. He only had a few hits at that time but he was coming to Phoenix and the show would be at the Fairgrounds. That's all Sharon and I could talk about. My folks would not let us go alone to see the show so they went with us. I don't know what they thought we would do but they insisted. He was quite the performer and the way he moved those hips was something we had never seen before. He gyrated all over the stage and some of the girls tried to climb the chain link fence to get to him. Of course this is the picture they chose to show on the front page of the newspaper the next day. I was glad we got to see him. I joined his fan club and bought all his records. He will always be the King." Pam grinned at her grandmother.

"There'll never be another performer like him, I'm sure, Nana. I'm going to leave you now unless there's something I can help you do to get ready?"

"I'm fine dear and I know the nursery is in good hands."

"Joe and I will pick you up this evening so be ready at about 6 PM."

"I'm looking forward to it and I'll see you then." Pam gave her a big hug and kiss and walked to her car. She would miss her Nana a lot as they had gotten much closer since Pam moved to Mission Park. It had been quite an experience these past eleven months.

She returned to the apartment and kept busy until Joe showed up at 5:30 PM. He couldn't wait to show her what he had bought Lee. It was something she might need on her trip. He pulled a small case out of a bag.

"I thought she might be able to use a highway emergency kit for her trip."

"Joe, this is just perfect for her. I know she has nothing like this." He showed Pam jumper cables, flashlight with red and amber lights that flashed, flares, and a few other items. "You're so nice to think of such a useful going away gift."

"Maybe it isn't me but my cop mentality that made me think of it."

"It doesn't matter, she'll love it and you will make a lot of points with her."

"Did you tell her about your mom still wanting you to have the abortion when she e-mailed you?"

"No, I thought I wouldn't bring it up. I don't want to worry Nana and spoil her nice trip. It isn't something she could change and I don't want to upset her. She needs to enjoy her trip and have a great time."

"What about you?" He looked at her with concern in his eyes.

"Part of me wants to tell my mother off and the other part thinks I should be quiet. What do you think I should do?"

"You should do what your heart tells you. I don't want you being stressed about it."

"I've been thinking that she's home and we don't have to see her but what'll happen in the future. I think she'll be coming down here more often just to stay involved in our lives and try to tell us how to live."

"Have you felt the baby today?"

"No, he must be taking a very long nap." Babies do sleep a lot."

"I'm glad you can feel him move. I know I told you that I would give you more time but I've been thinking so much about things we could do. I don't want to raise a kid in an apartment. I thought that maybe we could buy a two bedroom condo for now and in few years sell it for a real home. I have the van now and that'll be perfect for the little guy."

"Joe, we can start making plans soon. Would you mind going by the store so I can buy a plastic container to put things in for the baby? I need to start buying little things that he'll need."

"Not at all, we have plenty of time." They got into his van and went by the store and picked up a plastic container. Is there anything else you need?"

"This will be fine for the time being. I can't wait to get started filling it up."

"Are you going to let me buy the baby things since I'm going to be in his life?"

"Sure I will. I'll make a list of things we'll need."

They walked out to the van and Pam asked him, if she could drive it to her Nana's. He handed her the keys and she got in behind the wheel. She was delighted to be driving such a nice vehicle. They pulled up to Lee's front gate and she came outside. Joe got out to let her sit in front with Pam.

"This van is beautiful, Joe, and you're letting Pam drive it." She grinned as she knew Pam was a good driver. "I love the new car smell so fresh and wonderful. Almost as good as a baby after his bath." Lee was not wearing her usual jean pants and jacket but chose a nice pair of navy blue slacks and a red blouse.

"Nana, you look so nice tonight. I really like your outfit." Joe agreed

"Thanks you two, it's nice to look a little spiffy once in awhile." On the way to the Den Pam told her about buying the container so she could fill it up for the baby. Pam walked a little slowly into the Den. It was a little eerie but she was glad she wouldn't have to see Suzy anymore. Lee sat next to Joe and Pam across from him. She didn't like sitting next to her guy but wanted to look at him at all times.

"This does feel a little strange to me, does it you?" Joe asked Pam.

"Yes, it does but I feel relief, also. Chris is giving me hell right now for being here and he not able to be." She smiled at her own comment.

"He's up in heaven entertaining God," Lee said to them.

"Lee, he's gay so maybe he's in the other place," Joe said to the women. Pam was instantly upset at Joe.

"So Chris was a mistake of God's, is that what you're saying, Joseph?" Pam asked.

"Now, you both need to calm down because I want my last meal to be nice," Lee said to the couple. "I figure I'll be gone 10 to 14 days because we don't want to rush this trip. It'll be so much fun. "I've never been to Tennessee or Arkansas so it will be a new experience. Back in '55 we drove out West from Maine on the old Route 66 and I'll be traveling the same highway except it's now Route 40. They shouldn't have changed the highway number. We stopped at every Stuckeys on the old highway."

"What is a Stuckey's, Nana?"

"It was a company that had shops all along the old route. They carried post cards, souvenirs, junk, and, of course, candy. They knew what it took back then to make traveling easier on the whole family."

"Lee, did you look like the people in *The Grapes of Wrath* movie?" Joe asked.

"Young man, we were in a brand new 1955 turquoise and cream colored Pontiac. It was a grand car and the trip was exciting, also."

"I like hearing about your family, Nana, and moving out West. You were true 1950's pioneers and it was what made the west as nice as it is today." Pam reached over and took her Nana's hand and gave her a squeeze.

"Pam, I'm going to miss you a lot and you too, Joe. You both mean so much to me." Pam was sure she saw a tear in her grandmother's eye but in the dimly lit room she was not sure. She enjoyed her meal and some more stories from Lee about the big trip West. Joe seemed to be enjoying them, too. He never had much of a life nor any good memories of his childhood.

"Pam, there's something I want you to have and right away," Lee said to her. "You know the old rocking chair in my bedroom, well, I want you to have it. I figured Joe could take it tonight in the back of the van so you could start using it."

"Oh, Nana, the one you had when mom was a baby. I do want one for the baby very much. I can start using it now and get him used to it."

"It's still in pretty good shape and I hope you'll enjoy it."

"Lee, you know Pam will start using it as soon as she gets home." Joe gave Pam a big smile.

"Maybe, if I rock him every night and make him sleepy, he'll let me sleep through the night." They finished their dinner and took Lee home. Joe got her gift out of the trunk and gave it to her when they got inside her house. Lee was so pleased and she gave him a big hug. Pam gave her one, too. They both told her to drive carefully and enjoy her trip to the max. Pam was talkative on the way to her apartment making comments about the rocking chair. Joe carried it in for her and she immediately sat down to try it out. "This is so nice and I had already thought about buying one real soon," she told Joe. "There's something bothering me and I'm sure you know what I'm talking about. You need to stop making bad comments about Chris. It isn't fair when he isn't here to defend himself. You don't have to like him just don't make me feel bad."

"I do apologize, Pam, and I promise to stop doing that. I guess he still irritates me and I shouldn't let him." She missed Chris a lot and Joe should not be tearing him to shreds now that he was gone.

"I should be going since I seem to keep upsetting you so much."

"You don't irritate me, Joe, just your mouth does at times."

"Pam, I hate leaving you all the time. We get together and it feels so good for me.

The next thing I know we're saying goodbye and acting like friends only. Am I the only one who is bothered by this? Because, if I am, I'm waiting for you to give me an answer that I don't want to hear."

"If you only knew how this bothered me, Joseph, those thoughts wouldn't even cross your mind. I've never wanted you to leave me but you made the ultimate choice and you're going to have to be more patient. I thought we would be together forever and in just a few minutes, you packed your bag and was gone. I was cast aside by you and it is hard to get past that." Joe turned and walked out of the apartment. The tears started as she knew he hurt and she did, too. There was something inside her that could not forgive him just yet. She got ready for bed and thought, if he only how much she wanted to go to bed with him every night.

Chapter 42

The next week passed quickly for Pam. Her Nana called her every couple of days to give them a progress report on her trip. She, also, wanted to find out how her nursery was holding up. She told Pam she would be back in Phoenix on the 13th and would spend a night or two with Sharon. She should be back in Mission Park on Friday the 15th. Pam would be so happy to see her.

At work she and Julie were being fairly civil to one another under a businesslike atmosphere. She knew they would never be any kind of a friend to each other. Joe still did not talk with Julie privately, Pam was sure of that. She knew Julie would tell her, if they still had contact with each other. She would throw it into Pam's face.

A week after her Nana left on her trip there was a little bit of excitement generated for her and Joe during their shift. On this Sunday evening the shift started out rather quiet. Pam was working the police radio and Julie was on the phones. A couple of hours into the shift Julie received a call from a citizen about an officer wrestling with a man. He gave the location and Pam knew it had to be Joe as the incident was occurring just south of the downtown area on his beat. It was not a good area for a cop to be alone and fighting in. She immediately alerted all units and asked the adjacent beat officer to respond to the call. Her stomach took a tumble after calling for Joe to answer his radio. She kept trying and he was not answering. The citizen described what he saw when he drove by and it was not good. Another officer arrived on the scene with Joe but no one said anything. This always drove the dispatchers crazy by being left out and not hearing or knowing what was going on. What seemed like several minutes Joe came on the radio and he had a chuckle sound in his voice. "Mission Park, we're Code Four and I'll explain later." This was all he said and then the dispatchers got pissed because they felt they deserved more than just a little blurb.

"Isn't that just like a fucking officer to reply like that," Dave told them. "We're sitting here thinking the worst and he comes on the air laughing and not saying another God damn thing."

"As Chris would have said, we'll have to find him some dogs to chase and see how he likes it," Pam told her two partners. "Pay back can be hell and more."

"Oh, you two are not nice and he wouldn't like you saying those things about him," Julie said.

"He'll hear about it from me at the end of his shift so I'm not saying it behind his back," Pam added. "Gee, Julie, you have said much worse about officers and that was okay, I guess, coming from you?"

"Since I'm been seeing Ken I'm not like that anymore. I have more respect and patience for the officers." She was not sounding like the person they had known for a long time.

"Julie, you sound like you wouldn't say shit, if you had a mouthful so when did you become a 'born again' dispatcher?" Dave asked her.

"You two spend all your time at work making fun of everyone and I don't like it one bit. You're disgusting and I don't want any part of it."

"You tell me one person I have made fun of and been vicious to, Miss Perfect Woman?" Pam asked to her. "We all joke and include each other and we have never been vicious."

"You both have short memories but I don't want to repeat some of the stuff you have said. It's too bad to repeat." Joe told Pam he was on his way into the office. She thought that he must be reading her mind because she wanted to know what was going on and why was he wrestling with a guy.

"I'll tell Joe what you two have been saying and see how he likes it," Julie said. Pam and Dave looked at each other and shook their heads. It wasn't long before Joe came into the Center. As soon as he walked in the atmosphere got thick. "Joe, tell us what happened, I was so worried," Julie told him. Pam looked at him but didn't say anything. He proceeded to tell them that he stopped a man because the car was weaving going down the street. The guy pulled over and he asked him to get out of the car. Joe could smell booze as soon as the man rolled down his window. The citizen stood next to his car and was having trouble standing up. He kept leaning into the car and Joe was trying to handcuff him. The guy was cooperating but as soon as Joe got the older fellow's hands behind his back his pants fell down. Joe was trying to keep him handcuffed and trying to keeps his pants pulled up at the same time. It may have looked like they were wrestling but it was not that at all.

"I could hear you calling me and I heard the concern in your voice but I couldn't get to the radio," he told Pam. The sergeant gave me permission to come in and explain what had happened.

"Joe, you shouldn't explain anything to them. When they found out you were okay, they were pissed," Julie told him.

"You lying piece of shit, Julie, we joked a little but we were glad he was okay," Dave said to the group.

"You're just trying to cause more problems between us all and I don't appreciate it," Pam said to Julie.

"What's going on here?" Joe asked them all.

"Don't ask them anything, Joe, but I'll tell you what went on. You didn't answer you radio fast enough for Pamela so she mentioned something about sending you out on a call to chase some dogs. She and Dave have no patience when they are working the radio. They make fun of everyone and I'm getting tired of it myself." Pam was so upset she couldn't even speak. The tears came to her eyes and her radio was getting busy. They all knew she was crying. "She's crying, Joe, because she got caught not being nice to you," Julie said. "You and I know how she can be." Pam was getting too busy to say anything more to Julie. She would explain to Joe later. He got quiet and finally left the Center not knowing who to believe.

Later her radio quieted down and she and Dave were only talking to each other. Julie was doing everything she could to make this a major issue. She couldn't have Joe so Pam couldn't have him back either. Pam had had it with her former friend. When their shift was over she noticed that Julie was taking her time getting ready to leave. She, now, knew that Julie planned on talking to Joe when his shift was over. She would take care of everything. Pam even went slower than Julie and after Julie left the Center, Pam followed her. She got outside and saw Julie waiting outside the locker room for Joe. She looked into the briefing room and saw Ken. He looked like he was just finishing some paper work and was getting ready to leave.

"Hey, Ken, lets all go to the Den tonight like old times."

"That sounds really good, Pam, I'll meet you there." She smiled at him and left. She saw Julie now talking with Joe and she called out to them.

"Let's go to the Den and have a good time. I just asked Ken and he's willing to go." Joe thought it was a good idea but Julie was hesitating. "I'll see you all there." Pam went out the office entrance and drove straight to the bar. She was able to find their old booth empty and the waitress came by all excited to see her. It wasn't long before Joe and Ken walked in together. Julie was not with them. Ken sat next to Pam and Joe sat across from her. This was not going exactly the way she had planned. She looked him in the eye but didn't see anything. The guys ordered a beer and Pam a 7-up. The waitress brought the drinks as Julie showed up. She seemed glad to sit next to Joe, although, he got up so she could be across from Ken.

"Okay," Ken said looking at Pam why are we here?"

"I just thought we all needed to have an adult conversation since there're still problems between some of us." Pam told them. "It's difficult working with someone who's always making obtrusive comments and causing a plethora of problems in our working and personal environments."

"Look, Pam, just get off your high horse and speak common English here," Julie said. "You love to throw those college phrases around because you're such a big phony."

"Hey, just wait a minute, Jules, this is not going to end up a name calling session," Joe told her.

"That's right let's keep it civil and let's keep acting as adults," Ken added.

"Well, Joe, I think you need to tell Pam what you said to me just after you met her, you do remember?" Julie asked. "Let me revive your memory a little. You said something like Pam would make a great trophy woman or have you forgotten?"

"I said that but I had just met her and thought she was very attractive looking." Pam did not dare look at Joe as she knew, if she did the tears would not stop.

"Well, I guess that's a little higher than being nothing at all as you found out when Joe wouldn't take you out," Pam said. "Maybe Ken needs to find out about the real Julie tonight, what do you think, Joe, shall we tell him who he's marrying?"

"It wouldn't solve a thing," Joe said.

"Ken will not believe anything from you two, he knows what you're like, Pamela."

"Okay someone had better start talking because I want to know what's going on," Ken told them.

"Since Joe was in charge of the punishment, he needs to be the one," Pam said. "Julie, you got such a light sentence in my opinion." Ken was getting exasperated.

"I'm waiting to hear from one of you," Ken said as his eyes went back and forth between Joe and Julie.

"Julie, I'll leave it up to you to be honest with the guy your engaged to," Joe told her.

"If you'll excuse me, I'm going to leave," Pam said.

"You bring us all together to cause big problems for me and then you are going to leave early, Miss Rich Bitch," Julie said. She was so angry her eyes were spitting fire. "You know, Pamela, I'd rather be a "wanna be" than a big fat obnoxious trophy woman. Look at yourself really good because you're going to die a lonely old woman. Your only accomplishment in life will be to have a bastard baby." Pam got up and left. She could not get out of the Den fast enough.

She was home and in the shower in record time. She was so riled up she couldn't begin to try and go to bed after what had just taken place. She sat in the rocking chair holding her belly with both hands and rocking. The tears finally came as she thought about the lonely life that she was already living. The doorbell rang and she looked out to see Joe. She slowly opened the door and didn't look him in the eye. She stepped back to let him come in. "I can't believe you would stoop so low as to get us all together like that and bring up what Julie did to you," he told her.

"I didn't say a word about it but she's going to have to come up with something for Ken. I'm tired of her Joe because she never lets up on me. You keep looking the other way or you just don't care. She hates me and it's obvious to everyone but you. Why did you come by here? I can't fight or argue anymore. You didn't even care that she called your baby a bastard. Julie can do and say anything she feels like and she doesn't ever get punished. She has it made and as long as she's allowed to continue like this, she will. There's no stopping her."

"I happen to like Ken and he's a good friend. I don't want to destroy his future with her. He should find out on his own what she's like and not find out from us."

"If you were such a good friend, why would you want him to have anything to do with her? There's no cure when you're deranged, Joe."

"I refuse to get involved in it."

"You know, Joe, you're right. I'm interfering when I brought us together to talk."

"I need to keep looking the other way no matter what she does or says. I don't like doing that so I'll never be in her company again except working with her. I'll just let her tear me to pieces and not defend myself. It wouldn't matter what decision I made about her, you would always defend her. Why don't you just go and be with her. You wouldn't even have to work at it. Just quirk your little finger and she would come running."

"I don't want her and I never have but you keep pointing me in her direction.

Maybe I should do what you suggest and get it over with."

"I'll tell you something right now. If you choose to do that you'll never be in this baby's life. I'll never allow her to take care of my baby not in a million years would I. You do what you have to do and please leave now."

"You're telling me, if you don't want me anymore and you don't happen to approve of any woman in my life, you'll keep my baby from me."

"I never said a thing about any woman, I just said that about Julie. I mean it, too. She would be cruel to him because I'm his mother. I don't think you would want that to happen."

"I think you're right about us trying to get back together. It isn't going to work out. We have way too many issues."

"Why don't you tell me what you really want to say, Joe? Tell me that you made a mistake about asking me to get married. Tell me you should have waited before popping the question. Just be honest with me, Joe, and you won't have to worry about me bringing it up again. I can have this baby and you don't even need to do a thing. I have medical insurance and I can afford to feed and clothe the baby by myself. I don't have to rely on you or anyone else to help me."

"I want to be with you, Pam, but you're right about us having too many problems. I'm actually getting tired of going back and forth and I thought I could do this for a while longer. I wanted to be with you forever but I'm a little nervous about getting married. It doesn't mean that I don't love you. You know my life was screwed up royally by my parents, especially my mother, and I'm trying to be cautious. I know you'll take this the wrong way and I'm sorry, if you do." Pam was instantly upset and didn't even want to have this conversation. "Are you not going to talk to me now?" He asked.

"I have nothing more to say to you, Mr. Pellerini." She turned away and would not talk with him. He left her apartment.

The next few days were very difficult for Pam. On Monday she woke up wishing the new day had never come. She didn't want to get out of bed. Everything about the night before was coming back and hitting her right between the eyes. The tears came and she could not stop them. She sat in the rocker and they wouldn't stop either. She would take her shower to try and wash them away. She had a doctor's appointment at 10 for the baby's ultrasound but she didn't know, if he would be there after last night. He didn't show up as she expected.

After the shift was over she waited for him outside to give him the ultrasound results. He was surprised to see her when he got to his car. She quickly told him he was having a son and she got in her car and drove home.

The only good thing in her life was that her grandmother was on her way home from Memphis. She was treated poorly by Julie and Joe was staying away from the Center while she was there. It didn't matter what she did, nothing was turning out right for her.

On Thursday she stopped by the nursery on her way in to work. Boots greeted her as she walked into Lee's office. She picked up the cat and started rubbing its head. Boots was purring loudly as she was missing Lee's presence very much. "I miss her, too, you spoiled cat but we'll soon have her back." She placed the cat back on the sofa and sat down at the desk. She wanted to go through some paper work and make sure the books were done up properly. Pam was missing Joe as she hadn't seen him since Monday night. She wondered, if he was happy he was going to have a son. Talking to him on the radio just wasn't the same. Julie hadn't made any smart remarks to her and Pam wondered what she had told Ken. He still came into the Center and seemed okay around Julie so Pam figured she made up some lies to appease him. It was something Pam would never bring up again to anyone. She was thinking about Chris and what he would be telling her right now. He would still be telling her to boot his ass out, even though, they weren't even seeing each other. She had no friends and in their place were numerous problems. She wished he had never proposed and she made a mistake by getting pregnant. She would love and take care of the baby but it would be much harder doing it alone. Pam got up from the desk and walked over to the file cabinet. As she walked across the small office she felt her body going through a chilly spot before she got to the cabinet. It was eerie and she felt a strange feeling going through her body. The clock on the wall said 1 PM. It was something that she had never felt before. She put the file away and decided to leave for the office.

Pam arrived at the police station a little earlier than usual because she always gave herself plenty of time to make stops on the way in. She stepped through the door and Joe was standing just inside. She knew he had been waiting for her. "Could we step outside to talk?" He asked her and she nodded her head. "You probably think I've been ignoring you and I guess I have been. It's hard for me to think the right way, if I see you and I've been doing a lot of thinking. I talked to Julie about calling our baby a bastard. That really upset me and I know it did you."

"I figured you would and I hope she doesn't ever say that again."

"Ken and I both got on her for saying it. Of course, she came up with all kinds of excuses. She didn't tell him either about the things that she did to you. Just brought up the fact that she had been hard on you at work and she would stop it."

"She's trying to be civil but it's hard for her. Not talking with her, is much better for me."

"I won't take up your time but I wanted to let you know what was going on and I want to know how you've been feeling. I know with Lee not around you don't have anyone to talk to and it must be hard."

"I'm doing okay just getting fatter all the time. I rock the baby every night and I'm trying to take care of myself for him."

"You didn't give me a chance the other night to tell you how happy I am that our baby is a boy. You said you would give me one and it's really going to happen. I hope you'll still talk with me and let me know how you're doing. I need to know how the baby is because I still care very much, Pam."

"I know you do and you can call me, if you wish. I know the two weeks is up tomorrow that I promised you a decision."

"If you're still waiting for one, why don't you come over after work and talk. I still have a couple of your beers in the refrigerator."

"I'd like that very much so I'll see you then." He took his index finger and ran it down the length of her nose and gave her a big smile. He opened the door and held it while she walked in. They walked down the hall together and stopped at the briefing room door. They both looked up as Julie came through the door. Joe told her he would see her later and Pam waited until Julie was past her before she continued into the Center. She was glad Dave was working as they could talk. Pam took the telephone position as Dave and Julie wanted to work the radios. They were just starting to get busy when Julie turned to her with her first snide comment.

"I see you're still trying to get back with Joe or make him feel sorry for you. Pamela, you play that role so well. I don't think he'll fall for it anymore."

"Julie, why don't you leave her alone. I'm personally sick of the way you keep hammering her and I don't want to hear anymore," Dave told Julie.

"Oh, so now Pamela has another knight in shining armor to her rescue. It must be those innocent looking eyes you think you have that has an affect on the male population. What do men know about life, love or the pursuit of happiness? They fall for sluts so normal women don't have a chance. How does it feel to be a slut with child, Pamela?" Pam was not going to talk with Julie.

"You know, Jules, you sound like a slut who's jealous because she isn't with child," Dave said to her. This amused Pam but she kept it to herself. "I wonder what Ken would say, if he knew how you talked to Pam all the time. Maybe I should enlighten him a little because he has no clue what he's getting into by marrying you. Guys talk as much as women and I wouldn't mind telling him about the real Julie."

"Dave, you need to butt out and fuck off," Julie said to him. Ken walked out of the kitchen much to their surprise.

"Jules, I thought you weren't going to give Pam a rough time anymore and I've heard enough to last her a lifetime," Ken said to her.

"Look, Ken, she came in here all high and mighty today and I had no choice but to tell her off," Julie said and he knew she was lying. Dave proceeded to tell him all that had been said by Julie to Pam.

"I'll see you when the shift is over, Julie, and I want to get to the bottom of everything." They never heard another word out of her mouth.

A little later some strange things started happening over the radio after Pam took a call from the California Highway Patrol in the Bakersfield Area. They requested a uniformed officer in charge to call them. She took all the information and Sergeant Wilson was told to contact dispatch for an important message. He told Julie he'd be coming into the office to pick it up. He soon was in the Center and Pam gave him the name and number to call. He left and told them he would be in his office. It wasn't long before he was back in dispatch and standing in front of Pam.

"Did the CHP tell you what the call was about?" he asked her.

"No, just that it was important."

"They're a very professional group," he acknowledged. "I'll be in my office for awhile. Julie, have Joe come in to see me right away, if he isn't tied up."

"He's not working any incidents," she told Wilson. She then told Joe over the air to come into the office and see the Sergeant. Wilson left the Center.

"What in hell is going on?" Dave asked the women. "Something's not right but no one is saying anything."

"It could be something important is being relayed to this area. Maybe the President or Governor is coming our way," Pam told them.

"I think your right, Pam and I guess they'll tell us when we need to know," Dave said.

"Joe's in the office now," Julie said to them.

About 15 minutes later Dave answered the inter-office phone. "Sure, I'll be right there. Hey, you guys, Wilson wants to see me in his office right away."

"I'll take your radio," Pam said to him. "Did it sound very serious?" she asked Dave.

"No, very businesslike but who knows, it must be about the very mystery phone call," Dave said. He left the Center. In about ten minutes he was back and had a serious look on his face. He took back over the radio and Julie started asking him what was going on. Pam started answering phones and couldn't tell what was going on between Dave and Julie. When she finished the call Dave told her to go and see Wilson. She walked down the quiet hallway and saw that the Sergeant's door was open. She looked in and saw Joe standing with his back to the door looking out the window.

"The Sarge wants to see me?" she asked. Joe still stared out the window.

"He isn't here, Pam." He slowly turned around to face her and she saw the tears in his eyes. "I have something to tell you." She saw love in his eyes for her and she saw pity. He walked over and carefully removed her headset from her head.

"What is wrong, Joe? Is it my Nana?" He pulled her into his arms.

"The CHP called and said that she was killed this afternoon just outside of Bakersfield. It was a very bad car accident."

"No, my Joe, no, not my Nana, it can't be. Please don't tell me that Nana is dead." She sobbed uncontrollably as he held her close and stroked her hair. It took her awhile but she managed to gain control of herself.

"Wilson wants me to take you home because they already called someone to come in and relieve you. Why don't you sit down and I'll put your headset away and get your purse from your locker." She nodded as he led her to a chair. He kissed the top of her head and left for the Center. He was back shortly as Wilson had come back in and was talking to Pam.

"Joe, take her home and stay with her, if you wish. Rose just arrived so the Center is okay." She thanked the Sergeant and Joe led her out to his van. As they drove to her apartment her crying started again. He reached over, touched her hand, and squeezed it a little. He helped her inside and she slumped down onto the couch.

"Joe, she died not knowing, if we were ever going to get back together again. She really wanted us to be a couple."

"I know she did but she'll know when that decision is made. Do you want to know what happened?" he asked.

"Not right now please. What will Boots do without her or Dorothy and the ladies? How will I get through this, Joe?"

"You will because I'll help you. I'll be here for you as long as you need me."

"Thanks, Joe, but I need to be alone."

"Pam, this is not the time to be alone. I want to be here to help you through this." She looked into his face and outlined his chin with her finger. She saw love in his eyes but she still couldn't trust him enough to accept him back.

"I know that two weeks are up and I promised you an answer at this time. I need a little more time, Joe, because of Nana's death. I hope you'll understand and not be upset with me. Can you forgive me for taking so long and causing us more problems?" He put his hand on her belly and held it there. She gave him a big smile and he gave her one right back.

"I care about you, Joseph Pellarini."

"I care about you, Pamela Austin. You still shouldn't be alone tonight."

"Don't worry about me, I think better when I'm alone. I need to call my parents and that won't be very pleasant. I'll call you, if I need anything, I promise."

"You haven't had dinner so let me get you something," he said to her.

"I have plenty of food here that I can fix for myself later. You need to get back to work and I'll be fine."

"Can I check on you after work? I'll come by and if you aren't sleeping, we could talk."

"Sure you can but I may well be sleeping by then. I'll call mother and dad. I have to do it right away."

"Take care of our son." She smiled and nodded at him as he hugged her and kissed her belly. She called her parents and left a message on their answering machine for them to call her. She tried both of their cell phones but they were obviously old numbers and she didn't have any new ones. She didn't feel like trying anymore tonight. They could be away for a week or far away for a few days. She would wait for them to return her call. Tomorrow she would have to tell Dorothy and the ladies and that would be so hard. She sat in the rocking chair and thought some more while she rocked the baby.

Awhile later she went into the kitchen and fixed herself a tuna sandwich and poured out a glass of skim milk. It was 9:30 and she was starting to feel dragged out. She needed her bed and some rest. She showered and fell into the bed but sleep did not come very soon. She was sure she heard him at the front door but she was too tired to get out of bed. She would see him tomorrow.

Chapter 43

The next morning the sun was shining bright as Pam woke and found herself feeling so lonely and sad. What an awful day she had been through and an equally terrible night. She got out of bed and went into the shower. She made coffee and decided to go outside. Pam took a cup and went out onto the patio to try and enjoy the nice spring morning. She heard Atticus tormenting a cat in the neighborhood. She couldn't see him but what a commotion he was causing. She got up and walked over to the edge of the patio. A black cat was crouched close to the ground and slinking along trying to keep away from the mockingbird. The cat looked so much like Boots but she wasn't sure. It would be impossible for Boots to find her. She looked a little longer and then she saw the four white boots on the black cat's feet. "Boots, come here. What do you think you're doing?" The cat saw her and ran toward the complex. She leaped up onto the patio's stucco fence and Pam walked over to her. "I can't believe this, Boots. How did you find me?" The tears came to her eyes as the cat purred and she picked it up. "I wish you could talk and tell me how you found me. I can't believe you came across the city." Pam knew there have been stranger things happen. She drank more coffee and held Boots as she tried to figure out how the cat had gotten here.

Pam called for a taxi to take her to the office for her car. She then went back to the apartment to get Boots for the trip to the nursery. She arrived at the nursery just before noontime. Boots was running around the car not knowing what was going on. The cat dug a little into the seat with her claws but took the ride quite well. Pam was going to tell Dorothy first and then take the ladies into Lee's office while Dorothy took care of the whole nursery. She would not take long with the ladies. As soon as she got Dorothy into the office, Joe popped his head inside the door. She told him she would tell Dorothy first. He offered to help out for awhile and she said that he could. She never dreamed he would show up today after not letting him visit after work. Dorothy was devastated upon hearing the terrible news. Pam asked her to round up the ladies to meet in the office for her to let them know. She went out to see Joe in the front for a few minutes before she talked with the ladies. She looked out the front door and saw Joe reaching into his van for something. He pulled out a large wreath with a banner across that said: In Memory of Lee. She joined him in the parking lot. "I'll put this on the outside of the front door." Pam nodded but couldn't say anything. She already had some tears. She told him about Boots coming to the apartment and she had brought the cat back. He thought that was very strange. "I came by after work last night but you must have been asleep. I really wanted to see you."

"I was so out of it and needed rest and I'm sorry you made the trip for nothing. I need to talk with the ladies so I'll see you in just a little bit." He gave her a reassuring look. There were five ladies working at this time and Pam took a seat behind the desk. Joe stepped just inside the door to give Pam support at the beginning of her talk. They could all tell that Pam had been crying.

"Ladies, I have some sad news to tell you. My Nana was killed in a car accident on her way home yesterday afternoon." They all groaned in unison and the tears were flowing freely. "I'm so sorry to have to tell you this. I decided to leave it up to you, if you wish to work or if you would like to go home and you'll still be paid. I know she would not want the nursery closed for several days in her memory."

"Pam, I think we should work until 4 PM and then close early," Dorothy suggested. The other ladies were in agreement.

"We'll have a memorial service for her or an open house at her place in a few days. I'll make sure you all have time off to attend." The ladies nodded. "I don't have any details about the accident yet but I'll let you know soon."

"Okay, ladies, let's get back to work," Dorothy told them. "We'll work hard today for Lee and make her proud." The ladies filed past Pam and they each gave her a hug and words of kindness. When the last one left she put her head down on the desk and cried. Joe walked over and took her into his arms.

"Cry as long as you need to because you just made Lee proud. I'm going to put a sign on the front door about today's hours and do you know what you want to do for the rest of the week."

"Why don't you talk to Dorothy and she what she thinks. I need to rely on her a great deal because she knows this nursery so well. I'll have the service next week before I have to go back to work, probably on Tuesday. I have to look into getting her body back here." Joe hung his head at her statement but Pam didn't notice. They went out to the nursery and she thanked him for coming by to help out.

"I went to your apartment to take you to your car but you were already ahead of me. I knew you had to tell the ladies and I wanted to be with you. Is there anything else I could help you with?"

"I need to go by the lawyer's office to notify him and see about her will."

"If you haven't eaten, I would like to take you to lunch at the New Horizons. We could leave your car here and I can drive you around. Please let me do this for you."

"I'll have lunch with you," Pam told him. "I'll be out in a few minutes, I need to talk to Dorothy." He gave her a wink and she went back inside. She found Dorothy out back sweeping and pulled her off to the side.

"Dorothy, I don't have a clue what's in my Nana's will so I can't offer you anything right now. I may need you to run the nursery after I find out what it says. Nana depended on you and you know more about this business than I do." Pam told her about the cat and she would leave Boots here for the time being.

"Thanks, Pam, and I would be interested in staying with this job. I hope you get to own it now because you'll be as nice as Lee was to us ladies. I don't know what to say about Boots but we'll try and take care of her for you."

"I'll let you know as soon as I find out and I'll make a deal with you." The two ladies hugged and Pam left to go with Joe to the restaurant.

They arrived and he put his hand on her back as they walked in together.

"You did that so well, babe, and I know it was hard for you."

"I keep thinking that she would not want us grieving every second of every day." Pam was feeling so close to him, more than she had ever felt before.

"Pam, are you thinking about quitting your job now that you have the nursery to take care of?"

"I don't plan that at all. I need to hear from her lawyer because I don't even know that it's mine. She may want it sold or even given to charity. She wanted me to be very interested in the business but I was honest and told her I liked my job very much. Nana could have even given it to Dorothy. You just never know what that woman could come up with. She'll be very precise in her instructions, too."

"You need to be told about the accident soon, Pam. You didn't want details last night so let me know when you are ready." The tears came forth, even though, she tried to keep them in check.

They finished lunch and went back out to the van. "Where is the lawyer's office located?" She gave him directions to the lawyer's office on Main Street. He told her he would go in with her.

"You can if you want to but there'll be no reading of the will today. I can set up an appointment with him. I'll go in and it will take just a few minutes." She was out of the van before he could say a word. In a few minutes she was back. "He's not in and he'll call me later so I guess we can go now. I need to hear the details of the accident. My parents must be on a business trip or vacation because they haven't returned my call. Do you know how we'll be able to get her body back, Joe?" Pam was just jumping from subject to subject not really wanting to hear the details.

"As soon as we get to your apartment I'll tell you." They drove back to the nursery to get her car and they both drove to the apartment. They walked into the apartment and he guided her over to the couch. "Pam, this is not going to be easy for either one of us. I don't have an accident report just what the CHP told Wilson. We can get a report when it's finished. She was driving on a two lane stretch of road west of Bakersfield. She started to pass another car and she hit a tanker truck head-on. Why she didn't see the truck or what was going on in the car, no one knows. The sun was in her front windshield and that might have caused it. The truck driver tried to avoid her but he had no road or lane to turn into. Her car burst into flames and she burned up."

"Oh, my God, no, Joe, not that." He went to her and held her in his arms. She was crying very hard. "I don't want her to burn up, Joe. She didn't deserve that."

"Look she was dead on impact so forget the fire, Pam. She didn't suffer any and there's no body to bring home. They couldn't tell her body from the seat she was sitting on."

"Where is she? You mean there was nothing left of her?"

"She's in the car sitting in a tow yard." Joe was still holding Pam and finding it hard to continue.

"That's it, we just leave her in the car forever? She'll be surrounded by junked cars and we can't bring her home?" All of a sudden she stopped talking and crying. She was trying to let it all sink in. A calmness came over her and Joe took a good look at her to see what was wrong. He saw no tears and her eyes appeared dark for the first time ever. More like the color sapphire then the usual cornflower hue.

"Pam, are you okay, can I get you anything?"

"I'm fine, Joe, I just need to think about things." The phone rang and Joe went to answer it.

"Pam, it's Mr. Daniel's, he's in his office now." He brought the phone to her. She talked with him for a few minutes and took the phone back to the receiver.

"We have to go on Monday at 10 AM for the reading of the will. We both have to be there, Joe. Apparently you're in the will, too." Joe didn't know what to think.

"Pam, what's going on with you right now? You stopped doing anything, all of a sudden and your eyes are not normal. How do you feel?"

"She would be pissed if she knew I was carrying on this way so I stopped."

"That's fine but you scared me and I don't want anything to happen to you. You need to stay calm and take it easy on your days off. You're off today and tomorrow and then you get three days off for bereavement. You go back to work on Wednesday."

"I don't need that much time off, Joe."

"Yes, you do and you're going to take it."

"I don't want mother to come down here so how can I handle that?"

"There's probably not much you can do about it."

"If Nana's body won't be here, we can have an open house at her home on Tuesday for friends to visit. She would like a wake with no crying or roses being tossed onto her casket. She'll be with us in our hearts. I could not put up with my mother at this time. She must not be in Nana's will because she doesn't need to be there on Monday."

"Pam, this is not a good time to fight with your mom either."

"When she calls I'll try to convince her not to come. I don't want her taking control of everything. I'll have some deli food delivered for our friends. I have to go to the newspaper today for her obituary. They can announce the wake in her obit. I'll close the nursery four hours early on Tuesday so the ladies can attend. The wake will be from four to eight. Does that sound okay, Joe?"

"You have it all handled it seems."

"I must go now to the paper and then stop at the deli to order what I might need for food. I want it all to be nice for her. I just realized that's not a good time for you, Joe, because you'll be working."

"I can take some time off for the wake so don't worry about that. I just might not be able to help you as much as I'd like to."

"Just being here for me will help me." He insisted on going to the newspaper with her. Lee's obituary would appear in the Sunday paper. They stopped at the deli and ordered food to be delivered. If they should get low on food, the deli could deliver more. Pam knew that friends may bring some dishes, too. She would bake several wine cakes to have on hand.

She was going to spend a quiet evening alone but Joe was still worried about her. He wanted to stay with her and sleep on the couch. She let him and it did make her feel a little better to have him close by. She had to go to bed early because she was all worn out. She was starting a new routine and she did not like it.

As soon as she woke up Saturday, she remembered that Joe was on the couch. She put her robe on and walked quietly out to the living room. He was gone and the moment turned into a big disappointment for her. She was missing his closeness so much and she wondered, if they would ever be close again. Pam needed to give him an answer but she didn't know, if she could trust him. She could always give him another chance but she was so afraid to do that. The more they were together the harder it would be for her to let go, if things didn't work out.

Her phone rang after she got out of the shower and was on her first cup of coffee.

"It looks like I ran out on you but it got too much for me knowing you were in the next room in our bed."

"I understand, Joe, and I don't blame you for leaving."

"All it would take is one word from you and we could be back together. I'm trying not to put pressure on you but it's hard not to."

"I know that but I still have doubts that things will be good for us, if we get back. I don't deal well with rejection and I don't like you moving in and out of here. I feel, if the least little thing goes wrong, I have to worry, if you will stick around or just leave me anytime night or day. I don't want those awful feelings."

"Do you want it in writing because I can go to a lawyer and have it written in a legal document. It'll be a contract between the two of us. Just like a prenuptial agreement only this one will state that I'll never leave you again."

"I don't want a written contract to validate our status. I want it to come from your heart that you'll never leave me."

"I tell you that I want to be with you but you won't believe me so we're in a no-win situation. I don't know what can fix it. Do you have any plans for today?"

"No, I don't. I did a lot of things yesterday and I don't have much more to do. I'll go to the grocery store and get the ingredients for the wine cakes and start baking. All the arrangements have been made for the wake. It seems funny that I'm off tomorrow. I can bake on both days to keep busy. "

"You still haven't heard from your parents?"

"Not one word and mom will be upset, if she doesn't know about the wake. There's nothing I can do about that. I'll call them everyday and hope I can make contact. Will you be playing tennis today?"

"Ken asked me to so why don't you come over."

"I would if it wasn't for Julie. I can't deal with her, Joe."

"Why do you let so many people intimidate you? You didn't want to go to the Den because of Suzy. You don't want to play tennis because of Julie. To hell with them and live your life in spite of them."

"So you think I'm using people around me as an excuse for not doing things?"

"What do you think? It sounds like it to me."

"What time is tennis?"

"That's the way you should be and we meet at 9:30 AM. A couple of hours of workout and then lunch."

"I may not be able to keep up with you guys but Julie can hit you on the ass for my entertainment. I hate it when she does that. I can't say anything to her because we're not a couple. She wouldn't listen anyway."

"I'm looking forward to seeing you and we'll let you rest whenever you wish." They hung up as Pam glanced at the clock and knew she had one hour to be there.

She called the nursery to ask Dorothy, if she knew of anyone she could hire to clean Lee's house on Monday. She put Pam on hold to check with one of the ladies. She came back on the phone and said that Maria who was off on Monday would be happy to do the cleaning. Dorothy said she did a good job because she had cleaned for some of the other ladies. It was all set for Maria to get the house key from Dorothy to go and clean. Pam changed into another maternity outfit and put on some tennis shoes for her trip to Ken's. Joe was right she did let people intimidate her but she liked only being around nice people. She could depend on Julie to come up with negative comments all the time.

She arrived at Ken's and rang the doorbell. Joe must have seen her drive up because he opened the door immediately. He leaned over and kissed her belly. It felt great. She could still see love in his eyes. "You're growing bigger all the time. I think you're going to give me a football player or something."

"If that's what you want, I'll see what I can do." Ken and Julie both came out of the kitchen and greeted Pam. Julie was not happy she was there but Pam wasn't going to worry about it. The four went out to the tennis courts and started hitting the ball to loosen up.

"You know, Pamela, you might be going to have a little calf," Julie said to her.

"No, just a football player for Joe," she replied. She knew Julie would not be happy with that comment. She would have to keep it up and play Julie's game with words this fine April day.

"Joe told me you were having a boy and you made him proud but you already know that. I have to hand it to you, Pam, you don't act like a rich person at all. I would never have guessed it in a million years," Ken told her.

"I did not go to private boarding schools, thank God, and I didn't get everything in the world that I wanted. My dad taught me the value of money and how to earn it. I had nice clothes but I didn't dress the rich way. I wanted to be like all the other girls in school and dress the way they did. "I didn't want to stand out in a crowd."

"Hey, my parents treated me the same way," Ken told them. "Their money was not handed to them but was earned over the years by doing hard work."

"Let's change partners, you guys, and make it more interesting," Julie suggested. Pam knew this was coming so she walked over to join Ken on his side of the net. She would rather look at Joe than play side by side. She kept staring at him and he noticed, too.

"Am I doing something wrong or is my hair out of place?" he asked her.

"I'm staring at you to try and get to you so you'll play lousy. You know, just trying to put a little hex on you." They were hitting the ball back and forth and Joe reached to back hand the ball and Julie whacked him across the ass. Pam didn't say a word nor act like it bothered her. They were still hitting it pretty good when Julie did it again.

"Hey, don't hit me anymore," Joe said to her and he was pissed.

"My, God, I didn't know you were so sensitive about your ass," Julie told him. Pam was so proud of him for speaking up. After this exchange, Julie started hitting the ball to Pam and making her move a lot and stretching to return it.

"I'm getting a little tired out so I'll sit for a little bit," Pam told them.

"Oh, come on, Pamela, don't be such a spoiled child. You need more exercise or you could be having an elephant."

"I believe in exercise and I know my limit so don't worry about me, Julie. I haven't gained much weight and the doctor says I'm doing fine. Someday you'll be in this predicament and you'll know what I'm talking about."

"When did your pregnancy become a predicament? I thought it was a blessed event and not a mistake for you," Julie told her. "Let me clarify that, it was a blessed event for you and a mistake for Joe. You're lucky he stuck around when he found out you tricked him."

"Thank you, Joe, for sticking by me. I should tell you more often how much I appreciate you." Joe did not know what to say.

"Are you two seeing each other on the sly?" Julie asked. "Something isn't right about your relationship."

"It's none of your damn business what we're doing. Every time Joe and I are together as a couple you start in on me, Julie, and I don't know why. You keep ridiculing me by bringing up off beat stuff and anything negative you can think of. Jesus, don't you get tired of it or am I your little pasttime?"

"I didn't know you were a couple. Joe lives here and you came to visit and play tennis. Does that make you a couple now?" Julie asked. "Just because you're having a child together doesn't make you a couple."

"Do you want me to leave, Julie, is that what this is about?"

"You need to keep your hormones in check, Pamela, because I'm always nice to you. You look for bad things and you find them. You're good at twisting shit around to make everything that comes out of my mouth sound bad." Ken walked over and sat down next to Pam. He was tired of hearing the women bicker. Joe came over and sat down. "You're all giving up so soon," Julie said. "We all need more exercise. Joe, you used to be more easy going but since you got tangled up with Pam, you're not the same guy."

"I'm the same guy, Jules, we have all changed this past year."

"I'll have lunch served a half our earlier so it's no problem but everyone stays and everyone enjoys," Ken said to the group. Pam was sitting next to Joe and she deliberately touched his leg with her leg. They looked at each other. He knew she needed a hug so he put his arm around her shoulders. Pam was enjoying it so very much. Julie was seething. They talked about work through lunch and Pam excused herself to leave when they finished eating. Joe said he would walk her to her car.

"Thanks so much for the hug, Joe. I needed it so badly. Also, you told Julie off about hitting you on the ass and you know I enjoyed that too."

"I'm trying to show you that I care, Pam."

"Does Julie talk against me much when I'm not around? I just have a feeling that she does. She'll soon be trying to fix you up with other women, if you won't have her."

"She does talk against you and I tell her to knock it off. She hasn't tried to get me hooked up with anyone else." Pam went into his arms and hugged him tightly.

"You know that I only want you, Pam. Take me home with you now?"

"Joe, I promise right after the wake I'll give you my final decision. Just be patient a little longer. Three more days and you'll know."

"Will you let me pick you up Monday to go to the lawyer's office?"

"I'll be ready at 9:45 or you can even come a little earlier for breakfast. I'll fix you a super duper Italian omelet."

"I'll be there at 9 and I'll be hungry." He kissed her softly on the lips and she let him.

"Joe, I meant it when I said I appreciated you standing by me for the baby and now for my Nana. I don't know what I'd do, if I didn't have you to lean on."

"I just want you to make me happy on Tuesday. That kiss meant a lot of hope for me."

Chapter 44

Pam woke up on Monday to beautiful rays of sunshine hitting her bed. She had not closed her blinds the night before. She was glad to be cooking him breakfast and she bounded out of bed and into the shower. It was 8 AM so she didn't have a lot of time. She wanted the omelet to be ready as soon as he arrived. She was preparing the food when the doorbell rang. She flew out to open the door. He was standing with a beautiful bouquet of flowers in his hand. "None of the florist shops are open so I had to buy these at the grocery store. I hope you don't mind."

"They're beautiful and I wouldn't care, if you picked them off the dump. It's the thought that counts. Come in so I can cook the omelet, it's ready for the frying pan." He was enjoying the omelet and she was having a bagel and fruit.

"This omelet is so good. Did you add that little extra ingredient of love?"

"I sure did and I hope it tastes good."

"It's delicious and I've missed your cooking. I'm lousy in the kitchen." They finished eating and he helped her clean up the kitchen. "I'm getting spoiled over at Ken's. The cooks and maids do everything and that bothers me some."

"You don't like all the pampering and being waited on?"

"I'd rather be here with you like this than have all the money and servants in the world. I guess I really like you pampering me."

"I understand that, Joe, you need a lot done for you to make up for your young life."

They left for the lawyer's office just before 10. "I have no idea why I have to be at the reading. I don't mind going but it has me wondering."

"Joe, we'll find out. The lawyer notifies all of the persons mentioned in the will and you and I are the only ones. That's what he said so you know as much as I do."

"I don't have any idea what this is all about."

"Pam, trying to guess will not help us. She was clever and I don't have a clue." Pam couldn't believe what a lovely day it was for such a dismal meeting. It would have seemed more right, if the day was dark and dreary.

The receptionist took them right into Mr. Daniel's inner office. He was sitting behind his desk with the will in front of him. He was tall and lean with graying hair and kind gray eyes. He looked like a lawyer with his expensive dark suit and flashy yellow tie. He stood up, shook their hands, and asked them to be seated in the two chairs in front of his desk. "First of all I want you to know how sorry I was to hear of Lee's death. She and I have known each other for the past 20 years that she lived in Mission Park. She was a fine lady and she'll be missed by many in this community."

"Thank you, Mr. Daniels. It's so nice to hear your kind words."

"Call me Ed, young lady, and what I said was very true. I'll get started as I know you probably have much to do. This will is unique as you'll soon find out and none like I have ever dealt with before." Pam looked at Joe with puzzlement in her eyes. "I'll not read the whole thing but will give you a copy to take with you. It's a little long. I'll tell you her wishes and the instructions that go along with her wishes. She is bequeathing all her worldly goods and assets to Pamela Austin and Joseph Pellarini. You'll share joint ownership of everything but you must follow her instructions. From this day forth, you both must live together, sleep in the same bed every night, and marry within two weeks of the reading of the will." Pam gasped and looked at Joe. He was almost in shock as well. "If either person fails to follow these instructions, the assets and worldly goods will be turned over Mr. Daniels. He will have the goods auctioned off and the proceeds will be given equally to a list of charities she has named in the will."

"I don't know what to say, Ed. We aren't even living together and we have no plans at all to marry at the moment." Joe was looking at the floor and had not spoken.

"You have plenty of time to get married, although, it won't be a big wedding," Ed told her. "You look like you might care about each other so I don't think marrying will be a problem. You have to report to me in two weeks and show me the marriage certificate. If you can't, you'll lose it all. The instructions after that is to let me know by some type of communication before the end of each month that you're still together and the will is being followed. It sounds simple enough and I'll see you in two weeks." He handed them each a copy of the will. The couple got up, shook his hand, and thanked him. They both walked out into the sunshine in a daze.

"Holy shit, Joe, what do we do now?" Pam was still shaking her head. They got into the van and sat there still stunned.

"We're going to the court house and get a marriage license. We'll go and have blood tests done. Then we'll be ready for almost anything."

"Joe, I believe you said recently, you didn't want to get married."

"Okay, we won't do those things in two weeks you can tell Ed that Lee's stuff is his to do as he pleases."

"I don't think Nana wanted her will to cause problems."

"Oh, really, so why do you think she put all those stipulations on our shoulders? This is one big fucking joke, Pamela? She changed her will just before leaving for Memphis. She did not know what our circumstances would be when it was read. Lee wants to make sure we're together and this is her manner of getting her way. We have to move in together today and then get married. At least, she didn't want a tape of us screwing so old Ed could watch and make sure we're a couple." Pam opened the van door and got out. "Did I hurt your little feelings, Pam?"

"Yes, you did. You do what you have to do and I'll be home sometime, Joseph."

"You get into this van now and I mean it."

"So what do you plan on doing, if I don't, move in but sleep on the couch tonight? That would break a fucking rule and we would have to give everything back. I don't think so." Pam started walking towards the apartment. Joe started following her in the van. He jumped out and stood in front of her. "I don't want to lose Nana's nursery or home. I'll do whatever it takes to keep those things. You need to get over to Ken's and start packing." She got back into the van. Her tears fell all the way back to the apartment. He took her into his arms when they got out of the van.

"I don't want you to be upset. I'll go and get some things to last me a few days here and then I'll take you out to lunch to celebrate our reuniting. I have a question, Pam, and I need the truth. Did you know anything about the will before it was read today?"

"I knew nothing until today. I would not lie to you."

"How are your plans going for the wake tomorrow?"

"The house is being cleaned today and the food will be delivered. I only have to put the paper plates out and plastic utensils. You'll help with the drinks. I made the cakes so that has been done. I won't have to do much but visit with the people and eat. Do you have any doubts about me? Joe, before the will was read I was going to let you back into my life. I can prove this, if you ever need the proof."

"What do you mean you have proof?"

"I sent an e-mail to a friend of mine last night and I told her we were getting back together. I sent a copy to myself. Joe, I'm not that evil woman who raised you and treated you so horribly. I would do anything, if I could go back and change your childhood so that it was nice. You need to talk about it and get it out of your system. You need to show that anger that has been building up over the years and get rid of it."

"I can't order it gone, Pam. I wasn't lucky to have your family and wealth."

"You know, Joe, forget the wealth. My family was not the great American family either but I was not treated poorly or abused physically. I was mentally pushed by my mother but it was nothing compared to what you had to go through. We can discuss this after work tonight."

"I had something else on my mind, Pam, for tonight.

"Okay, tonight you can have your way with me and tomorrow we can discuss your childhood. Is this a deal?"

"I think I'll call in sick and have my way with you all afternoon and evening."

"You would get tired of me after awhile."

"I'll never be tired of you and your beautiful body, I promise. I'm going to be worthless for the rest of the day just thinking about making love to you once more. I have to get over to Ken's so I'll be back soon." She hugged him, kissed him, and reached down and felt his hard penis. He had to push her away because he wanted her so badly. "I don't want to leave you for one minute." He dashed out of the apartment.

It didn't take him long to return and she had cleared out a drawer once more for him. She helped him put some clothes away. He grabbed her when they finished and laid her on the bed. He got down beside her and started kissing her face all over.

"Joe, you're going to spoil all my plans I have for after work."

"We can love one another now and then after work. I'll want you again,

I'm sure. Please don't let me leave for work so frustrated and depraved of sex. I'll be angry and take it out on the public all shift." She gave him a big smile and she started undressing him. She wanted him and couldn't wait to accept him inside of her. He was all over her breasts with his mouth and tongue and she moaned as her nipples turned hard. She could tell that he didn't want much foreplay as he was hard and ready to take her. He pinned her arms to the bed and kissed around her breasts leaving her nipples untouched. She moaned again as his busy tongue was doing its job.

"Joe, please come into me, I'm so ready." He raised up and slid his penis inside her moist body and they rocked back and forth in unison. Their bodies stopped rolling together and calmed down in a few minutes. She opened her eyes and kissed him again and again. "I love the way you feel inside of me. I love being with you like this, Joe. It feels wonderful and feels so right."

"When you love someone, Pam, making love is always the best. I hate to leave you but I'll love you again tonight. What did you have planned for tonight?"

"Oh, just candles and taking a shower together to start it all off."

"I'll take a rain check on the shower and I'll go slower so you can enjoy it more."

"I enjoyed this very much because if you're ready you don't want to take all night. I'll never let you leave me again, Joseph, remember this is a promise."

She spent the evening missing him and she did light a couple of candles in the bedroom before he came home. They showered together and enjoyed being close again very much. It was the happiest they had ever been and she knew now that they would be a couple forever. Nothing or no one could ever keep them apart.

They both woke up together with smiles on their faces. He nuzzled her and she did him. "You made a promise yesterday that we could talk about you and us today." She put her hand on his face and outlined his jaw with her index finger. "You're so good, Joe, there isn't a mean streak in you and I love you so much." He lowered his eyes. "You need to look at me. You need to tell me what she did to you. All the mean and rotten things that you remember, you need to get it out of your system."

"Pam, you don't need to hear that stuff. You would never be mean to me. Yesterday morning when you fixed me breakfast, I could tell you really enjoyed doing it. I could tell something else that you're proud of me. I could see it in those beautiful blue diamonds of yours. If I could have had one look from her that was half as good as what I saw in your eyes, I would have been thrilled. She did all kinds of mean things."

"Joe, you need to talk about what you went through. It'll help you."

"One of the worst was when she held my head in the toilet and kept flushing and flushing. She knew how far to go so I wouldn't drown but I felt like I was. I was six and I hadn't dusted furniture the way she wanted it dusted before I left for school. She found a spot I had missed. I had to be perfect in everything that I did or I would be punished." Pam was listening and looking into his eyes as he talked. She saw tears start to form in his eyes. "I'm not perfect anymore. When I lied to you about never leaving you is when I stopped being perfect. Pam, you have never told me one lie since we've known each other. I apologize for asking you earlier, if you knew about what was in the will before it was read. I shouldn't have asked you."

"You're still perfect to me, Joe, and you don't have to do a thing to prove it." He hung his head. She took his chin and tilted it up so that he looked into her eyes. "You need to tell me more."

"There's a lot I don't even remember anymore. I've just blocked it out because that was my way of coping and getting past it."

"Did she ever do anything to your private parts, Joe? There's something you are leaving out."

"She would pull really hard on my penis at times. I think she got a kick out of doing it." He turned away from her face and buried his face in her belly. He cried and so did she as she kept running her fingers through his hair. He got in control and continued. "When I hit puberty she didn't do much to me physically anymore. I was about as tall as she was and she was afraid of retaliation, I think. My younger years were full of abuse and maybe another time I can tell you more. I can't deal with anymore today." Joe looked into her eyes and she saw more than love. "When I left home I was desperate to find someone to love me. I was trying to make up for all the abuse and coldness I received from her. I have met quite a few women in the past seven years. I was looking for the woman with the kindest eyes. That was my number one goal. I didn't care what she looked like or how she was built. I would look into their eyes. When I stepped into the Center last May 1st and saw your kind eyes, I knew you were the one I had been looking for these past seven years. It's a bonus that you're pretty and you have a great body. I just noticed your kind eyes."

"I must remind you that, even though, I never lied to you, I withheld telling you I was pregnant or that I was even trying to get pregnant. Joe, no one is perfect in this world including myself."

"You got pregnant because you love me so much. It wasn't about revenge or trickery, you wanted to always be a part of my life. How could I feel bad about that. It's a great compliment." He leaned over and kissed her lips gently and sweetly. "You were more than worth waiting for." The phone rang and shattered their closeness. Pam reached for it. Joe was holding her in both of his arms.

"Hello, Mother, where in hell have you been?"

"We went to Puerto Vallarta for a few days, is anything wrong?" Pam paused and then continued.

"I have some bad news to tell you and I didn't have any other way to reach you. Nana, died in a car accident coming back from Memphis." The tears formed in her eyes as she heard her mother shriek and lose control. Joe heard her mother, also. "Is dad there? Please put him on."

"Pamela, what did you tell your mom, she's out of control?"

"Dad, Nana died in Bakersfield in a bad car crash. She almost made it home. She burned up in the car so there was no body to bring home. Today we're having a wake and I don't think mom should come down."

"Aren't you rushing things, Pamela? You must know your mother and I would like to attend."

"I had to have it today because I go back to work tomorrow. The announcement has been made and all the plans are completed. I couldn't possibly hold off any longer."

"We'll be down in our jet and don't worry about picking us up. Your mother will need this closure so expect us later. How are you doing?"

"I'm fine and I'll see you later at Nana's." Pam hung up and let out a big sigh.

"Joe, I don't need to deal with her today. How will I ever get through it?"

"You have to deal with her and I'll help you."

"Joe, I love you so much. You'll get to meet my dad which will be nice. Did you want to talk about getting married or is it too soon?"

"Do you think I'll need any weapons to defend myself when I meet him?" Joe said with a big grin.

"He'll like you very much but she's not a forgiving person. She should be happy when she hears we're getting married. We need to get moving because I want to go over to Nana's house and make sure everything is ready. My parents will stay there tonight, I imagine. The Queen will demand that everything is in order." They both got up, showered, and decided to eat breakfast out on their way to the house.

When they got to Lee's home, Pam marveled at how clean and nice it looked. She decided to make up the spare room bed for her folks with clean sheets. She didn't think her mom would like to sleep in Lee's bed. Joe helped her make the bed and he got out a couple of folding card tables. The main food would be put on the dining room table. There would be drinks on one card table and desserts on the other one. It didn't take them long at all to have everything in order. Joe went to the store to get ice and some more plastic glasses for the sodas. There would be no liquor served. She got out her Nana's collection of Elvis music while he went to the store. She didn't know what time her parents would be there. Joe left for work at 1:15 PM and she was left to stand by for the guests. Her parents arrived at 3 PM and her dad had to adjust to his daughter being pregnant. Her mother was dressed in black from head to toe, clad in the latest fashions.

"I have some good news for you both, Joe and I are getting married real soon."

"I was going to ask him about that," her dad admitted. Lake Austin was a handsome man with short wavy brown hair and blue eyes. His face was rugged looking and tanned from spending as much time outdoors as he could. He liked adventure and only participated in outdoor sports. He had given Pam her smile. Her mother was playing the grieving daughter role to the hilt. Pam told them about the will and Lee's stipulations.

"So you're only getting married because Lee said you had to or no inheritance?" Anne asked.

"We were planning to be married, we just hadn't set the date."

"You don't need any God damn inheritance from her, Pamela," Lake said to his daughter. "You have a trust fund coming in three years that'll take care of all your needs for years to come."

"Look, you two, I don't care about an inheritance or assets from Nana. She loved that nursery and I don't want it to be sold just to anyone. We'll take care of it the best way that we can. I, also, want to keep this house because it holds so many memories." Pam was glad when Joe came by as the other people started arriving. He was in uniform and she didn't care as she walked up to him to greet him with a hug and kiss him. She was eager to introduce him to her dad. The men shook hands and then her mother started in.

"Well, I can see why Pamela fell for you in your uniform, Joseph. You're a very nice looking young man."

"Jesus, Mother, can't you think of something nice to say. I didn't fall in love with his uniform. Being handsome is just a bonus in my opinion." Pam was very upset with her mother. Her dad started asking Joe all kinds of questions about his job and their future. She knew they would get along right away. Every time her mother was introduced to someone new she started wailing and carrying on. Julie and Ken came by. She had traded the day with Dave so she didn't have to go to work. Ken was in uniform and was stopping by on duty as Joe was. Pam motioned for Joe to go into the kitchen. She went out there first and he followed. She slowly walked over to him with the tears falling. He took her into his arms. She cried softly as he rubbed her back with his hands.

"I knew this would be hard on you today, Pam. I do like your dad very much."

"Mother is being her usual self and I should be used to it but I'm not." She looked him in the eyes and kissed his lips softly. "I feel so good in your arms."

"Hey, you two, you can't do that on duty, Joe," Julie said as she came into the kitchen. This was all that Pam needed to hear from Julie.

"If you weren't in here, Julie, no one would know."

"I'm just joking and I wanted to congratulate you both on getting married. I guess it took a will for Joe to make up his mind?" She added.

"It wasn't just the will," Joe said to her. "I was not going to have the baby born without us being legal." Ken walked in looking for Julie. She immediately told him she was congratulating the soon to be married couple. He, also, wished them the best.

"Joe, your future father-in-law is quite the entrepreneur," Ken told Joe. "Everything he touches turns to money." Joe grinned and nodded but didn't say anything.

"Joe, you and I are somewhat alike," Julie said to him. "We both fell in love with someone with money. Who would have thought this would happen to each of us?"

"Julie, there is a difference. Joe didn't know about my money before we started dating."

"Are you sure about that, Pamela? Is that what Joe told you? I brought up your family in December because Ken and I did read the article that Sunday in the Chronicle. We all knew about you way before that. Chris knew all about you and your family's wealth. He lived in the Bay Area and was quite the historian in regards to the rich and famous." Pam looked at Joe and then she knew that he had known about her family from the very beginning. She started to turn and walk out of the kitchen into the dining room.

"You don't have to get pissed off, Pamela because he knew," Julie said.

"I'm not pissed off because he knew but he didn't tell me that he knew."

"You'll get over it as you always do when things don't turn out your way."

"Julie, you can fuck off and leave me alone for the remainder of the wake. I don't even know why you came." Joe left and she walked him out to his patrol car. "I'm not real mad, Joe, because I fell in love with you that day, too. I knew nothing about you but I fell hard and I'll never leave you."

She spent the rest of the evening talking to friends of Lee and keeping her parents company. Ken had left earlier to get back to his beat. Julie stayed a little longer and then told her goodbye. When the last guests left she put away what was left of the food and visited with her folks until 10 PM. Her dad told her that he liked Joe and he hoped they would be very happy. Her parents would leave in the morning for San Francisco. They gave her a check as a wedding present for $50,000. It would buy a lot of wedding presents. She would have to go home and show him. She didn't know what he would say.

After Pam got home she took her shower and waited but he wasn't home at his usual time. It appeared he wasn't coming home at all. She got ready for bed. He was staying away because he knew she was rich when he asked her out. That didn't bother her as much as him carrying on about it as if he didn't know. Their whole relationship was turning out to be one lie after another. How could they ever live happily ever after? She turned out the light but couldn't sleep. She tossed and turned and finally heard his key in the front door. She was not going to let this go until the morning. She would face him tonight and have it out with him. Pam reached over and turned on the light as he was making his way from the bathroom to the bedroom.

"I didn't want to wake you up," he told her. He got into bed and turned the other way.

"Joe, we have a lot to talk about tonight. I'm not letting you go to sleep so that we can discuss this in the morning."

"You can talk and I'll just listen." He was still facing the wall. She reached over and tugged on his shoulder.

"You think this whole thing is a big fucking joke?" He moved in bed and sat up.

"I told you the truth when I said that I asked you out because you had the kindest eyes. After I asked you out, I found out your family was rich. I should have told you then that I knew but I didn't. I pretended I didn't know because I didn't want you to think that I asked you out because you had money. Now you know the exact truth." She lay down and didn't say anything to him. "Come on, you wanted to talk so keep talking."

"You can't reason with a drunk so we can talk in the morning." He moved over and pinned her arms down to her side.

"So I'm now just a drunk that you can't reason with?" She blinked her eyes and looked frightened as he held her tight."

"You tell me, Joe, how this relationship can survive under these conditions?"

"I think we should split the sheets and not even try to get married. Isn't that what you think, too? Pam, if you feel it isn't worth fixing then it is what should be done." He bounded out of bed and grabbed his pillow. He took a blanket out of the closet and headed for the living room. She couldn't believe he was going to sleep on the couch. The nursery would be sold to the highest bidder. She got out of bed and ran into the living room.

"I will not have you sleeping on the couch, Mr. Pellerini. You'll get back into our bed right now. If you sleep somewhere other than our bed, it'll not be on this couch."

"You want me in your bed or you want me to leave your apartment?"

"I want you in bed with me because I love you and I want to marry my baby's daddy. Please come to my bed and please love me, too." He followed her into the bedroom. He went into the closet and brought out an envelope.

"I bought these the other day because I was hoping I could give them to you." He handed her the envelope and she opened it up.

"Two tickets to Reno for Friday. We're going to Reno and get married in a few days? You didn't tell me this."

"I was waiting for you to give me the answer if I could be with you. You told me on the weekend you would let me know right after the wake. I got the tickets because I was pretty sure you would say yes. I love you with all my heart. I want to marry the mother of my baby very much." She went into his arms and they hugged. She had a smile on her face that wouldn't quit.

"I have something to show you, also," she told him as she reached over to the nightstand and opened the drawer. She pulled out the check from her dad and handed it to him.

The End